JULIA WOLF

More Books By Julia

MILE HIGH BILLIONAIRES
In The Details
By The Letter
To The Chase

The Harder They Fall (Billionaire office romance)
Dear Grumpy Boss
Sincerely, Your Inconvenient Wife
P.S. You're Intolerable
Not So Truly Yours

The Seasons Change (Rock star romance)
Falling In Reverse
Stone Cold Notes

Faded in Bloom
Where Waves Break

Savage U (college romance)
Soft Like Thunder
Bright Like Midnight
Sweet Like Poison
Real Like Daydreams

Savage Academy (academy romance)
Save One Thing
These Two Wrongs
Jump On Three

Blue is the Color (Rock star romance)
Times Like These
Watch Me Unravel
Such Great Heights
Under the Bridge

Unrequited (Rock star romance)

Unrequited

Misconception

Dissonance

Never Blue Duet (Angsty rock star romance)

Never Lasting

Never Again

Playlist

"MESS IS MINE" VANCE JOY

"Sun To Me" Zach Bryan

"Stubborn Love" The Lumineers

"Missing Piece" Vance Joy

"Hold The Line" Arizona

"Wildflower" Billie Eilish

"Hold The Line" The White Buffalo

"I Got You" The White Buffalo

"Walls" The Lumineers

"All The Pretty Girls" Kaleo

"chance with you" mehro

"Sleep On The Floor" The Lumineers

Chapter One

Phoebe

Not many people were awake this early in Sugar Brush. The quiet on Main Street was broken only by the crunch of my boots on the salted sidewalk and the faint hum of an old truck somewhere in the distance. This time of day, before the sun rose to kiss the sky, I was the only soul around. Sometimes, when I was in a whimsical mood, I liked to imagine this whole town was mine. The queen of an empty kingdom...or maybe just its overworked baker.

I yawned, fumbling to braid my hair while I walked. Multitasking this early could be a dangerous endeavor, but I refused to show up to work looking like I'd just rolled out of bed, even if it was painfully accurate.

I'd bet there were only a handful of bakers who weren't morning people, and I was one of them. I'd tried to train my body to rise with the sun, but my body was a rebel without a cause, and the sound of my alarm going off each day hurt.

As I reached Sugar Rush's baby pink door, which never failed to make me smile, the low growl of an engine made me pause. A silver truck I didn't recognize rolled down Main Street, its headlights cutting through the darkness. I turned, raising a hand to wave because that was what we did around here. Greeting my neighbors was an instinct born from a lifetime of living in a small town.

If the driver returned my wave, I couldn't tell, but I was curious where they were going. It wasn't often I had company on my way to work.

The truck continued past, slow enough to make my stomach twist. I brushed off the strange sense of unease—I really needed to lay off the true crime podcasts—but still hesitated before turning my key in the lock. My little kingdom suddenly didn't feel so quiet.

"Who are you, and where are you going?" I whispered to the fading taillights.

It was none of my business, obviously, but at heart, I was a Nosy Nellie. Half the reason I loved owning a bakery café was it serving as a town hub. I spent my days baking, serving coffee and treats, and soaking up little snippets of other people's lives. I'd never spread what I heard further than my older sister. Hannah and I passed the latest Sugar Brush news back and forth to each other like a cold in preschool, but it ended with us.

With no answers forthcoming, I let myself into Sugar Rush and filled my lungs with air that always seemed laced with sugar. It did more to wake me up than a strong cup of coffee. Oh, I'd have one or two of those too, but for now, I flipped on the lights on my way to the kitchen.

My favorite place on earth besides my family's ranch.

The air was even sweeter back here, and the stainless steel surfaces gleamed. I wasn't the most organized person on the planet, but when it came to my kitchen, I didn't play around. Messes were never left "for tomorrow."

I stashed my coat and bag in my tiny office—which was little more than a desk, computer, and filing cabinet tucked in the corner—and grabbed my favorite apron. I had a small collection, but this one reminded me of an old-fashioned housewife's dress, full-skirted with cute floral embroidery.

Sucking in another breath, I pulled my frilly apron over my head, checked my baking list, and got to work.

"Hey! What'll it be?"

The line had been steady since I'd flipped the "open" sign. We opened on the early side for the town-living ranch hands headed off to work. Sugar Rush was a little pink for all the cowboys we attracted. Then again, we were the only game around besides fast food, and, well...we were heads and tails above what they had to offer.

The rugged man at the front of the line blushed scarlet and averted his gaze to scan the bakery case. "I'll take a coffee, black, and one of your muffins. You pick the one you think I'll like. If that's all right."

"I can do that," I agreed, mentally cataloging the flavors we were serving today and landing on the one I thought this virtual stranger would enjoy. "We have a carrot cake muffin this morning. There's a dollop of cream cheese frosting in the center. Sound good?"

He swallowed, still looking over at the case. "Sounds good...Phoebe."

I grinned, unsurprised he knew my name. He'd been part of a crew coming into the shop for some time now. Not a local, and I surely didn't know his name, but his face was familiar.

He handed me his payment after I rang him up, and I passed his order over to Camille, my barista slash right-hand woman. I took note of his friends nudging him from behind, quietly cajoling him, and braced myself for what I had a feeling was coming.

I passed him his change and offered another wide smile. "Well, all right. It'll be ready for you at the end of the counter in just a minute."

"Thanks." He rubbed his nape and finally aimed his eyes at me. "Would it be possible for me to have your number so I can take you out sometime?"

The first time a customer had asked me out a couple years ago, I'd froze, and in my shock, I'd given him my number. That hadn't ended so well. Since then, I'd prepared myself for these situations. It happened more than I wanted, but I'd learned the kind of men who came in for my treats—men who worked long, hard days, doing backbreaking labor, often far away from home—liked a soft woman who could cook and surrounded herself in frills and pink. It wasn't *me* they were after, but the idea of me.

I leaned closer, dropping my voice. He seemed nice. The last thing I wanted was to embarrass him. "My personal policy is not to date customers. Thank you so much for asking, though. I'm very flattered."

His already ruddy cheeks burst into flames. If I'd been the slightest bit interested, I might've given him a chance just for that, but he didn't stir anything in me.

"Oh. I-I...all right. I'm just gonna be going now—"

The guy behind him threw his arm around his shoulders. He was bigger, rougher, and had a meanness in his pale-blue eyes I instantly didn't like. "What's this now, Thomas? You're giving up just like that?"

Thomas had been quiet and respectful, but his friend, who I also recognized from his big mouth and grating swagger, instantly put me on alert.

Thomas grimaced. "It's all right, Ry. She said it's her policy. Leave it."

The big-mouthed friend raked his eyes over me. "You think you're too good for Tommy?"

I didn't dignify his question with a response. "Would you like to order something? The coffee's hot, and our muffins are delicious."

Thomas tried to pull away, but his friend—Ry, he'd said—kept his arm tight around him. "I'd like you to get your head outta your ass and see that my friend Tommy is a real nice guy. He wants to take you out on a date and treat you right. You're not married. Far's I know, you don't have a man either. So, how about you make an exception this one time and give my boy your number?"

Squaring my shoulders, I kept my gaze steady and level, my tone still low and friendly but as firm as I could make it. "If you'd like to order something, that would be great. Otherwise, I'll ask you to step aside. There's a long line behind you, and everyone will be a lot less cranky once they have their coffee."

Ry grew rigid, and any semblance of friendliness faded. Luckily, he didn't get a chance to say whatever ugliness was about to drip from his tongue because Camille called out Thomas's name.

Thomas finally got it together and managed to drag his friend with him, nodding to me as they moved along. If I'd looked, I was sure I had earned a filthy, dirty look from the other guy, but I smiled at the next customer, not giving him any more of my time.

I only breathed easier when they were gone. Hopefully, they'd find themselves at the fast-food joint instead of Sugar Rush tomorrow. My mornings were way too busy to be catering to a couple cowboys' bruised egos.

Chapter Two

Phoebe

During the week, we stayed open until five, though there were always stragglers I had to shoo along. We were nearing closing time when I slid open my glass case to take stock of what we still had. Several trays were nothing but crumbs.

"They were hungry today," I remarked as I jotted down what I needed to make more of the next day. Cookies always went fast, today being no exception.

Camille paused in wiping down our espresso machine. Friends since we were kids, she'd been working with me since I opened three years ago, and fortunately for me, was as fastidious as I was. "They were. Seems like they went wild for the carrot cake muffins."

"They did." They'd cleaned me out by midday. I made a note to make an extra batch next time. "Think they realize they're eating their veggies?"

She snorted. "Think they don't care, as long as they get your cream cheese frosting with it."

I straightened, crinkling my nose. "Are you implying my muffins aren't health food?"

"Yep." She grinned as she moved to wipe the counter on the other side of the case. "That's exactly what I'm saying, babe."

The chimes over the door rang, and like clockwork, my sister Hannah strolled in, heading straight for the pastry case. If she didn't show up in the morning, she always appeared close to closing time. Sometimes, I got her at both ends of the day.

"What've you got for me today?" she asked in lieu of greeting, bending down to scan our selections.

If it'd been the beginning of the day, I would've plucked a blueberry muffin from a tray and handed it to Camille to bag up. Hannah liked to pretend she was mulling over her choices, but she'd been eating the same thing for breakfast every day for the past couple years.

Unless her boyfriend, Remi, made her waffles. Then she was willing to switch it up. That was how I knew it was true love.

As predictable as she was in the mornings, afternoons were a crapshoot.

"How about a lemon bar?" I offered, sliding the tray out of the case. "We've got a few left, and one looks like it has your name on it."

She twisted her lips, considering. "Oh, all right. You convinced me."

Camille laughed. "Wasn't too hard."

Hannah cocked her head toward Camille. "Think you could throw in a vanilla latte? I'll wipe down the tables while I wait."

Camille tossed her towel down. "Deal."

I rounded the counter to give my sister a hug. She hugged hard and fierce—it was just how Hannah did things. Three years older than me, I used to follow her around like a little shadow. When we got older, our interests had diverged—Hannah spent her days tending to horse hooves as a farrier, while I'd gotten hooked on creating in the kitchen—but no matter our differences, we'd always stayed close.

Up until a month ago, we'd shared a duplex, her half of the house above mine. She'd officially moved in with Remi—though she'd barely spent a night without him since they'd become an item last fall—but I'd hardly gotten a chance to miss her between her pop-ins at Sugar Rush and family dinners.

"You don't have to wipe down the tables," I told her.

She pulled back, giving my shoulders a squeeze. "You've got a couple people who look like lingerers. I'll get them moving along."

"They can linger," I protested, sweeping my gaze toward the two people pecking away on their laptops. They were both regulars and indeed had a habit of not taking a hint and staying well after closing.

I wasn't good at telling anyone to get gone, but Hannah had no trouble. Problem was, she wasn't as gentle as I would've liked. I adored everything about her, but Hannah Kelly had never been subtle a day in her life.

"Nope. You've been working for twelve hours. Closing time is closing time." She glanced over her shoulder at my customers. "I'll be nice. If they don't get the hint when I start wiping down their tables, I'll spray them a little. That should do it."

I laughed, though I knew she wasn't kidding. "You're not going to spray my customers with cleaner!"

She agreed, but I kept one eye on her as she made her way around the tables. By the time the clock struck five, my two lingerers had cleared out. I didn't even want to know what Hannah had said to get them moving. So long as it hadn't involved threats or chemicals, I was good.

I let Camille go, leaving Hannah and me as I shut everything down. She leaned her hip against the counter, her long legs crossed at the ankle, and sipped her latte.

"On my way here, I drove by the house. Noticed a light on in my old apartment and a truck parked out front," she said.

"Oh yeah? I guess someone moved in." My stomach twisted at the idea of someone else living in Hannah's place, as irrational as it was. Shoving that feeling aside, I reached for a to-go box. "Is it rude to bring leftovers as a welcome present? I don't have the energy to bake anything, but I'd like to say hello."

"If someone's offended by *anything* you make, they're an asshole," she stated. "Hope like hell your new neighbor's not an asshole."

"Joy wouldn't let an asshole move in."

"Yeah. Probably not."

Joy was our landlord and a Sugar Brush staple. She owned Joy's Elbow Room, a bar at the other end of Main Street, along with several properties around town, including the duplex I rented. In her fifties, Joy had been hardened from working in bars all her life and didn't tolerate nonsense. I trusted she'd fully vetted the new tenant. After all, I'd practically had to give blood samples, and Joy had known me all my life.

Hannah peered into the to-go box I'd loaded with pastries. "If the newbie doesn't think you're the best neighbor ever, let me at 'em."

I snorted a laugh and closed the box, sealing it with one of my custom floral stickers. "You have to stop threatening violence, Banana."

She held her hands up. "When did I say anything about getting violent? That's all in your mind."

She didn't have to say it. Hannah had become mellow with age and her ADHD meds, but back in the day, she'd been known to take on any guy who looked at me funny. My sister was tall and strong, both from genetics and working with horses, and she'd socked a jaw or two when she'd felt necessary. I couldn't picture her doing it now, but Hannah was good at keeping everyone on their toes. It was one of the best things about her.

As we walked out together, she bumped my shoulder. "By the way, Camille mentioned some guys gave you a hard time this morning."

I waved her off. "It wasn't a big deal, honestly. You know how those guys are. All bluster, no bite."

I locked up, and she rounded on me. "You sure? I can put Caleb on it. He'll find out which ranch they work on—"

The last thing I needed was our older brother dragged into this. If Hannah told Cay a guy had looked at me sideways, he'd wade in, no questions asked, and he had enough going on. There were four of us Kelly siblings, and we would all throw down for each other. My version of throwing down might've been a conk with a rolling pin, but still, I'd be there.

My siblings were more than protective over me, though. I wasn't tough or strong. I liked sugar, collected cookbooks, and surrounded myself in all shades of pink, so they saw me as weak. They'd never say it, but they didn't have to.

I laid my hand on her arm. "Banana, honest. I know you think I'm a wimp, but I can handle myself. I set them straight, and they went on their way. I'm hoping they're too embarrassed to come back, but if they do, I'll be fine. I mean, worse things have happened than some guy I'm not interested in asking me on a date."

Her brown eyes, which matched mine, examined me for a long beat before she nodded. "If that's how you want to play it. Now, hop in the truck. I'm driving you home."

"I can walk a couple blocks," I protested, though it was closer to a mile.

"You *can*, but you won't." She stole the bakery box from my hands and started walking toward her truck. "Not if you want this back!"

The drive to our place took a few minutes, but only because we had to stop at both traffic lights along the way. Our duplex was situated kitty-corner to a park with a gazebo and small playground. When it got warmer, the town held markets and summertime concerts there. All the small-town goodness right outside my front door. I understood why Hannah had moved out to the ranch she and Remi shared, but I liked living right in the thick of things—as thick as they got in a town this size anyway.

My good mood from time spent with my sister lasted until I saw the mess outside my door. The pots I'd bought from an artisan from the Wind River Reservation were in pieces, soil scattered around them. Heartbroken at the brightly colored beauties being in ruin, I crouched to inspect the damage. If the pieces were big enough, there was a chance I could glue them back together, but I was no potter. Even if I managed to reassemble them, they'd never be the same.

With a huff of frustration, I lifted my gaze, spying dirty footprints leading away from the crime scene directly to the stairs that went to the apartment above mine.

I wasn't anything close to a forensic scientist, but I also wasn't an idiot. I could've checked the footage from my doorbell camera, but it didn't seem necessary. All signs pointed to my new neighbor being the culprit. *Dammit.*

Dropping my bag by my door, I picked up the pastry box and headed up the stairs, the knot of anger in the pit of my stomach unraveling with each step. Most likely, it had been an accident. Surely, they'd be deeply apologetic. There was no sense in holding a grudge. I loved those pots, but they were just things, and I had to share walls with the person who'd moved in above me. We weren't going to be enemies before we even met.

Thoroughly talked down, I put on a cheery smile and knocked on their door, the pastry box in front of me. The thumps and grumbles that followed weren't what I'd expected. Then the door swung open, and the man who stood there was *really* unexpected.

Lean and rangy, like so many of the cowboys who worked on the ranches around town. That's where the similarities stopped, though. His arms, covered in gray and black tattoos, were crossed tightly over his chest, covered in a faded band T-shirt. Bracketing his mouth was a frown so deep it'd worn grooves. It was only when I got to his eyes—storms frozen in Jurassic-age amber—I recognized him.

Deacon Slater.

When had he gotten out of prison?

Chapter Three

Deacon

Pink.

Cheeks, sweater, box—all of it pink.

What all this pink was doing on my doorstep was a wonder. I didn't want visitors, least of all a woman like this, with her rosiness and long, shiny brown hair draping over tits I could tell were round and soft, even with a sweater covering them. All of her looked that way, like there wasn't a single sharp corner.

What was sweet little Phoebe Kelly doing knocking on my door? No doubt her daddy and brothers would not approve.

"Yeah?" I gruffed.

"Hey." She dug her teeth into her full bottom lip, waiting like she expected something from me. I didn't know what. She'd been the one to knock on my door. "I stopped by to say hi. It seems like we're neighbors."

"Ah." This news rocked me back on my heels. I hadn't given much thought to who rented the apartment below mine. Seemed I should have. "Sorry 'bout the pots. Hit 'em when I was moving my bed in. Give me the name of the store you got 'em from, I'll replace them."

She shook her head. "Thanks for that, but they came from an artist who lives on Wind River. Too far for you to be trekking to buy some pots. I'm going to try to glue them back together if I can. Otherwise…" She sighed as she trailed off.

"All right. Then tell me what they cost. I break something, I'm going to settle up."

Her brown eyes were big and bright, and she had them pinned on me, scraping over my face. With recognition? Doubted it. She'd know my name. Everyone in town knew the Slaters, and that was so they could steer clear. There was not a chance Phoebe had given a thought to me since we'd been in school together.

"Don't worry about it. I understand accidents happen." She smiled straight at me, confident and friendly. "I'm just glad to have a new neighbor. My sister, Hannah, lived here before you. It's been too quiet, not hearing her footsteps marching around upstairs."

"I don't plan on making much noise." I'd need to take my boots off when I got home so this soft, pink woman didn't have to put up with any extra racket.

"Well, as long as you don't set fire to your oven like Hannah, I think we'll get along fine."

I nodded. "I noticed the scorch marks on the wall. I've got no plans of adding to them."

Her giggle was sugar-laced. "Yeah, Hannah and cooking don't mix. Fortunately, our parents had supplied her with a fire extinguisher when she moved in. They knew all too well the kind of damage she's capable of."

I didn't have much to say to that. Having the kind of parents who cared enough to buy me a fire extinguisher was as foreign to me as Japanese—a language I'd never learned and only heard in passing.

Phoebe sucked in a breath. "Anyway, I wanted to welcome you to the neighborhood. I brought you some baked goods from my shop,

Sugar Rush. I don't know what you like, so I picked out some of everything." She tapped the lid of the box in her hands. "And I wrote my number in case you ever need anything."

I didn't need to look inside the box to know I wouldn't be eating the contents.

"No thanks."

Her eyes flared with surprise. "No...you don't want it?"

I shook my head, as much as it pained me. Something sweet on my tongue that'd been baked by this pink woman would have more decadence than I'd know what to do with. But life had served me a hell of a lot of lemons, including allergies that might kill me if I ate the wrong thing.

"Appreciate the gesture. Won't eat it. Might as well give it to someone who will."

She withdrew the box, hugging it against her middle. "Okay. I know not everyone likes sweets..." She put on another smile, this one a little wobbly. "I'll leave you to moving in. If you need anything, I'm downstairs at night or at Sugar Rush all day. Oh, and I'm Phoebe."

Confirmed what I already knew. She didn't have a clue who I was. Not that I was mad about it. The years hadn't been easy on me. I didn't look the same as I had back then, and it wasn't like we'd been friends. She had no call to remember me. I should've forgotten her too, but I hadn't been around enough good to replace those memories of Phoebe Kelly smiling at me like I'd meant something.

I tipped my chin. "Deke."

"Deke," she whispered under her breath, like she was testing the feel of it. Then I got a dose of her sweetness in the form of rosy cheeks and fluttering lashes. "I'll see you around, Deke. I hope you settle in nicely."

I didn't let myself watch her leave. Once she turned away, I closed the door and locked it, putting all thoughts of her aside.

Walking into my new bedroom, I took a seat on the side of my mattress to unlace my boots and placed them next to my bed before I lay on my back. I stared up at the ceiling, dappled with light filtering in through the curtains.

It'd been a year since I'd walked out of the prison gates, and this was the first place I was considering making my home, at least for a while. There wasn't much to it. A mattress and box spring in the matchbox bedroom. A camp chair and folding table in the living room. A few plates and silverware given to me by my aunt in the kitchen. But to me, it was a luxury. I didn't have to listen to anyone snoring or making other sounds I'd rather not dwell on. The air was clean and fresh. Lights went on or off when I wanted, and I'd never have to wait in line for the bathroom.

Luxury.

Without meaning to, my mind drifted back to Phoebe Kelly. I hadn't seen her since graduating high school almost ten years ago. I wasn't surprised she still lived in town. Her family's roots ran deep in these parts. The Kelly Ranch was twenty or thirty thousand acres. They owned so much land it went from prairie to rivers to mountains. Most of the town loved them, but there were plenty who resented them too.

My mom and dad hadn't thought much of them. The Kellys lording their fortune over the town while we'd struggled to get by. That was what they'd said, anyway.

I'd never thought Phoebe had lorded anything. I'd been the dirty kid in worn-out hand-me-downs with holes in my shoes. She'd been pristine in her jeans, boots, and girly, fussy tops. But the few times our paths had crossed, she'd talked to me like we were the same. She'd say hi when she was with her friends, like knowing me wasn't something to be embarrassed about.

She'd treated everyone that way, though. It was no wonder she'd forgotten about me. What'd been something special to me had been everyday life for her.

What were the chances she'd live right downstairs from me?

I guessed getting daily glimpses of her would be a luxury too.

That was all I'd get.

And that was all right with me. I'd learned a long time ago not to expect much so I was never disappointed.

I climbed into my truck before first light. My jobsite was a long drive from Sugar Brush, but that was the way in Wyoming—nothing was close, just how we liked it.

I turned the key in my ignition at the same time Phoebe walked down the steps and hit the sidewalk. She was bundled in a puffy black coat that went to her knees and a light-pink hat with something fuzzy on top. It was almost spring, but winter always clung hard around here, and she was out walking before the sun had even risen.

I'd caught sight of a woman walking down the sidewalk on my way to work yesterday. That must've been her.

Before she turned away from me, she stopped and peered directly into my windshield. The cab was dark, so there was no way she could see me, but that didn't deter her from walking straight to my window and tapping on it.

With no way out, I rolled it down. "Morning."

She blew out a puff of air. "Oh, good. It's you."

My brows rose. "That's good?"

"Considering the other option was some random man sitting here watching me, yeah, I'm glad it's you." She brushed a strand of hair off her face with her mittened hand. "I think I saw you driving down Main Street yesterday morning too."

I inclined my chin. "That was me."

"Going to work?"

"Yep."

Her nose was getting rosy as she stood here talking to me while I sat in my slowly warming truck. She needed to move along. I did too.

"I am too." She crinkled her nose. "I know you don't want pastries, but if you like coffee, I make a mean cup. We open at six, but if you're leaving now, I guess that's too late for you."

"It is. I have to be on my way."

She backed up a step, probably from the firmness in my tone. I hadn't meant to be so harsh, but I didn't have a lot of practice at exchanging pleasantries with neighbors. Truth be told, I didn't intend to make a habit of it either.

It took her a beat, but she pulled herself together enough to smile. "Well, all right, Deacon. Hope you have a good day at work."

"You too." It was on the tip of my tongue to tell her she shouldn't be walking alone in the dark, but I bit it back. She knew what she was doing, and this town was safer than most.

She raised her hands. "See you later."

I gave her a nod as I rolled up my window. It went against my instincts, but as soon as she was clear, I reversed out of my spot and drove off, watching her disappear in my rearview. She'd probably been getting herself to work without my interference for years. She didn't need my concern, and *I* didn't need to get caught up in thinking about what could happen to her out there on her own.

She'd be fine.

Besides, Phoebe Kelly was none of my business.

Chapter Four
Phoebe

I ALMOST MISSED THE envelope partially stuffed under my welcome mat but stopped just before stepping on it. Bending down, I scooped it up and carried it into my apartment. It seemed I always had an armful when I got home from work.

Aprons and towels to throw in the laundry, my lunch box, laptop, and my hat and mittens were unloaded onto my kitchen island once I'd kicked off my shoes and wiggled my toes in my thick living room rug.

I flipped the envelope over to examine it. On the outside, scrawled in pencil, was the word "Sorry." I frowned as I opened it, which turned into a full-on scowl at the stack of cash inside.

Deacon hadn't bothered to sign his name, but there was no doubt this was from him. It was way too much money. Not that I wanted any amount of money from him, but this? No way. I wouldn't accept it.

An apology for an honest mistake was all I'd needed, and he'd paid in full. We weren't going to start our neighborly relationship like this.

Tossing his envelope aside, I pulled out a card and envelope and wrote my own note.

Deacon,

Your apology is accepted. No grudges are being held.

Welcome to the neighborhood!

If you ever change your mind about pastries or coffee, you know where to find me, and you can always count on me to have sugar if you need to borrow some.

Your neighbor,

Phoebe Kelly

He probably wouldn't appreciate the handmade, pressed-flower notecard I'd bought from a paper artist at the town market last summer, but I wasn't a plain stationery kind of girl, so he'd have to take it.

Once I placed his cash in the envelope, I slipped my feet in my furry slippers, tossed on a sweater, and walked upstairs to knock on his door.

Like yesterday, there were a few bangs and heavy footsteps before he answered. The flick of his eyes was quick but unmistakable. He'd looked me over then let his gaze linger on my braid resting on my shoulder.

"Hey, Deke. I got your envelope."

He raised his eyes to mine. "That's good. Let me know if it's not enough."

"You left me two hundred dollars. How could that not be enough?"

His shrug was lazy. "Don't know how much things like that cost. Took a wild guess."

"Well, it's way too much and, like I told you, unnecessary. Accidents happen, you know? I'm not holding a grudge. In fact, I'd forgotten about it until I got home and spotted your apology envelope."

His nostrils flared as he rocked back on his heels. In the beat of silence that stretched and stretched, I really looked at him, cataloging the changes in his face since I last saw him going on ten years ago.

As a teenager, he'd never had much softness about him, but now, he was rawboned and chiseled. Golden stubble sprouted along the sharp planes of his jaw and shadowed above his flattened mouth. His lashes were thick and pale. Like downy chick feathers, his neatly cut hair was somewhere between light brown and strawberry blond, and his cheeks had a pink tinge, like they'd been bitten by the wind.

Deacon Slater had grown up hard, and it showed, but it didn't lessen how devastatingly handsome he was. I'd never found myself attracted to tattoos on men, but the ones covering his lean, sinewy forearms made my knees weak.

When we were young, I'd thought he was the most beautiful boy I'd ever seen. He'd never really looked at or talked to me, making staring at him for long swaths of time without getting caught easy.

I wasn't so lucky this time.

"What?" he gruffed.

I ripped my gaze from his arms, realizing I'd been biting my bottom lip. *Oh, my muffins. What the hell am I doing, and why am I doing it on this man's porch?*

"What?" I echoed, without the gruffness.

His lids lowered, and a ripple went through his jaw. "Never mind. Did you need anything else?"

"Actually, yes." I held out my own envelope. "This is for you."

He took it in his hand, frowning like he'd never seen pressed paper before—which might've been true. I didn't know what kind of mail prisoners received, but I had a feeling it didn't usually come on fancy stationery.

With unexpected care, Deke slid his thumb under the flap, opening the envelope without ripping it, and slid the card out. A harsh crevice took up residence between his brows as he read it. Then he replaced the card and stuffed it in the back pocket of his jeans, holding the cash out to me.

"Appreciate it, but you need to take this."

I raised my hands, taking a step back. "I don't want it, Deacon. Please keep it."

His fist balled around the bills. "I can afford to pay for a couple pots."

Though he was making a valiant effort to keep his tone void of...well, anything, I didn't miss the echo of injury behind his words. I was aware of what some people in this town thought of my family, especially when the disparity between the haves and have-nots was so vast. The Slaters were on the opposite side of the spectrum. I'd never seen their home, but I'd heard tales of crumbling foundations and boarded-up windows. No heat or indoor plumbing. And everyone said they cooked meth, though I wasn't certain that was true. If it were, surely they'd have the money to fix up their house.

There was probably a lot of veracity to the things I'd heard, though, and it had to be a sore spot for this man. I hated that he thought I was insulting him. That wasn't me. Then again, just because I'd carried a torch for him back in high school didn't mean he'd ever given me a second thought, let alone knew anything about my character. He might've thought I was a snobby bitch who looked down on the Slaters.

I wished he didn't.

"I'm not implying you can't. I'm sorry if it seemed like I was. I feel as though we're misunderstanding each other, so I'll start over."

He waited, amber eyes keen but darkened by the storms stirring behind them.

I sucked in a deep breath. "I bought those pots on a road trip to Yellowstone with my grandparents. We stopped at an art fair we'd spotted from the road and met the artist who made them. They weren't very expensive, but I thought they were really pretty. That was right before I moved into my apartment. They were the first purchase I'd made for the start of my new, independent life."

Deacon was as still as the dead, attentive but silent. I went on.

"The pots are gone, and while I'm sorry about that, it's okay because I had one of the best trips of my life with my grandparents. I don't need the pots to remember that. That's why I don't want your money, Deacon. It has nothing to do with whether I think you can spare it."

He cocked his head. "What was so good about it?"

"The trip?"

He nodded.

"A lot of things. We went out with a nature guide at sunrise two mornings in a row and saw wolves. They were just hanging out in a valley, living their wolf lives and letting us witness it. It was the coolest thing I've seen in my life. Plus, my grandmother is a little crazy, and my granddad loves the stuffing out of her. It's always nice to be around that. Love and wolves."

A little happy laugh bubbled out of me. Deke jumped as though he was startled. I'd have to remember not to laugh so suddenly around him.

He rubbed his chest like he was trying to calm his skittish heart. "Okay. Doesn't sit right with me, but if you won't take the money, I can't force it on you." He inclined his chin. "Is that all?"

"That's all." I had a lot to do tonight, but I was still dragging my feet. "Will tomorrow be another early morning for you?"

"Always is." He cupped his nape, scuffing his foot against the floor.

"Me too." I rubbed my lips together. "It's none of my business, but I'm going to ask anyway. What do you do?"

"Work on the roads. Maintenance and inspection."

No wonder his cheeks were so ruddy. He worked outside, and the wind could be brutal. If I thought he'd be open to it, I would have given him a salve to protect his skin, but he wouldn't take my pastries, so I doubted he would accept *that*.

"Do you do a lot of driving?"

"Yep." He glanced behind him then peered back at me with a pinched expression. "We don't need to do this. The whole neighborly thing, it doesn't have to happen."

"Oh." That knocked me down at the knees. Here I was, interested in being friendly since he was living right on top of me and had made my little teenage heart go pitter-patter once upon a time, and he didn't want any of it.

I couldn't say my feelings weren't a little hurt, but that was my fault, not his. I shot him my best, most gleaming smile. "Then I'm sorry for bothering you. I promise I get the hint. It won't happen again. Have a good night, Deacon."

I whirled around and started down the stairs, not even making it halfway before he closed his door with a firmness that struck me in my gut.

I didn't think that could have possibly gone worse. Clearly, Deacon Slater wasn't any more interested in knowing me now than he had been in high school. That was fine. I didn't need to be told twice.

He'd go his way, and I'd go mine.
No big deal at all.

Chapter Five

Phoebe

My older brother, Caleb, showed up at Sugar Rush near the end of the day with my nephew. Jesse was eleven, smart as a whip, and basically the light of my life.

He had the Kelly eyes—like the perfect cup of creamy hot chocolate—thick chestnut hair and feet too big for his gangly body. When he stood in front of my pastry case with his arms crossed, it was all I could do not to laugh at how damn cute the kid was. He'd told me more than once that sixth graders weren't cute.

I rounded the counter to tousle his hair. "What's up, Jess?"

His brows were pulled together in consternation. "No chocolate chip cookies?"

Caleb moved next to his son and sighed. "Kid…"

The two of them were a funny sight. While Caleb obviously hadn't carried Jesse, Jesse had inherited one hundred percent of his dad's DNA. Caleb's ex, Shelby, had just been the incubator. Same eyes, same coloring, same smile, same expressions. Caleb was essentially Jesse on a massively multiplied scale, at least in looks. In attitude, they were night and day. Cay was laid back, as easygoing as they came, while Jesse's mind spun a mile a minute.

Jesse turned toward his dad. "It's basically torture to bring me here when I can't eat my favorite thing. I should call the cops on both of you."

I put one hand on my hip, keeping the other behind my back. "Have you ever known me to torture you?"

He peered up at me. "There's a first time for everything."

Caleb's massive mitt landed on top of his son's head. "Be good to Aunt Phe, and I bet she'll be good to you."

It was hard to believe Jesse and I were blood related. The kid didn't like sweets, chocolate chips being the only exception. I'd tried to win him over with countless recipes, had even made my bakery nut-free so he could try anything he wanted without worrying about his allergy, but he'd refused all but my cookies.

"Good, like this?" I whipped a white paper bag from behind my back. I'd set a batch aside just for him. "I have all these chocolate chip cookies and no one to give them to. Do you know anyone who wants nut-free cookies?"

Jesse did a dance he'd learned from some video game then snatched the bag from me, gave me a quick hug, and ran to an empty table to demolish the cookies. If I were his mom, I'd probably tell them to save some for later, but as his aunt, I got to let his father deal with that.

Caleb draped his heavy arm over my shoulders. "Thanks, Phe-Phe. Kid's spoiled."

"He's cute. He deserves it."

His chuckle was like thunder rolling over prairies, deep and resonant. "I'd agree, except he has two aunts and an uncle who gives him everything he wants, and that's just on my side. His mom's not much better."

"And yet, he's the best boy in the world." I ducked out from under his arm and faced him. "How's Shelby?"

He lifted a shoulder. "We don't have much cause to have deep conversations. Jess says she's dating some new guy. Says he seems nice, but he doesn't hang around the house, so Jess doesn't know him too well."

I scanned my brother, gauging whether he felt any kind of way about Shelby dating. He was as relaxed as always. He and Shelby had never been anything serious, but after Jess was born, they'd tried for a while. It hadn't worked out, and as far as I could see, there were no hard feelings. Not that Caleb would share if there were. He wasn't a big talker.

"That's good he isn't hanging around the house yet," I replied. "Are you hungry? Want something from the case?"

"I'd never say no to anything you make. Pick something for me."

Cay ran a hand over his rounded stomach—a trait we'd both inherited from our dad. For Cay and Dad, the roundness was limited to their middles, while the rest of them were solid and strong from the backbreaking labor they did every day on the ranch. In contrast, I was plump all over, thanks to years of sampling the treats I baked.

I picked out a blondie and muffin for Cay then made him a coffee. He and Jesse hung around for a while, and I went back and forth between them and the few customers I had since Camille had gone home for the day. When it was almost time to close, the two helped me by wiping down tables.

"I don't like you being here alone," Caleb groused.

"I'm thinking about hiring an afternoon worker. I put in a job notice at the high school." I had someone who worked weekends, but I needed another person during the week. I couldn't keep asking Camille to work twelve-hour shifts. She'd burn out, and I'd be screwed if I lost her.

"That's good. You work too hard." Caleb frowned at the empty seating area. "You should close now."

I shook my head. "There are always last-minute customers. I'll close at five."

He huffed. "You sure you'll be okay on your own?"

"Of course. This isn't my first rodeo, you know."

"Yeah, I know." He put his hand on Jesse's shoulder, still seeming conflicted. "I'd stick around if I didn't have to get this kid to his mom's."

Jesse puffed up his scrawny chest. "I can't be late for spaghetti night. Mom and I are making meatballs. She hates to touch the raw meat, so that's all on me."

I smiled at him. "Get out of here then. Don't let your mom down."

"I won't."

They were off soon after that, leaving me in a quiet shop. I started my cleaning routine, keeping an eye on the clock. We still had a half hour before closing, and chances were there'd be a few stragglers. There wasn't much left in my pastry case, but I'd rather it not go to waste.

The bells over the door tinkled. Crouched behind the counter, grabbing extra cup sleeves, I yelled out, "Be right with you!"

That was how he'd gotten so close.

I stood, spinning around, and the asshole from earlier in the week was leaning over the counter only a foot or two from me. On instinct, I stepped back, my hands going to my chest.

He chuckled, mean and humorless. "Did I scare you?"

What was his name? Ry? He and his friend hadn't been back since the incident, and I'd been hoping that had been the end of it. I'd been wrong.

"You startled me, but that's my fault. My mind was elsewhere." Loosening my arms, I forced them to my sides. "How can I help you?"

Taking his time, he looked over the pastries I had left. While he did, I slipped my phone from my pocket, just in case I needed to use it. He hadn't done anything wrong, but I was less than comfortable being alone with him.

"Give me one of them brownies. I could use a coffee too, if you still have some brewed."

I jumped again at the sound of his voice, making him snicker. "Sure. Just a second."

I moved as quickly as possible, pouring his coffee and slipping his brownie into a bag. He followed me over to the cash register, using his phone to pay. I told him to have a nice day, crossing my fingers he'd get the message, but he didn't seem to be in a hurry.

He took a long sip of his coffee, peering at me over the lid. "He's still not over it, you know."

I gripped the edge of the counter. "I'm not sure what you mean, but we're getting ready to close. I'm sorry, but you'll have to take your coffee to go."

He leaned his hip against the counter. "Still got ten minutes 'til closing. Think I'll stay right here, enjoy my drink. You can go about your business. I won't be no bother."

I tucked hair that had slipped free from my braid behind my ear. "Actually, I have to close early tonight. Thanks for coming in."

Chuffing, he put his coffee down. "When I moved here, all the guys told me about this cute girl who baked like an angel. I tell you what, I got a look at you, expected something better, but your coffee and baking didn't let me down. Tommy, on the other hand? That boy's downright smitten. You're telling me you can't make an exception for him?"

"I explained that's not an option." I started to round the counter, intent on opening the door for him, but he moved when I did, blocking my path. I wasn't panicking yet, but my heart was in my throat, fluttering wildly. "You need to leave right now."

He loomed over me, dark eyes like a rake as they moved over my body. "Don't think so, darlin'. Not until we reach an understanding."

Gathering all my bravery, I lifted my chin and stood firm. "There won't be an understanding. Get out of my shop."

Quicker than lightning, he snatched my wrist and yanked me into him, knocking my breath out of me. "Not happening, ya cunt."

Now, I was panicking.

Chapter Six
Deacon

THERE WAS NO REASON for me to be walking along this end of Main Street other than curiosity. I'd driven by Sugar Rush a few times on my way to work, but I hadn't gotten a good look.

That was all I wanted: one good look.

My newfound freedom meant I could sate my curiosity whenever I wanted, and I rarely restrained myself. If I wanted to peek at Phoebe Kelly's bakery, that's what I'd do.

The first pass showed the bakery empty save for Phoebe and a man at the counter. He was paying for his coffee, nothing unusual or suspicious, yet my hackles rose the moment I spotted him.

None of my business.

I didn't go looking for trouble anymore. In fact, I stayed as far from it as possible. Going back to prison wasn't an option.

Forcing my feet forward, I made it half a block before turning back. Trust didn't come easy to me these days. A rough childhood had wrung most of it out of me, and four years behind bars had taken the rest. Made me suspicious of every shadow and wary of the intentions of strangers—I'd heard enough from other inmates to give me every reason.

I'd been hoping it was just my paranoia, but the sight through the shop window made my blood run cold. Phoebe was pinned against the counter, her wrist trapped in the man's grip. Even from the outside looking in, it was plain to see she didn't want this guy anywhere near her, let alone touching her.

Instinct took over. Yanking open the door, I crossed the room in a few long strides, grabbed the back of his jacket, and hauled him off her with a guttural growl.

Taken by surprise, he went down easy, ass on the floor in a flash. Phoebe's whimper struck me deep in the gut, but I didn't dare look at her. If she was hurt, if he'd done something unforgivable...nah, I couldn't go there.

I planted myself in front of her, blocking his view. "You put your hands on her?"

The guy scrambled to his feet, glaring. "What's it to you, dickhead?"

"You don't put your hands on a woman." My fists were tight at my sides. It'd been a long time since I'd used them, but I was ready for him.

"We were havin' a chat, brother. A private conversation." He sneered, peeling his coffee-soaked shirt away from his chest. "Don't appreciate you spilling my drink."

Sliding my eyes to the side, I addressed Phoebe. "You want to talk to him?"

"I don't," she stated, her voice firm.

"You heard her. Get out," I said evenly.

He didn't move.

I knew guys like this one. Bigger than he had any business being, eyes conveying how dirty and mean he was inside. He was taller and heavier than me, probably crazier too. He wouldn't like that I'd taken him down, and I could already tell he wasn't going to let it go.

"Not finished here."

His body tensed, his stance shifting. I recognized the tell a second before he charged and caught him around the neck, locking his big head under my arm. He flailed, getting some jabs in that'd surely smart later, but I wasn't feeling them much at the moment.

Our legs got tangled in all his chaos, sending us both tumbling. He landed with a thud, and I rolled over him, his shirt tight in my grip, my knees pinning his arms down. He bucked under me like a wild bronco, trying his mightiest to get me off.

The things he hollered wouldn't have bothered me if they'd been aimed at me, but he'd turned his head to shout obscenities at Phoebe. Ugly names. Hideous accusations.

I couldn't let it go on. Not for another second.

The first punch snapped his attention back to me. As soon as I had it, I jumped up and jammed my steel-toed boot into his ribs—once, twice, three times. By the fourth, he wasn't yelling anymore. He was crawling, headed toward the door.

I'd have gone after him if not for Phoebe throwing herself in front of me. "Deacon, stop. He got the message. Now, you need to stop. You can't do anything to get yourself in trouble."

She reached out, wrapping her fingers around my forearm. "Don't, please," she whispered.

The haze of violence began to clear, but black still edged my vision. The bells above the door jingled, and we both turned as the bastard bolted out into the street.

All my instincts screamed for me to run after him, but Phoebe's soft fingers stroked my arm, holding me in place.

"You okay?" I asked.

"I'm fine. It's over. He's gone now." She lifted on her toes, her eyes filled with urgency. "I don't want you tangled up in this."

"Do you know him?"

She shook her head. "Not really. His friend asked me out, I turned him down, and...well, he wasn't happy about it."

My jaw was rigid, but I managed to bite out, "You gonna call the cops now?"

Phoebe didn't appear shaken. Of the two of us, I was the one worse for wear. She seemed steady, quietly mulling over my question. If I'd been asked to guess how this soft, pink woman would have reacted to being treated roughly by a man, it wouldn't have been this. Instead of tears and wobbly knees, she had pushed her shoulders back and taken deep, calming breaths.

Her guileless eyes found mine. "I don't want them looking at you when you did nothing wrong. You protected me, but I don't know if they'll see it that way."

I wasn't a big fan of the law, but this woman needed more than me on her side. Chances were, the coward wouldn't be back, but having a more concrete guarantee would help me sleep easier at night.

"Doesn't sit right with me. Call 'em"

Her eyes bounced over my face. "Are you sure?"

I nodded once. "Do it."

She released a heavy breath. "All right, but you were never here. I'll tell them I chased him away with a rolling pin."

I blinked at her. "A rolling pin?"

Cheeks flushing prettily, she waved. "Baker here. It's my weapon of choice. They'll buy it."

A minute ago, I'd been ready to run. Now, I was hesitating. Leaving her alone didn't feel right, especially when I'd spilled the drops of blood on the floor.

But I couldn't go back...

"You sure?" I choked out.

She nodded, resolute. "Absolutely. If you got in trouble, I'd never forgive myself."

That got me moving. I was out the door and around the corner when what she'd said really hit me. Phoebe didn't want me to go back. She knew I'd been in prison.

She'd also called me Deacon, and I was positive I'd introduced myself as Deke.

I sank down to my ass between two buildings, my back against a cold brick wall, and flexed my hand. It wasn't too bad. My boots had taken the brunt of the hits.

Christ, what am I doing?

I was not a violent man by nature, even if my actions said otherwise. Every time I had to use my fists, I swore it killed a part of me. I didn't feel good about hurting anyone, even assholes who probably deserved it.

Knocking my head against the brick, I closed my eyes as my heartbeat settled. I'd get up in a minute. As soon as I was sure it was over.

No idea how long I sat there, waiting. Long enough for the cops to come and go. I climbed to my feet as a woman in a puffy black coat passed by, not believing what I was seeing.

Phoebe was walking herself home after dark. What the hell was she thinking?

I shouldn't have stuck around, didn't really know why I had, but since I'd made that choice, I couldn't stop myself from falling in step behind her. Far enough she wouldn't know I was there, but close enough to do something if needed.

She took her time, waving at a few people, saying hi to others, everyone enthusiastic about seeing her. It was no surprise Phoebe Kelly was the town's sweetheart. It served as a good reminder of how deep the divide between us was. No one would have been glad to see me if they'd known who I was.

She turned onto our street, and I picked up my pace, uneasy at losing sight of her. She had a car. It was parked in our shared driveway. There was no reason for her to be walking to and from work in the dark. Especially tonight. Why wasn't she afraid?

I hurried around the corner, exhaling when I spotted her retreating back. She was hurrying toward home, oblivious to me following her. She needed to pay better attention. Hadn't she learned her lesson?

Tonight, it was me.

Tomorrow, it could have been someone much worse.

She reached the stairs running along the side of our house. Five steps took her to her front door, but she didn't climb them. Instead, she stopped and swiveled around, finding me between the pools of light spilling from the streetlamps.

"I made it," she announced. "You could have walked *with* me, Deacon."

Not so oblivious after all...

With a defeated sigh, I closed the distance, boots echoing on the quiet sidewalk, hands firmly tucked in my pockets. "Just making sure you made it home safe."

She didn't look like a woman who'd been through anything out of the ordinary only an hour ago. Her eyes were lively, and her smile was soft, gently curving, plump, pink lips.

"Safe and sound."

"You okay?" I asked.

"I'm fine, honestly." She paused, looking me over in a slow, curious perusal. "Are you okay? You didn't hurt yourself, did you?"

I tapped the front of my boot on the ground. "Steel toes. Didn't feel a thing."

"I'm glad." She shifted the canvas bag hooked over her arm and continued her thoughtful examination. It didn't make me uncomfortable to have her look at me the way she did, but I wondered what she was thinking since it was clear a lot was going on inside her mind. "I told the cops the rolling pin story. They don't know you were there."

"You didn't have to do that."

"You helped me when *you* didn't have to, Deke. This was my thank-you." She nodded toward the pink box peeking out the top of her bag. "Ordinarily, I'd thank you with baked goods too, but that won't work with you, will it?"

I shook my head and chuffed.

"You didn't have to lie for me." I bet Phoebe Kelly had never lied once in her life. A short time around me, and I'd tarnished her. "I wish you hadn't."

"It's done. No sense in dwelling on it." She shrugged like it was nothing. "This won't come back to bite you. You're free and clear."

I wouldn't be free and clear for a long time. Another year of parole if I walked the straight and narrow, but that was no guarantee. I'd lived a clean life before everything happened, and that hadn't kept me out of prison.

It was easier if I didn't think about that. I set my mind on the problem in front of me—the one I could do something about.

"It'd be better if you weren't alone at your shop. Safer."

Phoebe's eyes crinkled at the corners. "You sound like my brother. I'm never going to hear the end of it when I tell him what happened. If I thought I could get away with not mentioning it, I would."

"But nothing stays quiet around here," I filled in, noticing she hadn't agreed with me about not being alone.

"That, it doesn't. Are you headed upstairs now?"

I shrugged. "Nowhere else to be."

She moved from foot to foot, letting her bag slip from her elbow to her fingers. "Well...if I thought you'd accept, I'd tell you you've earned free coffee and pastries for life."

"Not necessary. Anyone would've stepped in."

"I'm not so sure about that." She plucked her keys from her pocket and smiled softly. "But the fact is, you did. Let me be grateful. You're my personal hero, Deacon."

My gut knotted with discomfort. I turned my head, jerking my chin. "If that's what you need, all right."

I was nowhere near a hero, but if Phoebe Kelly wanted to make me one in her mind to feel safer, she could. My hands were empty. That was one thing I could give her.

Chapter Seven

Phoebe

IF MY SIBLINGS HAD been overprotective before the *incident*, they were practically velcroed to me now. My parents and grandparents were even worse, constantly calling and dropping by just to make sure I was still in one piece.

A week later, I could admit I was still a little shaky, even though there'd been no sign of Ry or his buddies. Camille had upped her hours so neither of us was left alone when the shop was open, but that wasn't a long-term solution. I needed to find another part-time employee—fast.

I'd sent another notice to the high school. So far, there were only a couple nibbles, no real bites.

That changed when a waiflike girl with strawberry-blonde hair finally worked up the nerve to step inside after pacing the sidewalk for several minutes.

I smiled at her. "Hi, how can I help you?"

Her grip on the edge of the counter was so tight her knuckles went white. "I was wondering if you're still hiring. My guidance counselor told me you were, but I didn't see a sign, so I thought maybe you'd already hired someone. I can go. I'll—"

"We're still hiring," I cut in gently.

"Oh. Good." She gave me a wobbly smile. Boy, this girl was adorably nervous. "Is there an application or...?"

Two people filed in behind her. With Camille on her break, I couldn't give her my full attention, so I pointed to the gap in the counter, making a snap decision. "Come on back. We can talk while I take care of these customers."

Her brows rose, but she didn't hesitate to duck behind the counter. While I filled orders, she told me her name was Hailey. She was almost sixteen, a sophomore at Sugar Brush High School, and had never held a job besides babysitting.

But she'd done a *lot* of babysitting.

I'd already been leaning toward hiring her, but I became sold the moment she started pitching in without being asked.

"There's one thing," she said during a lull.

I paused mid-wipe on a coffee spill. "What's that?"

"Well...I don't have a bank account, and I'm not sure my foster family would let me have one. I know this is asking a lot, but would it be possible to be paid in cash?" Her pale cheeks flushed bright red as she avoided my gaze.

It wasn't the first time a part-timer had asked for cash, and it was usually for a good reason. Hailey seemed motivated and eager. She needed the job.

"I can do that." I grabbed an application from the shelf. "Fill this out for me. You can skip the tax stuff. I'll need a reference if you can provide it and all your contact information."

Her mouth spread into a wide grin. "I can definitely do that. Thank you so, so much. If you hire me, I won't let you down, I promise."

I laughed at her unabashed enthusiasm. "I'm sure you won't. I have a good feeling about you."

Her eyes locked on mine, earnest and hopeful. "I have a good feeling too."

My grandparents arrived at closing time, claiming they'd missed me terribly. I didn't point out that they saw me days ago, and since spending time with them was no hardship, I happily agreed to let them treat me to dinner at Joy's.

Grandad walked between my grandmother and me, his arms linked with both of ours, chest puffed out with pride. That was how he always looked when he had one or more of his "best girls" by his side.

"Connell, tell Phoebe where you're taking me next," my grandmother ordered.

Granddad flashed me a conspiratorial wink. "She has me taking her to Croatia. Can you believe that?"

"I've heard it's beautiful," I replied, unsurprised they were planning another trip.

A stone's throw from eighty, they were as lively as people half their age. My grandmother had never been content to stay put, and Grandad would follow her anywhere just to make her happy.

So they traveled a few times a year, always coming back tan and hearty.

"Sure it is. I know because I've been made to watch not one but two documentaries on the place." Grandad made a show of grumpiness, but no one bought it. "What's the point of going now that I've already seen everything?"

My grandmother hmphed. "Making your wife happy—that's the point."

His mouth curved at the corners, and he waggled his white eyebrows. "That's right. The point is to make my lovely Lily happy."

I squeezed his arm. "What a good husband you are."

"You'll love it, and you'll love me for making you go," my grandmother said breezily. "Take note, Phoebe. Don't settle for a man who wouldn't follow you to the ends of the earth. The right one will, sweetheart. Gladly."

I arched an eyebrow. "As if I have time for *any* man."

"When the right one comes along, you'll find the time," she assured me.

If she'd known about the string of terrible dates I'd gone on recently, she probably wouldn't have been encouraging me. There were a lot of men out there who were either emotionally unavailable or just plain strange. I'd put a pause on dating for the time being. Maybe I'd try again when it wasn't so damn cold out. Sundress weather made me want to go out dancing or to a concert in the park. Until then, I was hibernating.

Joy's Elbow Room was a Sugar Brush institution—unchanged for decades and beloved for it. Neon beer signs, dart boards, an ancient jukebox, the best greasy food in town. We settled at a table in the center, my grandmother's choice. She liked to people-watch and hold court. She'd grown up in a family of politicians and had made her own career in politics. Schmoozing was second nature to her.

When our waitress, Alice, came by, my grandmother patted her arm. "Royal blue is your color, darling."

Alice blushed and tugged at her sweater. "Thank you. Is anyone else joining you?"

"Just us chickens!" Grandad boomed, his voice carrying like a roll of thunder. It'd always been that way.

Alice, the poor thing, flinched slightly. She'd been working at Joy's for a couple years and had yet to come out of her shell. I'd always wondered why she worked here when she had a full-time job as a librarian, but I'd never pried. I didn't think she'd appreciate it if I'd tried. I just assumed her salary wasn't large, so she supplemented it by waitressing.

My grandmother gasped. "We should have invited Caleb. With Shelby having Jesse this week, he won't cook for himself."

Alice swayed toward the table. "He was in last night."

I bit back a smile. Alice was so lovely, and Caleb was oblivious. Even if she threw herself at him, which she wouldn't, he'd probably just steady her and tell her to be careful. I didn't know a lot about his personal life since he was deeply private, but I'd never known him to date or be in a serious relationship. He was all about work, family and, most of all, his son.

Grandad chuckled. "Caleb would never turn down a meal at Joy's."

Alice shifted back and forth on her feet. "Well...are you ready to order?"

We took mercy on her and placed our orders. She scribbled them on her notepad and scurried off. Once we were alone again, my grandmother pinned me with a stern look.

"You'll be pleased to know I hired someone this afternoon," I said, cutting her off before she could start. "I won't be alone anymore."

Grandad covered my hand with his. "We're annoying because we care about you, darlin'. The idea that you had to chase away some...some *mongrel* who wouldn't take no for an answer makes me sick."

I sighed softly. "I know. And I'm grateful."

Grandmother tsked. "When I think about what could have happened..."

"Believe me, I agree." My gaze flitted between them. "I'm not so proud I won't admit it scared me. That's why I took action, making changes that will hopefully prevent something like that from happening again."

"Good," Grandmother stated, resolute. "I'm proud of you for being honest about your fear and doing something about it. It's not easy to admit you need help, but it's smart. And, my darling, you've always been so very smart."

I leaned in, knocking my head against hers. "Thanks for saying that."

Grandad folded his arms across his barrel chest. "Doubt you'll have any trouble from that particular guy again. Not after you scared him away with a rolling pin." He grinned at me, deep crinkles bursting like sunshine next to his eyes. "If I could have been a fly on the wall for that scene..."

I did not feel great lying to my family about what had truly happened last week, but since I'd set the ball in motion with the police, I had to let it roll. Besides, it made them feel better thinking I'd successfully defended myself.

I sucked in a deep breath and slowly let it out. "How about we talk about something else? Absolutely *anything* else, please."

Satisfied, they let the conversation shift to other topics. I relaxed, letting their easy banter and warmth soothe the lingering unease.

At one point, while they bickered playfully about Croatia, my gaze drifted to the bar. My stomach flipped when I spotted Deacon Slater carrying a heavy crate. His tattooed arms flexed as he moved, and he disappeared down the hall to the back.

What was Deacon Slater doing here? And why did my stomach feel like it was suddenly filled with a thousand newly hatched butterflies?

I hadn't spoken to him since he saved me. He seemed to be avoiding me, and maybe that was for the best. He'd done a nice thing for me, but that didn't make us friends. He was just going about his life, and I wasn't part of it.

I told myself this, but when he returned from the dark hallway with another crate, I nearly melted in my chair. After all this time, he still had the same intangible quality that had drawn me to him when we were teenagers. Tangible ones too, of course. His ass still looked incredible in a pair of Wranglers, and the tattoos had only added to his appeal.

My grandmother demanded my attention, so I set my mind off Deke, giving it to her. Soon after, our food came, and I was so swept up in eating and laughing I mostly forgot everything else.

After our plates were cleared, Grandad asked his wife to dance. Joy's didn't have a true dance floor, so they made their own near the jukebox. I strolled over, wanting to watch and pick out a few songs I liked. The choices had been popular twenty or more years ago, but the classics worked for me.

Grandad twirled my grandmother around, making her cheeks rosy with happiness. Looking at them, no one would guess they'd been divorced and estranged my entire childhood. They were a reminder that bad situations didn't have to be permanent. People could change, grow, become better, and have a happy ending.

When the last song was over, my grandmother spoke into Grandad's ear. He nodded, and she meandered off, then he held his hand out to me. I took it, and he pulled me in close. He clutched my hand in his then placed his other on the center of my back and swung me around the makeshift dance floor. For a man of his size and age, he had smooth moves. He'd been dancing with Hannah and me since we were little, balancing our feet on top of his.

He patted my back. "You're really doing all right, darlin'?"

"I really am. It shook me up when it happened, but I'm okay now. I'm glad it was me and not Camille or any of my part-timers."

His chest rumbled. "Love you and how selfless you are, but I'll never be glad a man put his hands on you."

I squeezed his hand. "I didn't even have a bruise."

His rumble became deeper. "Lucky for that man you didn't. You wouldn't have been able to stop your father or brothers from hunting him down."

"Or my mother and sister."

He nodded. "True enough." His bottomless brown eyes darted around my face, and he sighed. "We're not going to keep talking about this. What's done is done, handled and over. You built something special, all on your own, and that's what we're going to focus on. Now, tell me, what recipes have you got up your sleeve?"

Relief thrummed in my veins. I should have known my grandad would understand I needed to put the incident behind me. He knew me like the back of his hand. I wasn't a dweller. I didn't have time for it.

I laid my head on his chest for a beat or two and smiled. Tipping my head back, I showed him that smile then launched into my plans for the bakery while he listened like what I was telling him was the most important thing in the world.

Then he spun me until I was dizzy.

On my final spin, I caught sight of Deacon at the hallway entry, his sharp eyes fixed on me. A jolt of awareness traveled down my spine. I mouthed, "Hello," and added a small wave before returning to the familiar warmth of my grandad's arms.

Our dance carried me into another turn, and I glanced back, half expecting to still find him there, but only an empty hallway remained. Deacon wasn't watching me anymore.

How disappointed I was by that surprised me down to my core.

Chapter Eight

Deacon

Joy gave my shoulder a tap. "You've done enough for one night, kiddo. Why don't you take a load off and have a drink?"

I placed the last bottle from the crate on the shelf and straightened, tucking my hands in the pockets of my jeans. "If you don't have any other work for me, I'll head home."

She sighed. "You're not getting it. I want you here so I can get a good look at you, not so you can break your back for me."

I narrowed my eyes. "You need to look at me? I haven't changed since the last time you saw me."

She shook her head. "Do an old lady a favor and park your ass on a stool, all right?"

"You're not old," I gruffed, pissed at the idea of Joy ever getting old. She might've been nearing sixty, but I refused to think about her aging. "And if I don't do the heavy lifting around here, you'll try to do it yourself."

She raised her arm, gesturing toward the shelves. "You stocked me up. Even if I wanted to carry a crate up front, there'd be nowhere to put anything. That's why you can sit your ass on a stool and take a load off. Let me feed you."

There was no arguing with Joy. I'd been about to do as she said when a guy who'd already had too much to drink hollered at her from the end of the bar.

"You hirin' felons now, Joyful? Watch your cash register." He snickered as the man next to him leaned away.

Joy whipped her head in his direction. "What did you say?" she hissed.

The guy kept laughing. "I'm just sayin', having a Slater near your money is like having a paper cut and swimming with sharks. You're living on the edge, Joyful."

And there it was. I'd been stupid to think I could show up here to help my aunt out and fly under the radar. Didn't matter I'd done my time and paid my due. The yoke of my last name would always hang on my shoulders in this town. I was used to it. And if it hadn't been directed at Joy with Phoebe Kelly present to heat it, I wouldn't give a damn what some drunk had to say.

That made it worse. She was dancing with her grandfather, looking so shiny and happy it was nearly impossible for me to tear my eyes off her. And her regal grandmother was perched near the asshole at the bar, taking in the entire scene.

Joy walked right up to the man and snatched his half-empty beer off the counter. "You're done here, Bill. Get the hell out and find yourself a new drinking establishment."

Bill raised his hands, still laughing. "Come on, Joy. You know I'm just joking around. If you can't laugh at the Slaters, what can you laugh at?"

Joy fingered the bat under her bar. "That's my nephew you're talking about. I don't play around when it comes to him, and I certainly won't allow you to run your mouth about my boy. Now, are you going to get out, or am I going to have to force the issue?"

The men around Bill scooted away from him, making it clear he had no allies. That didn't mean they disagreed with what he was saying; they were just smart enough to keep it to themselves. Joy's was the only bar in town. They got tossed out, they were up shit creek, and they knew it.

After some grumbles and curses, Bill pulled his hat low on his forehead and stomped out. Joy scanned the other guys sitting at the bar. When no one had anything to say, she nodded and started refilling their drinks.

I took that as my cue to leave. Empty crate in my arms, I headed toward the end of the bar. As I passed Phoebe's grandmother, she reached out, her manicured fingers snagging the sleeve of my shirt.

"He embarrassed himself, you know," she stated.

I nodded, agreeing. Though only halfway. He might've made a fool of himself, but I hadn't gotten off unscathed. My skin felt like it was burning from the cloak of shame I couldn't seem to shrug off no matter how much distance I put between me and my family.

She huffed an elegant laugh. "Clearly, you don't believe me, but as an unbiased third party, I have no reason to lie to you."

That much was true. I'd never spoken a word to this woman, but I knew who she was. In Sugar Brush, Lily Smythe-Kelly stuck out like a sore thumb. Where most women wore jeans and cowboy boots, she lived in silk and high heels. She was older than Joy by a couple decades, but she was well kept, with pretty blonde hair and subtle makeup.

When I didn't reply, she held up her near-empty wineglass. "Would you be a dear and pour me a refill before you go?"

"'Course." I put the crate down and bent to check the cooler. There was only one wine bottle open, so I lifted it up. "This one?"

"That's it." She smiled, faint crinkles bursting next to her eyes. "Joy buys that brand for me. As far as I know, I'm the only one who drinks it, but she always has it when I come in."

"She's good like that," I said as I filled her glass.

"She's wonderful. Now, I'm not usually one to listen to gossip, but I couldn't help overhearing you're her nephew."

"That's right. She's my mother's sister."

"Ah." She picked up her glass, swirling the white liquid around. "Lucky her, she escaped the Slater name."

I grunted in agreement and picked the crate back up so I could get out of there. I'd had enough for the night. Before I could, though, Lily grabbed my shirt again, bringing me to a halt.

"I grew up in a political family. In certain circles, the Smythe name was mud. In others, it brought expectations I always worried I couldn't fulfill. But over the years, I learned someone was always going to have an opinion of me, and frankly, that was none of my business. The people who knew me didn't give one damn about my last name, and they were the only opinions I valued." She arched a brow. "Joy thinks very highly of you."

"I think highly of her too," I replied, unsure why this woman thought I mattered enough to tell me anything about herself, let alone find some way to relate to me.

"Don't you think that means a whole hell of a lot more than what some idiot who can't hold his drink thinks?" She raised her glass to her lips and winked. "I know I do."

"Wish you weren't the only one who thought so." I tipped my chin. "Have a good night, Mrs. Kelly."

"You too, Mr. Slater."

I'd never had many friends. I'd stopped trying early on since most bailed when their parents found out who my folks were.

Chris had never cared about that. Rough as they came but loyal to the end. Besides my aunt, he'd been the only one who'd visited me in prison then had gotten me a job with his dad's construction company when I got out. It wasn't my dream, but it paid more than I'd ever expected and allowed me to breathe easy. With a felony on my record, landing any job was a feat, let alone one with security and benefits.

The thing about having a friend like Chris was he knew me well. When I did something out of character, he noticed.

"What's that you're making?" he asked, roaming his shed where he'd let me set up a carpentry workshop. The space offered me the opportunity to restart my side business, building custom furniture. And work was trickling in—enough to keep me busy when I wasn't on a jobsite.

I kept my eyes on the pieces of wood clamped in a vise. "Planters."

"Planters? Last I knew, you were working on a storage piece. Is this a new commission?"

I sighed, wiping my forehead with the back of my hand, then leveled my gaze on the hairy, sloppy bastard. Chris and razors didn't mix. His beard reached his chest, and his hair was a scraggly mess on his shoulders. When he wasn't wearing work clothes, he had on sweats that had seen better days years ago. It was a wonder his wife

Tilly had given him a chance, but he'd managed to charm her. Tilly was always neat as a pin, while I'd never known him to dress up or make any kind of effort with his appearance.

They said opposites attract, and it seemed that was true. I didn't know a lot about healthy relationships, but it was clear as day the two of them loved the hell out of each other.

"They're not a commission."

Chris stuffed his hands in his hoodie pocket. "You making them for yourself? Never knew you were so domestic, Deke."

"They're a gift."

"A gift? Hope not for Tills. Love the woman, but she kills every plant she touches. Makes her sad every time."

I couldn't stop my grin. "That's cute."

"Cute? Sure. To *you*. Me? I've banned her from buying more. Can't take it when she gets herself all heartbroken over a fern."

"Well, don't worry. They're not for Tilly." Since he wasn't going to let it go, I continued, preparing myself for his onslaught of questions. "They're for my downstairs neighbor. I broke her pots when I was moving in. She won't take cash to replace them, so I'm making her new ones."

His brows popped the way I'd known they would. "Your neighbor is a woman? Is she, by any chance, a pretty woman?"

"That has nothing to do with why I'm making her planters."

"Mmmhmm. You not saying she's pretty is answer enough. I like her."

I frowned. "You don't know anything about her."

"I know she wouldn't take your money. That tells me a lot about her character." He ran a hand down his beard and tugged on the end of it. "This neighbor have a name?"

Chris and Tilly lived in town, and Tilly worked on Sugar Brush River Ranch, so they were well aware of the Kelly family. Besides that, he and I had gone to school together, so he knew exactly who Phoebe was. If I thought I could have gotten away without answering him, I would have.

"Phoebe," I grunted.

"The only Phoebe I know is...oh, damn. You're tellin' me Phoebe Kelly's your neighbor? And you're building her some planters?" His laugh sounded like a witch's cackle. "What are the chances?"

"It's a small town," I answered wryly.

"True, true." He managed to contain his laughter, but mirth danced in his eyes. "Remember our senior year when you—"

"I remember." I didn't need him walking me down memory lane. The moment Phoebe knocked on my door, every interaction with her had come rushing back to the forefront. "Not a dumb kid anymore. I'm just being a nice neighbor and making up for breaking her pots. Nothing more."

He scratched his beard. "Why not? You're good-looking, gainfully employed and, as far as I know, bathe on a regular basis. If you asked her out, I bet she'd say yes."

I turned back to the wood pieces on my worktable. Phoebe Kelly was a nonstarter. Watching her grandpa twirl her around the dance floor at Joy's a few nights ago had only served to remind me how far apart our worlds were. There wasn't a bridge long enough to close that gap.

Not that it had stopped me from wanting to experience a moment of twirling Phoebe around a dance floor for myself—to know what it would be like to live snatches of time that were nothing but smiles in the arms of a loved one. Soft, pink moments that were so commonplace, it probably didn't even register how rare they were for others.

But thinking and talking about it was a waste of breath.

"I wouldn't know the first thing about taking a woman on a date, and I'm not dating anyway. I've got other things I'm working toward. Even if I wasn't...yeah, not happening."

He went quiet for a beat, and I braced myself for what he was going to say. Chris was always honest and could be as blunt as a baseball bat to the temple when he thought it was needed.

"They took four years from you. That time is gone. Wasted in a cage. Sometimes, I think you forget you're allowed to live how you want now. Why are you locking yourself down voluntarily? I don't get it, Deke."

"Don't expect you to get it. I'm glad you *don't*."

I wouldn't wish what I went through on my worst enemy, let alone my best friend. I was glad Chris had lived a life so good and clean he couldn't begin to fathom the way I was moving forward with mine.

Sighing, he came closer, bending his head to look at the planters I was making. Constructed of reclaimed barn wood, they were about two feet tall and square. I'd added thin, crisscrossing strips of teak to the sides to make them more interesting. I didn't know if Phoebe would like them, and it wouldn't make up for the ones I'd broken, but I had to do *something*. I repaid my debts and repaired what I broke.

"These are incredible," Chris said. "Really, don't let Tills see them. She'll want a pair of her own, and that'll only lead to tears."

I chuffed. "She wants some, I'll put fake plants in them. No tears."

"Nah, you need to focus on work you're getting paid for." He clapped his hand on my shoulder. "We both know you wouldn't let me pay you if I tried."

"Damn right. I'm using your shed for free."

"It was full of junk you cleaned out for me. That's all the payment I need." He propped his hip on my worktable and leveled me with a hard gaze. "Friends do shit for each other and don't keep score. When are you gonna get that through your thick skull?"

"Might be a while."

He groaned. "How'd I know you were gonna say that?"

I smirked. "Think we've had this conversation before."

Until I felt like we were on an even playing field, we'd probably keep having it. With all Chris and his family had done for me, it'd be a long, *long* time.

Chapter Nine

Phoebe

THIS WAS THE THIRD time I'd come home to a surprise since Deke had moved in, and this one...

Well, I was speechless.

On either side of my doormat were two of the most gorgeous planters I had ever seen, with absolutely no explanation of where they'd come from. Except I knew, without a doubt, they'd come from Deke.

I crouched to run my fingers over the crosshatched details and smooth rims. Some of the wood looked aged while the rest was newer with a darker hue. I had never seen anything like it.

"Beautiful," I whispered.

These had to have cost a fortune. The craftsmanship was so intricate and skilled there was no way they were from a factory.

I would have liked to have said I wasn't going to accept them, but I loved them so much I was considering bringing them inside so I could look at them all the time.

I wasn't giving them back.

But I also couldn't allow him to give me something so beautiful without letting him know how much I loved them. He might have been tired of me knocking on his door, but he was going to have to handle it one more time.

I threw my things into my apartment, locked my door, and climbed the steps to Deke's landing. I knocked, and a few seconds later, I heard him moving through his apartment.

He cracked his door, his body filling the opening. "Hey," he grunted.

"Deacon," I sighed. "The planters are so beautiful. You really didn't have to do that."

He leaned his shoulder against the jamb, slowly crossing his arms. "You needed a spot for your plants. Now you have it."

I shook my head, wondering if he thought life was as black and white as he made it out to be. Every action had a reaction, and that was just the way it was.

"Well, thank you. I would say you spent far too much, but I love them, so I won't. I'd like to know the name of the artist, though."

His mouth twitched slightly. "Why's that?"

"So I can follow them, and maybe when I save my pennies, buy another piece."

"You like 'em that much?"

"Love them, Deacon. I'm considering bringing them inside."

"They'll do just fine outside." His gaze traveled down to his socked foot as he scuffed it on the floor. "They're weatherproof."

"I wasn't worried about that, though that's good to know. I thought I might like to have them where I can look at them more."

"Ah." He raised his eyebrows first, then his eyes, though they didn't meet mine. I couldn't tell if I was bothering him, but he didn't seem in a hurry to close the door on me. "Then you still wouldn't have a place for your plants."

"That *is* a conundrum."

His mouth moved, and I stopped breathing when I realized he was silently forming the word "conundrum." When he didn't say anything else and the silence stretched to a point where it might have been uncomfortable if I didn't like looking at him as much as I did, I broke into a gentle grin.

"The artist, Deacon? Will you give me their name?"

He jerked, running his hand down his chest and abdomen. "It's me. I built 'em. You want something else; all you have to do is ask."

My breath caught in my throat. "*You*? I—wow, you made them? That's incredible."

He lifted a shoulder. "They're just planters."

"I don't know a lot about carpentry, but it takes a special talent to make an everyday item beautiful, and you did. I'm so impressed." I bit down on my bottom lip, giving him room to speak if he wanted—he didn't—while considering my next words. "You don't eat sweets at all? Or not my sweets?"

He chuffed. "It's not personal, swear it."

"So, no sweets." I snapped my fingers in disappointment. "You build beautiful things and give them to people. I bake delicious things and give them to people."

Arms falling to his sides, he worked his jaw back and forth. "I'd eat 'em if I could."

My head tipped to the side, curiosity piqued even more. "Why can't you?"

"Nut allergy." He looked like it pained him to admit that, and I felt bad for having pushed the issue.

"I see. Well, in that case, we're both in luck. Sugar Rush is nut-free. My nephew can't have peanuts or tree nuts, so I'm about as mindful as they come. Everything I make at the shop is safe for you to eat." I pressed up on my toes, excited I'd be able to feed him. "I have a box of pastries I brought home. Wait right here. I'll be right back."

Before he could reply—or, in Deacon's case, stare at me in silence—I darted down the stairs. When I got to my stoop, I took a moment to sigh over the pretty planters then unlocked my door, grabbed the pink box I'd set inside, and returned to Deacon.

He frowned at me and practically scowled at the box I held out to him. "You sure?"

My mouth opened, then closed, then opened again to ask, "About what?"

He eyed the little pink box like it might've been a bomb. "It's safe?"

"It is." I tapped my fingertips on the lid. "Is your allergy really severe?"

Nostrils flaring, he jerked a nod. "Surprised it hasn't killed me yet."

Flat, emotionless, like it didn't mean anything. But it did. Trusting food was safe wasn't easy when one wrong ingredient could be the difference between life and death. Deacon didn't know how careful I was. Couldn't understand the love I had for my nephew was my driving force.

"Okay." I pulled the box into my body. "I completely get it. Eating something from a kitchen you're not familiar with is too big of a gamble. I'll stop trying to feed you, I promise. Just...thanks again for the planters. They're amazing."

I turned to go, determined to really leave him alone this time, getting one step before his fingers ghosted over my shoulder.

"Wait...Phoebe. I'll try it."

I swiveled around, locking eyes with him, hoping he could read the sincerity in mine. "You don't know this about me, but I love my nephew Jesse most in the world. I am meticulous about my ingredients because if anything I made sent him into anaphylaxis, I'd never be able to live with myself. Do you understand?"

His eyes darted back and forth between mine, solemn and serious. Then he nodded, seemingly finding what he was looking for, stepped back, and swept his arm out.

"You wanna come in?"

"Yes." I smiled at him. "I'd love to."

I'd been in this apartment countless times, but when Hannah lived here, it had been warm and cozy. Our mom had helped her decorate since she didn't really care about that kind of thing, so she'd had pretty curtains and lots of plush throw pillows on her comfortable sofa.

By any standard, Deacon's place was barren. Nothing on the walls, and all he had for sitting were camp chairs. He'd lived here for a few weeks, but it looked like he'd just moved in.

Stopping in the middle of the living room area, he glanced around like he was just seeing it for the first time. "It's not much."

"No, it's not," I agreed.

He twisted his head around, forehead crinkled with surprise. "Didn't expect that. Thought you'd drop some niceties."

I went to his kitchen, placing the bakery box on the counter. "What's the point of blowing smoke when we can both see you're living like you've got one foot out the door? Do you need furniture? I'm sure I could ask around—"

"You're right. I'm not sure how long I'll be here."

A sliver of disappointment cut through my gut at the thought of him moving away. "Oh. Well, even if you're only in Sugar Brush for a short time, you should at least have a couch."

"I'm not leavin' town anytime soon." He rubbed his nape, his expression somewhat sheepish. "I want a house with another bedroom and a workshop."

"A house? So you're staying?"

"That's the plan." He moved to join me at the kitchen counter, frowning at the bakery box. "We'll see how it pans out."

"Then you should definitely buy a couch. You can take it with you when you find your house. No sense in being uncomfortable in the meantime."

He shrugged. "I don't need much. I'm used to living without."

"That might be, but the point is, you don't have to." I tapped my chin. "Actually, my sister put her furniture in storage when she moved in with her boyfriend. I'm sure she—"

"I can afford to pay for my own things," he said softly but with a firmness that brooked no argument.

Rightfully put in my place, I pressed my hand to my chest. "Sorry. I can't help myself sometimes. When I see a problem, I like to fix it. I'll butt out, though. That camping chair looks pretty comfortable."

That got his eyes on me, something like curiosity tugging at the corners of his mouth. "You're being sarcastic."

I held my thumb and forefinger an inch apart. "A little. But I really won't bring it up again. Your furniture is your business. Even if it sucks."

The laugh that shot out of him froze me solid. A powerful blast of surprise and mirth that broke free without warning, there and gone so fast, I could have convinced myself I'd imagined it if not for the goose bumps crawling up and down my arms.

"Don't spare my feelings."

I grinned back at him. "My other bad habit is being honest to a fault."

"I don't think there's anything bad about that at all."

All traces of his frown had disappeared, unveiling a light in his amber eyes that made me want to lean in to feel its warmth. Then he flipped the lid of the box open, turning his attention to examining the contents.

"Tell me what's in here."

Edging closer, I pointed to each item, naming them and their main ingredients. He considered for a beat then selected a s'mores brownie. As he brought it to his mouth, I fought the urge to knock it from his hand. His first bite of my baking, and it wasn't fresh from the oven. I wished he were trying a warm, gooey brownie with oozing marshmallow and melted chocolate.

Deacon's low groan brought me out of my mental spiral, raising the hairs on the back of my neck. I watched his mouth move as he chewed, taking his sweet ol' time. His throat bobbed when he swallowed, and I exhaled a breath I hadn't realized I was holding.

Without saying a word, he took another bite, this one bigger. We stood facing each other, my eyes on his mouth, his on the floor, as he slowly but eagerly consumed the entire brownie. No words passed between us. Neither of us moved any more than necessary. I didn't ask what he thought, and he didn't offer his opinion.

He didn't need to, though. He'd put away the huge brownie in four bites then searched through the box for something else. Finding a strawberry shortcake cookie, he broke it down the middle and offered me half.

"Don't make me eat by myself," he gruffed.

"Oh, all right." I slipped the piece of cookie from his hand and brought it to my mouth. This time, he watched me take a bite. Only when I started to chew did he tuck into his, making a sound of pure pleasure that I felt all the way down to my toes.

"Good?" I asked.

"Best thing I ever tasted."

My breath caught for a moment. "Then I'll make you your own batch."

He wiped his mouth with the back of his hand. "You don't need to do that."

"Just like you didn't need to make me the most gorgeous planters I've ever seen." I lightly touched his forearm. "I *want* to. It's kind of my thing."

The sinews in his arm rippled under my fingertip. I wasn't sure if it was from discomfort or something else, so I dropped my hand to my side. Deke glanced around his apartment then set his gaze squarely on me.

"Thinking you might be right about needing a couch." He scratched his jaw. "I'd offer you a seat right now, but you deserve better than a flimsy camp chair."

I laughed. "Wow, all it took was a brownie and half a cookie for you to see the light. Don't worry about me. I'm used to being on my feet all day. Anyway, I'm not going to stick around bothering you for much longer."

"You're not a bother." The corners of his eyes pinched. "You remember me? From when we were younger?"

"Of course I do." I brought my hand to my chest. "Did you think I didn't recognize you?"

He gripped the edge of the counter, his index finger tapping the grout between the tiles. "It was a long time ago. We weren't friends, and I was a year ahead of you."

His saying we hadn't been friends wasn't false, but it was still a light punch to the gut. Back then, I'd wanted to be so much more than friends with him; I'd scribbled his name all over my notebooks like the little starry-eyed teen I'd been.

"And you introduced yourself to me," he added.

"Well, I couldn't tell if you remembered *me*." He chuffed as if the idea was preposterous, but it *had* been a long time since we'd last seen each other. What reason had he had for me to be a memory he'd kept? "I knew exactly who you were when you opened the door, Deacon Slater."

"You knew me." He turned his head, giving me a full view of his rippling jaw. "Then why the hell do you keep coming around here, Phoebe Kelly?"

I jerked, staggering back a step. "What's that mean? You said I wasn't a bother."

"You aren't. Not to me." His jaw clenched so hard I was concerned for his teeth. "But you know who I am and where I was the last few years, and where I came from before that. Why are you wastin' time with me? If you feel some kinda obligation because I stepped in when that asshole was hassling you, forget it. You're absolved. We're square."

"You just said a lot." I sucked in a breath, measuring my response. "I'm glad we're square. Anything I do going forward, like bringing you your own batch of cookies, you'll see as an act of friendship, not obligation. Further, I don't have a lot of spare time, Deacon. If I choose to spend some of it with you, it's because I want to. But I am good at taking hints. I'll go. Next time, if you don't want company, simply don't open the door, and I promise I'll leave you be."

He followed me to the door, putting his hand on the knob before I could. My back was to him, but I felt his warm, solid presence close. His breath ghosted near my ear, and my pulse tripped over itself.

"I'm just trying to figure you out."

The next breath I took was shuddery and deep, drawing me back just enough my shoulders brushed his chest. The contact was fleeting, barely there, but his body went rigid, his fingers flexing on the doorknob.

"I don't have ulterior motives," I said softly.

Time stretched as my heart stuttered. Neither of us moved. We barely breathed. We weren't even really touching, but those inches of fleeting contact had felt electrified and important.

Then, as if snapping himself out of it, he took a step away and twisted the doorknob. Moving aside for him to open the door wider, I dared a glance back at him. His cheeks were flushed, and tension radiated from the corners of his eyes and the clench of his jaw.

"I'm gonna go." I offered him a smile so we didn't end on a sour note, then barely made it two steps onto the landing before his voice caught me.

"Phoebe."

Heart in my throat, I turned back. "Yeah?"

His fingers curled at his sides. "I'll answer the door."

A thousand butterflies took flight in my belly.

"Okay," I whispered.

One shoulder braced against the jamb, the weight of his gaze followed me as I slid my key into the lock. Before stepping inside, I hesitated, my eyes flicking up to him.

He nodded to me. "Night, Phoebe."

"Good night, Deke."

Chapter Ten

Deacon

WHAT WAS THAT?

Phoebe Kelly wanted to be my friend?

Why the hell would she want to go and do something stupid like that?

I sat down in my camp chair, the bakery box in my lap. There weren't any more otherworldly cookies, so I tore into a muffin that tasted like carrot cake.

I'd never eaten anything like this in my life. Growing up, what meals I hadn't eaten for free at school had mostly been scraps I'd scrounged up in our kitchen. No one had been making gourmet, and my cooking skills were severely lacking. I ate because I had to. This...it was an extravagance I'd never consider giving myself.

And Phoebe had handed it to me like it was nothing then stood in front of me, watching me eat like it was no big deal at all.

Phoebe Kelly, with her thick rope of shiny hair draped over her shoulder. A woman so distinctly outwardly feminine, she might as well have been a different species—one I sure as hell had never been this close to. Her floral shirt had hugged her full breasts before trailing over the gentle roundness of her tummy. The denim of her jeans had followed the generous lines of her full hips and thick thighs. And she had this...curve right at the apex of her thighs, where her jeans creased. My eyes continued to stray to that spot, wondering how it looked without clothes, how it would feel to slide my fingers into. Would it be as soft and warm as my head told me it was?

I'd tried as hard as I could not to look, but it'd been impossible. Just like it'd been impossible to keep my body from reacting to hers.

Luckily for both of us, she hadn't noticed the bulge in my pants from my half-hard cock. Her offer of friendship would've been rescinded fast enough to make both our heads spin.

Forcing my mind from spiraling, I examined the rest of the pastries in my lap. I should've saved the rest for tomorrow, spread out the decadence and spared my stomach, but once I'd had a taste, I didn't want to stop. One by one, I ate everything in the box. When it was gone, I tipped the corner up to my mouth to get every last crumb.

With a full belly, I sank down in my chair and closed my eyes, letting the good settle over me.

Strawberry shortcake cookies, lemon bars, carrot cake muffins. Phoebe's shoulders touching my chest, the scent of sugar radiating from her pores, the look of sheer wonder when she'd discovered I'd made her planters. Comfortable, quiet home. Freedom. Joy, Chris, and Tilly. So much goodness, it was hard to believe it was all mine.

My phone vibrated in my pocket, tearing me out of my reverie. Pulling it out, I checked the screen, expecting a message from Chris or Joy. Instead, I found a text from an unknown number.

Unknown: *Heard you're out and back in SB. How's it going? Enjoying the smell of freedom?*

Dread pooled in my gut. I'd expected a text like this last year when I first got out. It never came, and I'd let my guard down. That it would come when I was feeling somewhat optimistic made sense.

Unknown: *Disappointed I haven't heard from you. Got no time for your big brother?*

Dammit. I couldn't have just had tonight—one night to feel all the good before I had to deal with this?

As much as I would've liked to ignore him, when Richie wanted something, he didn't stop until he got it—and I knew my brother well enough to know he wasn't texting for a family reunion.

Time would only tell what kind of havoc he intended to wreak.

Chapter Eleven
Phoebe

Our family didn't do regular, scheduled dinners, but they tended to happen at least once a week anyway. Midafternoon Sunday, I headed out to the ranch. Since moving to my apartment a few years ago, I became intentional about spending time with my parents. I liked being with them, so I always carved out room.

Driving through the gate marking the entrance of my family's ranch, I sighed like I always did. There was nothing like coming home.

On either side of the road, cattle grazed on patches of grass where lingering snow had melted. A couple ranch hands on horseback rode along the fence line, nodding in greeting. I didn't recognize them, but that wasn't unusual. The ranch employed a lot of workers—some long term while others were seasonal.

Long before I was born, part of our property had been turned into a luxury resort. A grand main lodge housed a spa and restaurant, and several private cabins had been built farther out, offering guests a secluded retreat. People visited to get a taste of cowboy life while enjoying every creature comfort they could want.

Our family homes were set well away from the guest areas. My grandparents, parents, and Caleb had built houses on our land, and once Cormac settled down, I figured he would build here too. As for me, I wasn't sure yet. Though I'd been making good use of the resort's spa since I was a teenager, living in town felt right for the time being.

I knocked before walking into my parents' house. As happy as I was they were still crazy about each other; there were some things a daughter should never see.

Fortunately for me, they were fully clothed when I entered the kitchen. My mother was standing at the island, tapping away on her laptop, with my dad behind her, his arms around her middle, his face pressed against the side of hers.

They were a picture. My mother, a gorgeous, silvery blonde who oozed sophistication. My father, equally gorgeous, but rougher, with thick, dark stubble and chestnut hair that always looked like it needed a trim. While she was tall and willowy, he was as solid as a Redwood and even taller. He worked with his hands running the ranch and looked the part in his worn jeans and flannel. My mother was the head of marketing at the resort and didn't believe in dressing casually. Even now, on a Sunday afternoon, she was wearing a fitted pair of trousers and a cashmere sweater. She'd never owned a pair of sweatpants in her life.

They were opposites in many ways, but Elena and Lachlan Kelly had a love story for the ages. I couldn't imagine ever settling for anything less than their example of what a strong, respectful, and happy marriage should look like.

Dad broke away from his wife and enveloped me in a hug, tucking me against his massive chest. I'd only seen him a few days ago, but he held me like it had been a year.

"What's shakin', kid?"

I pulled back, dropping my bag on the huge, rustic farm table that fit our whole family with room to grow.

"I brought blondies."

My dad's mouth hitched. "You know you don't have to bring anything when you come over."

"And you know Phoebe would never show up empty-handed." My mother closed her laptop and rounded the island, kissing the side of my head when she reached me.

She always kissed and hugged with a little more strength than necessary. She'd once told me it was because she hadn't been taught how to properly do it when she was young. I liked her forceful hugs and kisses. They made me feel loved, and I was happy to be the one to help her make up for lost time.

"You know me so well." I lifted the storage container out of my bag and passed it to my mom as the back door burst open.

"Aunt Phoebe!" Jesse plowed into me, wrapping me up in his little iron limbs. He'd been hugged plenty, but he shared the same affliction as my mother. Maybe it was a little bit genetic too. "What'd you make?"

"Blondies...and chocolate chip cookies." The myriad of emotions Jesse's face broadcasted in the two seconds he thought I hadn't brought his favorite treat made me laugh. I looked at my dad. "Do you honestly think I could let this kid down?"

He chuckled and ruffled Jesse's hair. "You've Pavloved him. He sees you and thinks dessert."

My grin split my face. "I have absolutely no problem with that."

My grandparents were off doing their own thing, but all my siblings and Hannah's boyfriend, Remi, were gathered around the table, eating dinner.

Hannah had just finished telling us about a horse with chronic laminitis. She and the vet had been trying to help this horse for ages, and she was frustrated as all get-out. My sister was a horse whisperer, so it had to kill her not to be able to fix this problem.

But she had Remi, and Remi adored her. He couldn't do anything to alleviate the horse's pain, but he could lessen Hannah's. Wrapping his arm around her shoulders, he murmured sweetness into her ear.

I caught my mom's eye across the table and sighed wistfully. She shot me a satisfied little grin. We were both big fans of Remi with Hannah.

"Phoebe, my love, were you ever going to tell us about your new neighbor?" she asked.

I straightened, surprised at the swift change of subject. "If the topic came up, sure. It isn't a secret."

Cormac nudged my arm with his elbow. "You didn't tell me someone moved in."

Hannah waved her hand. "A month ago. I completely forgot to ask you about them. Guy or woman? On a scale of one to ten, how much worse are they than me?"

I snorted a laugh. "He's quiet as a mouse. I don't know where that fits on your scale."

So quiet I hadn't heard a peep in days. Not that I had expected Deacon to come knocking on my door, but I'd thought...well, it didn't matter. We were both busy people who worked long hours. It wasn't much of a surprise we hadn't run into each other.

Caleb turned his attention to me. "A man is living above you? Who is he?"

"I actually know him from school." I paused in what I knew would be the calm before the storm, taking another second or two of peace. "His name is Deacon Slater."

Grumbles and hisses came from all sides like surround sound. Hannah was the first to speak, turning to fully face me.

"Richie's little brother?"

Hannah had dated Richie for a while after she graduated high school. I wouldn't have said he was a bad influence since Hannah had always had a penchant for getting in trouble, but he'd gleefully brought out the worst in her.

I nodded. "He was a year above me in school. We were...well, not friends, but friendly."

My father's brow pinched. "Thought he was in prison."

My mother's head whipped in his direction. "Prison? Richie or Phoebe's neighbor?"

"The neighbor," Dad gruffed. "Though Richie should most certainly be too."

My mother whipped back around to me. "Your neighbor was in prison? What did he do?"

Before I could say I didn't actually know, Caleb interjected, giving us the answer. "His friend, Chris Jacobson, was working on the ranch the summer it all went down. From what I remember, he went in for robbery. Chris ranted to everyone who'd listen about the judge having it out for Deke because he was a Slater and throwing the book at him."

"He's been out for a year," I told them. "He does roadwork and carpentry. And like I said, he's really quiet and keeps to himself, so I don't know any of the details."

My mother clucked her tongue. "What was Joy thinking, renting to a felon—especially when Phoebe's living below him?"

I bit my tongue so I didn't leap to defend him. The truth was, I had no idea what Deacon had done to land in prison. The quiet, gentle boy he'd been when we were teens was a memory. He'd lived a lot of life since then. But my instincts told me he wasn't dangerous—not to me or anyone else.

Fortunately, my father jumped in, taking my mother's hand in his. "Come on, Ellie. You know better than anyone people can change. The man paid his dues. On top of that, Joy'd never rent the apartment to anyone she didn't fully vet."

She sighed, leaning into him. "I suppose that's true. Well, I liked it better when Hannah was the one sharing the duplex with Phe."

"Sorry for moving," Hannah mumbled.

Remi cracked a grin. "Sorry for needing my girl under the same roof as me."

Dad huffed a laugh. "Never apologize for that, son."

"He's Joy's nephew," Caleb supplied. "But knowing her, nephew or not, she wouldn't have rented to him if she didn't trust him."

"Joy doesn't mess around when it comes to her properties," Cormac added.

"She doesn't," I agreed. "Anyway, Deke is a fine neighbor. I'm not worried."

Hannah raised her eyebrows at me. "I seem to remember you had a huge crush on him back in the day. How is he looking now?"

"Better than ever. And he has tattoos."

She let out a loud laugh. "I think I'm going to have to stop by to get a good look."

I aimed a glare at Remi. "Please don't let her stalk Deke."

He raised both hands. "You know your sister does what she wants."

My mother didn't look very amused. "Be careful, love. He may have paid his dues, but he still has connections to the Slaters. No good can come of that."

Cormac chuckled. "Look at Hannah. She dated a Slater and got herself a record."

Hannah snarled at him. "It was a misdemeanor."

At the height of Hannah's rebellious phase, she'd been with Richie in a stolen car he'd crashed right in front of a cop. Luckily, she'd been okay. Double luckily, it had ended her relationship with Richie and the path of self-destruction she'd been on.

Jesse's eyes bugged. "Does that mean you were arrested, Aunt Hannie?"

"I made some bad, *bad* choices when I was younger." Hannah wagged her finger at him. "Take it from me, Jess, you don't want to go to jail. The mattresses are rock hard, and the food is mush."

He scrunched up his face like she was nuts. "I'm not going to jail. I don't even like crossing the street unless I'm at a crosswalk."

Caleb palmed his son's head. "Good, kid. Keep that attitude, and you'll do just fine."

Hannah winked at him. "I don't know...breaking a few rules is pretty fun—just don't get caught."

Caleb groaned. "Don't listen to your aunt."

Jesse shook his head vigorously. "Don't worry. I'm not going to."

After dinner, Hannah, Remi, Cormac, and Caleb played a card game in the living room while my dad took Jesse outside to look for a constellation. Since I refused to play games with my ultracompetitive siblings, I helped my mom clean up the kitchen.

She waved a wooden spoon over the leftover pasta. "Do you want to take some of this home with you, love?"

I almost said no but hesitated. "Yes, actually. That would be great."

She narrowed her eyes. "You never take leftovers."

That made me laugh. "Then why did you offer them?"

"Because I always do, and you *always* say no. It's our thing." She folded her arms across her chest. "Have you not had time to cook for yourself lately? You work far too much, Phe. You should—"

"No, it's not that. I was going to take them to Deacon. But it's fine. I don't have to."

She considered me for a long beat. "You're being a good neighbor?"

"That, and I'd like an excuse to talk to him."

Her pale brow arched. "He's that cute?"

"The tattoos, Mom." I fanned my face, making her laugh. "I don't know, there's something about him. I want to get to know him better."

"Hmmm." She considered me closely. "I haven't heard you say that in a while. As much as I like that you're interested in someone, couldn't it have been anyone else? Really, a Slater?"

"It could have been, but it's not."

She knocked my shoulder with her spoon. "Smart-ass."

"Hannah's busy. I had to fill the slot."

"You really didn't. One Hannah is as much as I can handle." She pointed toward a cabinet. "Be a love and grab a container and lid."

I kissed her smooth cheek. "Thanks, Mom. I'm sure he'll appreciate it a lot."

"He'd better." She filled the container to the brim, using a lot of force to get the lid on, then tapped it with her perfectly manicured fingernails, turning to me. "So, tell me about Deacon."

"I'm not sure there's anything to tell yet. He's sort of a closed book. I don't know if what I'm feeling is nostalgia or something more, but I keep finding reasons to knock on his door."

Her eyes narrowed. "I don't have a problem with a woman doing a little of the chasing, but I don't think I love that this man isn't jumping for joy at your attention."

I almost giggled at the idea of Deacon jumping for joy. Something told me that kind of effusiveness was not in his wheelhouse. "I'm not chasing him, Mom."

She tapped the container of leftovers again. "Really?"

Some people mistook my soft, thoughtful nature as shy, but I wasn't at all. There were probably even more people who suspected I was self-conscious because of the size of my ass...and other parts, but they were wrong too. If I was interested in a man, I had no trouble pursuing—but I wouldn't chase. That would mean he was running from me, either because he was playing games or not interested. I'd rather cut my losses than engage in games, and I'd never had a shortage of dance partners when I was in the mood for one, so lukewarm wasn't my thing.

"Really," I stated firmly. "I'm attracted to him and definitely intrigued, but we'll see where it goes from here."

"Hmmm." She didn't appear convinced. "I'd rather him be jumping for joy, Phe. You are stunning and wonderful. You deserve that kind of enthusiasm."

"I hear you, and I promise I'm not rushing headlong into anything."

"Of course you're not." She patted my cheek. "Even as a toddler, you examined situations from every angle before making a decision. Of all my kids, your judgment is not something I've ever worried about."

"I'm just figuring things out, the same as everyone else."

That earned me an eye roll. "The way you figure things out is not the same as *anyone* else." Then she sighed. "Have fun with your tattooed bad boy. I have one word of warning then I'll drop it."

"Mom..."

She leveled me with a sharp gaze. "I can accept he might not be like the rest of them, but if more Slaters start showing up, please forget about him. I don't want you tangled up with that family."

That I could promise her.

If Deacon was still involved with the other Slaters, I'd have no trouble walking away.

Chapter Twelve
Phoebe

As luck would have it, I didn't have to go knocking on Deacon's door. He pulled in moments after I did, so I waited at the rear of my car, my canvas bag hooked on my elbow.

He climbed out of his truck and ambled toward me. "Need help with something?"

"No, I don't. I wanted to see if you've eaten dinner yet."

He rubbed his nape, his gaze dropping. "Got caught up in a project and haven't had the chance. I should probably get on that."

From the look of him, he'd been doing some carpentry. Chips of wood were scattered in his hair, and a fine layer of sawdust coated his navy-blue hoodie. His jeans were old and worn, ripped at the knees and stained here and there.

He looked like he'd been working hard all day with his hands, and I liked that very much. So much so, I became preoccupied in my perusal of him and forgot to reply.

He took a step toward our house. "I'm gonna go get cleaned up. Have a good night, Phoebe."

"Wait." I grabbed the back of his sleeve. "I brought you leftovers from dinner with my family. Are you interested? It's pasta, roasted chicken, salad, rolls—"

He cocked his head. "You brought food for me?"

"Well...yes. My mother would be pretty offended if you didn't eat it," I teased.

"She knows who it's for?"

"She does."

He scuffed his work boot on the pavement. "I appreciate it more than you know, but I can't eat it."

I moved in front of him, catching his lowered gaze. "My whole family is nut-free for Jesse. He ate this meal with us. It's safe."

It took a moment for him to agree, but he finally did. "All right. Thank you."

"Do you want to eat at my place? I can warm it up for you, and I have an actual table and chairs. Not to mention cutlery and real plates."

He chuckled, smoothing a hand down his front. "I'm filthy. You don't want me in your apartment."

I wanted to tell him I didn't mind that at all. That his version of filthy was sexy as all get out to me. But I had a feeling he'd get spooked if I was that forward with him. "Get cleaned up then. It'll take me a few minutes to heat up your dinner anyway."

We parted at my door, and I bustled around my apartment, straightening pillows and putting away the few odds and ends I'd left around.

He was back in under ten minutes, in a fresh band T-shirt and clean jeans, his hair wet and combed away from his face. I let him in, catching a whiff of soap and something spicy. Maybe aftershave or cologne. I liked that he'd taken that extra step before coming over.

He stood at the edge of my living room, his head swiveling left and right. The bones of our apartments were identical, but everything else was different. Tapestries and prints I'd picked up at fairs and markets hung on the fresh celery-painted walls. A comfy couch piled with plush pillows sat in front of a thick wool rug, facing a small TV on my vintage credenza.

"Looks like someone really lives here," he said.

"Well...I do. I don't know how long I'll be here, but I don't have any plans to move. I like pretty things."

"It's nice. I'm guessing you decorated your bakery too."

"I did. Camille and my mom gave a lot of input and helped me shop, but the basics were all me."

He nodded. "It smells good in here."

"Come eat."

I waved him over to the kitchen and ordered him to sit down while I dished up his food. I piled the plate high and placed it in front of him.

"What do you want to drink? I have water, beer, an open bottle of wine..."

He looked up at me, the ruddiness in his cheeks deepening. "I'll have a beer if you'll join me."

"Sure." I smiled at him. "I like the sound of that."

I grabbed one for us both and settled across from him, watching him dig into his food. He started slow but once he'd gotten his first taste, his speed picked up, shoveling huge forkfuls of pasta and chicken into his mouth. There was something about the way he ate, an urgency that pricked at my nerves like he was worried it would be taken from him at any moment. I wondered if that was something from a shitty childhood or a habit he'd picked up in prison. Or maybe he was simply hungry after a long day at work.

"Can I ask you a question about prison?"

He paused midchew, lifting his eyes to mine. I thought he'd turn me down, but after a moment's hesitation, he jerked his chin.

"How did they handle your allergy there? Were you able to eat what everyone else did or...?"

Swallowing hard, he wiped his mouth with a cloth napkin. "There are supposed to be procedures in place, but they don't follow them. My first week on the inside, I went into anaphylaxis from contaminated food. Almost died because no one knew where they kept the EpiPen."

"Shit." My fingers tensed around my beer bottle. "I'm not surprised, but I'm sorry you had to go through that."

"I won't pretend it's not scary as hell to feel my throat closing up, especially in a place where I had no autonomy. Couldn't carry my own EpiPen, no access to check ingredients in food, nothing. Just had to trust people who didn't care if I lived or died." He stabbed his pasta with his fork. "After that, they served me prepackaged food. It was terrible, but I didn't have to worry about it killing me."

My stomach dropped. "That's awful. God, I'm so sorry you had to endure that."

He lifted a shoulder. "Some would say I deserved it. Part of my punishment."

"And some people are assholes, so there's that."

One beat. Two. Then laughter burst from somewhere deep within Deacon. Dropping his fork, he tossed his head back, letting it roll out of him.

Delight curled inside me. Giving that to him felt so good I could have melted into a happy puddle. Something told me Deacon hadn't done a lot of laughing in his life. I didn't consider myself an especially funny person, but I'd gotten him to do it twice since we'd become reacquainted, so I must have been doing something right.

He grinned at me as his laughter died off. "You're right, Phoebe. A lot of assholes out there." Picking up his fork, he paused. "That wasn't the question I'd expected you to ask me about prison."

"What'd you think I'd ask?"

"I dunno. What I did to get in there, what it was like—that kinda thing."

"I'm curious about that too, but what I asked seemed less invasive." I nodded toward his plate. "Maybe I'll ask something else in a bit. Eat first."

He waved his fork over his food. "Besides your baking, this is the best thing I've ever had."

I had to stop myself from showing any reaction. My mother was a great cook, but this wasn't anything special, just an everyday dinner in the Kelly house. That pasta and roasted chicken were a big deal to Deacon killed me. I wished we'd been better friends when we were younger and I'd invited him over. I wished he'd had a better life. I really wished things had been different.

I swallowed my emotions and smiled. "I'll have to tell my mother. She'll be honored."

"She really knew this was for me?" he asked.

"She really did."

His eyes narrowed. "Your family's okay with you spending time with me?"

"They had questions, but in the end, they trusted my judgment. If I'd been able to tell them you were the one to rescue me that day, you'd be invited to family dinner every week."

He lifted a brow. "In that case..."

I laughed. "If you're free next time I go, you're welcome to join me. My family is protective, but they won't bite."

As soon as I said it, it was like a curtain fell between us. Deke concentrated on his food, answering me with a grunt I interpreted as, *"No way in hell is that happening, lady."*

"Or I can bring you leftovers again," I added.

"I won't turn that down."

When he finished, he washed his plate and utensils, even though I told him he didn't have to, then turned to me as he dried his hands.

"Ask your questions."

"All right." I opened the container of blondies I'd brought home from my parents' house and slid them across the counter toward him. "First one: do you want dessert?"

Huffing a laugh, he grabbed a blondie. "If you're making it, the answer is always yes."

"I like that." I tipped my head toward my living room. "Would you like to sit down and hang out for a while?"

His eyes darted back and forth between mine. "I'm having trouble not wondering what's in it for you."

"Remember what I said the other night? If I get tired of your company, I don't have a problem asking you to leave."

He grinned and bowed his head, following me to the couch. "You're forthcoming."

"I am."

"It's a good thing."

I hoped he still thought that after I asked him everything on my mind.

Chapter Thirteen

Phoebe

SITTING WITH MY BACK against the arm of the couch, I tucked my feet under me and faced him. He took the opposite end, keeping as much space between us as he could. That was okay since it gave me a spot to put the rest of the blondies.

"Caleb said you were in for robbery."

Deacon nodded. "That was the charge, yeah."

"Did you do it?"

"I was there and shouldn't have been. My brother...he convinced me to drive that night. I made the mistake of thinking my being there might have kept him from doing something stupid. In the end, it was my vehicle spotted, and I was the only one whose alibi fell apart."

It didn't surprise me Richie had been the catalyst to Deacon's downfall. When he'd dated Hannah, he'd given me the creeps. The only reason my parents hadn't barred him from our house was because they'd known it would drive Hannah straight into his arms. My sister was stubborn like that. And Richie had had a way of sweet-talking his way into getting what he wanted—which had usually been trouble.

"Caleb knows your friend, Chris." I trailed my nail along the seam of the couch cushion. "He told us Chris believed the judge had sentenced you harshly because of your family."

"Probably. I had a shitty public defender who had no interest in being there, a judge who'd seen my brothers, cousins, and dad in his courtroom more times than anyone wants to count, and my alibi...well, it had been a perfect storm. My lawyer had convinced me I'd get probation and community service. Instead, I got six years—out in four for good behavior."

He polished off the blondie in his hand and grabbed another, quickly demolishing it too. I liked feeding this man, but it hurt me how starving he was—and not just for food. Anyone who spent more than a minute speaking to him would see he was hollow. Had he always been that way, or was this from being locked up for four years?

Every little bit of Deacon I uncovered made me want to dig for more. But I sensed he was brittle, and if I dug too hard, he might crumble.

"But you didn't come back to Sugar Brush right away," I prompted gently. "Where did you go?"

"Wasn't sure I ever wanted to come back here. I sure as hell wasn't ready when I got out, so I found a spot in a bunkhouse about an hour from here. Spent my days working for Chris's dad on the roads and nights in my bunk. Took me a year to feel enough like myself again to want to rejoin civilization. Lucky for me, your sister moved out, and Joy offered me the apartment."

"I never knew Joy was your aunt."

He lifted a shoulder. "You can see why she doesn't advertise a connection to my family. She's my mom's sister, so not a Slater herself. But she hasn't always lived a clean life. Has a record of her own from her younger days. She'd tried to take me in when I was a kid, but the state wouldn't give me to her. Someone out there had truly thought I was better off with my parents, who'd only wanted me around for the government benefits."

"At least you have her now."

"A whole lot better than nothin'." He took another blondie and bit off a corner. "I don't want me being around now to rub off on her in a negative way. You were there that night. I'm sure you heard what was said."

I'd heard some of the ruckus from where I had been dancing with Grandad, and my grandmother had filled in the rest of the blanks later. It made me furious for Deacon and Joy. I hadn't brought it up to him since I was certain he'd been embarrassed and would rather have forgotten all about it.

"What I heard was she banned that asshole Bill Keller from her bar. And that he deserved far worse."

"He was tellin' the truth. If Joy wasn't family, she wouldn't trust me in her business."

"But she is, so it doesn't matter." I huffed, frustrated. "People around here are so adamant about law and order, then when someone does the time for his crime, they can't let him get on with his life."

"People in this town were never going to trust me, Phoebe. I was born with a reputation, and I did exactly what was expected of me."

"Then why'd you come back?"

"It's all I know." He ate the rest of the blondie in two bites then wiped his mouth with the back of his hand. "It's not all bad. I've got Joy, Chris, and his wife, Tilly. I have a workshop in their shed, and I'm slowly getting carpentry commissions. Not all bad."

"And we're friends now," I added.

"Yeah," he gruffed. "That too."

I laughed lightly. "You sound thrilled."

He looked back at me seriously. "Can't imagine being any luckier than having you as my neighbor. Still wrapping my head around you being interested in knowing me."

"I think I've made myself clear on that subject."

"You have." He almost smiled. "I'd be out on my ass if you were through with me."

"That's right." I rubbed my lips together as little butterflies attempted to fly up my throat. "You know, you're welcome to knock on my door too."

"I don't have anything to offer. No baked goods or delicious dinners."

"Your company is all I need."

He inclined his chin. "That, I'll be happy to give any time you want it."

Silence descended as our eyes locked. Part of me wanted to crawl across the cushions and plant myself in his lap so I could kiss his mouth, while the other part was content to stare at him from a cushion away. That part won. My pulse fluttered, and my stomach swooped dangerously. I sucked in shallow, sharp breaths, getting whiffs of his soap and spice. Deacon was still and steady, drawing his eyes along my face.

Then I screwed it all up by yawning. Big and obvious, there was no stopping it once it started. I was tired. Not so tired I wanted to stop whatever this moment was, but Deacon took it as his cue to leave.

"You must've gotten up early. I'll let you get some rest." He climbed to his feet and twisted his body left and right to stretch.

The bottom of his T-shirt lifted to show a sliver of skin and a peek of tattoos on his abdomen, and my mouth went dry.

Oh, this man...

He truly had no idea how devastatingly beautiful he was to me. When had I ever thought of another man this way?

Refusing to answer myself, I grabbed the rest of the blondies and stood. "You have to take these with you."

He patted his stomach. "Don't think I ate enough?"

I had to bite back a smirk. He'd eaten a lot, but I bet he'd eat the rest when he went home. "I don't. Take them, please."

"I won't turn you down." He slipped the box from my hands, our fingers brushing. "Thank you, Phoebe. I had a good night."

"I did too." I opened my door and leaned against the side. "I'll see you around, Deacon."

He took a step back, then hesitated, rubbing his knuckles against the wood frame. "Do you ever get off work around four?"

"I can. If I have a reason to." Camille and Hailey could close just fine without me.

He shifted back and forth between his feet. "I'm heading to Laramie this week to get a couple tattoos touched up. Think you might want to come with me? I'll treat you to dinner afterward."

I did not hesitate. "Yeah, I'd love that."

His shoulders dropped a fraction like he'd been bracing for a different answer. "Good." He rubbed a hand down the side of his jeans, his eyes darting away before finding me again. "Wednesday work?"

"It works great." I dug my teeth into my bottom lip to stop from grinning. I got the impression Deacon was nervous and as surprising as that was to realize, I thought it was sweet. "I'm looking forward to it. I can't say I've ever been to a tattoo shop."

"I don't guess you have." He gave me a quick once-over. "You'd look good with some ink. You decide you want something; my guy's talented."

"I'll think about it."

"Okay." He retreated from my doorway, but his eyes were still locked on me. "Pick you up at the shop?"

"I'll be there with bells on."

His mouth curved—just a little. "Night, Phoebe."

"Good night, Deke."

I closed the door, pressed my back against it, and sucked in a sharp breath.

Oh, my muffins.

Did that just happen?

I think Deacon Slater just asked me on a date.

Chapter Fourteen

Deacon

I'D MADE THE DRIVE to Laramie plenty of times, but never like this. Sugar and spice spiked the air in my cab, along with grisly details of a serial killer.

Phoebe Kelly had a keen interest in true crime. When she'd hopped in the truck, she'd asked if I'd like to listen to one of her favorite podcasts. I'd had no clue what I'd been in for, but by the time I'd parked my truck outside the tattoo shop, I couldn't say I wasn't invested in the story.

I turned off the engine, and Phoebe twisted in her seat. "Well? Did you hate that?"

I chuckled. "Didn't hate it. Wondering where you hide your darkness under all that pink."

She looked down at her jeans, dark-pink sweater with the ends of a floral T-shirt poking out the bottom, and pink suede sneakers. Then there were the dainty little rose earrings and floral headband pushing her hair back from her rosy-cheeked face. I would've never guessed this woman would enjoy listening to the fine details of a murder spree.

She lifted her head, grinning. "I guess you know my favorite color, but I don't think I'm dark on the inside."

"I don't think you are either," I agreed. From what I'd gleaned, her core was just as soft and pink. "That's why I'm surprised you like listening to this kind of thing."

"I get it. But you know, women are actually the top consumers of true crime. I once read a theory it's because most women's worst nightmare is to be taken, hurt, or violated, and learning about true crime is a safe way of understanding the psychology behind the perpetrators so we can protect ourselves."

When Phoebe spoke, she took care with how she formed her words. Her plush, rosy lips moved with precision, and when I looked into her eyes, I could almost see her brain working. I'd never known anyone who'd expressed their thoughts the way she did. I kept catching myself leaning closer so I didn't miss anything she said.

"Do you think that's true?" I asked, wanting to keep her talking.

"Probably. On some level." She rubbed her lips together like she was revving her engine. "I'm a curious person. Learning about others so inherently different from me is fascinating. And you know what it's like growing up in a small town. I love most parts, but I've been intentional about keeping my world big. It would be too easy to think the people I see every day are all that's out there."

Before I could tell her how rare that way of thinking was, especially around here, someone knocked on my window. I whipped my head around, finding a face plastered against the glass.

"Shit," I muttered. "I wanna keep talking to you, but there's not a chance he'll leave us be."

Phoebe leaned around me to check out the idiot with his cheek smooshed against my window. "I hope you know him."

"That's Jett."

Jett had been giving me tattoos since I was twenty. He'd been just starting out in the business, and I'd had no money at all, so we'd worked out a barter system. I'd built furniture for his shop, and he'd covered my body in art. I'd always thought I'd gotten the sweeter end of the deal, but he'd disagree.

Soon as I stepped onto the sidewalk, Jett swept me into a hug so tight, my ribs creaked. Hugs weren't something I'd had an abundance of in my life, but I took it even though I wasn't too sure what to do with my arms or face.

"Happy as hell to see you, man." He slapped my back hard enough to take my breath away. "Real, *real* happy."

When he pulled back, he looked me over, a wide grin on his face. "Dear god, you're skinny. They forget to feed you in there?"

"Food was shit," I muttered, aware Phoebe was witnessing our interaction.

"Figured it wouldn't be great. You need to come around more often and eat Mama's cooking. She'll fatten you up on her tamales and carne asada. Mmmm, I'm getting hungry just thinking about it." He glanced over my shoulder. "You know there's a pretty girl standing by your truck?"

"That's Phoebe."

His brows popped. "Oh shit. Your girl?"

"Friend. Just a friend," I grunted.

But Jett was already off, shaking her hand with the enthusiasm of a kid in a candy store. And it was no surprise Phoebe was into it. Everyone liked Jett. It was a good thing he wasn't into women, or I'd probably lose her to him.

Christ, what was I even thinking? I'd have to have her in order to lose her, and we weren't there. Phoebe wanted to be friends. She'd made that clear. And I wouldn't have had the first idea of what to do with a woman like her.

I strode back to my truck as Jett draped his arm around Phoebe. She was already telling him about her bakery, clearly having no problem with it.

I did.

I opened the tailgate. "Jett. You want to help me get this out?"

"Oh, yeah, man." He gave Phoebe a squeeze. "Let's see what kind of magic this guy has made for me."

Phoebe followed him to the rear of the truck, both peering in to see what I had strapped in the bed.

I'd built most of the furniture in the shop, but Jett had decided to go with some shitty chrome monstrosity for his reception desk. Just like I'd expected, it hadn't aged well, so I'd built him a new one. He'd tried to decline, but the man had spent countless hours adding ink to my body. As far as I was concerned, we weren't close to even.

Jett ran his hand over the smooth walnut top. "Dude. What the hell did you do?"

"Built you a desk, like I told you."

He blinked. "I was thinking something simple. This is a work of art."

Phoebe came closer, her soft tits brushing the back of my arm. "Oh my...can I help you guys take it out? I'm dying to see it."

Jett and I barked, "No," at the same time. We didn't agree on a lot of things, but not letting a woman carry something heavy was something we did.

Laughter burst from Phoebe, and she raised her hands. "Okay, I hear you. You guys can do the heavy lifting. I'll go wait inside."

Tongue-tied, I watched her strut into the tattoo shop like she'd been there a hundred times. She'd been that way from the first time I'd seen her. Like she knew she'd be welcome in every space she entered. Watching her never failed to fascinate me.

I turned back to the truck, and Jett waggled his brows. "Just a friend, huh?"

"Yep," I stated.

"I bet you're hoping not for long." He nudged me with his elbow. "She's pretty as hell."

"I know." I pushed him toward the tailgate. "Now, are you gonna help me or what?"

In the time it took us to carry the new desk inside, Phoebe had already made a friend in the waiting area. Standing at the flash wall next to a tall, lanky tattooed guy, she was looking at the art. He was looking at her.

She whirled around at the sound of us putting the desk down, her eyes lighting as she took it in. "Oh, wow. Deke…" she whispered, her hands clutched at her chest.

I rubbed my nape. "Yeah?"

She crossed the space, her arm brushing mine. "It's stunning. I can't believe you made this with your bare hands."

"There were a few tools involved too."

Her laughter was light and tinkling, like a delicate wind chime. "Don't make jokes. This is gorgeous. You're a true craftsman."

Jett clapped a hand on my shoulder. "It's sick, dude. How in the hell did you brand my logo on the front?"

The desk's base was built from stained walnut strips. I'd mounted a circular plaque on the front bearing the shop's branded logo. The top, also walnut, was lacquered to a smooth, glossy finish. It was my first reception desk, and I was pretty damn proud of it. Still, it was nice to know I wasn't the only one who liked it—even if taking compliments wasn't my strong suit.

"Trade secret," I replied wryly. "If I told you, you wouldn't need me anymore."

It'd been a lot of work. I'd never done well in school, had never taken an interest, but when it came to woodworking, I always wanted to challenge myself to learn and expand my knowledge.

Jett shook his head. "Nah. Even if you laid it out step by step, I'd never come close to replicating what you do. I'll stick to the needle, thank you very much."

"Speaking of needles, you ready to get working on me?"

He jerked, like up until that second, he'd forgotten why I was here. "Yeah. Yeah. Let's get into it."

Jett led us deeper into the shop. I trailed behind with Phoebe, pointing out the pieces I'd made years ago. They still looked good. Didn't seem anything had fallen apart while I'd been locked up.

When we reached Jett's workstation at the rear of the building, Phoebe hesitated. "Are you sure you want me back here? I can wait up front if you'd rather—"

I caught her wrist before I'd known I was going to reach out, and once I'd closed my fingers around the softest skin I'd ever felt, I wasn't in a hurry to let go.

"Stay. I'm sure Jett'll find talking to you a lot more entertaining than just me." And if she went back to the front, I had no doubt that scuzzy, rat-faced guy would slide right next to her again.

"All right. I'd love to watch."

I forced my fingers to open and let them slide down the front of her hand. My lungs seized as she rotated her wrist to put us palm to palm. I looked at her. Her eyes were on Jett as he readied his station, but her lips were curved in a small, secret smile.

My index finger twitched, and hers curled, hooking around mine. Her nail grazed the inside of my finger in steady, purposeful movements I felt in my gut, brain, chest...everywhere. Like my nerves had been miswired and she was tripping them again and again.

Felt like I should've said something. Or maybe twined my fingers with hers to make her understand just how much I liked what she was doing. Anything other than standing stock-still, staring at the side of her pretty face.

"All right. I'm all ready for you," Jett announced, prompting Phoebe to let go of her featherlight hold.

Like it had never happened, the moment we'd been having, whatever it was, was done and dusted.

Chapter Fifteen

Phoebe

I HAD NEVER GIVEN tattoos much thought. None of the men I'd dated in the past had had more than one or two at most, and I hadn't paid them any attention. But when Deacon Slater whipped his shirt off, my tongue got stuck to the roof of my mouth. Not only were his arms fully sleeved, but across his chest was the silhouette of the Rocky Mountains and unraveled spools of barbed wire running down his sides to the ridges of his hips. It was beautiful work, to be sure, but the fact that it was on Deacon's body made my knees feel like jelly.

He lay down on Jett's table, his arms behind his head, staring at the ceiling. Jett winked at me when he caught me staring. I wasn't embarrassed, though. If I were lying in front of Deacon with my shirt off, I hoped he'd be staring too.

Jett got to work on touching up Deacon's side piece, low music playing in the background. I asked Jett questions about his business and tattoos in general. He was easy to talk to and enthusiastic about sharing his knowledge. He also seemed to enjoy hyping Deacon up.

"Met him at a show. He came into the shop I used to work at the next day and showed me his measly portfolio. Even back then, the kid had talent." Jett rolled away on his stool to grab a paper towel then returned, bending his head to keep going. "I thought he was full of shit, though. Never figured he'd really follow through on building all the cabinetry for this place."

"I wanted a tattoo," Deacon muttered. "'Course I followed through."

Jett chuckled. "Yeah, *one* tattoo for all that work. I'd said no, brother, you're getting sleeves. Then he built my mom a vanity, so I inked his sides. The chest piece was payment for the molding he installed. Never been to a tattoo shop with fucking molding. Customers are always noticing it too. Details like that set us apart. Top-notch art and nice as hell environment."

I tipped my head back to study the crown molding. It was the same hue as the wooden furniture with ornamental detailing. It looked so nice I wanted crown molding at Sugar Rush.

I didn't think I'd ask Deke for it, though. Knowing what I did about him, he'd try to build me a whole new shop and ask to be paid in cookies.

"Did I hear Deke is on the premises?" A woman with long, black hair stuck her head in the doorway. "No one thought to call me down here?"

Jett raised his head. "I knew you'd find your way."

She sauntered into the space, hands on her curvy hips, focus on Deacon and Jett. Shiny ebony hair hung in loose waves over honey-brown skin decorated with classic-style tattoos. Her jeans molded to a really nice butt, and her T-shirt revealed a slice of narrow waist. It was only when she turned to the side I noticed the lines around her eyes and mouth and silver at her temples. This stunning woman had to be closer to my mom's age than mine.

Once she'd reunited with Deke, Jett pointed me out to her, and she threw her arms around me with the same enthusiasm Jett had.

"Oh my god, you're stunning." She pulled back, fluffing my hair around my shoulders. "Deke's never brought a woman around. It's about time."

"You are too. I'm Phoebe, by the way."

"Giselle, sweet thing. Though most of the guys around here call me Mama." She jerked her thumb toward Jett. "I only birthed one kid but managed to be a mom to a dozen."

I grinned. "Nice to meet you."

Deacon stayed quiet, his lips rolled in a tight line, eyes on the ceiling. I had a feeling all this hustle and bustle was taking him out of the zone he needed to be in to get through the pain.

"Is there somewhere I could grab something to drink nearby?" I asked Giselle.

"Sure is. I'll take you." She slipped her arm around mine. "Phoebe and I are going to get drinks. We'll be back in a bit. Don't trash the place while we're gone," she singsonged, pulling me with her to a coffee shop down the block.

After ordering, we grabbed a table and sipped our drinks while she told me everything she knew about Deacon—which wasn't a lot. At least I wasn't the only one he was closed off around.

"We sent him care packages when he was on the inside." She shook her head. "He didn't want any of us visiting, like it would've been an inconvenience or something. It pissed me off, but Jett talked me down. Said we had to help Deke get through how he needed to. Being reminded of life on the outside wasn't what he wanted, so we sent him books and magazines and stocked up his commissary account for him to buy toiletries and snacks for himself. Showed him we had his back and hadn't forgotten him the only way he'd accept, you know?"

"Yeah, I do know. Every time I'm nice to him, he's surprised."

She laughed, but it was a sad sound. "That's Deke. I don't know a lot about how he grew up, but I know there wasn't a whole lot of love there. Like the song goes, instead of kisses, he got the shit kicked out of him. I'm paraphrasing, of course."

"That's probably what Annie really meant," I said, laughing with the same sadness. "The Slaters have a bad reputation, and they've earned it. They live on the outskirts of town in an off-the-grid compound. From what I've heard, most of the crime in the area can be traced back to them. I can't imagine they were a loving family to grow up with."

"Nope. It's a wonder Deke turned out the way he did. He was like Jett's scrappy little brother. It took him a while to get that wild look out of his eyes. Like he was expecting an attack at any second, but once he relaxed, he'd get us laughing with his smart-ass comments. That boy would do a favor for anyone at the drop of a hat. He's just good down to his bones. It killed me when he went away."

We finished our drinks and headed back to the shop. Deacon and Jett were finishing up when we arrived. I bit my lip as Jett cleaned and bandaged Deacon's fresh tattoo. Beside me, Giselle laughed. She probably knew exactly what I was looking at.

After he slipped his shirt on, Deacon faced me, giving me a long once-over. "You all right?"

"I'm great." I held out the bottle of juice I'd picked up for him. "I checked the label. It's safe."

"Appreciate it, Phoebe." He took it, twisted off the lid, and took a deep pull without double-checking the ingredients. Warmth blanketed my chest at the trust he'd just shown me. There was nothing better.

The four of us headed to the front. Giselle had to take a phone call, and Deke and Jett started in about the care of the wood on the desk, so I ventured back to the flash wall. I still wasn't convinced I wanted a tattoo, but the idea was creeping in.

The same guy who'd greeted me when we'd arrived sidled back up. His name was Phil, he was a tattoo artist, and he'd been trying to convince me to let him give me my first tattoo.

"Did you make up your mind?" he asked.

"I did not. If I ever get a tattoo, it won't be on a whim."

"I'd be honored to draw you something custom."

I smiled at him. "I'll keep that in mind."

He took his phone from his pocket. "I'd love to take you out to dinner and talk about it more. Would you give me your number?"

Of course I'd been aware he was flirting with me, so why was I so thrown off guard? Probably because I was here with Deacon. The audacity it had taken for Phil to ask me for my number when I'd shown up with another guy was pretty astounding.

I was so surprised, I accepted his phone before I could give it a thought. He leaned in, his head almost touching mine, and swiped the screen. When his contacts lit up and my name had already been input, I snapped out of my daze.

Phil was cute, but I wasn't at all interested. Still, there were people around, and we were at his workplace. Not wanting to embarrass him, I kept my voice quiet.

"Thank you for asking, but I'm not available." I returned his phone and smiled. "Besides, I think Jett would be offended if I went to someone else for a tattoo."

He cocked his head. "Ah, no worries. Figured I had to shoot my shot while I had the chance. No harm, no foul."

Still smiling, I stepped away and turned around, finding Deacon staring blankly in my direction. Concerned, I crossed the waiting room, stopping in front of him. His eyes lowered to mine.

"Are you okay?" I asked. "You probably need to eat after getting tattooed, huh?"

"Right." He jerked his chin. "I was thinking we'd grab a pizza on the way out of town. Is that all right with you?"

"It's perfect." I brushed my fingers along his forearm featherlight, and his muscles rippled. "Are you sure you're okay?"

"I'm good." He drew his arm away from me. "Like you said, I probably just need to eat."

I hoped that was all it was.

Deacon stayed quiet and remote through dinner. After spending the last few hours with the boisterous group at Jett's shop, the shift was jarring, but I tried not to take it personally, assuming he was all peopled out. From the time we'd spent together, I'd gleaned Deacon was far more introverted than I was.

We listened to my podcast on the way home, and I shifted between staring out my window into the dark and studying Deacon's rigid profile illuminated by the truck's panel lighting. I wondered if reuniting with Giselle and Jett after being away for so long had been somewhat heavy for him. Not to mention, he'd worked a full day at a physically demanding job before picking me up, driving an hour, and getting tattooed.

Yeah, it was no wonder he was quiet. That would have been a lot for anyone.

The episode ended as we entered Sugar Brush, and I switched on the radio, keeping the music soft to spark a little conversation.

"Giselle, Jett, and everyone else at the shop were pretty great."

He tapped the steering wheel with his thumbs as he nodded. "Yeah."

"Thanks for bringing me with you. I really liked meeting everyone. I'm still not sold on getting a tattoo, but if I ever decide on one, I'd trust Jett in a heartbeat."

"Not Phil?"

It took me a second to remember who Phil was. When I did, I wondered why in the world Deacon was asking about him. "Oh, no, I don't think so. I really love Jett's style. Plus, I think he'd have me laughing through the whole thing. Maybe one day…"

"Maybe."

That was all I'd gotten out of him the rest of the drive. My stomach twisted with disappointment. It had been such a lovely evening, but it wasn't looking like it was going to end on a sweet note.

Once we were home and parked, we walked up the steps together. Deacon stopped with me on my landing, keeping a good distance between us.

Definitely not having a sweet ending.

I unlocked my door but stayed on my welcome mat, hoping for…something—a clue of what had gone wrong or why Deacon was so withdrawn.

"I had a really wonderful time, Deacon."

He looked down at the leftover container clutched in his hand. "Good. I'm glad you did."

I rubbed my lips together, searching for something to say to prolong this. "The piece you made for the shop is truly incredible." I touched my toe to one of the planters he'd made me. "I knew you were talented, but that was beyond."

"Thank you, Phoebe." His gaze lifted, landing on my face. He took a slow meander over my features before locking onto my eyes. "I don't know Phil, but if he works for Jett, he's probably a stand-up guy."

My brow dropped. "Okay...well, I'm not sure I want a tattoo, but like I said, I'd go to Jett."

"I'm not talking about tattoos."

"I—what are you talking about then?"

He scrubbed the back of his neck, puffing a heavy breath. "Aren't you going out with him?"

I blinked hard. And again. "I thought this...tonight...oh my god!" I slapped my forehead, finally understanding what he was saying and how incredibly wrong I'd been. "Oh, I feel so stupid."

He took a step toward me. "You're nowhere near stupid. Why would you say that?"

I blinked a few more times, processing the concern etched in his expression. I'd never made such a misstep with a man in my life. Here I'd been thinking I'd been on the best first date ever and it hadn't been a date at all.

"I misread things. That's my fault." I tried to sound nonchalant and waved him off as if I wasn't mortified. "Phil did ask me out, but I turned him down. Partially because I'm not interested, but mostly because I thought I was there with you."

"*With* me?" His eyebrows shot up, his voice laced with disbelief like the idea was so absurd it couldn't possibly be true.

"It's my own fault for thinking tonight was a date. Don't worry at all." Reaching behind me, I twisted my doorknob, beyond ready to disappear and lick my wounds. "It's late, and we both have to get up early. Thanks again for a lovely time. Good night."

I managed to push my door open and take a single step into my apartment. Before I could slip inside and pretend this never happened, though, a warm hand gripped the back of my neck and spun me around so fast I collided with his chest. His other hand came up to cradle my jaw, his touch firm but gentle, his thumb brushing my cheek.

We stared at each other for one breath, then another. Before I could take my third, his soft lips touched mine, light and testing. I shifted closer, fisting the fabric of his shirt in my fingers, and he tipped his head, slotting his lips with mine.

At first, that was all it was: a press of tender flesh and slow exchange of breaths. Then, gradually, his lips parted, and mine followed, and it became more. The touch of his tongue to the bow of my lip. His fingers threading into my hair. The front of his hard body pressing, flushing with the soft give of mine.

It wasn't a burst of fireworks. It was an incremental rise of a promise for what was to come. And somewhere in the haze of being kissed breathless, younger me was cheering. I was finally getting to kiss *the* guy, and it was more than I ever imagined back when I was doodling his name in hearts.

Opening my hands, I slid them down his sides and circled my arms around his narrow waist. He was only a couple inches taller than me, and I liked that very much. It put us on the same level, neither of us straining. We could have comfortably stood outside my door kissing for hours. And the way he tasted and felt, I would gladly have done that.

Deacon pulled back, his warm breath ghosting across my lips as he stared at me in a daze.

"You're not stupid," he uttered, low and raspy. "That's me. I'd never been in a position to take a woman out before I went in. If I'd known you wanted tonight to be a date, I would've brought you flowers."

"You've never been on a date?" That surprised me. Looking the way he did, with the tattoos, voice, and everything else…

But maybe he'd kept things casual with women. After all, he'd been in his early twenties when he'd gone to prison. Deacon didn't strike me as a hit-it-and-quit-it kind of guy, though.

The corner of his mouth hitched. "Guess I have now."

My toes curled in my shoes. "I guess so." I leaned in, touching my lips to his. "I like flowers, but they're not necessary. I really did have a great time with you."

His thumb dragged back and forth on my cheek. "I'm wrapping my head around this."

"I think I am too."

"You want to do it again?"

I nodded. "Yep, I definitely do."

"Good." He kissed the side of my mouth. "This kind of thing is new to me, Phoebe. You're gonna have to tell me when I'm messing things up."

"You won't. So long as you don't assume I'd ever take another man's number when I'm out with you."

He chuffed. "I think I got that."

"Then you'll do just fine." Smiling, I let my arms slip from his waist and backed into my doorway. "See you soon, Deke."

The slow, lazy grin he returned would keep his name in heart doodles for years to come. It was that good.

"Yeah. You will," he drawled in a promise I fully intended to cash in on.

Chapter Sixteen
Phoebe

HAILEY HAD BEEN WORKING at Sugar Rush for a couple weeks now, and she fit in like she'd always been there. She showed up on time, did her work well, and had gotten comfortable enough to show her personality, albeit slowly. I'd learned we shared the same taste in music, she'd lived with her foster family for five years, and she wanted to be a nurse—though that was subject to change.

We had a lull in customers, so I decided to show her how to make a cappuccino. Usually, she just ran the register, but knowing how to make coffee would help.

"By the way, is the guy who picked you up yesterday your boyfriend?"

Why had that question made wild butterflies take flight? "No, he's not."

Her nose crinkled as she examined me. "Do you *want* him to be your boyfriend?"

I laughed. "That was our first date, so we'll see. I'm not in any rush to find a boyfriend."

She worried her lip with her fingers as I explained the parts of the machine and the different types of coffee drinks we offered.

"Is he nice?"

I turned from the machine to look at her. "Who?"

"The guy you like. What's he like?"

"Well..." I poured the coffee we'd made into a cup, adding cream and sugar, then slid it to Hailey. "He's very nice. I knew him in high school and always had a thing for him, but nothing ever happened. Now he's my neighbor, so we're getting to know each other."

"That's cute. So, I guess...you're dating him?"

"It's really new, but yes. I think so."

"I bet he really likes you. You're so pretty and sweet. Plus, you make great desserts."

I snorted. If that was all it took to win over a man I liked, I guessed I was a shoo-in. "Thank you, sweetheart. I really like him, so I hope he really likes me too."

"I don't think you have anything to worry about."

She sipped the coffee I'd made, and her lips puckered, making me laugh.

"That's a strong one."

She pushed it back toward me. "I don't think I'm a coffee drinker."

"That's okay." I brought the straw to my lips and winked. "I drink enough for us both."

A customer came in, ending our chat. Hailey rang him up, and I made his coffee. That was the beginning of our late afternoon rush. The two of us moved around behind the counter like we'd been choreographed, grabbing drinks and pastries in a smooth dance.

Hailey stayed until we flipped the "closed" sign, and her foster mom pulled up in a minivan to drive her home, like she did at the end of every shift.

Her foster family included six children—some biological, some not. When I'd first hired her, I'd worried she might have a troubled home life, but that didn't seem to be the case. She was shy and lived in a crowded house, but as far as I could tell, she wasn't being mistreated. I'd never asked why she preferred to be paid in cash, but I hoped if I was wrong—if something was happening at home—she'd eventually trust me enough to tell me.

My heart kicked up when I spotted the silver truck idling in a parking spot out front and the tattooed arm hanging out the window. I walked straight up to the door, fighting to keep a silly grin off my face.

"Waiting for someone?"

"I was." Deacon opened his door and climbed out to stand on the sidewalk in front of me. Still in his work clothes, he looked good as ever. Maybe better. There was something about a man in a canvas jacket, dirty jeans, and scuffed-up steel-toed boots. He'd worked hard all day, yet here he was, giving me his time. "Can I give you a ride home?"

"I'd love one."

He walked with me to the passenger side and opened the door. There, sitting on the seat, was a bouquet of wildflowers. I spun around to face him, eyes wide and a wild heart.

"To make up for yesterday," he murmured.

"You had nothing to make up for." I picked them up and held them to my nose. "They're beautiful, Deacon. You really didn't have to, but thank you."

"Glad you like 'em." He patted the seat. "Hop in, sugar."

My heart pinged. "Sugar, huh?"

He pitched forward, bringing his nose close to my hair, and inhaled. "You always smell sweet, but when you leave work, you smell like pure sugar. Didn't mean to call you that, though. Slipped out."

"That's okay." I turned my head, my cheek brushing his. "It was sweet. I liked it."

All he did was grunt and give a little push to guide me into the truck. That was a good thing since I needed a second to collect myself. I'd been called plenty of nicknames, but I liked being called "sugar" by Deacon Slater the very best.

The drive down Main Street was slow going. Between the two stop lights, people returning home from their jobs, and pedestrians crossing the road, we were moving at a snail's pace. So slow, I had to laugh.

"I could have walked faster."

Deacon's mouth quirked. "Thought I was doing you a favor, giving you a ride. I slowed you down."

"I'm sitting next to you, so I'm not complaining."

He glanced at me. "You want, I could pick you up every day."

"The thing is, I sample a lot of the sweets I bake."

His eyebrow shot up. "Oh yeah?"

"Oh yeah. So, every morning, unless the weather is treacherous, I walk the half mile to Sugar Rush. And every evening, unless one of my family members waylays me, I walk the half mile home. That's how I make up for the sampling. I also just like the walk."

"Lucky I work with asphalt. No danger of wanting to sample it."

I laughed. "No, I guess not."

I'd hoped he would ask if he could join me on my walk home sometimes, but he'd made me laugh instead. Grey's Diner was coming up on our right, and suddenly, I didn't want this encounter to end. "What do you think about stopping for dinner?"

Deacon looked from me to the diner and back to the road. His grip on the wheel tightened to the point of his knuckles blanching.

"I'm not feeling like going out. It's been a long day," he replied flatly.

"That's understandable." At least, it would have been had he not reacted the way he had.

"Phoebe..." he sighed, "I'm just getting used to being in town. Going out in public is still a real challenge for me. I see the way folks whisper and react when they recognize me. Doesn't feel great, and Grey's is full of a whole lot of people bound to look and whisper. I can handle it, but I don't want to put you in a position to deal with that. Not yet."

I reached across the console to rest my hand on his leg. "I hear you, Deke. I wish I could assure you that wouldn't happen, but we both know that isn't true. It'll take time, but they'll get used to seeing you around."

"You've lived in this town your whole life. You know how slow things are to change."

"The best and worst part of Sugar Brush—love it because it's always the same, hate it for the same reason." I squeezed his leg. Feeling how rigid he was had me wishing I hadn't asked him to go to dinner with me. The mood had started to nosedive, though I wasn't quite ready to admit it as ruined. "I've had enough people for the day anyway. I'll make us dinner."

"You don't need to do that. Not after working all day."

"Then you can help so I don't have to cook all by myself."

His hand came down on top of mine, warm and rough. "I don't know what I'm doing, but I'll try the best I can."

"That's all I ask," I whispered.

Later, after dinner, Deke was washing up while I quizzed him about his favorite things—chocolate cake, dogs, blue, football, Sundays, the sunrise. It wasn't like my questions were deeply personal, but he gave the answers easily like he had nothing to hide, and I liked that. After dating one too many men who'd lied as naturally as breathing, honesty was critical to me.

"Do you like to dance?"

Finished with the dishes, he shut off the water and grabbed a towel to dry his hands. "I can't say I've done much thinking about it. Don't know if I like doing it or not."

"I take that to mean you've never been out dancing."

He chuckled. "Yeah. It's never come up. Chris and Tilly like to go to some country joint near Laramie. They've asked me to join, but being their third wheel is the last thing I want to do."

"Boots Up Bar? I've run into those two there at least twice. Cam and I like to go when it gets warm and let guys spin us around the dance floor. We should go. Maybe with Chris and Till."

Tilly stopped into Sugar Rush fairly often, and Chris swung by on weekends to pick up a coffee and muffin for his wife. I didn't know either of them well, but they were both friendly as could be. Getting to know them better wouldn't be a hardship—especially since they were Deacon's good friends.

"I wouldn't know the first thing about spinning." The muscles in his jaw jerked. "And I don't think I'd like sitting there while other men spun you around the dance floor."

"Didn't I make it clear? If I'm on a date with you, I'm not going to entertain other men."

"Yeah, you did." He tossed the towel onto the counter and slowly reached out, setting his hand on my hip. "Still wrapping my head around that, Phoebe."

I stepped into him, laid my hands on his chest. "Instead, how about you wrap your *arms* around *me* and take me for a spin in my kitchen?"

He slid his hand from my hip to the base of my back. "There's no music."

I called out to my home entertainment system, asking it to start my dancing playlist. "Problem solved."

His brow furrowed. His entire body was rigid. "I'm going to step on your toes."

I puffed a frustrated breath. "If you don't want to dance with me, you can say it."

His hold on me tightened, and he pulled me against him. "You like it, I want to do it. I just don't want to let you down or demolish your feet."

I smiled, wiggling my toes on top of his. "We're both in our socks. I think we'll be okay. I'm not expecting fancy moves. Let's just sway and take it from there."

"I think I can do that."

I hooked my arms around his neck, and he held me around the waist. So close I felt him breathing. We moved in slow circles in the center of my kitchen floor. Too slow for the music, but it didn't matter, not with Deacon holding me close.

"Why do you like dancing when it's warm?" he asked.

"So I can wear my sundresses."

His head cocked. "You can't wear them in winter?"

"No, they're for sunny days and hot nights." I grinned at his perplexed expression. "I promise it makes sense. If I wore a sundress and had to put a coat on top of it to go outside, I'd fall into a deep depression."

His fingers splayed on my back. "We can't have that."

"No, we can't."

"I guess I'll have to wait a couple more months to see these sundresses."

"You'll need to stick around."

"There's no danger of me not sticking."

My heart leaped. It was too early for those promises, but from Deacon, it sounded more like a statement of fact. I liked to think of myself as pragmatic in most ways, but my whimsical side seemed to always emerge around him. That he was holding me so sweetly and trying his hardest not to step on my toes as we danced didn't hurt.

Leaning in, I touched my lips to his. Just a graze, letting him know I liked him very much. He responded by palming the back of my head and molding his lips to mine. Not a graze but a collision. His mouth moved over mine, his tongue sweeping along my lips. They parted, letting him in, and he went deep, tasting me, lapping at my tongue like it was covered in nectar.

I clung to his shirt, and his fingers tangled in my hair as he kissed me and kissed me. Through it all, we kept dancing our uneven circles, swaying to the beat, matching our hearts instead of our movements.

The hand he'd braced on my back slid upward along my spine then trailed down again, lower, stopping right at the top of my ass. He could've kept going, and I wouldn't have objected, but he stilled, flattening his palm at the cusp.

"Deke," I murmured into his mouth.

"Sugar," he murmured back, the tip of his tongue tracing the line of my lips. "Just like sugar."

My eyelids fluttered. "I'm spinning."

His forehead rolled on mine. "No, you're not." Then he let go of my hair to take my hands in his. Before I knew what he was going to do, he pushed me away from him then pulled me back. "Now you're spinning."

I laughed, pushing off his chest. "Again. Until I'm dizzy."

Holding my hand above our heads, he spun me like a top. Each flash I caught of him, his grin widened, until he was laughing with me. When he finally took hold of me and wrapped me in his arms, I was dizzy, so dizzy.

My smiling face fit in the crook of his arm and neck. "Dancing isn't so bad, is it?"

He dragged his nose back and forth in my hair. "With you? No, not bad at all."

Chapter Seventeen

Deacon

"We need to go dancing."

Chris whipped his head in my direction, his brow dipped so low his eyes were nearly hidden. "What'd you say?"

I wasn't good at conversation. There might've been a better way to introduce the topic instead of just blurting it out during our lunch break, especially with Chris fully engrossed in the meatball sub Tilly had made for him, but when we're working with heavy machinery all day, there wasn't much time to talk. I had to take my opportunities when they arose.

"We need to go dancing," I repeated.

Chris wiped his mouth. "How's that?"

It'd been a week of me doing the bare minimum with Phoebe. Some nights, when I got home early enough, I'd book it to Sugar Rush to walk home with her. Other nights, I'd meet her on her porch. We ate dinner together—dinner she cooked since I didn't have the skills and she insisted she liked doing it—listened to music, watched TV, talked, and always ended up dancing in her kitchen.

She was happy to spend time with me, and I'd had a week to let that settle. I was starting to come around to it, not that I understood it. I had nothing to offer her, and she...well, she had pretty much everything. But she liked me for no reason I could see, so I was determined to do more—give her more than cloistered dinners and piss-poor dancing.

And kissing. God, that woman's mouth. I couldn't get enough of kissing her.

I wasn't ready to face what it'd be like to take her out in Sugar Brush. Outside of town, though? Hell yes. I wanted to experience pretty Phoebe Kelly by my side, and I wanted her to know how proud I was to be out with her.

Trouble was, I didn't have the first clue how to go about all this. I'd stumbled into our first date, not realizing I'd been asking her out, and now that I wanted to do it for real, I needed help.

It pained me to ask Chris. Not because I thought he'd say no—I knew he'd be all in—but he'd have *questions*. And enthusiasm. Far beyond what I was prepared to handle.

"Phoebe likes to dance at the place you take Tilly." I tossed my half-eaten sandwich in my lunch bag and reached for the cookies I'd saved for last. "I wanna take her there too."

"Now, wait a damn minute. Did I miss a few chapters?" He blinked hard. "Are you seeing Phoebe Kelly?"

I jerked my chin. "I am."

His grin was Cheshire cat wide. "Well, look at you, keeping things from me. Till's going to flip her shit."

"Maybe don't let her flip her shit to Phoebe. Or spread this around. It's only been a week."

He smacked my shoulder. "You don't need to say that. We know you like your privacy. Tilly will flip her shit behind closed doors. Don't worry your pretty little head about it."

"Thanks." I wasn't going to touch his calling my head pretty. "You in for doing…I guess, a double date kind of thing? Maybe next Saturday?"

He swiped a finger under his eyes, and I stared, waiting for a response. "Sorry, I'm just trying not to cry."

I groaned. "Never mind. This was a dumb idea. I'll figure it—"

Before I could finish, Chris tackled me into the grass. Luckily, we'd been sitting, so I hadn't had far to go, but his big, heavy frame had knocked the wind clean out of me. If he'd been anyone else, my fight-or-flight instinct would have kicked in, but since it was Chris, I just blinked up at the sky.

"Nope. Don't say it. We're in." He lifted himself off and pulled me upright. "Sorry for tackling you. I got excited."

I shook the daze out of my head and caught my breath. "Get it all out before next weekend, all right?"

"I've got you, Deke." He finally grew serious. "Till and I will be there to support you. And we're gonna have fun."

I hoped like hell that was true.

A couple nights later, I'd let Phoebe convince me to go with her to a furniture store—not that she'd had to try too hard. She was determined to make my place nicer, and though it didn't bother me either way, if it made her happy, I had no problem spending the money. And I guessed her wanting me to live somewhere comfortable, surrounded by nice things, made me feel cared for and valued, worthy of having a decent home. It wasn't a feeling I was all too familiar with, but if Phoebe believed that about me, who was I to argue?

After I'd agreed to buy the couch she liked, we moved on to tables. She kept sitting at them and asking me what I thought, but I couldn't offer much of an opinion since she made everything look beautiful.

"Aren't you a carpenter?" She tapped my chest, teasing. "You should care about the construction of the furniture you're buying."

She had a point. I could've built my own damn table and chairs, but that would've taken time I'd rather dedicate to paying customers and the woman in front of me. "I care more about which table you like sitting at best."

Her cheeks flushed with pleasure. "That was an all kinds of sweet thing to say."

"Just being honest." I touched my lips to hers. It still blew my damn mind I was allowed to do that whenever. And that she *liked* me doing it. "Pick the one you like the most. I'll like it too."

She slipped her hand in mine, weaving our fingers. "If you're sure..."

"I am."

I stood next to her while she spoke with a salesperson, zoning in and out of their conversation. My phone vibrated in my pocket, so I slipped it out to check the text.

My stomach bottomed out.

Richie: *I was thinking about swinging through town to see you Friday. Maybe visit Joy's. Unless you want to meet me in Rawlins. It's up to you.*

I'd put him off the last time he'd texted, having no interest in seeing him, let alone speaking to him, but I'd known he wouldn't be done just as well as I understood the threat behind his words.

There was no way he'd be setting foot in Joy's. She could take care of herself, but I wouldn't have her being put in a position where she had to. Joy had done enough for me. Putting herself between Richie and me wouldn't be added to that list. No way.

Me: *Tell me where you want to meet that's not in Sugar Brush.*

I'd get this shit over with as soon as I could. Friday, I'd deal with Richie, then Saturday, I'd get to take Phoebe dancing. She had no idea what I had planned. It was a surprise for her and a reward for me. Just had to get through this first.

Phoebe squeezed my hand. "You're frowning. Bad news?"

"No." I turned off the screen and put my phone back in my pocket. "It's nothing."

She tilted her head, her eyes trailing over my face. "Okay," she whispered. "But if it turns into something, you can tell me."

I pulled her close and pressed my lips to her jaw. "Know I can, sugar."

But I wouldn't. This would never touch Phoebe.

Chapter Eighteen

Phoebe

DEACON HAD A COUCH. The rest of the furniture he'd purchased was on back order, but at least he had somewhere to sit besides a camp chair. I liked seeing him allow himself to have nice things, even if I'd had to push him to do it. I was coming to realize he didn't believe he deserved to spend the money he'd worked hard to earn. Not on himself, anyway.

He stood over me as I sank into the soft cushions, his mouth curving into a grin.

"It was worth the shopping trip, seeing you comfortable in my place," he stated.

"It was worth it because it's a nice couch and looks good in here." I patted the cushion beside me. "Sit with me. Try it out."

He sank down, propping his feet on the matching ottoman. Pulling my leg up, I twisted to face him and patted his stomach.

"What do you think?"

He caught my hand and tugged me closer until I was almost splayed across his chest. His other hand came up to cup the back of my head.

"I like it." He tipped his face closer to mine, our noses brushing. Then, with a tilt, our lips met. He kissed me softly, a whisper of contact. "Anywhere I can have you in my arms is a place I want to be."

Free fall.

What was happening to my stomach had to be what skydivers felt in the moments between jumping and releasing their parachutes. Deacon had a tendency to say the sweetest things out of nowhere, and he did it so earnestly I didn't doubt he meant them.

This was why I was falling hard and fast for this man.

"Deacon," I murmured.

"Sugar," he murmured back, dipping in again to taste my lips. "Just like sugar."

"That's probably from the mango sorbet I had at my parents'."

I'd had dinner with them tonight. Deacon had been invited, but I hadn't been surprised when he'd declined. Disappointed but not surprised. We were new, and he was still unsure—of himself, this town, *us*. Probably my family too. He'd find out eventually they'd accept him so long as he treated me right. But we weren't there yet, so I didn't push.

I'd come straight to his apartment afterward, though. Oh, I was hooked.

His tongue dragged along my bottom lip, and he hummed. "No, that sweetness is all you."

"The things you say." I sighed against his lips. "Are you sure you haven't had lots of girlfriends? You're good at this."

"I haven't. You're my only girl." He nudged my chin with his knuckle, drawing my eyes to his. "If I'm good at anything, it's because of you. You make me feel like I'm free to say what I'm thinking. I've never had that with a woman."

My insides went so soft they were barely solid. Being told I made him feel free after he'd been locked up was too big of an honor to put into words. I would have to remember that. And be careful with it. I never wanted him to second-guess his choice to be fully open with me, especially when that was a huge part of what I wanted in a partner.

"You can always tell me what's on your mind. I want to hear it."

"It's a whole lotta you these days." He took my jaw in his hand. "Tell me something."

"Like what?"

"Like something about you. Did you go to college?"

"No. College wasn't my thing. I went to culinary school." I shifted slightly so my arm was draped over his stomach and my shoulder was tucked under his arm. "I did a two-year program at a school in California then spent six months in France doing a pastry course."

He blinked hard. "I didn't know you'd left Wyoming."

"I did. I always knew I'd be back, but I had to see more of the world for myself before I settled here."

"You went all by yourself? To California and France?"

"Well...I went alone to California, but I had friends from school I moved to France with. They'd done their damnedest to talk me out of coming home. As much as I'd loved that experience, that hadn't been an option. I love to travel, but my roots are here." I moved my hand over his stomach, tracing the ridge of muscles beneath his T-shirt. They tensed, and I leaned my head back to see his face, mine mirroring the frown he wore. "What's that about?"

"What?"

I touched the downturned corners of his mouth. "You look unhappy."

"I'm not. Just thinking. I don't have a passport."

"Oh. Well…it's not hard to get one. Is there somewhere you'd like to go if you had one?"

He shook his head. "No, you don't get my meaning. I'm not allowed to have one. I've got a year of parole left, and after that, from what I hear, getting a passport and leaving the country as a felon isn't always cut and dry. Don't know if I'll ever have one, and I'm not wasting time dreaming of places I might not ever be able to go." His gaze leveled on mine. "It's too soon to talk about this kind of future, but you should know what you're getting into with me. I may never be able to go with you to all the places you wanna go."

I swallowed down this information. It was too soon, but I wasn't dating for the sake of dating. I wanted someone to share my life with. I never would have considered Deacon's past could follow him for a long, long time. That record would stay with him and, if we lasted, with us.

"God, that sucks, but I get it." I flattened my hand on his stomach. "Thanks for telling me, honey. I'll think about it, but just saying, there are lots of places I haven't seen and want to go to in the US."

"I don't ever want to hold you back."

"I don't want that either. Not for either of us. If we stick long term, we'll figure out how things'll work for us. We're two smart people. I think we can handle it."

He curled his arm around me, bringing me close, his face in my hair, mine in his neck. He was warm and so tender my heart ached. This man wasn't built for the harsh life he'd been handed. If I started thinking what he might've been like if he'd grown up with a family like mine, I'd become unbearably sad, so I focused on his soapy scent and the goodness of being wrapped up in him.

"For the record, I earned an associate's degree while I was on the inside," he said as he sifted his fingers through my hair.

"Oh yeah? What's your degree in?"

"Business accounting. Thought it'd help me to manage my books if I ever got my business off the ground again."

"See? Like I said, smart." I touched my lips to his thrumming pulse. "I love that you spent your time that way, thinking ahead. And I really have no doubt your business will pick up. Actually, I can see if the ranch needs—"

He tapped my lips, cutting me off. "No, Phoebe. Let's not mix this with anything else, all right? I appreciate it. Love that you want to help me, but I don't want this to turn into you trying to rehab me. Just be my girl. That's all I need from you."

I opened my mouth, then closed it. I hadn't thought that was what I'd been doing, but I had to stop and consider if I was. Of course I wanted more for Deacon. He was insanely talented and deserved recognition. But would I have made that same offer to another man, one who hadn't been dealt the short end of the stick from birth, this early into our relationship? I couldn't say with any certainty I would have.

I brought my head out of his neck, finding his eyes again. "When I graduated and moved back to Sugar Brush, my parents assumed I was going to work at the ranch's restaurant as a pastry chef. Technically, I wouldn't have been working for them since neither has anything to do with managing the restaurant, but it's still theirs. They own it. I hadn't been sure what I wanted to do, but I'd known working for my family wasn't it."

Deacon listened intently, a furrow between his brows as he nodded along.

"Back then, I hadn't been able to put a name as to why I'd been so viscerally against it, but I think I finally can. They're my parents. I don't want them as bosses. It would change things. So, I worked at a couple different bakeries in Laramie until I figured out what I wanted to do. That happened to coincide with a storefront opening on Main Street, and the rest is history."

He raised his hand to cup my cheek, his thumb pressing on my bottom lip. "So you understand me then?"

I nodded. "I can just be your girl, honey."

We melted into the couch until we lay together, Deke on his back, me on my side, wedged between him and the back cushions. We'd put a podcast on, but I was only half listening, my attention more on his hand resting on my waist and the kisses he kept planting on my forehead.

Antsy, I moved my legs so one draped over his, my foot hooking beneath his calf. He lowered his chin to his chest, watching me shift around.

"Comfortable?"

"Getting there."

"C'mere," he demanded softly. "Give me your mouth."

I scooted up his body, putting us face to face. Once he had me there, he didn't hesitate to slide his lips over mine and coax them open. I parted, allowing him entry, and he clutched my head, kissing me long, wet, and deep. Tongue dancing with mine, I was lit from head to toe. Turned on and ignited. Cozy and languid. In no rush to take things further, I bunched his shirt in my fist, letting this kiss consume me.

Deacon didn't move quickly, and I liked that. If all he wanted to do was make out on his new couch, I was game. It was different, but so was he. I couldn't remember ever being this *into* a man. Excited to see him, talk to him, *know* him.

I drew my leg up higher and twisted, aligning my core with his thigh. I rocked, and it wasn't intentional, just my heated body seeking his, but he felt it.

Oh, had he felt it.

Pulling away from my mouth, he looked down, then flicked his eyes back to mine.

"*Sugar*," he drawled. "What're you doing?"

"Feeling you." I slid my palm from his stomach to his chest then curved my fingers around the side of his neck. "I love the way you kiss me."

He shook his head. Close enough, his nose brushed mine. "Can't get enough of your mouth."

He rolled into me, letting me feel just how much I affected him. The thick ridge of his cock pressed into the soft give of my stomach as his fingers dug into my sides and hips like he was trying to gather me up. Then he roamed lower, slowly, tentatively, until he reached my ass.

"This all right?" he asked thickly.

"More than," I assured him. If he was a little less careful with me, that would have been all right too.

Perfectly, delightfully, ecstatically all right.

I took my own journey of his body, tracing my fingers along the length of his back to his backside. I tucked my hand into his pocket, curving my palm around his tight, round ass, and pulled him even closer, though he was already flush against me.

Grunting, he kneaded my bottom, roving from side to center. Then he squeezed, his fingers delving in as far as the seam of my jeans would allow. Not far enough, if his frustrated groan was anything to go by.

"Deacon," I moaned, latching onto his lips.

Hot and swollen at my core, my nipples beaded and tingling, I was breathless, swirling with him in this in-between place of pleasure we'd yet to explore.

I sucked his bottom lip into my mouth. He tasted so good I wasn't able to resist rocking my hips into him.

Then I was on my back, and Deacon was over me, his face buried in my neck, hips snug between my thighs. He nipped at my throat, teeth, lips, tongue, making me quiver. My knees tightened at his flanks, bringing his cock in line with my clit. I felt him, even through two layers of denim, and my body arched on instinct.

His groan vibrated my throat. "You feel so good." His lips trailed along my jaw to meet mine once more.

"Stay there," I said into his mouth. "Right there."

He rolled his hips into mine. Right where I needed him. "Here?"

"Yeah," I whispered. "Do you like that?"

"Don't ask me that," he gritted out, dragging his cock along my clit. "Your voice, I can't—"

Oh, he liked it.

I smashed my lips to his, riding the wave our bodies were on. Colliding, retreating, coming back together. Friction and desire heating our cores to the tipping point. His weight on me, his hands all over me, rubbing me where I needed. Tension stretched taut in my belly, yanking and curling, in and out, until it was almost unbearable.

I pressed my heels to the backs of his thighs, raising to meet his steady, impatient thrusts. My body bloomed, opening for him. Even through too many layers of fabric, I felt him like we were almost skin to skin.

I writhed, overheated from the fire building within me, and grappled with his shirt. I found my way beneath it, and the moment my hands met his rippling back, he released a desperate groan I felt all the way down to my bones.

My head tipped back, eyes startling open. He was there, over me, watching as I fell apart without warning. Pleasure barreled over me, lifting my hips into his, aching to take him inside. Warmth spread across my skin and through my veins, as something within me ripped to pieces.

Deacon cried out, gripping the cushion on either side of me with savage strength. He thrust wildly, slapping against me hard and fast. My already tender clit was a live wire, sparking with each pass of his covered erection.

"Phoebe," he moaned. "Oh, fuck."

He let go of the cushion to grip my jaw, his eyes locking onto mine. Then, it was me watching him find his pleasure and slip into it. A shudder started at his shoulders, traveling down until he was one shaking mass. He held my gaze as long as he could, but he couldn't stop his head from jerking back as his body stilled, pressed so tight to mine, I felt him pulsing.

"Yes," I urged, lifting my head to kiss wherever I could land my lips. "That's right, honey. That's exactly right."

Another broken groan, and he collapsed on me, rolling us to our sides. He held me tight, huffing into my hair. I tucked my face in his throat, clinging to him just as fiercely.

"What the hell was that?" he uttered hoarsely. "I'm—fuck. I hadn't expected that."

I giggled, happy he sounded as discombobulated and shocked as I was feeling. "I don't know, but it was so good."

He pulled back, and I tilted my chin to look at him, unsurprised to find a worried frown tugging at the corners of his mouth. I leaned in, kissing each side of his lips then the center.

"You...came?" he asked.

"Yeah." I smiled at him. "Really hard."

He closed his eyes, exhaling heavily through his nose. "Hottest thing I've ever seen in my life. Most beautiful too."

"Same, Deacon. I loved watching you come."

His eyes flashed open, intent on my mouth then my eyes. "I didn't mean for that to happen. I couldn't stop it. You're just...god, I don't have words."

"I think we're on the same page."

He hesitated, then dropped his forehead to mine. "Blows my mind."

"Mine too," I whispered. "I'm really glad you bought this couch."

A long beat, then he chuckled, low and warm. "I promise you, nobody's more glad than me, sugar."

I wasn't sure how that could possibly be true, but I wasn't going to argue with him.

Chapter Nineteen

Phoebe

LEAVING WORK EARLY ON Fridays pained me…except when it was to take a class. I thought of myself as a perpetual student, always eager to learn more about my profession, so months ago, I'd booked an afternoon off work to attend a class on bread baking at the cutest bakery in Rawlins.

I spent a few hours in baking heaven, exchanging ideas and techniques with others in the profession and adding a few new skills under my belt. We didn't offer bread at Sugar Rush, but I'd been toying with the idea of selling loaves once or twice a week.

As if I needed to add something else to my plate.

As the class neared the end, everyone made plans to head to a bar for dinner and drinks. I decided to check in with Deacon first to see what he was up to. We'd been spending most of our free time together, and it surprised me how much I could miss him after twenty-four hours apart. Being with him was so sweet and cozy, with all the excitement of something brand new and sparkly.

I sent him a text, hoping he was free.

Deacon: *Thanks for asking. I'm going to work in the shed tonight. Hope you have fun.*

Me: *You too. Don't work too hard!*

Deacon: *Will do. Drive safely.*

I put my phone down and looked out a nearby window. A prickly feeling crawled along my neck at his short and curt responses. Not that we texted often, but something seemed off. It could have been that he hadn't asked how my class had gone or when I'd be home. Hadn't tried to make plans for later or even called me "sugar." It might not have been any of those things but something else I couldn't pinpoint.

Or maybe I was imagining things.

That was probably it.

"All right, you guys. I should hit the road." I pushed back from the table amid groans from my classmates. I'd tried to be present but hadn't been in a social mood. I wasn't too certain I'd be missed, but at least they were putting on a good show of being sorry to see me go.

We were in the back of an Old West–style tavern. The crowd seemed to lean older and a little on the rough side, but despite basically being a dive, the food had been good, and the half a beer I'd drunk had been icy cold.

I'd have to come back another time when I could really enjoy it.

Once I'd said goodbye to everyone and grabbed my bag, I stopped to use the restroom then wandered toward the exit. I took a different route, checking out the rest of the rustic tavern. The wood floors were beaten up and creaky, and the animal heads mounted on the walls looked like they had a thick layer of dust on them.

Distracted by the decor, I didn't notice the people sitting at the table near the door until I was almost upon them. I stopped in my tracks, his hair catching my attention first. The overhead lights glinted off the fine strawberry-blond highlights, making them brighter. Then I caught his smile, rare and lovely as it was, tugging the corners of the lips I'd come to know so well.

What was Deacon doing here?

My heart lifted like it always did when I saw him. Without a second thought, I raised my hand to wave. His gaze met mine, but just as quickly, it was as if he were looking right through me, lodging my breath in my throat. It was like I was a stranger. For a split second, I might have convinced myself he hadn't recognized me in the crowded bar, but then his eyes flicked back, a glimmer of something unreadable crossing his face before he shook his head.

It was subtle, but there was no denying he had just told me no.

No, I don't want to see you.

No, do not come over here.

No, we're in public, which means I don't know you.

No. Just...no.

I staggered back a step as my breath blew out of me. *What...?*

This wasn't happening. Deacon wasn't at a bar when he'd explicitly told me he'd be working in his shed. He wasn't sitting at a table with Richie Slater and two women I did not know. *Smiling* at them.

This *really* wasn't happening.

But it was.

Fortunately, my self-preservation got me out of there and into my car. I sat there in the dark, waiting out the pounding of my heart. When I felt it was safe for me to drive, I got going, putting distance between me and whatever the hell that had been.

I was so damn disappointed, I could have screamed. Technically, I guessed he hadn't done anything wrong by going out tonight. Except...he'd *lied*. I could forgive and understand a lot, but lying was my line in the sand.

I didn't abide by liars.

The ride home had given me ample opportunity to think. By the time I flopped on my couch with a groan, I'd sorted myself out.

The sharp pain in my chest was an overreaction. Once my body caught up with my brain, it would dissipate. Deacon and I had only been seeing each other a couple weeks. Our proximity had intensified what should have still been casual, and I'd let myself get carried away from the nostalgia of it all.

When it came down to it, we were so new we were barely a blip. We hadn't gone public with...whatever we were, so ending it would be like it had never happened. Being neighbors might be awkward for a time, but that would fade. I was sure of it.

If this pain in my chest would just get the message.

I'd allowed myself to be hidden away by a man once, and it hadn't ended well. I should have known this time would be the same. But

Deacon was so different from Jared. I'd let myself believe his reasons for not wanting to go to Grey's or spend time at Sugar Rush.

I groaned again, wishing Hannah was still upstairs. She'd be down in an instant to stroke my hair while cussing out Deacon and every other man who'd done us wrong. Just thinking about what she might've said made me smile. I could almost hear her voice.

"Goddamn no-good men. What use are they anyway?"

"I know a good place to bury the body. They'd never find him."

"No one ignores my Phoebe."

The sound of Deacon's truck pulling into the driveway made me stiffen. He must've left the bar shortly after I had.

Was he bringing one of those women home with him?

I couldn't stop myself from going to the window even as my stomach clenched. As hard as I'd worked to convince myself none of this mattered, the wave of relief that crashed over me at seeing him alone was so immense my knees went weak.

It seemed my body was still warring with my brain. I hadn't made the decision to open my door until it had already happened.

Deacon paused with one foot on the stairs, his head jerking up to find me standing there. Neither of us said a word. I folded my arms around my middle. He stared.

No, staring wasn't the right word. His eyes scanned me inch by inch, like he was committing every facet to memory.

"Deacon," I whispered.

The sound of my voice snapped him out of his momentary pause. His boots hit the stairs hard. When he reached my landing, he stopped but didn't face me, giving me the rigid lines of his profile.

"You always knew I was a piece of shit."

His eyes slid sideways toward me then darted away just as quickly before he continued up to his apartment. The door closing behind him sounded like finality—the ending of some of the sweetest weeks I'd ever experienced.

"You always knew I was a piece of shit."

I hadn't thought that. Not once. Even now, with my chest cracked down the middle, I didn't think it.

But it didn't really matter what I thought. Whatever Deacon and I could have had was over before it had really begun.

Chapter Twenty

Deacon

My sandwich tasted like sawdust, but I chewed by rote anyway. Chris's eyes were on me, waiting for me to start talking. If I kept my mouth full, I could put him off until our lunch break was over.

"You're not getting out of this."

I took another bite.

"You canceled our Saturday night plans without an explanation, and today, you look like death warmed over. Do you really believe I'm going to let you off the hook?" He nudged my shoulder. "Talk, dammit. What happened?"

I swallowed hard and looked out at the highway. We were on our asses on the side of a grassy hill next to the road, the sun bathing our spot with warmth, the traffic whizzing by in a nice, low hum. It wasn't the worst place in the world to be, not with my best friend sitting next to me and a few other decent guys on our crew around us, but I might as well have been back in prison. Looking over my shoulder every day wasn't freedom.

"It's over," I muttered. "It was never going to work."

"What's that mean?"

I shrugged. "I don't have anything to offer."

He shook his head. "That's bullshit, and you know it. Did she break up with you?"

"She didn't do anything wrong."

What I'd done to her on Friday night had been inexcusable. How I'd convinced myself I could compartmentalize, I didn't know. But the second I noticed Phoebe walking up to the table I shared with Richie, I knew I had to keep her away. Even if it meant hurting her.

The stricken look on her face when I'd shaken my head had just about killed me, but if Richie had seen she meant something to me, it would've been worse. So much fucking worse.

"Wasn't that Hannah Kelly's little sister?" Richie craned his neck to watch her as she calmly walked out of the bar. "What the hell's her name? Penny? No, Phoebe."

The woman on my right snickered. I'd been told her name, but it didn't matter to me, so I couldn't remember what it was.

"There was nothing little about her," she said.

"Shut up, Janie," the woman on my left admonished. Didn't know her name either, just that she was Richie's girlfriend. "You only wish you had hair like hers."

"You shut up, Jennifer. You don't have to be rude." Janie picked up a piece of her lank, straw-like hair. "I guess her hair was all right. At least she had one thing going for her."

My hands balled into fists beneath the table, and I bit my tongue hard enough to taste copper to keep myself from roaring at all of them to keep their mouths shut. They didn't deserve to breathe the same air as Phoebe, let alone talk about her.

Richie turned back around, his brows raised. "That was her, wasn't it?"

I shrugged, my mind whirring to come up with an answer that'd make him lose interest. If I denied knowing whether it was her, he'd latch on, but if I acknowledged, maybe he'd let it go.

"Could've been." I picked up my beer. "It's been a while since I've seen her."

Twenty hours, when she'd been in my arms, and I was kissing her good night. My gut knotted into an impossible tangle.

"Remember when you had a thing for her in school?" He chuckled to himself, mean and dirty, like everything about him. "You were fucking awful at hiding the hearts in your eyes. Like a little cartoon character..."

The straw-haired one, who Richie had brought to turn this whole thing into some kind of hellish version of a double date, trailed her nail along my arm. It took all my power not to jerk away in disgust. My skin was not hers to touch. The only hands I wanted on me were Phoebe's.

"Is that your type?" she simpered.

"Yeah, is she?" Richie glanced back at the door. "Should I run after her for you?"

"High school was a long time ago," I muttered. "Lot's happened since then."

"I guess so." He crossed his arms over his chest. "My baby brother finally has his freedom back. No sense in wasting your time on anything less than the finest life has to offer."

Janie scooted closer, and I had to swallow back bile. "Like me, baby," she cooed.

I'd gotten out of there as quickly as I could, but the damage had been done. In some small way, it was a relief. Phoebe saw for herself who I was. There'd be no more knocking on my door. No more trying to see the good in me. And I wouldn't be waiting for the other shoe to drop.

It'd already happened.

"Talk to me," Chris urged. "You were excited about her. I've never seen you like that."

"It was a mistake to think I could have her."

He grumbled, and I could tell he was getting angry at me. I didn't like that, but I didn't have it in me to make it right.

"This song and dance is getting old. I get you think you're the worst man in the world and everyone is better than you, but that's a lie you internalized a long time ago, and it's time to shake it the hell off. Do you think I'd let you around Tilly if you were actually the piece of shit you claim to be?"

"I'd never let any hurt come to Tilly." I tossed the rest of my sandwich in my bag. There weren't any cookies in there today. Just a whole lot of emptiness.

He shoved my shoulder, harder this time. "Jesus, man. I know that. That's exactly my point. You are what you make yourself. Would you ever tell your sister she's the sum of where she came from?"

"No." I narrowed my eyes on him. He knew I didn't like talking about my little sister. "She's a kid, and she has a chance now."

"So do you, Deke. If Phoebe doesn't see that, it's her loss, not yours."

"I heard you. Appreciate the sentiment, but I'm done talking about this."

"Might as well still be wearing shackles," he mumbled, knowing full well I would hear him.

He wasn't wrong. If this was freedom, I sure as hell didn't like the taste of it.

Chapter Twenty-one

Phoebe

I sliced two pieces of fresh, warm rosemary bread. One went to Hailey, the other to Cormac. This was the first loaf I'd made since my class last week. Hailey had smelled it baking during her shift and asked if she could taste it when it was done. Cormac had stopped in right before we closed, so now they were both my guinea pigs.

I hadn't intended to bake bread this week, but I'd needed to keep myself busy. Any downtime I'd had had been spent with my family, cleaning like a madwoman, and baking. I'd managed not to have a single sighting of *him*.

My heart was a little less achy, but not by much. For the most part, in those few quiet moments I'd allowed myself, I vacillated between confusion and anger.

But it didn't matter why he'd behaved that way, only that he had. I was moving on, baking bread and spending time with people who wanted to be with me.

"Mmmm." Hailey's eyebrows popped as she chewed. "I don't think I've ever tasted rosemary before, but I like it."

Cormac nodded in agreement. "This is your first loaf?"

"It is," I preened.

"I shouldn't be surprised; it's the best bread I've ever tasted." He wrapped his arm around my shoulders and tucked me against him.

Everyone in our family was tall, but my baby brother towered over even Caleb at six and a half feet. "I'm going to have to forbid you from selling it, though."

Twisting under his arm, I gave him the side-eye. "Why's that?"

He wagged his finger at me playfully. "Young lady, tell me where you're going to get the time to add baking bread to your insane schedule? Do you want to start going to work at four a.m.?" I wrinkled my nose, and Cormac laughed. "Yeah, I didn't think so. Maybe lay off the bread until you bring in another full-time employee."

Hailey stole another piece. "But wouldn't selling a lot of bread pay the salary of a new employee?"

I tapped my temple. "I like the way you think, smarty."

Cormac gave me a shake. "How many loaves are you going to need to sell to pay that salary?"

I sighed, reluctantly admitting defeat, even though I really didn't have plans to hire anyone else so soon. That idea was a year or two down the road.

"Okay. I concede. I won't start selling bread."

Hailey slid the rest of the loaf across the cutting board, bringing it closer to her. "But maybe, on occasion, you could bake some for your very best employees."

"And your best younger brother," Cormac added, eyeing the bread Hailey had very obviously laid claim on.

I patted his arm. "It's okay to let her have that one. You don't have to fight her for it." With a flourish, I whipped a towel off the second loaf I'd baked. "You can take this one home."

He grinned wide. "I knew you loved me. Thanks, Phe."

Cormac stayed to help Hailey and me close up, then drove the two of us to my place so I could grab my car. Hailey's foster mom hadn't been able to pick her up from work today, so I'd volunteered to bring her home. My brother would have done the driving, but he had a real live date he had to get to. Since he'd had his heart broken years ago, he rarely dated, and it seemed I was more excited about it than he was. Still, he was trying, and that was the first step.

After waving Cormac off, I unlocked the doors of my car, ignoring the big silver truck parked next to it. Hailey climbed in beside me, eyeing the truck and my house.

"I like your house," she said.

"I do too. During the summer, I can open my windows and listen to the concerts in the park."

She settled back in her seat with a sigh as I pulled out of the driveway. "I'd love that. My house is loud, but not that kind of loud. If I want to listen to music, I have to wear headphones. There are *definitely* no live concerts."

I glanced over at her. "But is it a good kind of loud?"

She pursed her mouth, considering. "I guess so. I mean, it had been loud when I was little too, when I'd lived with my real parents, but that had mostly been screaming and slamming things." A knot formed in my throat. "My foster family is nothing like that. They're loud because someone's always talking or laughing, and Linda, my foster mom, likes to run the vacuum a lot. We're kinda messy, and we have two dogs. So, yeah, it's loud, but the good kind."

The knot unfurled. That kind of loud I was intimately familiar with, and it was definitely the good kind.

Hailey's eyes were on me as I drove. "Can I ask you a question?"

"Sure."

"Well...I was wondering what happened with the guy you were dating. He doesn't pick you up anymore, and...don't get mad, but you've seemed pretty sad lately. Did you break up?"

I sighed, wishing I hadn't agreed to answer her without finding out her question.

"It didn't work out," I hedged. "I'm sad about it because I really liked him."

"So he dumped you?"

A surprised laugh burst out of me. "No one dumped anyone. It just didn't work out."

"Did you break up with him then? I thought you liked him. You said he was nice."

"Hailey..." I groaned softly.

"I'm sorry if I'm being nosy." She twisted in her seat. "I've been a little worried about you, and I guess Deke too. He's got to be sad he lost you."

"I understand." Fortunately, I pulled up to the curb outside of her house, ending the inquisition. "I'm a little bit of a Nosy Nellie too. But you're right, I'm disappointed things didn't work out, so right now, it's easier if I don't talk about it, okay?"

"Of course." Hailey's gaze was sympathetic as it swept over me. "I hope there's some way you guys can work it out. You smiled a lot more when he was around."

With that, she hopped out of my car like she hadn't just landed a solid punch to my gut.

If I had thought I'd be able to move on peacefully, I'd obviously forgotten what living in a small town was like. After the morning rush, I disappeared into the kitchen to bake more cookies. I'd gotten one batch in the oven when Camille stuck her head in the door.

"Hey, Phe. Tilly McMannis is asking for you. She's doing some work on her laptop and said it's no rush."

My brows drew together. "Tilly? What could she want?"

Camille shrugged. "She didn't say. Should I tell her you're too busy?"

"No, that's okay." I waved her off. "The cookies are baking, so I have a minute."

I didn't know Tilly well. She'd been ahead of me in school and we hadn't shared friends, but I'd always had a good impression of her. She and her husband, Chris, had been together forever. They were an odd couple that somehow fit. Her, with her neat bob and headbands, sweet sweaters and corduroy slacks, and Chris, with his mountain-man beard and rugged work clothes. Whenever I saw them together, he doted on her—opening doors, holding her hand, swinging her gently around the dance floor.

She smiled at me and closed her laptop as I approached her table. "Hi, Phoebe. How are you?"

"I'm great." I nodded toward her computer. Tilly worked in the accounting department at the ranch. "Are you working?"

"No, not really." She stacked her hands on top of it. "It's my day off. I was trying to clear out my email inbox, which is pretty much an impossible feat."

"That's why I don't bother trying." I pulled out the chair across from hers and perched on the edge. "Camille said you needed to speak to me?"

"Yes. I'm sorry if you were busy. I would have called, but I don't have your number."

I waited for her to continue, which she did.

"Well..." she blew out a heavy breath, "I want to talk to you about Deke. I'm sure you know he's Chris's best friend and a good friend of mine."

Blood rushed to my head in an instant, making my cheeks burn and my brain buzz. "Tilly...I don't think there's anything for us to talk about on that subject."

Her eyes slid back and forth between mine, and she whispered, "He was happy."

I couldn't stop from flinching. "I don't—"

"Hear me out, *please*. Deke is a good man who's been dealt a really rough hand. Chris and I have tried our hardest to help him build a new life since he got out, and on a professional front, that's happening. But personally...you have to understand he's never had a girlfriend, much less dated. Before he went in, he had so many family issues I don't think he even considered it. You're the first woman I've heard him talk about since high school, and you were the *only* girl he talked about back then."

I swallowed hard, trying to take in what she was saying, even though it felt like there were razor blades in my throat. I'd assumed, after everything, he'd kept me a secret. To know he'd talked about me to his closest friends and still did what he had hurt even worse.

It didn't seem Tilly knew what had happened last Friday. If she did, if she knew I'd spotted him on what had looked very much like a double date and he'd ignored me, she might not have been riding so hard for him. Yet, I couldn't bring myself to tell her. Deacon might not have been mine, but that didn't erase everything. Despite myself,

I cared for him, and I refused to make him look bad in his friends' eyes.

Tilly went on. "Whatever happened, if he pulled back from you or messed up in a way that made you end things, I'm asking you to be patient with him. Hold the line, Phoebe. He'll return when he gets his head on straight. I know it. He was so excited about you, and Deke doesn't show that emotion often. Maybe never." Her hand darted out, grabbing mine. "He asked Chris and me to go dancing with you two. We were all supposed to go out last weekend. I don't know why the plans got canceled, only that Chris said Deke had shown up to work on Monday looking like he'd died."

"Dancing?" I whispered. That was news to me. I didn't know how to feel about that, so I tucked it away for later when I was alone and could roll it around in my mind.

She laughed. A manic burst that faded as quickly as it had begun. "I know. I didn't believe it when Chris told me, but it's true. That's how I know how real his feelings are for you. Deke dancing?" She shook her head. "I can't even picture it."

We danced in my kitchen. Every night, he spun me like a music box ballerina.

I didn't tell her that. Those nights had been sweet, and they were mine to hold tight. I also didn't figure Deacon would like me sharing them, not even with one of his good friends.

"I understand why you're here, Tilly. You're being a loyal friend…but this isn't going to turn out how you want."

She squeezed my hand tight. "I'm asking you to be open when he comes to you. Please, just let him have the chance to make it right."

I withdrew my hand, balling it in my lap. "I don't think he'll be coming to me." I hadn't even seen him in almost a week. "I'm sorry."

"Don't be sorry." She straightened her spine and leveled me with a direct gaze. "He'll come to you. Just hold the line until he does. He's worth it."

Long after she'd left, the shop had closed, and I'd gone home for the evening; I was still thinking about Deacon wanting to take me dancing. I would have loved that so much, even if it was too chilly to wear a sundress.

Something told me there might have been more to what had happened in that tavern. If he'd come to me like Tilly had assured me he would, I would have listened to his explanation.

But he'd stayed away.

There was nothing to forgive, even if I'd wanted to.

Chapter Twenty-two

Deacon

I HADN'T LOOKED FORWARD to going home in a week, but today I was. I'd never been so tired in my life. Not even in prison, where I was lucky if I got four hours of consecutive sleep. Exhaustion ate at my bones like a crippling disease.

Chris looked over at me from the driver's seat. "You look like shit. Are you feeling okay?" For once, luck had been on my side. Chris and I sometimes carpooled to jobsites, and most of the time, when we did, we took my truck. Today, he'd volunteered to drive. Good thing, too. I wasn't sure I would have been able to safely get us home.

I rubbed my sweaty forehead, but it did nothing to relieve the ache behind my brow. "Pretty sure I'm coming down with something. Try not to breathe my air. Tilly'll kill me if I get you sick."

It'd come out of nowhere and hit me like a freight train. I'd barely been around anyone lately, but I must've picked up a bug during the few interactions I'd had.

"You need to stop to get some meds?"

I shook my head. We were nearly home. The thought of being in this truck for more than a few more minutes was almost unbearable.

"I've got what I need in my medicine cabinet." I'd be lucky if I could find a Tylenol, but he didn't need to know that. "I just need to sleep it off."

"Good thing it's the weekend. I see you working in the shed; I'm kicking you out. You need rest."

My arm dropped to my lap, heavy and lethargic. "I'm not arguing that." I didn't know how I'd gotten through my workday. Pure adrenaline, probably, and I was experiencing the crash. My body said, "No more," and I had no choice but to listen.

Chris pulled up in front of the house, putting his truck in park so he could look at me. "Are you sure you're gonna be okay on your own? I can run out, get you soup or medicine—anything you need."

"I must really look like shit if you're offering to get me soup."

He guffawed. "Hell yeah, you do."

"I'm good." Using every ounce of my remaining strength, I pushed the door open and climbed out. Once I was upright, my legs were anything but steady and my head started to spin. "Just need to crash. I'll be fine."

I took a step back—staggered, really—and closed the door, lifting my hand in a wave. That act alone almost sucked out all the energy I had left, and I still had a long flight of stairs to climb.

Dizziness struck me from all angles, but I managed to put one foot in front of the other. Behind me, the steady sound of a big engine faded as Chris drove away. The act I'd put on had been good enough to convince him I wasn't on death's door.

At the bottom of the stairs, I stumbled, narrowly avoiding falling by grabbing onto the railing. I looked up. The steps had multiplied since I'd been gone. There were now ten thousand, most of them moving.

"*Fuck.*"

This was going to hurt.

I climbed two, and I was breathless. Black spots danced in my vision. Pushing through it, I made it up another two. Sweat flowed down my back and dripped off my brow freely, and my vision narrowed to little more than a pinpoint.

Just need to make it to my door.

Then inside.

I'll crawl to my bed.

I staggered onward, somehow lifting my leg high enough to climb another step and another until I reached the top. My door...Christ, I could barely get my eyes to focus on it.

I braced one hand on the frame, my head hanging between my shoulders until I caught my breath. Then I reached into my pocket for my keys, but my fingers weren't wrapping around them.

Frustration swamped me, making it hard to do anything other than groan. Actually, that might have been the virus running rampant through my body. Hell, maybe I could take a nap right here and worry about getting inside later.

Yeah, that sounded like a really good idea.

As soon as I decided, my legs gave out, and I dropped to my knees on my welcome mat.

When had I gotten a welcome mat? I must've forgotten. Didn't seem like me, but what the hell did I know? Glad I had it, though. Cushioned my ass when I fell on it.

With a ragged groan, I let my head drop back against the door. I'd just rest here a little while.

My eyes fell closed.

Just for a while...

Chapter Twenty-three

Phoebe

For the past week, I'd been hyperaware of my surroundings when I came home, which was why I spotted the man slumped against my door immediately.

I stopped on the sidewalk and blinked, letting my brain catch up to what I was seeing. It wasn't just a random man.

For a second, I thought Deacon was waiting for me. It was a strange place to wait, but whimsy got ahead of logic as I rushed forward. It was only when I got closer I realized something was very wrong.

Deacon was hunched, his spine bowed, his arms gathered in his lap in a distinctly vulnerable pose. Eyes closed, head hanging limp. He was sleeping...on my porch. Was he drunk? That didn't seem right, but nothing about this did.

Reaching him, I crouched down and touched his knee. Heat radiated off him through his jeans even though it couldn't have been above sixty outside.

"Deacon?" I shook his knee. "Deacon, wake up. You can't stay here."

His eyelids fluttered open into little slits. "Just for a while," he croaked.

"Oh, Deacon. Are you sick?"

His brow furrowed. "Sugar."

"That's not an answer." I rested the back of my hand on his forehead and nearly yanked it away at how hot he was. "You're sick, honey. We need to get you inside. Can you stand if I help you?"

He grunted. "Resting."

"You'll rest so much better in bed."

One eye cracked. "Bed sounds good. Gimme a second."

With a lot of my help, we got him to his feet, but he was leaning on me hard. One arm around his waist, the other on his abdomen to keep him upright, I guided him into my apartment. When we reached my bed, he all but flopped onto the mattress.

"Don't fall asleep. We need to get water in you—" My words cut off when his hand wrapped around the back of my thigh.

"Why's my bed so soft?" He squeezed. "Like you, but you're softer."

Leaning down, I brushed his hair off his forehead. "We're in *my* apartment, Deke. You're in my bed. I need to find a thermometer and medicine. You have to let me go for a minute, okay?"

His glazed eyes roamed erratically over my face. "Think I'm dreamin'. Have to be. Best goddamn dream I've ever had, sugar."

Despite my worry, I couldn't stop from smiling. My heart was not hard enough to handle Deacon Slater, sick and adorable as he lay in my bed. I had to get away from him.

"I'll be right back. We're going to get you better."

His brow pinched with panic. "Don't go." His hold on the back of my thigh tightened, but he was so weak I could have easily broken free. "Stay with me."

I slid my fingers through his hair until the lines on his face eased. "I'm not going far. You need medicine to bring your fever down. You have to let me go. I'll be back in a minute."

Slowly, his fingers opened, and I stepped away. Only when I was out of my bedroom did I start to freak out. I wasn't sure I had a thermometer. I wasn't sure what to do to bring down his fever. I hadn't been sick in ages. When I was younger, my mom—

My mom.

That was who I needed.

My mother arrived with supplies and confidence and went right to work helping me sit Deacon up to get medicine and fluids into him. His temperature was alarmingly high. She had me take his socks and shoes off, then run a tepid washcloth along his forehead and down his arms. Through it all, he was pliant, lethargically moving where we wanted. He barely seemed to notice my mother had joined us.

While I ran the washcloth over his skin, she called our family doctor. He didn't make house calls on a normal basis, but for Elena Kelly, he made an exception.

Deacon grumbled a little more as the doctor poked and prodded him, but the moment I slipped my hand in his, he settled.

The good news was his lungs were clear. The bad news? He had the flu and the next few days would probably be rough. There was never a question of whether I'd be taking care of him. But how I would do that and run my business, I did not know.

The medicine kicked in, and Deacon finally fell into a deep sleep. My mom pulled me out of my bedroom and into the kitchen, a slight furrow between her brows as she looked at me with worry.

"Is there someone you could call to stay with him?"

I shook my head. Though that wasn't true. I now knew a list of people who cared for Deacon, but I wasn't going to call any of them.

"I'll feel better being the one to take care of him," I admitted.

"Of course you would." She ran her hand from my crown down the length of my braid, tugging the end. "You haven't mentioned him in a while. I was under the impression things between you had petered out."

Despite the way he'd hurt me, I hadn't had the heart to tell anyone Deacon and I had ended. Deep down, I still wanted to protect him. And maybe, even deeper, I held a small bit of hope he'd somehow make things right, and if I'd told my family what he'd done, they would have never been able to forgive him.

"They have, but I can't leave him alone right now."

She sighed and patted my cheek. "I blame your father for making you this way. Too selfless for your own good. If you get the flu, who's going to take care of you?"

I leaned into her hand. "You, obviously."

That made her roll her eyes. "Obviously. I'm here taking care of your sort of ex-boyfriend. Of course I'd take care of you. But I'd rather you not get sick. As good as I am at nursing my ailing children, I can't bake worth a damn. If you're down and out, who's going to make your muffins?"

I crinkled my nose. "I won't breathe his air."

"That's a realistic solution."

"Actually, I was thinking about going to work in the morning while he's here..." I trailed off, hoping she would fill in the blanks and offer.

"I see what you're doing, Phe. I'll come back in the morning to check on you both." She took my hand in hers. "Please be careful."

She didn't have to say she meant that in every way. She'd seen me give with my whole heart only to have it stomped on, and she'd been there for the aftermath. I supposed I was still living in the aftermath since I'd never felt the same again.

"I will," I promised.

At least, I would try.

After my mother left, I was in and out of my bedroom all evening, running a washcloth over Deacon's head and rousing him enough to drink some water. When he'd sweat through his clothes, I took his keys from his pocket and ran upstairs to his apartment to grab some fresh, comfortable ones.

Passing the kitchen, I stopped in my tracks. The card I'd given him weeks ago was hanging on his refrigerator, pressed flowers stark against shiny stainless steel. I wondered when he'd hung it there. After the tavern? We'd spent most of our time at my place, but I'd been in his on occasion, and that card hadn't been anywhere in sight.

For reasons I couldn't name, seeing it there made my heart skip a few beats, and I had trouble taking a full, deep breath.

Oh, Deacon, how can you be so unbearably sweet and still have screwed up so massively? It isn't fair.

When I returned to my apartment, Deacon was sitting on the edge of my bed, shoulders slumped, head low. His elbows rested on his knees, and his fingers dragged down his face before he looked up at me through bleary eyes.

"You came back," he croaked.

"I had to. This is my apartment."

His gaze drifted away, his eyes wandering around the room as if seeing it for the first time. "Yeah," he muttered, confusion twisting his features. "What am I doing here?"

Ignoring his question, I put his things down and moved to his side, pressing the back of my hand to his forehead. His skin was clammy, but the fever seemed to be easing. "I think you might be a little cooler. Are you up for getting changed?"

"Think so." Gripping the mattress, he tried to stand, but his legs gave out, and he plopped back onto the bed with a defeated groan. "Might need some help."

I placed my hand on his shoulder, looking over him. "I'm here."

The hand that'd been on his thigh reached out to brush my leg as I stood in front of him. "You really are. How's that?"

I swallowed the lump in my throat, brushing his damp hair back. "Let's get your shirt off first, all right?"

Deacon wasn't a lot of help, but at least he cooperated. Getting him changed into a clean T-shirt and soft sweats took effort, his sluggish movements making everything twice as difficult. By the time I was done, his remaining strength was spent. Eyes closed, his head lolled on my pillow. I stood over him, hugging my arms to my chest, unsure of what to do next. I was bone-tired, and my couch called to me. But leaving him alone didn't sit right.

"Don't go," he murmured, almost as if in a dream. "Stay, sugar."

I brushed my fingertips along his jaw, feeling the rough stubble beneath my touch. "Okay, Deacon," I whispered. "I'll stay."

Chapter Twenty-four

Deacon

I HAD TO BE dreaming.

Had to.

Except I'd never had a dream this good. I lay on something so soft, it might've been a cloud, sugar all around me, warmth at my side, cocooned in a comfort I'd never experienced...

So how could I be dreaming it?

I cracked one eye open. A distant light broke through the shadows in the room, outlining the rounded woman who lay in the bed beside me. There was no mistaking her. That was when memories came to me in flashes.

Phoebe's face, her hands on me, her supporting my body. Cold water, medicine, moving. Icy blue eyes peering at me, a stethoscope on my chest, bitter medicine in my mouth. Phoebe's voice reassuring me, staying beside me when I basically begged her not to go.

I'd never felt as shitty as I did right now, but if I were given the choice to feel better in an instant, I wouldn't have taken it if it meant leaving this bed. I knew I'd never get back here.

I must've made some sound because Phoebe shot up on her elbow, her hand going to my forehead.

"You're burning up again." Her face moved closer to mine. "Deacon?"

"Right here," I forced out the words with a whole lot of effort. As good as it was to be beside Phoebe, I felt like I was moving and breathing in a thick layer of sludge laced with spikes. My entire body ached, and the simple act of speaking took more energy than I had.

"I'm going to help you sit up so you can take more medicine." I must've groaned because her voice dropped, low and soothing. "I know, honey. I know you don't feel good, but you'll feel so much better after a little medicine and water."

I couldn't say I helped her much in getting me upright. My body was pretty much deadweight, but she managed. Her touch was gentle but firm, guiding me without a hint of hesitation. I watched her bustle around the room. The way her hair caught the light, the way her brow furrowed with worry...it didn't make sense. None of this did. Why was she here? She had no good reason to be taking care of me. Hell, she had every reason to turn her back and leave me to fend for myself.

Then again, that wasn't who she was. She was a much better person than anyone I knew. Of course, she'd take pity on me. But that didn't explain how I'd ended up in her bed. I racked my fever-fogged brain, trying to piece together the fractured memories. Last thing I remembered was stumbling toward my door, the world tilting sideways. Everything after was a blur.

The mattress dipped as she perched on the edge of the bed, her hip pressing against my side. My arm fell across her lap, heavy and clumsy, fingers curling instinctively into the soft warmth of her stomach. She stilled, her breath catching for just a second before she relaxed, letting me hold on to her.

"Dreamin'," I mumbled, my voice a rasp. "Know it."

Her lips twitched, a faint smile breaking through her worried expression. "You think I'd be in your dreams?"

"Always are. This is the best one, though."

She huffed as she dabbed a washcloth along my forehead. "You're very sick, honey. I can't imagine how this could be a good dream."

I blinked open my eyes, looking up at her. She was haloed by the light behind her, golden and soft, her edges blurred. Or maybe that was just her.

"Angel girl."

She shook her head. "It's probably better if you don't talk so much. You might end up saying things you'll regret when you're better."

I slid my hand up her side. Here, in my dreams, I was allowed to touch her. "How do you feel so good? Can't be real."

"Deacon." Her hand, cool and a little wet from the washcloth, landed on mine. "You need to rest."

Rest. I was already sinking, my limbs heavy with fatigue. But I didn't want to let go—didn't want to leave this dream where she was mine to hold. I fought to keep my eyes open, to memorize her parted lips and the flush in her cheeks. So damn beautiful, my angel.

Sleep was stronger, though. It pulled me down, dragging me into darkness. Just before I went under, I felt it.

A whisper of warmth.

The ghost of her lips brushing against my knuckles.

Next time I woke, I was alone in bed, but I knew I wasn't by myself. My eyes flew open in a panic. My head rolled sideways, finding the other side of the bed as empty as expected. Rolling my heavy head the other way, I nearly pissed myself at the woman sitting in a chair two feet away.

She calmly looked up from the book she'd been reading. "Phoebe went in to work for a few hours. She asked me to stay with you until she gets back."

Unless my eyes were playing tricks on me, I was pretty sure this woman was Elena Kelly, Phoebe's mom. This continued not to make sense, but the way I was feeling, that wasn't a surprise. My brain wasn't working at full steam. None of me was.

"She's gone?" It wasn't easy, but I pushed myself into a sitting position.

"I offered to make the muffins, but she declined. Not that I have any clue why." Elena stood, leaving her book on her chair, and closed the small distance. Like her daughter, she pressed the back of her hand to my forehead. "Don't worry, I wasn't watching you sleep. I heard you stirring and rightly assumed you'd be waking up soon, so I came in here to wait. You're still running hot. We need to get more medicine in you. Do you think you'd be up for taking a shower? You're starting to get ripe."

I blinked at her, taking in everything she'd said and getting stuck on me stinking. Sweating all over Phoebe's sheets. Disgusting and gross. She'd be glad I was gone when she finally turned me out.

Elena put her hands on her hips. "Meds first, then we'll see if you're steady enough to get in the shower. I brought the stool my father-in-law had to use after he had surgery so you can sit. Phoebe would murder me if she came home to you having cracked your skull on my watch."

"I—thanks. Thank you."

Making my mouth move was difficult, but I wanted to tell her thank you for being so kind to me. I shouldn't have been surprised Phoebe came from a mom like this, acting like her generosity was nothing special.

Her movements were fluid as she flitted around the room. First, she dosed me up and made sure I drank as much as I could. Then she opened the curtains and cracked a window. "Letting the sickness out," she'd said. After, she brought me breakfast and fed me by hand when my arms proved too damn weak to do it myself.

"Thank you," I said again.

"That's not necessary, Deke." She shook her head. "I would hope if one of my kids were in your position, someone would help them too."

Elena Kelly had always been a mythical story I'd only heard bits and pieces of. The queen of the Kelly fortune she ruled with her husband, Lachlan. I'd seen her in town plenty. With her icy-blonde hair and height putting her above most women and a lot of men, she was impossible not to notice. Never thought I'd have the opportunity to spend time with her, though. Hadn't even considered what it might be like. If I had, it wouldn't have been like this. Feeding me, caring for me, being nicer to me than my own mother had ever been. It made me uncomfortable. I didn't understand it.

Didn't know how to handle it either.

"Lotta people wouldn't," I said.

Her eyes narrowed. "I think there's more good in the world than you know." She lifted a shoulder. "But suppose you're right. Suppose most people wouldn't help someone in need. Should that stop me? Honestly, Deke, once upon a time, I tried being like everyone else, and it made me utterly miserable. Ages ago, I decided to do what I wanted, damn what anyone else thought, and surprise, surprise, I found my happiness. *I'm* helping you because I love my daughter, and she cares about you. There's nothing more to it."

Fortunately, she wasn't waiting for a response. I couldn't begin to formulate one. Even if I hadn't been sick and sluggish, I didn't think I'd know what to say to her. I did see where Phoebe had gotten her straightforwardness from, though. Knowing that poured a good kind of warmth into a hollow part of me.

Elena dragged my smelly carcass into the bathroom after breakfast. I was so damn wobbly she had to help me take my clothes off but refused to let it be awkward.

"It's either me or Phoebe. I have a husband and two sons. There's nothing you have I haven't seen before, kiddo."

By the time I was finished with my shower, I felt steady enough to put on my own pants. Dressed and clean, I shuffled into the bedroom, finding she'd stripped the sheets and replaced them with fresh ones. Shoved back into bed, I had my temperature taken then was bundled under the covers.

As I fell back to sleep, I thought this must've been what having a real mother was like. *Wouldn't that be nice...*

I woke to warmth and softness, but this time, I could easily discern it as real. Not a dream anymore, even if it felt like one. Phoebe was stretched out beside me, her side flush with mine.

"Did I move?" I croaked.

With a gasp, she dropped her phone onto her chest and turned her head. "You're awake."

"Yeah." I scrubbed my face with my hand. "Did I move over to you?"

"No." She rolled to her side, propping her head on her hand, and reached over, tentatively stroking the edge of my jaw with her other hand. "When I got into bed, you kept writhing and groaning like you were in pain. I scooted close to check on you, and you settled down, so I stayed."

I exhaled toward the ceiling. "I'm not surprised I wanted that. Surprised you stayed, though."

"Really?" I turned back to her, and her eyebrows lifted. "I've been taking care of you for twenty-four hours, and you're surprised I stayed beside you?"

"Surprised about that too." I rubbed my dry lips together. "Thank you. You want me gone, I can go. I'm feeling better."

She shook her head. "I'd like you to stay at least one more night. You're still feverish and, from what my mother said, pretty weak. You shouldn't be on your own."

"I don't wanna get you sick."

"I took extra vitamin C. I'll be fine."

"Not gonna be happy if you get this." That was an understatement. I'd be pissed as hell, and it'd be aimed squarely at myself.

"Worry about getting better. I'm fine."

Not waiting for me to argue—not that I had it in me to do so—she hopped out of bed and started fussing over me. Temp, meds, water, then she brought me soup and fed me herself like her mother had. I couldn't begin to guess why she was doing this, but I soaked up every ounce of her attention while I had it because I knew it was temporary.

I'd keep on dreaming, just a while longer.

Chapter Twenty-five

Phoebe

I held my breath as I unlocked my door after work on Monday, my heart thudding unevenly. I had no idea what I'd find on the other side. Deacon had been occupying my bed for three days, his fever coming and going, his strength wavering. He had insisted he was leaving multiple times, but I wasn't in a rush for him to go—not when he was still sick and wouldn't take care of himself the way he needed. He'd tried to go to work this morning, still running a fever and barely able to keep his eyes open longer than ten minutes.

I exhaled the moment my gaze landed on him, half reclined on my couch, a blanket tangled around his legs. His head rested on the back cushion, eyes closed, his chest rising and falling slowly. Relief softened my tense shoulders. "You're still here," I whispered.

His eyes fluttered open as I stepped inside, his gaze locking onto mine. He sat up, the blanket slipping on his lap. "I can go." He rubbed a hand over his face, scrubbing at the stubble on his jaw. "I should."

"No, you shouldn't." I dropped my bags and shrugged out of my jacket, hanging it on the hook by the door. "If I don't keep an eye on you, you'll probably go build a bookcase while your teeth are clacking from shivering so hard."

His mouth moved like he was trying to smile. "It'd end up crooked and wobbly. Probably best I don't try." He nodded in the direction of the refrigerator. "Tilly dropped off soup earlier. She told me not to hog it all. Thought we could share it for dinner."

I perched on the couch beside him. "Do you have an appetite?"

He flattened a hand on his abdomen. "It's coming back, I think. I can handle soup."

I studied his face, taking in the pale hue of his skin and the dark shadows beneath his eyes. He looked better than he had yesterday, but that wasn't saying much. "I hope that means you're on the mend."

Without thinking, my hand lifted to brush his hair off his forehead, but I stopped myself just in time, curling my fingers into my lap instead. It was one thing to touch him when he was delirious with fever, but his gaze had cleared and was locked on me with an intensity that made my pulse skip. If I hadn't known better, I would've thought that look was...yearning.

His eyes flicked down to my clenched hand before sliding back up to my face. "I'll be out of your way soon enough."

The thought of him leaving left a hollow ache inside me. Having him here felt natural. Easy. Too good.

I'd spent Sunday taking care of him. He'd been too weak to talk much, but he'd managed to mumble an apology. I'd let it lay. He'd been in no shape for any kind of conversation, and I wasn't sure I wanted one.

Oh, who was I kidding? Of course, I wanted that conversation. I wanted him to explain away his hurtful behavior so we could pick back up where we'd left off, but the realist in me was overruling my whimsical side. I was helping him because it was the right thing to do. Once he was better, we were done. We had to be.

We shared a quiet dinner, then I helped him to bed. I stayed up a little while after him, but not long. After showering and putting on my pajamas, I crawled in beside him.

Deacon stirred, cracking his eyes open. "Sugar," he whispered, his voice rough around the edges.

"It's my lotion," I whispered back.

He reached for my hand under the covers, curling his fingers around mine. "It's you."

A shiver slid up my spine, and my breath caught in my throat. "Deacon—"

"Go to sleep, Phoebe." His thumb brushed my knuckles in a slow, lazy caress. "You need your rest. I saw how hard it was for you to get out of bed this morning."

Like it was *every* morning. Deacon was still too sick to have gleaned me and mornings never mixed; we just had a temporary accord. The thing was, it was even harder to get out of bed when he was still in it.

"Good night, Deacon."

His hand tightened around mine. "Night, sugar."

We had one more night. One more coming home to him, sharing dinner, and falling asleep together. Wednesday evening, I was greeted with an empty apartment and a note on my kitchen island.

Phoebe,

Thank you for everything. It couldn't have been easy having me stay with you. You'll never know how much I appreciate all you and your mom have done for me.

I'm sorry for hurting you. I think I said that, but it bears repeating. I'll let you get back to your life now.

- *Deke*

And that was that. No trace he'd ever been here. Even the sheets had been changed. Deacon was gone.

Saturday afternoon, I returned home to flowers in my planters—flowers I hadn't put there. It might've been too early in the season for them, but they were bright and colorful and made me smile.

I checked my doorbell camera app. Sure enough, there was video of Deacon on my stoop, planting the flowers.

As I stood there looking at the flowers, my smile faded.

How dare he?

I didn't want this kind of gesture from him. Being sweet after making me feel so rotten was like rubbing salt in the wound. I had to move on, but he kept reminding me of what could have been—or what I'd *thought* we could have been.

I spun in a circle, at a loss. Deke's truck wasn't in the driveway. Even if I wanted to tell him to shove his flowers, I couldn't. Not that I would have. The flowers were innocent in this.

Just as I decided to go inside to cool my jets, the rumble of Deke's truck stopped me. Moments later, he parked in the drive and hopped out. He lifted his head, spotting me on my landing. I was too far away to read his exact expression, but he didn't avert his gaze. We both stood staring at each other for a long, drawn-out moment. So long, I began to think he might turn right back around and hop into his truck. Eventually, Deke moved, slowly approaching the stairs.

I backed up until I hit my door. I had no clue what I wanted to say, but I knew something *had* to be said.

He arrived on my stoop, rooting himself two feet away. Dark circles ringed his eyes, and his cheeks were sunken. He'd lost weight he hadn't been able to afford to lose while he'd been sick, but I wondered if he was fully better. Probably not. He should have been resting. He should have been—

Deke finally spoke, breaking me out of my worried spiral. "Almost ten years ago, you asked me to catch a movie with you, and I said no."

He really didn't need to remind me of that. "I remember. It sucked."

"Yeah. For me too. I would have given any damn thing to be able to say yes." He shoved his hands in his pockets, a pained expression crinkling his brow. "I don't know why, but messing with me has always been one of my brother's favorite pastimes, and I knew, if word got around I went out with you, he'd find a way to ruin it. Having Richie's attention on you has never ended well. I couldn't do that to you."

"I—" *didn't know what to say.* "It would have been good to know that back then. I just thought you didn't like me that way."

He took a step forward. "That's the furthest thing from the truth. I'd never let myself like anyone until you, and that was less about letting myself and more me being bowled over. I used to think about you all the time. Changed my route to class so I'd pass you. When you smiled at me, it made me feel important in a way I never had." He chuffed. "And haven't since. Not until you shined your light on me after I moved in here."

I rubbed my chest, but it did nothing to alleviate the tightness. "Why are you talking about this now? What does it matter?"

"It matters because a lot's changed"—he moved into my space, so close, his toes hit mine—"but two things haven't: how I feel about you and my asshole brother."

I closed my eyes. If I allowed myself to continue looking at his face bathed in sincerity, I wouldn't be able to stop from leaning into him. "You lied to me."

"I did, and I regretted it even before I did it. I thought I could meet Richie and keep him separate from what I'm trying to build for myself here, so it never touched you." Rocking back on his heels, he sighed. "I should've told you where I was going and why, but all I could think about was keeping him far, far away from you, Joy, this town."

"Lying to me isn't protecting me."

"Know it." He started to bow his head but raised it again, keeping his eyes on mine. "I'll never forget the look on your face that night. *Never.*"

I lifted a hand to ward off him and all the feelings flooding me. "I still don't get why you're telling me all this."

He was direct and unwavering. "I want another chance."

My heart kicked up even as my eyes narrowed on him. "I don't understand why you're trying now. That night, you didn't even apologize to me, and now you're here, planting flowers, being sweet, and—what am I supposed to do with this, Deacon? How do I trust this one-eighty? I saw you on *a date.*"

He shook his head hard. "Wasn't a date, Phoebe. There's only been one woman who's ever turned my head, and that's you. Richie blindsided me with that woman, and I left as soon as I could. I couldn't even tell you her name or anything else about her. But when I saw you, I couldn't acknowledge you. Not with Richie there. Knowing you mean something to me, I don't know what he would have done, and I don't care to find out." He scrubbed the side of his face. "It's no excuse. I made the wrong choice by not telling you I was meeting Richie. I got myself where I am."

"Where *we* are," I whispered.

His head jerked, recrimination twisting his features. "Where we are, yeah. I got us here. Messed it all up. I was going to let you go. If I were better, I would. But for once in my life, I want something good. I will work my ass off to be worthy of all your good. I'm asking if we can try to start over. You don't have to answer me now. Think about it as long as you need. I'll be here. I'm not going anywhere."

"What about Richie? Is he going to be a part of your life?"

"No, he isn't." His jaw rippled from how hard he clenched it. "I have no control over him, but he also has no control over me anymore. If he comes calling, I'll turn him away. That night, I made it as clear as I could we were one and done. And after I went to prison for helping him, he owes me that. Whether he'll give it to me is up in the air, but I'm done with him. I won't give him any more."

I chewed on my bottom lip, mulling over his words. My gut told me this was too important to rush—not that I was prone to making snap decisions anyway. When it came down to it, I believed what he was saying. That didn't mean I'd automatically trust him. He'd purposely lied to me. Albeit, he'd done a bad job of it since I'd sensed something was off, but that didn't mean he wouldn't do better next time.

"Hold the line."

Tilly had been right about him coming to me. Whether he was worth the risk was yet to be seen.

But my instincts screamed I already knew the answer. And it wasn't childhood nostalgia leading me there—it was the man I'd come to know now.

"When I first opened the bakery, a customer asked me out. He was a regular. We'd chatted a few times, and he seemed nice, so I accepted. We started seeing each other, and even though he'd just moved to Laramie to teach at the university, our dates were always here, in town. I never questioned it, but I should have. Turned out he was married. His wife had moved to Wyoming a few months after him, and that was it. He'd told me himself why we were over, and I'd been devastated."

Deke grunted, displeasure written all over in the hunch of his shoulders and a deep frown dragging his mouth south. "I bet."

"It wasn't some grand love affair," I clarified. "I didn't miss him when it was over. What crushed me was realizing I'd been the other woman without even knowing it. He lied to me over and over, and I never saw it coming. That changed me. I never date customers, which is no skin off my back, but in here"—I tapped the center of my chest—"I can't see the world the same anymore. My glasses had been rosy before Jared, and he'd knocked them right off in one fell swoop. Now, there's always this voice in my head, wondering if I'm being lied to. And, Deke, I can't do that with my person. I can't fall for someone if I'm constantly questioning their honesty."

His jaw tightened, regret softening his eyes. "I get that, and I'm sorry as hell you crossed paths with that guy."

"Me too."

"I see why you wouldn't want to forgive me. I gave you good reason not to take me at my word. All I can promise is I'll prove to you I won't ever keep anything from you again. I need time to do that." The tips of his fingers brushed my knuckles. "I'm standing here, asking for you to give that to me. I know full well I don't have the right, but I'm doing it anyway."

My fingers moved on their own accord, catching his as they passed. He stilled while I scoured him for the truth behind his promises. It was there, plain as day. The same ways his lies had been obvious to me when he'd told them.

His fingers curled around mine, making my heart stutter and my mouth dry.

I licked my lips, but it did little to help. I wanted to say yes and launch myself at him, but the hurt of that damn headshake held me back.

I pulled my hand from his. "I need to think, Deke. Can you give me that?"

He let out a jagged breath and nodded. "Of course, Phoebe. I'll give you space, but I'm not going to be far."

He kept his promise, leaving me at my door. But the next day, I caught him watering my flowers through the doorbell camera. The morning after that, the low rumble of his truck greeted me as I left for work. And when I walked home, his footsteps echoed mine.

A week passed with Deacon as my shadow—always near yet respecting the space he'd promised. He cared for the flowers he'd planted in the planters he'd built, proving with each quiet act he was all in.

And each day, I softened more and more until I questioned whether I was dragging this out too far. No matter what test I threw at this man, I had a feeling he would pass, but I was beginning to think it was unfair. Deacon had hurt me, yes—but maybe I was punishing him for wounds another man had left behind.

I could not allow my fear to be used as a punishment against this man, who had already paid more than his fair share of dues.

Saturday afternoon, halfway home from work, I stopped on the sidewalk and turned to face him. At first, he stilled, but when I curled my finger to beckon him, he closed the distance between us.

I reached for his hand, hooking one finger around his. "That night I texted you...I knew you were keeping something from me. You're not great at lying—not even through words on a screen."

"No. I'm not." He huffed a low laugh. "You'd think I'd be better at it, coming from a family who wouldn't know the truth if it bit them in the face. But I can't lie to save my life. More than that—I don't *want* to lie to you."

I nodded, believing him. "Tilly told me you were worth it. She said if I held the line, you'd come back. I didn't believe her. Even when you showed up last week. But here you are—you keep showing up."

"Here I am," he murmured. "I'm sorry it took me so long."

"You came to me two weeks ago—passed out on my welcome mat."

His mouth flattened. "Not my finest moment, dammit."

"Well, I'm glad you chose my porch to take a nap on."

He cocked his head in wonder. "Phoebe...?"

Making a decision I truly hoped I didn't regret, I turned my hand to lace our fingers together. "I'm going to hold the line, Deacon, and give you the chance to prove it."

"Hold the line," he repeated, tasting the words. "Are you sure?"

I nodded. "I've had weeks to think it over. I miss you. And if we're going to close this breach, I need to be with you. It might take time to get past what happened…but I'd like to spend that time with you."

"I'd really like that too." His free arm curved around my waist, drawing me closer. "Can I start by taking you to dinner?"

I slid my hand up his chest and over his shoulder. "A date?"

"Yeah, sugar." His lips brushed mine. "I'd like to take you on a date."

Just like that, this man made me glad I'd chosen to hold the line for him.

Chapter Twenty-six

Deacon

I'D GOTTEN MY ONE and only second chance with Phoebe, and I wasn't going to waste it by keeping her locked up behind closed doors. We were doing this right this time—that meant facing down public opinions head-on.

No sense in delaying the inevitable.

Knowing Phoebe how I now did, she could withstand anything thrown her way. The trouble was, I didn't want her to have to, not on my account or for any other reason. But she'd chosen me, and I had to trust she was going in with open eyes.

Joy caught sight of me the second I pushed through her door, and her eyes lit up how they always did when she saw me. Had been that way for as long as I could remember. But they brightened in a way I'd never seen when she locked on my hand, joined with Phoebe's.

"Come with me to say hi to Joy?"

"Of course," Phoebe replied. No hesitation.

I led her around a few tables, pausing so she could greet a couple people. I tried my best to put on a friendly face for her sake, but I wasn't sure I was doing a great job. I'd have to ask her to give me lessons when we were alone—I was far better at avoiding polite conversation than engaging in it.

We sidled up to the bar together, and I pulled a stool out for Phoebe before parking myself on the one beside hers. Joy strolled over to us, her curious gaze bouncing back and forth between us.

"I wasn't expecting you tonight. Are you feeling better?"

I nodded. "Yep. I've been back at work all week."

Phoebe hissed. "You didn't tell me you worked the whole week. You should've been resting. What if you'd hurt yourself? It's too soon, Deke. Way too soon."

"I'm doing fine," I assured her. "Chris put me on light work this week, and today, I just finished up a project in the shed. I didn't push too hard."

She didn't look convinced. "I can't believe Chris let you come back to work at all. Then again, he didn't see you at your worst. I bet you didn't tell him exactly how sick you were. If I see him—"

I squeezed her hand. "I'm good. I'm gonna take it easy tomorrow. Swear it."

Her eyes narrowed. "Considering tomorrow's my day off, I'll make sure you do."

"I won't mind that at all."

Joy had watched our entire interaction. When I finally turned my attention back to her, a wide grin split her face.

"I see," she drawled. "I understand it all now."

"Uh...what do you see?" I asked.

Joy braced her elbows on the bar opposite us, her grin turning into a smirk. "Why you've been in a good mood recently. You've been hiding things from your aunt, haven't you?"

"Not hiding." I lifted our joined hands. "Taking things slow and keeping it private until we were solid."

Joy's brows rose. "You're solid now?"

I turned to Phoebe. She nodded, and I turned back to Joy, smiling. "Yeah. We're solid."

"Well"—Joy cleared her throat, and I swore I saw a flush rising up her cheeks—"I couldn't think of two better people. Though, I can't say I saw this coming when I rented you your apartment, Deke. Wish I could claim I had."

Phoebe laughed softly. "If you want to, you can. I won't contradict you."

Joy reached across the bar to pat Phoebe's cheek. "I'm not saying I will, but if you hear rumors about me being a matchmaker swirling around, you'll know who it came from, sweetie. Now, what can I get you two to eat and drink?"

We placed our orders before moving to a table tucked in a corner. Phoebe had been the one to choose it, and she didn't give me a chance to wonder why.

"It's quieter over here." She glanced over her shoulder at the screens above the bar. "I love coming to Joy's, but she keeps the TVs too loud on game nights. Drives me nuts."

"Not a sports fan?"

She huffed a laugh. "I can't say I am. I love hitting one or two Rockies games during the summer, but I mostly like going to watch the sunset. Have you ever been to a game?"

"I haven't, but I do like baseball."

"We'll have to go." She paused, worrying her bottom lip with her teeth. "Are you allowed to leave the state? Denver's so close, but it would mean crossing state lines. And...well, can you?"

"Hate you have to ask me that. Can't even take my girl to a baseball game without the shitstorm of my past getting in the way." I pressed on my stomach, which was a tangle of knots. "It hasn't come up since I've been out, but if I check in with my parole officer first, it shouldn't be a problem."

"Good. Then we'll look at the calendar for the season and plan ahead." She kept right on going, swerving around my torn-up guts, so I had no choice but to pick them up and put myself back together. "Like I said, I can take or leave baseball in general, but there's something about watching a game while the sun sets behind the Rocky Mountains."

Took me a minute, but I did what I had to do. Swallowing down the jagged pill of my past, I became fully invested in planning this future with the girl sitting across from me.

"I like the sound of that. I'm all in."

She leaned forward, dropping her voice. "I was worried I'd jumped the gun, making plans for the summer."

"I'm not going anywhere, Phoebe. Pleases the hell out of me to think of you in your sundresses."

That earned me a laugh. "You haven't even seen my sundresses yet."

"I haven't, but I know reality's gonna be ten times better than my imagination since I'm no women's fashion expert."

She giggled harder. "I don't think I want to know what you're dreaming up in your head."

I grinned at her, all the heaviness I'd been carrying the past couple weeks set aside so I could share this light moment with her.

"There's not a lot to it." I tapped my temple. "Up here, it's pretty damn skimpy, if I'm being honest."

"Oh my muffins." She cupped her forehead, still laughing. "I fear you're going to be disappointed at the amount of fabric that makes up my sundresses."

"You're wrong about that. You wear a paper bag; I wouldn't be disappointed." I flicked my gaze over the soft-looking sweater hugging her curves just right. "I've seen how you dress on a daily basis. You're always so pretty I have trouble believing you're real."

The laugh on her lips flowed into a whisper. "Deacon, god, you really know the right things to say. Are you sure there isn't a horde of girlfriends in your past?"

"I really don't. When I say you're the only one, I mean it." I scooted my chair closer so I could impart a fact about myself I'd thought she'd understood. Brushing her hair over her shoulder, I put my mouth next to her ear. "You're my first date. The first woman I've held hands with. The first woman I've made come, and who's made me come. And if I'm lucky and we get there, you'll be the first woman I make love to."

She pulled back, her brown eyes wide. "What? Surely not..."

"I know you didn't get in this to be my teacher." I cupped the side of her face, my fingers sliding into her silky hair. "As natural as we've been together, I'm thinking I'll catch on pretty quick. That is, *if* we get there, and you want that with me."

"Deacon...of course I want that with you." She blinked a few times. "I'm trying to make this make sense. I know you were away, but before...you're so...I'm just...well, I'm surprised."

"Turned off?"

She didn't immediately reply, but I was getting used to that with her. If she was asked a question, she made sure of her answer before she gave it.

Finally, she responded, giving me what I'd been hoping for. "No, I'm not turned off. Not at all." She curled her fingers around my wrist, stroking my pulse with her thumb. "I'm curious why you've never been with anyone, though."

"I spent a lot of my life just trying to make it through. Once I was done with school and had a job, I brought my little sister to live with me. Finding a girl was the last thing on my mind. After I got out, I don't think I really started breathing easy until I moved into my apartment. I don't know if it's God smiling down on me or finally catching a break, but I happened to find the girl of my dreams is my neighbor, so...well, now I'm thinking about it."

Her lips tipped. "A lot?"

"Oh yeah, sugar. I want all that with you." I leaned close, my nose gliding along hers. "But we're going to take our time getting there because I want everything else with you too."

"Sorry to interrupt, lovebirds," Joy announced, putting a halt to our conversation. She bent over the table, placing our plates and silverware down beside our beers. "I tried to wait you out, but the rate you two were going, your dinner was going to get cold."

Phoebe's laugh was melodic and sweet. Goddamn, had I missed hearing her laugh. And the way she looked at Joy, like she was genuinely happy to see her, made me fall even deeper for this woman.

"Thanks so much. This looks great," she said.

Joy winked at her. "Just trying to keep up with all the deliciousness you come up with in your kitchen, darlin'. You two have a nice dinner."

"Thank you, Joy."

"Of course, Deke. Happy to have the two of you here together. Real, real happy."

She caught my eyes. Hers twinkled, startling the hell out of me. My aunt had always cared for me and made no bones about showing it, but I couldn't say I'd ever seen a twinkle in her eyes. Not even close.

The conversation we'd been having before Joy's arrival was best left for private, so we ate our dinner, switching to lighter topics. I got to hear about the bread she'd been baking in her spare time and how her brother had forbidden her from adding it to her menu—something I agreed with once I'd learned his reasoning. I told her about the desk I'd finished today for a client and a potential new commission for custom cabinetry I was bidding on.

"Do you have a picture of the desk?"

"Sure I do." I spun my phone in her direction, holding my breath as she scrolled through the pictures I'd taken. "I started documenting my process so when customers questioned my pricing, I could show them how much I put into my projects."

She tapped the screen with her nail. "If anyone questions the cost of your work after seeing the finished product, they're being purposely obtuse. You make incredible pieces, Deacon."

She huffed but didn't say anything else.

"What?" I asked.

"Nothing really. I was thinking I wish you'd been around when I was opening Sugar Rush. I would have loved to hire you to build pieces for me. But then it occurred to me I wouldn't have been able to afford you."

"You think I'd let you pay me?"

"I think it would be a bad business model if you didn't." She grinned, then flicked the thought away. "Soon, you'll be too busy. Even if I had the cash, you wouldn't have the time for me."

"Never. That'd never happen," I stated firmly.

"I mean professionally," she amended.

"Same answer." I pushed back from the table and held my hand out to her. "We're gonna pick a song on the jukebox and dance to it."

She raised a brow. "We are?" Her hand slipped into mine like it'd always been there, and she rose to her feet before me, her lips curled in a happy little smile. "We are."

Joy's didn't have much of a dance floor, but it was enough. I felt eyes on us as I twirled her the way she liked but decided not to care since it was obvious she didn't give a single damn.

She proved that when a woman bumped into her as she passed.

"Oh, I'm sorry." The woman was fortyish, dressed a little too sophisticated for her to be a local, and when her gaze landed on Phoebe, recognition lit her features. "Phoebe, darling, it's you!"

Phoebe twisted in my arms to face her. "Margot, hey. How are you?"

"I'm great. Just grabbing a drink. You look like you're having fun." The woman's eyes darted from Phoebe to me then back.

"We definitely are." Phoebe's hand slipped from my waist to find mine, grabbing hold. "Margot, this is my boyfriend, Deke. Deke, this is Margot. She runs the spa at the ranch."

It took me a beat to recover from Phoebe calling me her boyfriend. I'd only just gotten her to give me a chance, and here she was, giving me more than I'd asked for. I liked the hell out of it.

I lifted my chin. "Nice to meet you, Margot."

"You too, Deke." Margot smiled, and not unkindly, then addressed Phoebe. "Your mother told me you've been seeing a tattooed cutie."

Phoebe laughed. "Well, I'd say he's more than cute, but since my mother has one type and it's my father, it's understandable she undersold Deke."

"Those two. I've never met a pair more suited on the inside and opposite on the outside." Margot shook her head. "Well, I'll leave you to your night. Have fun."

I pulled Phoebe back into my arms, splaying my hands over the upper curve of her backside.

"You called me your boyfriend." I tipped my head toward Margot, now laughing with a cowboy by the pool table. "That'll get back to your mother."

Phoebe slid her palms up my chest and looped her arms behind my neck. "Are you more worried about me calling you my boyfriend or my mother finding out?"

"Not worried about either."

"Then there's no problem, is there?"

"No." I tilted my head, brushing my lips over hers. "No problem at all, sugar."

That was how the rest of our first real date in town had gone. Laughing, dancing, keeping my girl close. If anyone had something to say, they'd done it quietly enough I hadn't heard.

After another beer, a game of darts, and saying good night to Joy, we ended our night, walking home hand in hand.

I'd started the week damn near certain Phoebe would never let me touch her again. Now, I had her pressed against her door, her mouth as hungry for mine as I was for hers.

One hand cradling the back of her head, the other cupping her sweet ass, I rolled my forehead against hers. If I'd been the crying sort, I might've let a tear slip for how *right* the last few hours had felt. I wasn't much of an optimist—life had taught me better—but right then, I was feeling it.

She nipped at my lips. "You could come in."

"I could." I exhaled, already regretting what I had to say. "But I don't think I should. Not tonight." I smoothed my thumb along her jaw. "I want to take my time with this—make sure we get it right."

"Okay." She pressed her face to the crook of my neck. "I'm glad you showed up on my porch. Thank you for making things right, honey."

"Always." I held her tight, touching my lips to the side of her head. "*Always*, angel girl."

She sighed, slowly letting her head fall back against the door. "You remember calling me that?"

"A lot of those days are a blur, but that? Yeah." I nodded toward her door. "Go inside. I'll stay here until I hear the lock."

One more lingering kiss, then she slipped inside, and I stayed right where I was until I heard the soft click of the dead bolt as it slid into place.

When I headed upstairs, my boots were lighter than they'd been in years.

Chapter Twenty-seven

Phoebe

"Do you want to do something fun?"

I was always up for adventure. Growing up on a property so vast, I hadn't even seen all of it. There was never a shortage of places to explore and fun to be had. The trouble these days was finding time.

I had my Sundays, though, and now that Deacon was a real part of my life, I intended to make full use of them. So I asked the question. Deacon had given a resounding "Yes," and that was how we ended up on a side-by-side, bumping over the hills and rocks at the ranch.

Deacon was gripping the bar above his head, his eyes wide as he took in the scenery. This part of the ranch was all rocky hills, the occasional pronghorn bounding out of nowhere, and no structures in sight.

Cattle were visible in the far distance, and in a month or two, Caleb and the other ranch hands would probably move them over this way. There was a lot to take in—miles and miles of pristine land—and I was eager to show Deacon all of it.

"Next time, we'll ride horses."

He glanced my way. "Never done it."

"Don't worry. We have a lot of horses who go on trail rides with tourists. They're so used to first-timers, they barely have to be guided."

"I'm guessing you have your own horse."

"I do, but that's not unusual. At least half the kids we went to school with had horses at home."

"Probably. Chris didn't, but his uncle has stables, so he knows how to ride. What's your horse's name?"

"Princess." His grunt made me laugh. "I know, not very creative, but I named her when I was seven. She's an old girl now. I don't ride her anymore. We can visit her before we leave, though. She's supersweet."

"Can't imagine any animal of yours *not* being sweet." He turned his head to peer at the land. "Glad you had this life. Sweet animals, gorgeous land, all this freedom. Glad it was you who got it."

Reaching across the vehicle, I squeezed his thigh. "I'm pleased I get to share it with you."

When we made it to the bank of the river running through the ranch, I parked the vehicle and hopped out, circling around the back to grab my bag from the open bed. Of course, as soon as I did, Deacon took it from me and slung it over his shoulder, taking my hand in his.

He stared out at the river. "Is the fun freezing our asses off?"

I snorted a laugh. Spring was in full force, but it was still way too cool to take a dip in the river unless...

"There's a thermal seep at the bank." I pointed toward the rings of rocks in the water. "A long time ago, my grandad put those rocks there to trap the hot water, and now we have natural mineral hot pools."

He took a deep breath and exhaled. "I thought that was the cattle I was smelling. It's sulfur, isn't it?"

"Yeah. That's the downside, but you get used to it." I tugged on his hand. "If you hate it, we don't have to stay."

He turned to me, scanning my leggings and baggy sweatshirt. Not my usual style, but easier to get in and out of than jeans and a sweater. "Are you going to be wearing a bathing suit?" I nodded, and he grinned. "Then I'm not going to hate it."

At the water's edge, he dropped our bag. I didn't bother hiding that I was looking at him as he undressed, and neither did he. We stood a foot apart, stripping down to our bathing suits—his, a pair of black trunks; mine, a magenta, high-waisted, vintage-style two-piece. Our clothes at our feet, we looked at each other, long and slow. Goose bumps pricked my skin, mostly from the cool breeze but a little from having his eyes on me.

Deacon in his work boots, worn jeans, and snug T-shirts made me weak on a regular basis, but in swim trunks with all his ink on display? Oh, that was something else. I reminded myself he wanted to go slow, and we'd only been back together for a week, so my hands stayed at my sides, but they were twitching to touch him.

Especially with all the heat burning in his gaze. He was making no bones about appreciating what my full body looked like in very little clothing. When his gaze stopped at the apex of my thighs, where my bathing suit disappeared between them, I couldn't resist rubbing my legs together. His eyes jerked to mine, then he grabbed my hand and tugged, striding into the river.

He had to slow down and release his hold so we could climb over the rocks, but once we were in the little natural pool, he grabbed me again and sank down, me practically on top of him.

The groan he released as the water lapped over his shoulders sent waves of satisfaction down my spine. His eyes locked onto mine, something like wonder softening them.

"This is natural?"

I nodded. "Yeah. Only the rock formations are man-made."

"Christ." His head fell back as he blinked up at the clear blue sky. "This land...do you get used to it? Or are you always amazed?"

I thought about his question and how I could respond in a way that didn't make me sound like a spoiled, rotten brat. In a lot of ways, this was my backyard. It just happened to be thousands and thousands of acres. But I understood how vastly different my experience growing up here was from almost everyone else's—especially Deacon's.

"As a kid, I don't think I ever thought twice." I skimmed my hand along the surface of the water. "It was when I moved away and came back I was really able to appreciate all the beauty around me. There's nowhere else on earth like this."

"Yeah." He rolled his shoulders and let out a long, low sigh. "Remind me to tell your grandad he's a genius."

I shifted in the water, my breasts skimming his chest. "Relaxing, right? The minerals are supposed to have healing properties too."

He lifted his head to stare me down, then he captured me around the waist, plastering me against him. I opened my legs so I could straddle him, settling my ass on his thighs.

He gripped my hips beneath the water, the tips of his fingers grazing my bare midriff. His erection prodded my inner thigh, hard and thick. He had to have been that way before he pulled me onto him. Maybe since we'd taken off our clothes. Since I'd been turned on all this time too, it was only fair.

"I'm feeling healed already," he drawled.

"Funny, I am too." I slid my hands along his arms, my breath catching as his taut muscles rippled beneath my touch.

"I'm about to ask something out of jealousy," he said.

"Okay." My hands stilled. "You can ask me anything."

"Have you brought other guys here?"

"No, I haven't. Well...my brothers, but they don't count." I leaned down, my lips over his. "This spot is a little bit of a family secret. I'm not saying other people haven't stumbled upon it, but we don't bring anyone here. That's how it stays special."

His fingers dug into my flesh. "You brought me here."

"That's right. I trust you." My lips curved. "Plus, I made sure to distract you on the way so you won't be able to find your way back. You're going to have to stick with me if you want these hot springs."

He chuckled. "That's no trouble. You can throw a bag over my head on the way back. I wouldn't wanna be here with anyone but you."

"I told you I trust you." I nipped his bottom lip. "But I do like you being a little jealous. I have to tell you, I'm jealous too."

His head jerked back. "Of what, sugar? There's no one else. Never has been."

"I know, but look at you, Deacon. You walk around looking like a hot, sexy bad boy. You might not notice it, but women drool over you just like I do."

His lips tipped into a grin as his eyelids lowered to half-mast. "You're drooling over me?" He sounded more than a little pleased.

"I am, and I'm not ashamed of it."

He pressed me down on his lap. "I might not be drooling, but you have me at least half-hard most of the time. Right now, with all your soft, pretty skin on display, I'm a rock. You feel that?"

I rocked against him. "I couldn't miss it, honey."

He groaned, his jaw rippling as he clenched it. "When you call me that..." He shot forward, burying his face in my neck, his breath warm and heavy. "Jesus, Phoebe, the way you make me feel...it's like I'm going to burst out of my fucking skin sometimes."

"Is that a good thing?"

"I don't know." He dragged his tongue along my collarbone. "It's hard to go slow with you when I'm losing my mind."

"I'm all in for your pace, Deke." I slipped my fingers into the sides of his damp hair, pulling his head back. "But if you want more, I'm all in for that too."

He blinked hard. "I want..." His hands slipped from my hips to cradle my ass, then farther, sliding into the valley between my cheeks. "I want to make you come again. This time, with my hand."

"Yes," I whispered. "Touch me."

He slid his finger along the edge of my bathing suit, his eyes studying mine, then slipped beneath the fabric to touch my bare, swollen skin. Our breath caught in unison. When I didn't stop him, he continued trailing his fingertip along my seam as the heated water slapped against us.

He wasn't hitting any of my most sensitive spots, but I was already panting, and my stomach ached from how tight it was knotted. It wouldn't take much. Not much at all. Then again, we'd been kissing for weeks. I was primed for him.

I didn't rush him, though. The sweetness of his exploration was part of the pleasure, and the look of pure awe on his face would stick with me long after this moment was over. I couldn't remember a time I'd felt this desired.

He dipped his face to my throat, kissing along my collarbone and chest. I let my head fall back, giving him all the access he wanted. His kisses started sweet and light, then he became more firm, adding teeth and tongue when I moaned for him and told him it felt so good.

His other hand glided over my breast, hesitating at my bikini top. I arched into his touch, giving him permission to touch me everywhere. That was all he needed. In the next breath, he tugged my top below my breasts.

"*Jesus*," he gritted out. "Holy fuck."

He dropped his head to my exposed breast, rolling his cheek along the top. His stubble rubbed my soft skin, causing a delicious friction that made me moan. Then his mouth covered my beaded nipple, so warm and wet I felt like I was melting.

I grabbed his shoulders so I didn't float away and rocked my hips languidly with his roving hand. He slid his arm around to my front and into my bathing suit bottoms. Finally, *finally*, his fingertip pressed on my pulsing clit.

"Yes," I cried. "Right there, Deacon. Keep going."

His mouth on my nipple, finger on my clit...I flew high, riding a powerful wave of bliss. A spool within me wrapped tight, tight, tight, until there was no more, and with a snap, it unraveled.

Deacon curled his fingers around the base of my neck as I pressed myself onto his other hand, taking all he had to give me. Black, then bright white, flashed behind my eyelids as I spiraled into a soul-shaking climax.

All the while, I felt him, his thighs quaking beneath me, arms trembling around me, his panting breath hot on my skin. The way my coming affected him only spurred me on.

My eyes flashed open to find his wild and slightly feral. "Deacon," I whispered.

He looked away, his jaw sharp and tight. "I gotta get out."

"Are you—are you okay?"

He shook his head. "If you don't get off me, I'm going to lose it, baby. I need—"

Understanding dawned. I put my hand on his abdomen. "Sit on the rock. You can lose it in my mouth."

His head whipped around, and I took back my thought of him being slightly feral. There was no "slightly" about it. My sweet Deacon had been overtaken by a powerful need my mouth was watering to slake.

"Do it," I urged softly.

He shoved himself out of the water to sit on the flat rock right behind him. I pushed his knees apart, fitting myself between them, and hooked my fingers in the waistband of his trunks.

I looked up at him. "Can I pull these down?"

"You can do anything you want," he rasped.

He lifted himself up a little to help me yank them down enough to free his thick, angry erection. I'd take my time admiring it later. Deacon was on the cusp of desperation, and I refused to make him wait a second longer.

One hand braced on his thigh, I wrapped the other around his base and lowered my mouth over his smooth tip. The groan he unleashed sounded like it'd come from the center of the earth. Primal and deep, I felt it in the pit of my belly.

Not wasting a single moment, I took him all the way to the root, wrapping my tongue around his hot skin. He jerked in my mouth, hitting the back of my throat.

"Sorry, fuck...I'm sorry," he scrambled. "I didn't mean to—"

I sucked him deeper and squeezed his thigh, assuring him he'd done nothing wrong and I was all in. I wanted him to stop thinking and lose it for me the same way I had minutes ago with him.

His fingers threaded through my hair, pulling it back from my face. I flicked my eyes up to find him watching me, his bottom lip caught between his teeth, a flush crawling up his cheeks. He looked both enamored and out of control. It was such a turn-on, I would have slipped my fingers between my legs if I hadn't been devoted to giving him the best first taste of everything he'd been missing out on.

"Phoebe...I'm so close, baby." He cupped my jaw as I slid down his length. "I don't want it to end, but I'm gonna lose my mind if I don't—"

I sucked him deep, cutting off his words—and hopefully his thoughts. I wanted him to only think about how damn good I was making him feel. My toes curled from the pleasure *I* was giving *him*.

His stomach contracted, then his hips rose, pushing his slick cock deeper into my mouth. I hummed around him and cupped his tight sac in my palm. The noises he made were almost inhuman, the release of pain and desire from somewhere buried deep within him.

He gripped my hair into his fist as my nose hit his abdomen and he surged upward, going as deep as he possibly could and staying there. I lapped at his pulsing cock until he let out a crackling roar. Hot liquid hit the back of my throat, and my mouth filled with him until I swallowed every drop.

Slowly, his grip on my hair loosened, and I eased up his length. He didn't pull out, and I was in no hurry to lose him. I suckled him gently, stroking his stomach and thighs as he began to soften. Emotion struck me out of nowhere. We'd just shared something brand new, solely mine and his, and we'd done it in one of my favorite places in the world. He'd trusted me to give him this, and I loved that I'd been the one to take care of him this way.

Finally, I made it to the top, and he fell free from my lips. I placed a soft kiss on his tip, and a shudder ran through his body.

"Phoebe." He took my hands in his, pulling me upright. On my knees in the water, he curled forward, putting us face to face. He touched his lips to mine and sighed into my mouth. "There aren't words."

"There don't need to be, honey. I felt it too."

He went in to kiss me again, but the sound of a rumbling motor had us both whipping our heads to the side. Still in the distance but getting closer by the second was another side-by-side, and if I wasn't mistaken, my brother was the driver.

I yanked on his hand. "Get down in the water with me."

Without a beat of hesitation, he slid back in and righted his trunks. "You know who's coming?"

"Pretty sure that's Caleb. Let's thank our lucky stars he wasn't a few minutes earlier."

Deacon shoved his hair off his forehead, looking at me with wide eyes. "Don't even say it. I'm having enough trouble figuring out how to act normal. I can't have that in my mind."

I leaned into him, grinning wide. "You're really cute when you're panicking."

He wrapped his arm around my waist. "Glad you're amused."

I snickered. "I really am." I couldn't even say why I found the situation funny, just that once I'd started laughing, I was done for. Caleb parking and hopping out of his vehicle made me laugh harder.

He stopped at the bank of the river, his hands on his hips. "What's she laughing at?"

Deacon shrugged. "Can't say I know. She's got the giggles."

I snorted, making me laugh even harder. I tried to greet my brother, but I couldn't collect myself enough to get any coherent words out. Beside me, Deacon chuckled, but he didn't give in to the complete mayhem that'd overtaken me.

Caleb shook his head. "I expect this lunacy out of Hannah." He watched me for a beat then grinned softly. "I like seeing it out of you, Phe."

"I do too," Deacon agreed, pressing a kiss to my temple.

Caleb tipped the bill of his hat. "My guys told me you'd taken one of the side-by-sides out here. Thought I'd check in, say hey since I was nearby. Looks like everything's good. I'll leave you to your soak."

I waved. "Bye, Caleb. See you soon."

"See ya." He nodded toward Deacon. "Keep her laughing like that; we'll all be happy to have you around."

Then he strode off to his vehicle and rumbled away, leaving us alone again.

I grinned at Deacon. "If only he knew I was laughing because he almost caught me blo—"

Deacon smashed his lips to mine, cutting me off. "You're killing me, sugar. You gotta stop."

"Okay." I pecked the corner of his mouth. "I don't want to kill you. I like you too much."

He rubbed my bottom lip with his thumb. "Like you too. More than words."

I closed my eyes, happy and calm in his arms. "Remember? Words aren't necessary."

He wrapped me in his arms, illustrating my point, and held me close and tight, letting me feel exactly how much he liked me...

And it was a whole lot.

Chapter Twenty-eight

Phoebe

DEACON SENT ME A text saying he was getting off work a little early and was going to actually come in to Sugar Rush today and hang out until closing. Since he normally showed up after we were closed to walk home with me, this would be a rare treat. Even if it meant only a few extra minutes together, I'd take them. With my hectic schedule and his, every second counted. And considering the time we *did* have together was always sweeter than the last, I was eager to have him in my space.

Hailey slid next to me as I grabbed a cookie from the bakery case. "Do you have the schedule for next month ready yet? I need to tell my foster mom the dates I'm working so she can make sure she can pick me up."

"Yes, I do." I handed the customer his cookie and turned to Hailey. She really was the best worker. Never late and kept complaining to a minimum. I still didn't know her story, but I liked what I did know. "I printed a copy this afternoon but spaced. It should still be in the printer. If you want to go grab it, you can have that copy."

"Okay." She tucked a stray strand of strawberry-blonde hair behind her ear. "Mind if I get it now before I forget?"

"Sure. We're not exactly packed to the rafters. Go ahead."

She disappeared into the back at the same time the door chimed, drawing my attention. My heart slid into my throat as Deacon sauntered in, his head swiveling left and right, checking out who was in the shop. It was almost closing time. My two lingerers were pecking away on their laptops, but otherwise, it was pretty quiet.

When his eyes landed on me, I was already circling the counter, on my way to him. He met me halfway but stopped before touching me.

"Hey," he uttered, low and cool.

"Hey yourself."

I wanted to reach for him, but more than that, I wanted him to grab hold of me. So I waited. He looked around, tipping his chin to Charlie, our resident budding author who'd been working on his book for the three years Sugar Rush had been open.

His warm gaze came back to mine, sweeping up the length of me before settling on my eyes.

"Busy day?" he asked.

"Busy in a good way." I smooth my hands over my apron, drawing his attention to it. This one had ruffles along the edges and heart-shaped pockets. Of course, it was pink.

He lowered his voice to barely a whisper. "You look so damn cute. I wanna gather you up, haul you out of here, and keep you for myself."

My silly heart flipped like a turtle. "I'd like you to do all that, but could we start with a hug?"

"If you're all right with me hugging you in the middle of your workplace."

"I'm more than all right with it, honey. I'm kinda asking for it."

Breaking into a grin, he stepped forward, caught me around the waist, and pulled me against him. I got my hug, warm and tight, and a sweet, firm kiss on my neck when he buried his face there.

"That's a much better greeting," I said, shoving my arms beneath his canvas jacket to wrap them around his middle.

"Exactly the kind I like with you." He pulled back, but not before brushing his lips over mine. "This is new territory for us, and I know how seriously you take your business. I didn't want to presume anything."

"Thank you for that." I flattened my palms on his chest. "But I'm pretty much always going to want a hug from you. You can presume away."

"Got it."

I tilted my head toward the bakery case. "Do you want to pick out something to eat while you hang out?"

"Never turn down your baking, baby."

As he leaned over the counter to survey what was left, I glanced toward the back, spotting Hailey approaching. My smile grew. "Oh my gosh, you've got to meet my part-timer. She's always asking about you and me. It's so cute. She's going to flip when she meets you."

Deacon straightened, and his gaze slid past me, locking onto the doorway. He jerked back as though he'd been struck. Heart thudding, I spun around to find Hailey frozen and wide-eyed, her mouth gaping.

"Hailey," Deacon rasped. "You—"

A panicked yelp interrupted him. Before I could process the sound, Hailey bolted. Darting around the counter, she yanked the door open and fled onto the sidewalk.

"What was that?" I gasped.

Deacon staggered after her, his movements heavy and unsteady. Shock rooted me to the spot as he shoved the door open and stepped outside, stopping just beyond the threshold, shoulders tense, fists clenched at his sides. His head dropped forward in what looked like defeat.

He didn't come back inside.

Not when I shook off my stupor and began the necessary process of cleaning the shop. Not when I ushered my two stragglers out and flipped the sign to "closed." Not when I turned off the lights and set the alarm.

I found him waiting at the mouth of the alley between my building and the one next to it. He fell into step with me, taking the canvas bag from my shoulder and slipping it onto his own. His fingers found mine and clasped tightly.

He did this without uttering a word. My mind had been whirring since Hailey had streaked out of my shop. I'd come up with a guess as to who she was to Deacon, but I would rather he told me himself.

But he seemed like he'd gone offline. We walked in silence until we turned off Main Street and onto our road. It was quieter here, fewer people around to overhear our conversation.

One of us had to start, and I decided it would be me. "She asked to be paid in cash and used the last name Spellman on her application." His hand twitched around mine. "But that's her foster family's name, not hers. I never pressed her on it since she's a great worker and really sweet. It never raised any flag how often she asked about you. I just thought she was a curious person like I am. But I think...well, is Hailey your sister, Deacon?"

He nodded. "She is."

I exhaled, slow and heavy. "I should have seen it. You have almost the same hair color. Her eyes are darker, but they're the same shape as yours. And you've talked about your sister, but I didn't—"

He tugged me closer, his hand stiffening. "Is she okay? I mean, is she safe? Healthy?"

I opened my mouth to ask a dozen questions but thought better of it. Slamming my lips shut, I nodded. "She says her house is loud but the good kind. Her foster mother, Linda, picks her up every day from work. And Hailey is...well, she's wonderful. So, yes, I'd say she's okay."

His exhale was jagged. "Good. That's good to know. All I ever wanted was for her to be safe, even if she's gettin' that with other people."

"I think she is." I looked at him, but his gaze was far away, like he wasn't even beside me.

I needed more from him after both their reactions, but I could wait until he came back to himself.

First, I'd get him home, make sure Hailey had gotten home too, then we'd talk.

Chapter Twenty-nine

Deacon

Phoebe was perched on my bed when I came out of the bathroom, steam billowing around me from my burning-hot shower. She waved her phone before dropping it onto the bedside table.

"I just spoke to Linda, Hailey's foster mom. She picked Hailey up at the diner not long after she left Sugar Rush. She's doing fine now."

I nodded and walked to my dresser, taking out a pair of sweats. I yanked them up my damp legs then roughly dried my hair with my towel. My head was in too much of a fog to properly respond. I couldn't believe she'd stayed—especially after she'd witnessed my little sister run from me in horror.

Once I ran out of things to do, I walked to the bed and sat beside her. Curling forward, I braced my elbows on my knees and held my head with both hands.

"I know you have a lot of questions. It'll be easier if you ask me instead of me trying to sort out my muddled thoughts."

I felt her moving closer—the exact opposite way she should have gone. She pressed her cheek to the back of my shoulder and circled her arms around my middle.

"She was living with you when you went to prison?"

"Yep. Parents didn't give a damn as long as they kept getting her check from the government. As soon as I graduated, I took her out of that hellhole and sorted a place for us to live. I'd been looking after her since she was born. I was still a kid too, but I couldn't leave her there to fend for herself. It was a struggle—taking care of her and myself—but I did it. Tilly's mom watched her for next to nothing while I was working. We were poor, but we'd always been poor. That didn't matter. She was safe, and that's worth more than a bank full of money."

Then I made decisions I'd always regret. I screwed up so badly my sister couldn't even look at me without running away.

"Deacon..." she whispered, her palm moving in slow circles over my flank, "what happened?"

"Richie," I uttered. "He kept coming around to visit Hailey. During his visits, he was always reminding me how easy it would be to pull the rug out from under us—he could snap his fingers and make sure Hailey went back to our parents."

I'd been almost certain he'd been bluffing, but there'd been no way in hell I was willing to take my chances with Hailey. Not when our parents' house was a revolving door of criminals and lowlifes who wouldn't have thought twice about hurting a little girl.

"For a while, all he'd done was dangle that reality, but a few months before I got arrested, he'd turned it into a noose, and my neck had been all the way in. He had me driving him and his buddies to jobs. I'd never asked what they were doing, but I knew. The fourth one had done me in. Someone saw my truck, saw me driving, and I was done."

"Not Richie?"

I shook my head. "They tried to get me to turn over on him, but that's not me. Even if it was, Richie promised he'd make sure Hailey went to a good family, not back to our parents. He's a piece of shit, but he cared about her. That, I knew for sure."

"So, Richie's done one good thing in his life." She hmphed. "Actually, he probably had nothing to do with Hailey's placement. Why would social services listen to him? I won't be giving him credit for the Spellmans—not when he let you go to prison for his crimes. He doesn't get credit for a damn thing."

I straightened, twisting around, one knee bent on the bed, and cupped the side of her face. Her cheeks were flushed pink, and her eyes were lit from within. Pretty and angry, my girl was.

"You're mad."

"Well...yeah."

"I'm not innocent, Phoebe. I *was* there. I knew he was committing crimes. I could've said no and found another way to protect my sister. I chose the shortest route instead and ended up losing her for good."

She shook her head. "There's no reason it has to be for good. You're here, and now you know where she is. You could rebuild your relationship—be her brother instead of her guardian. You could—"

"She doesn't want to be around me, and I understand." I blew out a heavy breath. "Remember the shitty lawyer I had?"

"I do."

I dropped my hand from her cheek to her leg, resting it on the soft bend of her knee. "His genius idea of a defense was getting Hailey to lie for me. He wanted her to say she saw me at home that night."

Her lips parted. "Oh no. Your alibi that fell apart?"

"Yeah. I didn't know any of it was happening. My parents had let him work her and gotten her to talk to the cops. All it had taken was a light grilling, and her story fell apart. There was so much pressure on her to lie for me, and she couldn't do it. That was when I lost her. She wouldn't see me after that. I wrote her a handful of letters, but I can't say if she ever got them. Don't know if she knows I'd *never* hold *anything* against her, let alone not being able to lie for me."

My girl. So much more than just my little sister. I'd let her down in a huge way. It was pure luck she was doing as well as she was, and it had nothing to do with me. In fact, my going away had probably been the true favor. Now she had a real family and a nice home.

"I'm sorry I didn't tell you all this before." I squeezed my eyes closed, but there was no chance of blocking any of this out. Opening them, I met hers. As always, her gaze was soft and thoughtful. "I should've told you, but I—it's really hard for me to even think about losing her. I've tried, but I don't know how to get rid of this...dirty, oily shame all over me."

"I won't tell you you have nothing to be ashamed of. There's nothing I can say to convince you of that." She took my hand from her leg and held it sandwiched between hers. "I don't think you've lost Hailey, though. Recalling the conversations we'd had about you when I thought you and I were over, she told me she was worried about you being sad. And before that, she asked me what kind of guy you were. So I think she still wants to know you, but today was a surprise for everyone, and maybe she wasn't ready."

"She was worried?"

A trickle of something that felt like hope made its way through my system. I didn't usually let myself hope. If I wanted something, I worked for it, and I *wanted* my sister back. I was socking away money to use toward a house big enough for us both. A place she'd feel was hers, not like she was living there on borrowed time. The problem was, I knew how to do the work, but I didn't have the faintest idea of how to get her back in my life.

"She was," Phoebe confirmed gently. "I bet she's been worried about you for a long time now. She really liked hearing we were back together."

Phoebe leaned into me, pressing her cheek against mine. "You haven't lost her, honey. Today might've been the beginning of you two finding your way back to each other."

My chest constricted from the enormity of that possibility. I tried to suck in a deep breath but only managed to pull in strawfuls. Phoebe saw me struggling and whispered tender, sweet words in my ear as she stroked my hair. Slowly, she pushed me back on the mattress and stretched out beside me. I rolled to my side, needing to feel the solid weight of her in my arms.

"She's safe," she whispered. "You're safe. We're here together, and we're going to figure this out. Nothing's lost, honey. I promise you that. As long as you keep trying, it won't be lost. Nothing will."

She gave me soft reassurance, murmuring variations of the same words over and over, until I could take a full breath. I held her close, taking everything she was offering.

"For what it's worth, I'm not angry you didn't tell me about Hailey." Her fingers trailed along my chest, slow and methodical. "We don't know everything about each other yet, but I'm eager for every piece of you you give me. Thank you for trusting me with this one. I know it wasn't easy to share it with me."

"I'm glad you know," I said gruffly. "You want to know me, I'll give you all of it. It might come slowly, though. There's a lot of ugly, and laying that on my beautiful girl doesn't sit right with me. But I won't ever withhold anything from you."

"I won't either." She shifted her legs, sliding one of them between mine. "It's not the same, but I know something about shame. I don't think I'll ever get over being the other woman. For a long, long time, I felt dirty. I'd done another woman wrong. I can't think about those months with him without wanting to claw my skin off. So, I get it, even if it's in a small way."

"Not your fault," I stated firmly. "You don't need to carry that."

Her fingers traveled to my jaw, flattening to cup it. "A lot of your shame comes from circumstances that weren't your fault either, but I don't know if anyone could convince you to lay it down."

I blinked at her. She was right. There was no convincing me. The fact that she wanted to, though...that affected me. It made me want to always live up to her good opinion. I was no stranger to working hard, so it wouldn't be a burden to put in that work for her. Not at all.

"Yeah," she breathed. "I didn't think so. But, for what it's worth, the more I learn about you, the harder I fall for you. Today being no exception."

"Baby...that's worth everything." I rolled my forehead over hers. "I'm in so deep with you, Phoebe. *So* deep."

That earned me a tremulous sigh. Then her mouth found mine in a searching kiss. Closing my eyes, I gave into all the goodness in my arms and sipped from lips so sweet they might've been made from spun sugar. She parted them, inviting me to slip inside, giving me so much more of her sweet.

I slid my hand down her side, over the round curve of her hip, and around to her plump ass. Squeezing her cheek, I pulled her closer, bringing us flush.

Her body was something else, so incredibly soft and wildly feminine. Pink where she blushed, peach in other parts. And *hell* if I didn't want to discover every other shade her clothes hid from me.

I could've gotten lost in her. It'd be too easy to forget the world outside her curves—curves shaped by sunshine and sweet things—but I kept my head, focusing on who I was with and where I was. She wasn't an escape from my pain. Phoebe was *my* girl, and I'd be damned if I missed a single detail of what she gave me because I was trapped in regret.

Pulling back from her, I watched her eyelashes flutter as her eyes cleared. "Are you okay?" she asked.

"Getting there."

Her breath shuddered. "We don't have to go further." Her legs scissored between mine. "I just want to feel you, Deacon."

"How do you want that?"

She brought her hand to my chest, smoothing it down my torso. "Your skin on mine." Pushing up on her elbow, she tugged her T-shirt over her head, then she reached back, unhooking her bra and tossing it aside. "Like this."

She lay back down in front of me, pressing her bare chest to mine. An earthquake racked my insides, shifting things permanently within me. I shoved my face into her neck, my hands skimming down her back, tracing the dips and swells that fit against me like they'd been made to.

"Phoebe, angel, I don't deserve this."

"Shut up, Deacon," she cooed, no sharpness to her words. "It's up to me to decide who gets to touch me, and I've decided on you. Can you let it be as easy as that?"

I huffed into her neck. "Nothing's as easy as that."

"What if it is this time?"

I kissed her shoulder and pulled her impossibly closer, her breasts molding against my chest. "I don't know how to do this."

"Just hold me. We'll figure the rest out together."

Chapter Thirty

Deacon

WE LAY THERE FOR a long time, eventually shedding the rest of our clothing. Skin on skin, we touched and petted. Slow and easy, gentle exploration and warm comfort. My mind settled after a while, all my previous panic a shadow in comparison to the light in my arms.

The girl I'd never allowed myself to dream about, more real than I could have imagined if I had. I trailed the rough pads of my fingers down the curve of her back, over the slope of her ass, then back again. I moved to her side, along the dip of her waist and the dramatic swell of her hip to her upper thigh.

Phoebe studied my tattoos, tracing the lines of the Rockies on my chest with her nail, placing light kisses on the peaks.

My cock had been hard for a long time, and it was getting difficult to ignore, especially when she moved her legs between mine, her hot pussy sliding along my thigh. She'd done it a few times, always shifting away quickly, except this time, she stayed, the slick heat of her core pressed against my leg.

Cupping the side of her head, I tilted her face back and peered at her. Her cheeks were rosy, bright eyes a little glassy, and her lips were pink and parted.

"You turned on, baby?" I gruffed.

She nodded. "But it's okay. We don't have to—"

I rolled her to her back before she could finish her sentence and braced my hands on either side of her head.

Bending my neck, I took a long look at all the valleys and swells of her decadent body, getting stuck on the brown curls at the apex of her creamy thighs. Then I found her eyes again, wide and alert.

"Do you have any idea—any idea how sexy and beautiful you are?" I dragged my nose along her jaw to her ear. There, I nipped her velvet lobe and whispered, "I really hope you do. You're the most beautiful thing I've ever seen. I look at you, and I have to blink to make sure you're real."

She brought her hands up to her breasts, holding them up like an offering. "Everything about you and me is real."

I stared down at her, my brow drawn to the middle. "Do you want this? With me?"

Her nod came quickly, and it was vigorous. "So badly, I can barely think of anything else."

There was nothing I could do but believe her. "I don't know if I'm going to be any good."

She brought her knees up, parting them slightly. "Then we'll have to practice until we get it right."

I was already so close to the edge I knew it'd be fast, and I'd be damned if I didn't make her come first. Sliding my hand down her sloped stomach and over her nest of curls, I slipped my fingers into her folds, finding her wet all over. Her clit was beaded and hard, rolling like a marble beneath the pad of my finger. She shivered and quaked as I rubbed her and even more when I took her nipple in my mouth.

This, I knew how to do. I'd made her come in the hot springs like this. The sounds she'd made were burned into my brain, along with what she'd done to me after.

I can't think about that, or I'll make a damned fool of myself.

She dug her fingers into my shoulders. "Baby, I'm so close. I don't want to—not without you." Her legs clamped around my wrist, stopping me in my tracks. "Please, Deke."

Popping off her nipple, I panted. "You don't want me to make you come?"

"With you inside me." She let her legs fall open. "I need you. *Please.*"

Every bit of self-control snapped. I wouldn't be asking if she was sure again. Didn't think I'd be able to get those words out of my mouth even if I'd wanted to.

Moving between her spread thighs, I slotted myself against her. The second my cock came in contact with her sleek pussy, I had to bite the inside of my cheek to stop myself from coming.

Some sanity prevailed, and I pulled back. "I don't have a condom, baby."

She raised her knees to either side of my hips. "I'm on birth control, and I've been tested. We don't have to use a condom if you're okay with it."

I shook my head, biting down even harder. "I'm going to make a mess of you."

"Then make a mess." She reached up to cup my jaw. "I'm one-hundred-percent sure of this, but if you're not ready, that's okay."

"No, I'm more than ready." I lowered myself onto her again, bringing my face close to hers. "I want to be good enough for you."

"You are." She rocked herself against me. "Be with me, Deke."

I dropped my forehead to hers, taking a moment to lasso the last of my restraint before aligning the head of my cock with her entrance. I tried to go slow, pushing into her a little bit at a time, but once I felt the warm grip of her all around me, there was no hope. Driving forward, I seated myself fully inside her and nearly lost my shit.

"Phoebe," I bit out. "Oh *hell*, baby. I didn't know. I—"

"Move, Deke. Let me feel you," she cried softly.

The last thing I wanted to do was pull back, but I did, then thrust forward again. And dear god that was even better. I stared down at her in disbelief. How was this real?

"Everything about you and me is real."

I fisted the sheets on either side of her head, going back and forth between staring at her flushed face and watching her breasts bounce as I plunged into her. I tried my hardest to go slow, to prolong this as much as I could, but her inner walls were wrapped around me so tight I was helpless to the call of her.

My mouth covered hers, kissing her wet and deep as I drove into her faster, harder. She moaned into my mouth, clinging to my shoulders, her feet on the backs of my thighs. I had to give in. There was no stopping it. Not with all her softness beneath me, her heat surrounding me, her sweetness on my tongue, all of her imprinted on my mind.

The frayed rope inside me snapped. I plunged into her deep, hard, planting myself at the end of her, filling her to the brim and spilling over so our mingled arousal coated us both.

We kissed breathlessly, grappling to get closer even though it was impossible. She tugged at my hair, and I kneaded her breasts and hips—anywhere I could get my hands.

We rolled to our sides, still joined, her leg over mine. I slipped my arm between us to give her clit the attention it needed, rubbing it the way I had before. Her lips broke from mine, but only far enough for her to cry out my name. Then I captured her bottom lip between my teeth, tugging sharply as her inner walls clamped down around my still-hard cock.

"Deacon—oh god, you feel so good," she moaned.

Seemed impossible she could get more beautiful, but Phoebe losing it while I was inside her had set a new record. Her hair was wild around her shoulders, flowing like chestnut banners on my pillow. The flush on her cheeks had traveled down to her chest, and her lips were little swollen rosebuds. I already knew I was irreversibly hooked on making this woman come.

I rolled my hips into hers, wanting her all over again. "I'm not done. Are you?"

"Nowhere close." Her eyes flicked open. "Fuck me, baby."

The angle was different this way. More shallow but no less hot. I tried to take my time—hell, I should've been able to, considering it had only been a handful of minutes since I came—but the combination of my seed in her and...*her* proved to be my downfall.

"How do you like it?" I asked through clenched teeth. "Talk to me."

"I like what you're doing." She rubbed her leg along my side, hooking her foot over my ass. "Those hard, fast strokes are hitting me just right. If you keep doing that, I'm going to come again."

I gave her what she asked for, a steady drive into her velvet heat, only stuttering when I bent to take her nipples into my mouth. I felt her getting tighter, swelling for me. The level of pride it gave me, knowing she liked what I was doing to her, struck me dumb. It instantly became my mission to make her come as many times as I could. I already knew I wouldn't be able to get enough of it.

"Right there, right there, right there," she chanted. Her neck arched, and her mouth fell open in a soundless cry as I ground my pelvis into her, hard against soft.

I fucked her like that, planted deep, rocking against her clit, until a faint scream broke free and she bowed into me, hands slapping on my shoulders, head thrashing wildly.

Beautiful.

Once again, my control was yanked from my hands, and I had no choice but to move with the tide slamming me into her. Primal instinct guided me. Shoving her onto her back, I hooked my arms beneath her knees, lifting them high and wide. Her nails clawed at my biceps and shoulders as I pounded relentlessly.

We were eye to eye, locked on each other. Sweat glistened like dew on her flesh. Our bodies were slippery from it. My gut was taut, cock so hard it was painful, and my chest ached from the emotion pouring out of my heart. Glorious pain rode me, and there was no shrugging it off. I had to take the pain to get to the blissful pleasure within reach.

Her hands clapped onto my cheeks. "Come in me, Deke."

"Deacon," I grunted. That was hers. I only ever wanted her to call me that.

"Deacon, honey. Come inside me."

There was no denying this woman a single thing. My body answered her call again, spilling so forcefully I fell over her, unable to hold myself up anymore. Her arms came around me, clasping me to her while I shook.

"Honey," she whispered beside my ear. "Perfect."

I didn't know if that was true, but right now, feeling like I did, I was inclined to believe her.

"Yeah, baby." I touched my lips to her temple and sighed. "Perfect."

We ended up in Phoebe's apartment a little while later since my fridge was barren. She had food, and we were both starving. We ate, talked about nothing of consequence, and watched a true crime documentary.

We'd had a couple heavy hours, and my emotions were still a little frayed, but Phoebe had worked a miracle and pulled me back with her. By the end of the night, I was prepared for whatever came next.

At least, I thought I was until Phoebe invited me to sleep at her place. I should've seen that coming, but I hadn't been thinking too far ahead.

She took my hand in both of hers. "Stay."

"I, uh"—I looked away, unsure how to answer her—"I don't know if I can sleep next to you."

"Oh." It was like I'd punched her in the face. Her hands slipped from mine, and she fell back against the couch cushion, deflated.

"Shit, Phoebe, I meant...I don't know if I can sleep next to *any-one*." I squeezed my eyes shut. "It's hard for me to shut down at night. I've had to be alert since I was a kid, and my years in prison didn't help. I'm up and down all night when I'm on my own, and I can't be sure how I'll handle sharing a bed with you when I'm not delirious with fever. Believe me when I say I want to. More than anything, but—"

"Okay." She leaned into me, wrapping her hand around the side of my neck. "That's a much better answer than your first one."

I exhaled a heavy breath and gripped her nape. "After everything you gave me tonight, I don't want it to end. Not ever. I just don't know how it'll go."

"I hear you." She rubbed her lips together, and I could almost see the gears turning behind her melted chocolate eyes. "How about this? Come to bed with me. If it's not working, you can go right upstairs to your place. I won't be offended if you leave since I understand the reason now."

I nodded, liking her plan even though I was already sure I'd end up at home before dawn broke. "It's not like I have to go far." And if I got to spend a little more time with her, it'd be worth it.

"No, you don't. So, we'll try it and see."

I waited in her room while she got ready for bed in the bathroom. When she was done, we switched places, but I stopped short in the doorway, my gaze locking on what had been left for me on the counter.

A toothbrush, new in the package.

My mouth twitched at the color: bright pink. I checked the toothbrush holder. Phoebe's was baby pink. We'd be able to tell ours apart.

My stomach knotted. A tangled mix of pleasure and something a lot like pain. Every little thing I learned about Phoebe pulled me in deeper—made me like her even more than I already did, and that was a lot. But moments like this, her quiet, simple gestures she probably didn't think twice about, staggered me.

I wasn't used to this sort of kindness—not when it didn't come with strings. Accepting I could be given something for absolutely no reason other than the person wanting to do it was hard for me. It drove Chris and Tilly crazy.

But Phoebe? This was who she was. A giver. If I pushed back, if I let my own hang-ups get in the way, I'd only hurt her.

I knew that because I was the same way. Giving felt good. And if someone turned it down, it stung. I wouldn't do that to Phoebe. Not ever.

I tore open the package and used my pink toothbrush, grinning the whole time. My girl was cuter than she had any right to be with all her pink, but I didn't mind being surrounded by it. Not one bit.

After I was done, I strolled out of the bathroom, still grinning. "Thanks for the toothbrush, sugar. Made me feel extra special, you sharing your pink with me."

"I'm glad you appreciated it. I don't share with just anyone." Smiling, she folded over the covers and patted the spot beside her. I stood at the edge of the bed, looking her over. She had on some kind of raspberry-colored silk slip.

"What're you wearing?"

She looked down. "A nightgown. It's what I always wear to bed. A lesson my mother imparted on Hannah and me from an early age—silky, pretty nightwear always makes for a better night's sleep."

I tugged on my cotton T-shirt. "Is that where I went wrong?"

She snorted a little laugh. "Could be. Though I think I like you in your sweats better than I'd like you in my pajamas."

"I think I agree." I crawled into bed with her, lay on my side, and hooked my arm around her waist. Her nightgown was smooth as glass beneath my palm. She snuggled in close, slotting her leg between mine and tucking her hands against her chest.

"How are you?" she asked softly.

"A lot better than I would've been without you. How about you? How are you?"

Even in the dim lighting, I couldn't miss the way her cheeks had pinkened. "If I didn't have to get up in six hours, I would want...well, I'd want to start all over again."

I raised a brow. "Start all over?"

She nodded and brushed her lips over mine. "I'm already aching to have you inside me again."

If I hadn't been hard just from seeing her in her nightgown, that would have done it. As it were, my arm jerked her against me out of pure instinct.

"You are?" I bit out. If I opened my mouth any wider, it would latch onto her and not let go.

"Of course I am." She wriggled against me, sighing. "We both need to sleep, though...right?"

I chuffed at her indecision. "You're putting it in my hands?" I dipped my head to kiss the crook of her neck. "It kills me, but I can't have my girl losing sleep. We're gonna turn off the lights and get some rest."

"That's what we *should* do." She hesitated until I gave her a gentle shove. Not that I wanted to but because we both had jobs where we needed to be on our game. "Fine, honey. Let's go to sleep."

She rolled away to turn off the lamp on her side of the bed, then returned to me, scooting into the same position. Legs tangled, my arm around her waist, her hands tucked against her chest.

I wasn't going to fall asleep, but I'd stay until she did.

"I'm glad you're with me," she murmured in the dark.

"I am too." My lips touch her forehead. "Good night."

"Night, Deacon."

I'd leave soon, but not yet.

Relaxing with her soft, still body alongside mine, I closed my eyes...

Just for a while.

Chapter Thirty-one

Phoebe

MORNINGS WERE ALWAYS THE pits, but this one was a bright, beautiful exception.

For once, I woke before my alarm, and as soon as I opened my eyes, I knew why. Sound asleep beside me was my gorgeous boyfriend. Flat on his back, one arm slung over his forehead, the other stretched over my side of the bed, his hand splayed on my hip. From the looks of the smooth blankets atop him, he'd barely moved all night.

Joy bubbled up from my belly, and I had to bite down on my lip to stop myself from laughing. I couldn't remember ever smiling this big before ten a.m. In fact, I could almost guarantee I hadn't. Me and mornings *really* didn't mix.

Last night was...well, the best of my life. It didn't matter that Deacon was inexperienced. Our connection was so deep it would have been good no matter what. But it was so much more than orgasms and pleasure—and there had been a lot of that.

It felt like the beginning of something huge, like the embarkation of a journey that would change everything. And I adored that he hadn't hidden how special it had been for him too. *"Perfect,"* I'd said, and he'd agreed. The truth was, there weren't words to describe what being with Deacon had been like, so perfect would have to do.

I wished I could have stayed in bed all day, and I was even more loath to disturb Deacon, but life was life, and we both had to get a move on.

"Deacon," I called, stroking the back of his hand. "It's time to wake up, honey."

His entire body jerked at once, knifing upright. Head swiveling, he looked around the room with wild, bleary eyes. Fists at his sides, his chest heaved as he sucked in great gusts of air.

"Deacon." I sat up but kept space between us, sensing he needed it. "You're in my room. You slept here all night."

He twisted to face me, and the pillow crease on his cheek would have been sweet if he didn't seem so panicked.

"What time is it?" he rasped.

"Early. Just past five."

He blinked hard and scrubbed his face with his hand. "I slept for six hours straight? How the hell...I didn't wake up once. I've never...Phoebe, I *never* sleep like that."

It broke my heart to see him so confused about getting good sleep—a basic human need. It made me wonder what his nights were normally like and how he managed a labor-intensive job on broken sleep.

I put my hand on his rigid shoulder. "A lot went down last night."

"Yeah, it did, and you were right there with me." He sighed, opening his arms, and I crawled right into them, curling into his chest. He wrapped me up, burying his nose in my hair. "I slept, sugar. How'd that happen?"

"I hope that means you feel safe with me."

"I do. There's no doubt about that." He pulled back, his brow furrowing. "I can't guarantee it'll happen like that again."

"We'll take it as it comes. I'm not going to worry about it." I pressed my palm to his scruffy cheek. "Though I do like waking up to you. I'm not a morning person, but today, I'm wide awake and almost cheerful."

His chuckle was scratchy and low. "Almost?"

"*Almost.*" I nuzzled into his neck, letting my eyes fall closed. "I really hate mornings."

"How in the hell did you become a baker, baby?"

"That's one of the mysteries of the universe." I smiled against his warm, smooth skin. "Do we have to get up?"

"We do," he agreed, making no move to let me go. He trailed his fingers along my nightie, toying with the thin straps on my shoulders. "You really wear this kind of thing every night?"

"I suppose you'll have to come back tonight and see for yourself."

"As much as I like you in this, I was always gonna come back. Doesn't matter what you have on." He dropped his hand to give my butt a firm pat. "Now we have our day planned out—get up, or we'll both be late."

Hailey showed up right on time for her shift that afternoon. She barely looked at me as she zoomed in, heading straight for the back to drop her stuff.

Camille raised her eyebrows. "What was that about?"

I lifted a shoulder. "Teenage things, I'm sure. Mind if I go have a chat with her?"

She glanced around at the quiet shop. Charlie was pecking away at his laptop, but the rest of the tables were empty for now. "Sure. I'll give you a holler if we get a rush."

Wiping my hands on my apron, I headed into the kitchen, finding Hailey by my desk, riffling through her backpack. At the sound of my approach, her head shot up, and her eyes rounded.

"Am I fired?"

I stopped in my tracks. "Why would you be fired?"

Her cheeks flushed bright pink, and she couldn't seem to bring herself to look at me. Scuffing her feet on the linoleum floor, she said, "First, I used a fake name on my application. Even though I was sure you wouldn't have hired me if you'd known I was a Slater, I shouldn't have done that. Then I left early yesterday, and you closed alone. I shouldn't have done that either. I'm so sorry. Linda told me no matter what happened with...well, you know, I should have fulfilled my responsibilities."

I put my hands on my hips. "I hope you know by now my choice of hiring you had nothing to do with your last name. Sure, some people in our town can be close-minded, but I won't ever let myself be one of them. Got it?"

She nodded and whispered, "Got it."

"I didn't love you running out like you did, but not because of anything to do with work." She peered up at me, and I went on to explain. "I was worried about you, sweetheart. You were upset, and I was afraid you wouldn't find your way home."

"You're not mad?"

"Why would I be mad?"

She went back to looking down at her shuffling feet. "For running away yesterday...and not telling you Deke's my brother."

The way her voice cracked on that last word made my heart ache. I hated that she was hurting and even more that Deacon was feeling the same way.

"Not at all. That was your business to tell when you were ready." I took a couple steps closer and propped myself on the edge of my desk. Hailey wasn't a big girl, and with my height, I towered over her. Sitting put us closer to eye level. "I have to say, I'm glad it's all out in the open now."

She tilted her head. "Did he tell you about me?"

I nodded. "I knew he had a little sister who'd lived with him, but your name had gotten lost in the shuffle. Last night, after you left, he told me everything."

The breath she took was fractured. "Is he mad at me? Well, I know he's mad at me, but how mad? He hates my guts, doesn't he? He has to. I wou—"

I grabbed her hand. "No, Hailes. He isn't mad at you. Not at all. If he's mad at anyone, it's himself. Definitely not you."

"Oh," she whispered. "But I'm the reason he was sent to prison."

I had to stop myself from gasping. "Oh, baby, no you're not. Have you been blaming yourself this whole time?"

She shrugged both shoulders. "It's my fault. I should've said what they told me to. If I'd been able to keep it together, he never would've—"

Her hand flew up to cover her face, but there was no muffling the sob that broke loose. I didn't think; I just pulled her into me and curled my arms around her. She shook as I held her, crying softly.

"You didn't do anything wrong," I assured her. "No one's mad at you. *No one*. I promise you that, okay?"

"Really?" she squeaked.

"Really and truly. I don't think I'm speaking out of turn by telling you Deacon misses you a lot."

"I miss him too." She swallowed so hard her throat bobbed. "Before I moved in with the Spellmans, he was kind of...not really a dad, but way more than a brother. My birth parents pretty much gave me to him, you know? And he took me when he didn't have to."

"Do you think you'd like to talk to him about all this?"

Her eyes rounded with worry, but slowly, she nodded. "If he wants to talk to me."

"He does."

"Do you think today's too soon?"

I let out a thick laugh, loving how eager she was to reconnect with Deacon. I was just as excited. He *needed* that connection. One member of his family who was good and loving and cared for him. I hoped having Hailey back in his life would open him to seeing neither his last name nor the mistakes he had made defined who he was. And maybe he'd be able to forgive himself and move on from his troubled past to the beauty that lay ahead for him.

"Why don't I call Linda and Deacon and see if we can set something up?"

"Yes, please," she whispered.

Camille stuck her head in the doorway. "We have a few customers. I could use some help."

Hailey bounced on her toes. "I'll be right there." Then she turned back to me with an earnest expression. "Thank you for not firing me and being so nice to me and being my brother's girlfriend."

"All of that is my pleasure." I tipped my head toward the front of the shop. "Now, let's go help Camille before she starts a riot and fires us both."

Chapter Thirty-two

Deacon

THE LAST TIME I'D been up close to my sister, she'd been a slip of a thing. Ten years old but tiny for her age. Her face had been blasted with freckles—summer or winter, it didn't matter—and her hair had been cut just below her ears.

At fifteen, the freckles were still there but less intense. She'd let her hair grow to mid-back, and it had some wave to it now. She still wasn't very tall, but she was a hell of a lot bigger than she'd been five years ago.

All those changes and I'd still recognize her laugh with my eyes closed. I didn't know what I'd done right to be listening to it again, but here she was, sitting at my girlfriend's table, giggling with Phoebe about a customer who'd gone into Sugar Rush last week.

"He wanted twelve shots of espresso." She pressed her hands to her face in horror. "Twelve!"

Phoebe snorted. "And what did Camille say?"

Hailey's shoulders shook as she snickered. "She said, 'Sir, if you're determined to explode your heart, you'll have to do it elsewhere. I don't have time to clean that sort of mess up.'"

If I'd had time to dwell on my sister coming over for dinner, I would've driven myself crazy. But Hailey had asked to meet, her foster mom had agreed, and twenty-four hours after bolting from Sugar Rush, we were sharing a pizza.

I barely ate, spending most of the meal cataloging every change in my sister instead. Her expressions were the same as I remembered, but there was a lightness to her that was new. I liked seeing that. I liked it a lot.

The rest of the time, I studied Linda Spellman. My instincts told me she cared for Hailey. Hell, she wouldn't have brought her here if she didn't have good intentions. I'd rather Hailey be living with me, but with my record, that wasn't an option. I was coming to the conclusion the Spellmans were the next best thing.

When their laughter died down, I said, "You grew your hair out."

Hailey dragged her hand along the locks draped over her shoulder. "Yeah, I did. I...uh, learned to care for it myself. And Linda taught me how to do ponytails and braids when it got longer."

"I like it. I'm sorry I didn't have those skills when you were living with me."

I'd done my best, but the underside of her hair had gotten so matted we'd had to cut it. After that, we kept it short because it was easier for us both. It wasn't like I was any kind of expert braider. I could've watched tutorials, though. I should've done more.

"It's okay." She picked up her paper napkin, wringing it in her hand. "It looked pretty cool short. I was just ready for a change."

Linda lifted the end of Hailey's hair, rubbing it between her fingers. "I loved your hair when you came to live with us. But you can pull off any cut with your pretty face."

Phoebe nodded. "Isn't that the truth? Not to mention all that gorgeous hair. You and Deacon share that trait."

Hailey smiled at me, her cheeks a soft, rosy pink. "Only Deke and I have this hair color. We don't match the rest of the family."

I cleared my throat. "Have you talked to any of 'em since I've been away?"

"Not for a long time," she replied. "Richie visited me a couple times in the beginning, but I think he forgot about me. Mom and Dad aren't getting a check for me anymore, so they don't have any use for me." She scoffed, rolling her eyes, being big and brave. "It isn't like I have any use for them either."

"Our parents..." I shook my head, trying to formulate how to explain their neglect of her had nothing to do with her and everything to do with them. "Don't know why they had kids. I guess it was just a thing to do. By some strange luck, they produced you and gave you every scrap of good they had in them. The one decent thing they ever did was let you come live with me. I'm not saying I was some prize, but—"

"You were," she rushed out. "Remember, you gave me the bedroom in our apartment, and you slept on an air mattress in the living room? Back then, I didn't realize what a big deal that was, but now I know. You were giving me what you didn't have."

I shrugged. "Anyone would have done it, buddy."

"Deke," she whispered. "I slept on a couch at our parents' house. I'd never had a bedroom until I lived with you. You did that for me."

In my periphery, Phoebe covered her gasp with her fingertips. I didn't like talking about how it'd been growing up. Whatever most people assumed, it'd been ten times worse. Most of the time, there'd been no running water. Electricity had been iffy. We had feral dogs running wild on the property, so going outside wasn't safe, but staying inside was often worse. Strangers were coming and going, every surface covered in drugs, dirt, and only God knew what else. It'd only grown worse as I'd gotten older. I *knew* if I hadn't watched Hailey like a hawk, something irrevocable would have happened to her in that house.

"I did that for you," I conceded. "Then I got locked up and left you alone. I let you down, kid, and I'll never forgive myself for that."

Hailey's spine curled forward, her arms stretched like plants on the table in front of her. "I wish I could have lied for you. If I'd been stronger—"

Linda put her hand on Hailey's shoulder. "You did the right thing, and there's no shame in that. I'm sure Deke agrees."

I nodded sharply. "You were a scared little girl. That lawyer never should have put that burden on you. I hate that you've been carrying guilt around all these years. *Hate* it. Where I ended up is all on me. I made the mistake of going along with Richie. If I hadn't gotten thrown in prison when I did, I don't know how much worse it would have gotten. Things happened the way they needed to."

I glanced at Linda. She was rubbing Hailey's back, nodding along with me. She didn't have to allow any of this. By rights, I shouldn't have had any visitation with my sister. Them being here said all I needed to know, and seeing Linda comfort Hailey only raised my esteem for her.

I continued. "All you have to do is look at the woman beside you, how she cares for you, and you'll see that's true. I wish I hadn't lost all those years with you, but I'm in a lot better place to be your brother now, and I'm hoping, once we get past all this, we can start there."

Sniffling, she finally raised her head, peering at me with glassy eyes. "You're staying in Sugar Brush?"

"I am." I slid my eyes to Phoebe, who was watching our exchange with intense focus. She offered me her hand, and I took it, folding it between mine. "My whole world is here, so this is where I'm gonna be."

Hailey swiped her eyes with the back of her hand. "Good. I want you to stay." She turned to Linda. "Is it okay if I sometimes maybe hang out with Deke? Maybe we could have him over to the house so I can show him my room?"

"Yes, that would be okay," Linda agreed. "How about we start with dinner at our house next week and go from there?"

Hailey turned her bright gaze back to me. "Would you and Phoebe want to come to dinner at our house next week?"

When I went away, I thought I'd lost her for good. Thought she'd be angry at me or feel like I'd abandoned her and never want to see me again. I'd convinced myself it didn't matter so long as she was living a good, safe life. But now, she was offering me more than I ever would have asked for, and I was going to grab it with both hands. Maybe I'd gotten better at accepting gifts. There was no damn doubt this was the biggest I'd ever been given.

"Yeah, buddy." I swallowed down the thick lump in my throat. "I'd like that a hell of a lot."

Hailey and Linda didn't stay long after that. Linda had other kids to attend to, and Hailey had homework. Plus, we were all a little raw and needed some time. As I walked them to the door, Hailey stopped in her tracks and spun to face me.

She stared up at me for a long beat, her dark-amber eyes assessing. Then she took a deep breath and threw her arms around my middle so hard, they were like steel bars. Her head only came up to the center of my chest, but the last time I'd hugged her, it'd been much lower. I was tossed back and forth between past and present for a few thundering heartbeats before I steadied myself and wrapped my arms around my sister. I hadn't had a lot of hugs in my life, but this one ranked right up there with the best.

"Love you, buddy," I murmured.

She pulled back, grinning up at me. "Love you too, Deke. Like, a lot."

With a choked laugh, I ruffled her hair. "See you soon."

I stood at the door until they were safe in their car and driving away. In that time, Phoebe had joined me, curling her arms around me from behind and resting her cheek on my back.

When they were gone, I shut the door, letting my forehead drop against it. "*Fuck.*"

Phoebe held onto me even tighter. "That went so well."

"I know." I put my hand over hers, slotting our fingers together. "How did that happen?"

"You two need each other." She rounded me without breaking her embrace. "It's only going to get better as you get to know each other again. I'm really happy for you."

I pulled her against me, burying my face into her hair. *Sugar.* "I got her back."

"I know," she breathed, running her hand up and down my back. "You both did."

"I got her back," I murmured again. "Don't know how, but I got my buddy back."

"You did, Deacon. You did."

The more I said it, the deeper it sank. Tonight had happened. My sister, who'd been lost to me for five years, was back. I'd held her a few minutes ago, and despite everything, it'd been like no time had passed. She was still my girl, silly freckle face and all.

"I must've done something right. Don't know what it was, but I had to have done something right for her to turn out like that."

"You gave her the bedroom," Phoebe stated. "You made her feel like she was important enough to sacrifice for. You gave her safety and love. You screwed up, but before that, you gave her a solid foundation to stand on. I think you did a lot right. All you have to do is look at her to see that."

"I don't know how they made a girl like her."

She sucked in a breath and slowly released it. "You said they poured every scrap of good into her, but I have to tell you, honey, they poured it into you too. You both got all the little bits of goodness they had in them and turned them into something even greater."

"I don't know about that."

"I do," she said firmly. "Would I ever lie to you?"

"No." I didn't have to think about that, not for a second.

She pulled back, a cute little crease between her brows. "Then believe me."

The corner of my mouth hitched. I couldn't help it. No matter what my mood was or how lost I was in my head, seeing my sweet Phoebe get stern made me smile.

"Guess I have no choice."

Later that night, after we'd showered together for the first time and made love—slower, but I still didn't last nearly as long as I would have liked—we were in her bed, trying this sleepover thing again.

Phoebe was on her side with me curled around her back, stroking the silk covering her soft stomach. She'd fallen asleep a while ago. I'd tried, but I was too restless to let go. As much as I didn't want to, I'd have to go back to my place to get some rest. I couldn't go to work without sleep, but shutting down wasn't happening like this.

My sigh must've woken her. Or maybe it was me shifting against her plump ass. She turned her head, blinking at me. "Deacon?"

"Go back to sleep." I kissed her shoulder. "I'm probably going to have to head upstairs soon."

She latched onto my hand, and her brows dropped. "You can't fall asleep?"

"No, not sure I can." I blew out a heavy breath. "I want to stay here, baby, but I can't get settled enough to drift off."

She snuggled against me, her ass nestling closer. I was hard but not really turned on. My body was having a natural reaction to hers—something I had no control over. Not when it came to Phoebe.

"Can we try something?" she asked. "If it doesn't work, I won't be upset if you go back to your place."

"Yeah." I closed my eyes, pressing my face into her hair. "I'll try anything."

She lifted her top leg and arched her spine. "Put yourself inside me."

"Phoebe, I—"

"Not sex, Deke. Just plant yourself inside me." She twisted her neck to meet my sharp gaze. "I don't know if it will help, but it might, so let's try?"

After a beat, I nodded. "Okay." I had a hard time believing this would work. Then again, being inside this woman was the most right thing in the world, so there was a chance she was onto something.

I gathered the back of her nightgown, lifting it to expose her round backside, then I freed my cock and pressed into her. Her warmth enveloped me as I slid between her folds and found her entrance. She stayed still as I pushed inside, slow and easy, until I made it all the way in.

She let out a sweet exhale and lowered her leg, relaxing into me. "There," she whispered. "That's better."

Surprisingly, it was. As we lay in her soft bed, her warm body aligned with mine, joined in the most intimate way, something clicked within me. Like a light switch finally shutting off. My heart slowed, matching her steady, even breathing.

I curled my arm around her middle, and she laid hers on top, her fingers sliding between mine. I stared at the back of her head, waiting for the restlessness to return, but the longer I stared, the heavier my eyelids became.

I felt the moment she drifted back to sleep. Her entire body sank into the mattress, and she brought me with her. Little by little, muscle by muscle, I unfurled.

Before I knew it, my eyes were closing too. Drifting off to sleep, the safest I'd ever felt in my entire life, buried deep inside my woman.

Chapter Thirty-three

Phoebe

TWO WEEKS SLIPPED BY in a blink. There was work and family and evenings with Deacon. We'd had dinner with the Spellmans, then another with just Hailey. On the days she worked, Deacon made an effort to get to Sugar Rush early enough to talk to her before her shift ended.

The difference in him since he'd reunited with his sister had come in increments. The first day, I wasn't sure he believed it would stick, but when he'd shown up at Sugar Rush, Hailey had walked right up to him and hugged him.

After that, he'd held himself a little taller. Then we had dinner with her foster family, and she was so damn proud to show him her room—though she swore nothing could ever be better than the first bedroom he'd given her—and he'd shed some of the heaviness he'd been shouldering.

Each hug she gave him, each text she sent to tell him about her day, every time he watched Linda pick her up from work and give her shoulders a squeeze, he laughed easier and smiled more.

He was still the same quiet, introspective Deacon but freer, open to letting the light in—and with it, me. We'd spent every night together and, most often, fell asleep with Deacon snug inside me.

I had never dreamed this would be something I'd want, but I'd come to crave it. Drifting off, filled with him, his arms around me, his scent on my sheets…it was the coziest, most comfortable feeling.

This morning, I woke up on my stomach, Deacon over me, sliding in and out of me, and I smiled into my pillow.

I turned my head to show him how much I liked his wake-up call. "Good morning."

He dipped down to kiss my cheek and shoulder. His lips were impossibly soft and warm on my skin. "Morning, angel girl." He pushed in deep. "This feel all right?"

I wiggled my butt against him. "More than."

"Good, because I woke up with your pussy wet and warm on my cock and needed you." He nipped my earlobe. "We have time before we need to be up. I just need a nice, lazy fuck with my baby."

"Yeah, honey. Exactly what I need to start my day," I agreed.

He did as he said, sliding in and out at a slow, steady pace. My thighs were clamped shut, making me impossibly tight around him. He worked every nerve within me, turning them into crackling live wires.

Deacon always smelled so good in the morning. Warmer than normal, most of his soap had worn off, leaving his natural scent behind. My body responded to it with a Pavlovian reaction—relaxing and anticipating pleasure, whether from sex or a few minutes of cuddling before we rolled out of bed.

I pressed my nose into his forearm, inhaling him into my lungs. "I love how you smell," I murmured, rubbing my nose along the inside of his arm.

"Nothin' special," he declared.

"Mmmm…you're wrong. I would bottle this scent if I could."

He chuckled near my ear. "Are you dreaming, sugar?"

I smiled again, a little dreamy. "It feels like it." My inner walls fluttered around him. "Keep going like that. Right there. Love that so much."

"Like this?" He snapped forward, then dragged his cock out so slowly it was torture. "Is that how you want it?"

"Mmmm...yes." My channel flexed. "Please, baby. Do it again."

He carried on fucking me with agonizing deliberation. It was so perfect I sighed into my pillow, clutching the sheets around me, and gave in to all of it. His lean, strong body weighing down my much softer one, hot panting breaths on my skin, sweet kisses along my shoulders, being filled to the very brim. I was helpless beneath him, and knowing he wanted me exactly that way gave me a heady, floaty feeling.

I wouldn't come this way, but that was okay. I loved having him inside me too much to care about that.

I rode the meandering waves until he reached the breaking point. His huffs became heavier, retreats shorter, and he began grinding into me in earnest. Deep and hard, he slapped against me, my name uttered like a divine chant. Then, without warning, he yanked himself free, and liquid heat spilled along the valley of my ass.

There was no chance for me to find my equilibrium before he flipped me onto my back and dropped between my legs. His mouth latched onto my swollen pussy, so suddenly I nearly levitated off the bed. But he had a firm hold of my inner thighs, anchoring me to his face and the mattress.

I shoved my fingers into his hair, drawing him even deeper. He'd worked me up so well it wouldn't take much to get me there. My mind might have been catching up to what was happening, but my body understood and was fully on board.

"Deacon, yes," I moaned. "Please, keep going."

He groaned, the vibrations adding another layer of exquisite pleasure. My fingers fisted in his hair, probably too hard, but he didn't complain. He let go of one of my legs to slide two fingers inside me, curling forward to rub the tender spot he'd recently discovered.

His lips closed around my clit, giving me a pulsing suction that made me writhe and beg. I had no idea what I was saying, but desperate words began spilling from my lips as he sucked my clit and fucked me with his fingers.

He must have understood because he did not stop. Not when I cried his name to the ceiling and my thighs quivered around his ears. Not when I halfheartedly pushed at his head either. Deacon wasn't satisfied with one orgasm that had almost brought me to tears. He licked me straight through another one. Only when I cried, "Enough!" did he slip his fingers free and kiss his way up my torso to settle on the bed beside me.

I blinked at him with bleary eyes. "Hi."

He grinned, his lips shiny and pink from my pleasure. "Hey, sugar."

I stretched one arm over my head, the other hand cupping his jaw. "How am I supposed to go to work now? I'm ready for a nap."

He nuzzled his nose against mine. "You'll manage, sleepy girl. I have no doubt." Then he sighed. "I'm gonna need you to get up so I can change your sheets before I go shower."

I winced at the stickiness under my back. "We'll change them together." I brushed my lips against his. "I liked that, by the way.

Next time, I'd love it if you let me turn over so I can watch you come."

One brow winged. "You wanna see that?"

"I do." I stretched my thumb to trace his bottom lip. "I like you, Deacon, and I trust you. That means anything you want to try, I'm in. I have things I want you to do to me too."

His head cocked. "You gonna share what those things are?"

Grinning, I shook my head. "Not when we both have to get out of this bed."

"But later?" Biting my lip, I nodded, and he groaned. "Yeah, we have to get up, or it's never going to happen."

If I didn't love my job so much, I might've said screw the muffins, but alas, I had to be responsible. I had a feeling Deacon wouldn't have played hooky with me anyway.

We got dressed separately but walked out together, stopping at Deacon's truck. I was walking, and he had a long drive to his current jobsite, so this was where we parted.

I leaned into him, taking in his golden scruff, amber eyes, and long, pale lashes. My stomach swooped. "God, Deacon, I have such a crush on you," I blurted.

He gave me a bemused look. "What's that feel like?"

I tried to think of how to put it into words. There weren't really any that were accurate enough, so I went for the closest thing. "When I look at you, I feel like I'm on the first drop of a roller coaster. Anticipation, excitement, like I'm about to fly."

"Hmmm." He dropped his hand to my backside, giving me a squeeze. "Gotta say, I think I have a crush on you too."

I grinned wide. "Good. Keep it that way."

His eyes slid back and forth between mine, and he grew serious. "You have nothing to worry about in that regard, sugar. Not a damn thing."

Swoop.

Chapter Thirty-four

Deacon

ROADWORK WASN'T MY TRUE calling, but after years of seeing the same walls every damn day, I didn't mind all the driving. I hadn't been to a lot of places, but I was pretty sure there was nowhere prettier than Wyoming. Even where there was nothing but golden grass and rocks jutting out of the earth at random, it never failed to blow me away.

I'd been moved to a new crew, doing road inspection and maintenance on the route to Casper. Chris's crew was out toward Cheyenne, so we weren't sharing lunch breaks for the time being. Instead, I sat in my truck, ate my sandwich, and listened to a podcast Phoebe had recommended. She'd gotten me as hooked on true crime as she was, so I was catching up on all the episodes she'd already listened to.

A phone call came through, interrupting. That would have annoyed me, but it was worse seeing the name on the screen. *Richie.*

He'd sent me a couple texts over the last month or so. I'd been able to beg off seeing him, but this was my brother. He wouldn't be deterred forever.

I picked up before the call cut off.

"Hey."

"Hey yourself," he greeted. "Thought maybe you got locked back up you went so damn radio silent."

"Don't have much to say, Rich. I'm working a lot, sleeping when I'm not."

His chuckle was raspy from all the chain-smoking he did. "Aren't you out of prison? Why the hell are you living like a monk, man? It's not like you have Hailey under your feet anymore."

"I'm not looking for trouble. I work, sleep, and don't find trouble. And you know I never minded having Hailey around."

"Yeah, you never did." He whistles through the line. "She's got a nice family now, and you're young and free. Why don't we meet up in Laramie? I know you weren't into the last girl I brought you, but Jennifer's got plenty of friends—"

"I'm not interested, Rich." I kept all emotion out of my response. If he caught anything in my tone, he'd latch onto it. I was aiming to bore him enough he'd lose interest and move on.

"All right, all right. How about you and I get together? I'm into something big, and you're going to want to hear about it. It's—shit, where did you say that construction job is?"

"I'm on the road. It's always changing. Lately, I've been out in Natrona County."

"Oh yeah? You do a lot of driving, right?"

Uneasiness swamped my gut. "I have to drive to inspect roads," I answered carefully.

"Makes sense. Chris's old man make you drive your own vehicle?"

I didn't like his interest, and I had no clue what his angle was. And this was Richie. He always had an angle. "We've got company trucks."

"Hmmm." He paused, and I braced. Instead of pressing me more, he moved on. "I guess you gave up building furniture, huh?"

"Nope. I'm still doing that."

"Good, good. You always were talented."

My suspicions skyrocketed. Richie did not give out compliments unless he was trying to get something. I couldn't guess what he'd think he could get out of me, and I didn't want to find out. I'd had a lot at stake before, and I'd lost it. Now, I had even more on the line.

I did not make the same mistake twice.

"Appreciate it," I replied, neutral.

When I didn't give him anything else, he sighed. "Look, I should've said this a long time ago, but I'm sorry. You got dragged into my thing back then and took the fall. If Hailey'd toed the line like she should've, you wouldn't have served time, but that's all done and over with. Point is, I regret you went down for my shit, and I'd like to make it right. I've only got one brother, you know? Same as you."

Oh yeah, there it was. This was his apology tour. He'd aim to get back with me then pull me into whatever scheme he had going on. I'd tried to help him out more times than I could count. The last time, I lost four years of my life. Fortunately, I'd wised up. Some people did not want to be helped, and Richie was the captain of that team.

"Appreciate that too, Rich. The thing is, I'm on parole. One screwup, they throw me back in, and I'm not going back."

"All right, all right." I could picture him nodding like he agreed with me. "That makes sense, man. Like I said, I just want my brother back. You don't need to have anything to do with my side interests."

"Gotta stay clean," I stated. "That's how it has to be."

He grunted. "And I'm not clean?"

"You know you're not. I can't let any of that touch me. I go back inside; I'm not gonna make it out again."

I might walk out the doors, but I'd never be the same. I'd lost a piece of myself the first time; I couldn't afford to lose more.

That earned me a scoff. "Come on. I know plenty of guys who spent time inside. None of them came out being a drama queen."

"That's them. Me and prison didn't mix well. I'm not going back."

"No one's sending you back," he argued. "I'm just trying to hang out with my brother."

I didn't raise my voice, but I answered him as firmly as I could. "And I'm declining."

If I hadn't heard him shuffling and noise in the background, I would've thought he'd hung up. Finally, he spoke, and I wished he hadn't.

"All right, Deke. Your life. Maybe I'll see you around SB. I should really stop by Joy's. I haven't seen our dear aunt in years. A visit is overdue."

The threat was clear. It was how he'd hooked me weeks ago. This time, I wasn't going to bite. If I did, he'd keep coming back. It was past time for me to put my foot down.

"You do that, you'll see the kind of welcome Joy'll give you," I warned.

After a beat, Richie let out a maniacal laugh. "Oooh, I'm shaking in my boots. Joy's so, *so* scary." He kept right on laughing at himself. "Really, Deke, prison made you way less cool. Like, I don't even want to hang out with you at this point."

"Okay."

"Okay. Don't come running to me when you're hard up for cash. You're *clean* now, so what the hell could you want with me?"

I cleared my throat. "My lunch break's over. I need to get back on the road. Good luck, Rich."

"Sure thing, Deke. Sure goddamn thing."

I tossed my phone aside and sat in the silent cab of the truck, my head hanging in my hands. When did I get to move on?

I already knew that answer. Richie would keep grabbing at me until he got bored with me, and there was nothing I could do to stop him.

I walked into Sugar Rush a few minutes before closing, unsurprised to see Hannah Kelly there. She was a regular fixture, guarding her sister like a pit bull. She was unsure of me, but given her history with my brother, her wariness made sense. Still, I liked her.

Phoebe had a spine of steel but a soft heart. Left to her own devices, she'd probably let her customers linger all night, but Hannah charged in and got rid of them in minutes. Anyone who protected Phoebe that fiercely was more than all right in my book.

"Deke," Hannah cried, hopping up from the table she'd been sitting at drinking some kind of iced coffee. "You're here." She charged toward me.

I stopped short at her enthusiastic greeting. *This* surprised me. "I am."

From behind the counter, Phoebe called out to me. "Look at Hannah's ring, Deacon. Isn't it beautiful?"

Hannah was already in front of me, flashing her left hand. A silver band with a square emerald caught the light as she wiggled her fingers.

"You're looking at a fiancée, Deke." She beamed, sharing her happiness. "Remi proposed last night. What do you think?"

She shoved her hand closer, and I took it, tilting it left and right. I didn't know a damn thing about jewelry, but I knew she wanted me to be excited with her.

I looked up and smiled. "Congratulations. The ring's really pretty. Suits you."

"Doesn't it?" She took her hand back to gaze at her ring and sighed. "I didn't think I was a ring girl, but apparently I am."

Phoebe approached then, wiping her hands on her frilly pink apron. When she reached me, she leaned in and pressed her lips to mine.

"Hey, honey," she said softly.

"Sugar." I smoothed a hand down her shoulder and around her waist, pulling her a little closer. "Looks like it's been a good day."

"It has." She slung her arm around Hannah's shoulders and gave her a playful shake. "My sister's getting married. How can it be a bad day?"

"Can't be," I agreed.

While Phoebe finished up, Hannah made me sit with her so she could tell me about the proposal. We'd never been friends back in the day and had barely spoken, yet she spoke to me like we had been. Before Phoebe, I wouldn't have known how to handle this kind of openness, but I'd learned when it came to the Kelly women, going along for the ride was the only choice.

All Hannah needed from me was to listen and nod at the right moments of her story and she was happy. She even gave me a one-armed, bone-crushing hug before she took off.

The one she gave Phoebe was full-bodied and looked just as bone-crushing, but my girl took it like she was used to it.

On the way home, Phoebe held my hand tight. I studied her as we talked, trying to get a read on her feelings. It was clear she was happy, but there was something else I couldn't grasp.

"This guy, Remi, he's good to Hannah?" I asked.

"Oh yeah, he is." She bumped her head against my shoulder. "When I was growing up, he was like the fifth kid in our house—always over for meals and spent most weekends on the ranch. He lost his mom when he was young, and his dad was dealing with demons too big to make him a good father, so my parents filled in all the gaps they could. Now, he's going to be an official member of our family by marrying Hannah, who he pretty much worships. So, yeah, I'm pretty damn pleased."

"You've got some good parents, Phoebe."

"Luck of the draw," she said.

"Luckier than most."

"Yeah, I am," she murmured, bringing our joined hands to her lips to kiss my knuckles. "They're going to have a little engagement dinner on Saturday at my grandparents' house. I'd love for you to come with me."

This was a bridge we hadn't crossed yet. I'd met most of her family, one on one, but never in any official capacity. For the past couple weeks, I'd found excuses to skip their Sunday dinners, and she hadn't pushed. I didn't quite know how to handle being around a family like the Kellys.

Deep down, I knew exactly what was holding me back. I was afraid they'd see us together and know Phoebe and I didn't fit. That wasn't fair to them, but that was where I was, and the phone call with Richie hadn't helped my mindset.

"Not sure I can," I hedged. "Got some work in the shed—deadlines I can't miss. Plus, I'm planning on seeing Hailey. I'll let you know."

She let our hands fall between us on a sigh. "Okay. I'd really love for you to be there, and Hailey too, but I understand."

"Thanks, sugar." The words hovered on the edge of my tongue—*I'll come*—but I couldn't make myself say them. I just wasn't ready for this step.

Phoebe might've understood this time, but what about next time? She had more patience and forgiveness than I deserved. If I didn't get my act together, I knew I'd lose her.

I should've said yes.

I wanted to. Hell, I always wanted to be with Phoebe. There weren't enough hours in the day to spend with her and turning down any time together felt as unnatural as breathing underwater.

But the words wouldn't come.

I'd figure it out—I had to—for her. I just needed more time. I'd get there soon.

Besides, she didn't need me there to have a good time with her family.

Everything would be all right.

Then why the hell does it feel like I'm messing everything up?

Chapter Thirty-five

Deacon

"You're messing up, Deke!" Hailey screeched.

Startled, I looked up from the trim I was about to nail to the front of a drawer. "What're you talking about?"

She hopped down from the stool she'd parked herself on in my shed and stalked over to the wood I'd just cut. Bending down, she picked up a strip and waved it at me.

"This one goes *there*. The one you have belongs on the other drawer."

I frowned, glancing between the trim in my hand and the one in hers. *Dammit.* She was right. If I'd nailed the wrong piece, I would've set myself back even further on a project that was already running late.

"You're right, kid. Thanks for looking out."

Dropping the trim and my nail gun on my workbench, I blew out a heavy breath and swiped my forehead with my forearm. When I turned back, Hailey stood with her hands on her hips, her sharp gaze locked onto me.

"What gives?" she demanded.

"What do you mean?"

She gestured wildly around the shed. "This place is kind of a mess. *You're* kind of a mess. Last weekend, you were focused. Now, you're all over the place. What gives?"

Linda had dropped Hailey off again today, same as last weekend. She'd wanted to see more of my carpentry projects, and I figured having an assistant wouldn't hurt. The difference was, last time, I'd had my head on straight. Now? My thoughts were scattered to the winds.

More specifically, they were on the Kelly Ranch and how badly I was screwing up by not being there. Phoebe had gracefully accepted me turning her down, but I'd have to be blind not to notice she had been disappointed.

When we'd parted this morning, she'd told me she'd probably be home late. And it was there between us, the divide I'd caused—space that hadn't been there before.

It worried me.

No, it was consuming my brain.

Where Phoebe was concerned, space was my enemy. We were close, tight—hell, we slept joined together.

"I've got some things on my mind," I said.

"Like what?"

My brows pulled together as I looked at her. One trait she shared with Richie was her sheer determination. She did not back down when she wanted something, and I saw from the stubborn tilt of her chin she'd latched onto *this* and wouldn't let go until I answered her.

Propping myself on my workbench, I exhaled a long breath. "The Kellys are having an engagement party for Hannah and Remi today."

"Okay...so what's the problem?"

"I'm not going."

Her jaw dropped. "They didn't *invite* you?"

I hesitated, and her eyes flared. "They did."

"*What?*" she cried. "Why are you here instead of putting on your fanciest jeans and getting your butt to the ranch?"

"It's complicated, buddy." My sister didn't need to know the ins and outs of what went on inside my head. Hell, I didn't even want to know.

Hailey threw her arms out wide. "This doesn't make sense, Deke. Clearly you're upset not to be with Phoebe, and I *know* Phoebe wants you with her. I mean, I've seen you guys together. It's like little lovebirds tweet around your head. It's sort of gross but pretty cute and *obviously* true love. So, why in the heck are you here and not there?"

I folded my arms and looked at her. Her freckles were almost glowing from how pink her cheeks had gotten. I didn't want her disappointed in me, and I didn't know how to explain without letting her down. There was no way I was getting out of this without giving her *something*.

"This relationship business is new to me, buddy, but it seems like taking part in a big family event is a huge milestone." That was the truth, but only a sliver of it.

And Hailey wasn't buying it. Her eyes narrowed into slits. "Come on, Deke. If you were invited, that means you're supposed to be there."

"I'm hanging with you." The tips of my fingers dug into my ribs. "There will be other events for me to go to."

"You could have canceled on me. I would have understood." She slowly shook her head. "I don't believe you're telling me the whole truth. Do you think I'm a little kid who can't handle knowing everything? I'm not. I probably have more relationship experience than you do."

"*What*?" That had me standing straight. "The Spellmans let you date?"

"Well, '*let*' isn't the word I would use. But what they don't know won't hurt them, and they *really* don't know I had two boyfriends freshman year and went to homecoming with Kyle Thomas this year." She waved that bomb off like it was nothing. "I'm taking a break from boys for a while, though. They're all pretty dumb. I just didn't realize you were one of them. My own brother, *pfft*."

"Two boyfriends and Kyle Thomas at homecoming?"

She flicked her hand again. "Not important. The point is, you're being dumb by not being there for your girlfriend. Don't you think she wants a guy who's going to be there when it's important? Are you *trying* to get her to dump you?"

I jerked hard. If my worktable hadn't been behind me, I would have staggered back.

"I don't—" I shook my head, clearing the fog. "I'm not trying for that. When it comes time for her to end it, it won't be because I wanted it. She'll realize—"

I cut myself off before I said something that couldn't be taken back. I wasn't about to tell my sister it was the blood in my veins, my last name, my history. Besides, the more I went over that list in my head, the less it made sense. Being in this shed while Phoebe was on the other side of town without me was nonsensical.

My sister was too damn smart for her own good.

"You think Phoebe's going to end it with you? Like, it's a sure thing?" she asked.

I lowered my chin in the affirmative. In my mind, it was a foregone conclusion.

"Because...why? Does this have to do with the Kellys being rich or something? If it does, you're just as bad as all the people who give us a hard time for being Slaters."

My shoulders bunched. "People give you a hard time?"

She rolled her eyes. "Oh my god, of course they do. That's why I used the Spellmans' last name on my job applications. But that doesn't matter right now. You know what Phoebe said when she found out? She said she knows the town can be close-minded, but she'd never be one of them. And guess what, Deke? *You're* being one of them!"

"I love you, buddy, but you don't know what you're talking about." Although some of what she was saying rang true. "I haven't even told you why I'm not at the ranch. Like I said, it's complicated. I have a past that doesn't exactly make me the kind of man parents want their daughter to end up with."

"I'm not stupid. I can see you love Phoebe and kind of worship the ground she walks on. The only reason I think you believe she'd be doing the dumping is because you think you're not good enough for her. *She* doesn't think that. That's all you, being a close-minded dummy."

I chuffed. "Tell me what you really think."

"Fine, I will." She threw her arms out wide. "Phoebe and her family know you're a Slater. They know you went to prison, and you were *still* invited to their party. What else are they going to find out about you that will make them turn their backs? Come on, Deke, use some critical thinking skills here."

I pinched the bridge of my nose. "Critical thinking skills?"

"Yeah. Mr. Rosen, my English teacher, is always telling us that. Analyze the story and use the information we've been given to formulate our thesis. We're not to put our own thoughts and feelings into it. You're using selective perception to jump to a false conclusion. Mr. Rosen would not be impressed with you, Deke. In fact, he'd give you an *F*."

Dropping my hand, I stared at my sister, both impressed and horrified. She'd clearly been paying attention in school, had taken those skills she'd learned and used them against me. Appreciated that. But damn if she wasn't right. That was all there was to it.

Phoebe knew all the bad about me. No doubt her family did too. She'd known it going in, and she still wanted me. She showed it in her unabashed joy every time I walked into Sugar Rush. Her constant curiosity about every detail of my life. Warm hugs. Sweet kisses. Her cooking, sharing her interests and wanting to be a part of mine. Her quiet, easy acceptance of my ongoing struggles with my past.

Yet, with all the acceptance she'd given me, I'd still assigned her this unearned judgment when it was me being the judgmental one.

If I kept my head stuck in my ass, losing her would be a self-fulfilling prophecy.

God knew that was the last thing I wanted to happen.

So, what was I doing here when she was all the way out at the ranch?

"What am I doing?" I uttered.

Hailey *hmphed*. "That's what I've been asking!"

I straightened and slid my phone from my pocket, handing it to her. "Call Linda. Make sure it's okay that you come with me to the ranch."

Hailey squealed. "I'm on it." Then she stopped and looked me up and down. "You're not going like that, are you?"

I didn't have to look at myself to know I was a mess. "Nope. Going to do like my wise sister said and change into my best jeans."

I just had to hope I wasn't too late.

Chapter Thirty-six

Phoebe

HANNAH'S SMALL ENGAGEMENT DINNER had turned into a medium-sized party. Fortunately, Hannah was no wallflower, so she didn't mind having a bigger crowd to show off her ring to, and Remi...well, he liked whatever made Hannah happy.

Thirty or forty people milled around my grandparents' kitchen and expansive back patio, chatting and drinking champagne. It was easy for my mother to use the resort's resources to arrange for the flower sprays around the home, catering, and event staff. There wasn't much for me to do, but I found ways to keep myself busy anyway. I'd baked sweets and made continuous rounds, ensuring trays were filled.

I had to stay busy, or I'd get sad, and I refused to be sad while celebrating my sister's happiness. Maybe tomorrow, I'd indulge a little—definitely not tonight.

Not even when my parents masked their disappointment when I'd shown up alone.

Really not when I'd put on a cheery smile and explained again and again Deacon had something he couldn't possibly get out of but had sent his congratulations.

Margot cornered me in the kitchen as I piled fresh cookies on a tray that had been picked over. I hadn't seen her since the night we'd run into each other at Joy's, but from her smeared lipstick and the smirk her cowboy had given her before he'd walked away, things were still going well between them.

"Hey, Phe. Mind if I steal a cookie?" She perched on one of the stools on the other side of the massive marble island from me.

I pushed the tray toward her. "Go right ahead. I thought I'd overbaked for tonight, but the rate these things are going, maybe it's the opposite."

She bit into a warm cookie and moaned. "My goodness, darling. Somehow, your food keeps getting better. I don't think you're going to have to worry about leftovers."

I smiled, trying to feel it. "Let's hope. If there are, I'll send them home with Hannah and Remi." I winked. "Do you think I can call it my engagement present, or is that too gauche?"

She snorted a laugh and stole another cookie. "You've made all the desserts for their party. I'm quite sure that's going above and beyond the call of duty." She angled herself closer and dropped her voice. "Now, where is that handsome man of yours? I was looking forward to seeing you two together again."

My stomach dropped like an anvil. It had done that each and every time I'd been asked that question tonight. I had always been comfortable being on my own, and I would have been fine now if I was able to share a true, valid reason Deacon wasn't with me, but I didn't have one. Oh, he'd given me excuses, and I'd tried my hardest to believe him, but I'd never been great at lying to myself. If he'd wanted to be here, he would have found a way.

His absence spoke a thousand words without him even opening his mouth.

I was all in with this man, and it seemed he was keeping one foot out the door. When we were together, it felt like we were building a future. I'd thought he was on the same page, but now, I wasn't sure.

Not sure at all.

Margot raised an eyebrow, and I realized I hadn't answered her. "Oh...well, he's—"

She perked up, focusing on something over my shoulder. "There he is, and even more handsome than I remembered."

I whirled around, and my lungs seized at the sight of Deacon prowling toward me with Hailey nipping at his heels. He didn't stop until he reached me, slid his arm around me, and gently pulled me against him. Dropping his chin, he murmured, "I'm sorry I'm late, sugar," then firmly pressed his lips to mine, not letting go until my heart thundered in my ears and my fingers curled into his button-down.

Only then did he pull back, his eyes darting between mine. "I'm sorry, Phoebe," he whispered.

I nodded, forgiving him in an instant. "You're here. That's what matters," I whispered in return.

Then it registered he was wearing a button-down. I pulled back to look at him. Starched dress shirt, dark blue jeans, and cowboy boots—I hadn't known he'd owned clothes like these, let alone had seen him wearing them. "Wow, you're handsome."

His mouth quirked. "Trying to keep up with my gorgeous girl." He took a long, slow perusal of me. My dress was flowy until it hit my waist, where it nipped in nicely, and the square neckline dipped low enough to show the rounded tops of my breasts. Finally, his eyes claimed mine again, vivid with appreciation. "Love you in pink, Phoebe."

"And I just love you." In my relief and excitement at his presence, seeing him all dressed up for the occasion, the words just tumbled out. I meant them, but I hadn't intended to say them at this moment.

Deacon blinked at me. "Phoebe, I—"

"Phoebe!" Hailey cried, launching herself at me. She wrapped her arms around me from the side, her head hitting my shoulder. "This place is crazy. Did you really grow up here?"

Laughing, I let go of Deacon's shirt to hug his sister. "This is my grandparents' house. Mine is down the road. You'll have to come back during the sunlight hours, and I'll take you on a tour. I'm still trying to get Deacon on a horse. Maybe we can make a day of it."

Margot chittered and pressed her hands together beneath her chin. "Oh my, you must get that man of yours on horseback. There aren't too many things sexier than a cowboy."

Hailey wrinkled her nose. "Wow, I don't want to think about my brother being sexy."

That made Margot laugh. "You're a doll." Then she held her hand out to Hailey. "Want to come with me? I'll show you where the good food is, and we can let these two have a moment."

Deacon's gaze bored into the side of my face as I watched them go. When we were alone, he jerked me against him, putting his mouth to my ear.

"Is there somewhere we can be alone?"

My heart skipped a few beats. "There is." I took his hand. "I'll show you."

His hand was tight around mine as he followed me through the house. Most people were outside, so we were able to avoid being seen.

I led him into the attached garage and flicked on the lights. My grandad was serious about his vehicles and workshop. His garage was more of a showroom and body shop with six parking spots, a lift, and every tool anyone could possibly need stored neatly in gleaming red cabinets.

There was also no reason anyone would come out here during the party.

My breath caught at the sound of the door closing and the lock clicking into place. I spun around to face Deacon, his hand still gripping mine. His brow furrowed over an intense gaze so heavy it felt like a weight pressing into me.

"Hi," I whispered.

He tugged me closer, his free hand carving into the back of my hair. "Say it again."

I knew what he wanted, but my mouth was suddenly dry, and those three words weren't as slippery as they'd been a few minutes ago.

Lowering his forehead to mine, he pleaded, "Please, sugar. Tell me."

My lashes fluttered until they stayed up, and my eyes focused on his. "I love you."

His exhale was a blast of such sweet relief it was staggering. "I almost didn't show tonight."

"I know."

"And you still love me."

"You're here."

"I'm screwed up."

I didn't believe that. But he did, and that was what mattered. His wounds wouldn't heal overnight, but I'd keep loving him until he saw himself the way I did—a beautiful man who had overcome circumstances that might've broken someone with less grit.

"As long as you show up, we'll figure it out," I promised. I'd hold on until he had no choice but to believe he wasn't the sum of his past.

"Phoebe," he croaked, "how are you mine?"

"It's just the way it is, Deacon." I touched my lips to his. "Okay?"

"Yeah, okay." His fingers in my hair balled into a fist. "You have to know I love you too, angel."

Then his mouth was on mine, and there was nothing soft about it. He kissed me like he'd been away for years, yearning for me. Deep, hard, searching, he found every corner of my mouth and laved it with his tongue. He *loved* me, and he was showing me just how much he meant it.

His hands were all over me, moving with more freedom than he'd ever allowed himself to have. He didn't stop to ask permission before he shoved my bodice under my breasts and pulled my nipple into his mouth. Nor did he ask if he could explore beneath my skirt. He helped himself to all my softest parts as he kissed me into oblivion.

Something had shifted between us. A wall had been knocked down, and we were touching each other in a way we never had. I'd never been shy with him, but I *had* been careful. Now, all I wanted was to show him how much I loved him in every way I could.

I yanked his shirt free from his pants to get my hands on his smooth abdomen and the long, taut planes of his back. Then I dipped inside his waistband, cupping his ass and pulling him as close as we could be in this position. It wasn't enough, so I tugged at his hair, bringing his mouth back to mine.

Our kisses were messy and urgent. Our touches were bordering on desperate. He hiked my skirt up to my waist, and his fingers were inside my panties, sliding through my folds and over my clit. I shuddered as he caressed me there and latched onto my throat with his warm lips.

"Deacon," I cried softly. "I love you."

He sucked harder, groaning against my skin, rocking his thick erection into my stomach.

"I didn't intend for this," he murmured into my throat. "This isn't why I wanted to be alone with you."

"I don't care about intentions. I need you."

"Now?" he asked thickly.

I nodded vigorously, my nails digging into his chest. "Right now."

He walked me back until I collided with the wall and my breath whooshed out of me. Then he hooked his hand under my knee, lifting until he could prop my foot on a stool. He cupped between my spread thighs, dipping two fingers inside me. I was so soaked and needy. When the heel of his hand rubbed against my clit, I jerked and moaned.

"Yes, yes!" My head fell back, and I rode his hand as he thrust and ground exactly where I needed him. "Keep going, just like that."

From beneath heavy lids, I watched him pleasure me. His gaze roamed over my body, pausing for long beats on his fingers disappearing inside me. The way he looked at me turned me on to the point where it was impossible to hold back a second longer. His eyes came to meet mine at the last second, so heated they were the spark I needed to explode. Writhing and wild, I grasped at his shoulders so I wouldn't fall—not that he'd ever let that happen.

My orgasm had barely crested when Deacon slipped his fingers from my body, stepped between my legs, and drove into me—hard and deep. Raw nerves were set alight as he fucked me into the wall, and I continued coming around him, rasping my pleasure uncontrollably.

He covered my mouth with his, muffling the wild noises I was making, and I wrapped my arms around his shoulders. Our bodies were aligned, chest to chest, belly to belly, toe to toe. He kissed me like a tidal wave and fucked me like a tornado, leveling me to the ground. Consuming all in his path and leaving his mark forevermore. Even as it was happening, I felt changed and made over. I knew I'd never had anything like this before. This connection, this deep bond...it was something Deacon and I had formed, and it belonged solely to us. Special, hot, loving, and unbreakable, so long as we tended it.

"I love you," I uttered, shaky and thick, as he bounced me on his cock.

"Love you more," he gritted out, his gaze burning into mine. "I'm all yours."

"Oh, thank god." I took his face in my hands, memorizing exactly what my man looked like when he gave himself to me.

He indulged me for a few seconds before shaking free so he could claim my mouth again. That was where he stayed as his thrusts increased, faster, harder, our skin slapping each time we collided. My inner walls were swollen, gripping his sliding length to pull him deeper. There was no getting enough of him. I had him, and still, I wanted more.

He hooked his arm beneath my bent knee, lifting my foot from the stool to open me wider, then planted himself solidly inside me, stealing my breath. Shoving, grinding, he hit my clit so perfectly, I was struck with another teeth-rattling orgasm. Quivering in his arms, I held on tight, trusting him to keep me from falling apart.

His groan echoed in my brain, heart, lungs, and chest. It was so visceral and unleashed. He thrust through my climax, making his way beyond my flexing muscles to my farthest depths. With his mouth on mine, his hand on my ass, the other on my thigh, he went still except for the hot pulsing inside me, filling me to the very brim.

When it was over and our bodies began to relax, he placed my foot back on the stool and pulled back enough to look me over. His brow was pinched with worry, and his pink, puffy lips rolled into a flat line.

"Are you okay?"

Okay was such a silly word to describe what I was. So silly my mouth curved into a goofy smile, and I giggled softly.

"Oh yeah, I'm okay," I replied. "Don't I look it?"

He cocked his head, his concern giving way to something more amused. His fingers skimmed my throat, trailing down to my collarbone then tracing lightly over my chest.

"You're all red from my scruff and mouth."

I pressed my thumb to his bottom lip, feeling the heat still lingering there. "And you're red from how hard I kissed you."

He nipped at my thumb. "How am I gonna take you back out there with all your family?"

My grin widened. "We should probably clean up before we do that."

He cradled my face with both hands, his gaze locked on mine. After a moment, he released a long exhale. "You mean it, don't you? You love me."

"I do, honey." I curled my fingers around his wrists, the rapid flutter of his pulse beneath my touch. "I mean it, and I couldn't be happier that you came here for me."

He chuffed. "Just had to get my head out of my ass. Hailey did a lot of the dragging."

"We can talk about what was keeping you away later. For now, I'd like to go celebrate my sister, and I want you with me."

"I'm all in," he vowed.

Finally.

Chapter Thirty-seven

Deacon

I WAS AN IDIOT. That was all there was to it.

There was nothing intimidating about the night. Hell, Hannah and Remi had all the attention—and rightly so. I just had to hang with my girl and sister, and everything was right as rain.

Phoebe's grandad grilled chicken, and the rest of the food was catered by the resort. Her mom had made it a point to stop by and tell me all of it was safe for me to eat.

I shook the hands of her brothers, dad, and grandad, was introduced as her boyfriend to people I'd never met and got ordered by her grandmother to sit down and take a load off since Phoebe had told everyone I'd been working all day.

I could almost forget this family was richer than I'd ever be able to imagine if not for the uniformed waitstaff and view of the land they owned as far as the eye could see. They were down to earth, the food wasn't anything fancy, and the conversation centered around either Hannah and Remi's wedding or ranch business. The same things regular folks probably talked about at events like this.

Hailey was eating it all up. She'd made friends with Margot, the woman I'd met briefly at Joy's a month or so ago. Margot had taken Hailey right under her wing, plying her with food and introducing her to every single person in attendance. Then she invited my sister to a spa day—on her. And I was pretty sure Hailey's head almost exploded.

Phoebe and I were on one end of an outdoor sectional. My arm was curled around her shoulders, hers draped across my lap. Comfortable, close, no space between us—exactly as we should've been.

I tipped my chin, lowering my voice. "Is everyone who works at the resort as nice as Margot?"

She laughed. "No. She's an exception. She and my mom became fast friends because they're both into fashion and all things designer. It's tough being glamorous on a ranch, but they find a way. I'm sure Margot wouldn't mind recruiting Hailey as part of their glam squad. There's strength in numbers, you know."

Scanning the massive patio, I found Hailey tucked between Elena and Margot, looking happy as a clam, and blew out a heavy breath.

"Last time I spent time with her, she was a little kid. I'm not ready for my sister to be glamorous."

She giggled softly. "Don't worry. My mother has two daughters who didn't inherit her sense of fashion. She won't push anything on Hailey she doesn't want."

I rubbed the back of my neck and frowned. "Yeah, not sure that makes me feel much better, seeing as Hailey's got stars in her eyes right about now."

Phoebe's nephew, Jesse, plopped down on the opposite side of her, and she leaned over to ruffle his hair.

"Hey, dude. Where'd you come from?"

He pointed his thumb over his shoulder. "Did you know the cookie tray is empty?"

She nodded. "I noticed. I refilled it three times. Everyone cleaned me out."

He scrunched his nose. "I only had two chocolate chip cookies. Dad says that's enough, but I beg to differ. I asked him how many he ate, and he wouldn't answer, which tells me it was a lot more than two."

Phoebe snickered. "You're probably right about that. But...did you think I'd bake all those cookies and not set a few aside for my favorite nephew?"

He bounced in his seat. "You did? Where are they?"

"I stuck them in your backpack. They're all yours to take home with you."

He threw himself at her, and she had to let go of my leg to return his hug. It was only when he was right next to me he noticed I was beside his aunt.

He straightened, looking me over with narrowed eyes. "Hey. I'm Jesse."

I nodded. "Nice to meet you. I'm Deke."

"I know who you are. You were in prison," he stated, as blunt as a bat to the head.

"That's true."

Phoebe knocked his knee. "That isn't *who* he is. That's something he went through. Deacon is a carpenter, a big brother, and my boyfriend."

I squeezed her hand. "It's all right."

Jesse folded his arms across his bony chest. "I know that, Aunt Phoebe. I didn't mean it in a bad way. It's like if you met me and said, 'I know you. You're the kid who's allergic to peanuts.'"

"I'm allergic to peanuts too," I informed him.

"Whoa." He let his arms fall. "It sucks, right?"

I nodded. "Yep. Good thing your family is careful about it. Means I get to eat delicious food whenever Phoebe cooks for me or brings home leftovers."

"Yeah, we're lucky." He pushed his glasses up his nose. "I can't eat school lunch. It's probably terrible, but one day, I'd like to eat pizza on Fridays. Just out of curiosity."

"Believe me, I get it. I was on the free lunch program when I was in school, and all they had for me was prepackaged cheese and crackers. I eyeballed that pizza more times than I can count."

He took that in, gearing up with more questions. Before he could get any out of his mouth, Caleb sat down beside him, placing his big hand on top of his son's head.

"Looks like an interesting conversation happening over here."

Jesse twisted toward his dad. "Did you know Deke has food allergies like me?"

Caleb raised a brow. "I hadn't heard that." He lifted his chin at me. "Sucks big-time, huh?"

My mouth quirked. "That's what Jesse and I were just discussing."

Jesse leaned forward. "What'd you eat in prison?"

Caleb made a gurgling sound. "Kid, come on."

I waved him off. "No, it's all right. Believe it or not, that was one of Phoebe's early questions."

She pressed a hand to her cheek. "Oh god. It was, wasn't it? I'm as bad as an eleven-year-old."

I shrugged. "I didn't mind then, and I don't mind now." I gave Jesse the sanitized story I'd given Phoebe, leaving out the time I'd nearly died. I figured this kid had enough to worry about without adding my trauma to it.

Jesse was on the edge of his seat, his elbow on his knees, chin resting on his fists. "So what was prison really like? I've seen documentaries—"

"What documentaries?" Caleb barked.

Jesse grinned at him. "Educational, age-appropriate documentaries. Ms. Clark, at the library, helped me find them."

Caleb rumbled. "Maybe I need to have a talk with this librarian about the type of material she's showing you."

He threw his hands up. "It's age appropriate, promise."

Hailey approached, stealing Jesse's attention. His cheeks turned bright red when she waved at us and introduced herself. Caleb greeted her, but Jesse clammed up. I got the sense his going quiet wasn't a common occurrence.

Beside me, Phoebe giggled. I looked at her, and she mouthed, "Jesse has a crush."

Oh shit. That was what this was, wasn't it?

I wasn't ready for this either. Even if he *was* only eleven.

Hailey perched on the arm of the sectional. "So, what are you guys talking about?"

"Prison," Jesse yelped.

"Oh." Her shoulders fell. "Maybe I should've waited a few minutes for you to finish that conversation."

"Don't worry, kiddo," Caleb said. "We're all done with that topic. I was about to ask your brother what projects he's working on."

From there, things went up. Jesse might not have found woodworking as scintillating, but he got the hint from his dad to cut it out, and he did. I didn't blame him for being curious, nor was I angry, but I was relieved to move on.

Later, after we said good night to everyone and dropped Hailey off at her house, Phoebe and I headed to her apartment. As soon as we were inside, she put her bags down and pressed herself against me, her arms curving around my waist. Mine circled hers without hesitation, holding her tight.

We stayed like that for a long time, holding on to one another in the middle of her living room. Nothing really needed to be said. We'd had a great night after a not-so-good few days. But the not-so-good part was over. My head was out of my ass, and my eyes were wide open.

"You're my girl," I murmured into her hair. "My angel girl."

"You're mine," she said against my shoulder.

"I'm yours," I agreed. "I'm sorry I had a hard time showing it these last few days."

"Thank you for saying that." She pulled her head away to meet my gaze. "When you're having a hard time, you can talk to me about it. I'd rather hear it than be left in the dark."

I nodded. "Richie called me the day Hannah was at Sugar Rush. Hearing from him always puts me in a dark place that's hard to shake off."

"I wish you would have told me that," she whispered.

"I should've. I was dealing with it, but not well. Got in my head and convinced myself if I showed up at Hannah and Remi's party, your family would see me for what I am and want you away from me."

"What you are?"

"Yeah. Unclean. A felon. Not good enough."

Her eyes narrowed. "Only one of those is true, and they don't hold it against you. You have to know that."

"Knowing a fact and taking it to heart are two different things." I sucked in a breath. "I get it now, Phoebe. I was wrong. Hailey told me to use my critical thinking skills, and dammit, the kid was right. You know all the bad I've got behind me, and you're still here. I need to stop questioning it and count my lucky stars."

"That's right, you do." Her hands trailed down my arms, stopping to curl around my wrists. "You're finished with that now, aren't you?"

"I am. I might get dark, but I won't let it keep me from you."

"You better not."

I took her to her bedroom, and we made love, slow and sweet. Sliding over her, into her, holding her face in my hands, whispering I loved her. I said that again and again, and she answered, feeling the same. She loved me too, and she repeated it until the words blended, mine with hers.

After, we lay tangled in her floral sheets and each other. I told her I'd spent most of my life in places made of concrete and sharp edges—not just in prison but long before. Now, I was learning to live with comfort and softness, with sugary kisses and words as gentle as her touch. It wasn't always easy to believe it was mine—to trust it wouldn't be taken away. My mind knew how to survive in the rough and unforgiving. *This*, her, was so new, I had to rework some of my wiring.

She brushed her fingers through my hair and told me she had all the time in the world. Patience, she'd said, was her strong suit. She'd always been a little whimsical. Had always found magic in places others overlooked. Her hope was that someday, I'd learn to see myself the way she did *"and finally understand why she loved me so."*

I wanted that too.

When we were close to falling asleep, she rolled to her side, and I curved around her. She lifted her nightgown, allowing me to slip inside her. And there it was. The comfort and security she handed to me without question. Giving me her very body to help me fall asleep.

How could I even question if she really loved me?

I couldn't. I didn't. Maybe I didn't understand it, but I knew it to be true. Phoebe Kelly loved me.

"It was a good night," I said on the edge of sleep.

Her fingers threaded through mine, and she sighed. "A really good night, honey."

With my eyes closed, I kissed her shoulder.

Sugar.

Chapter Thirty-eight
Phoebe

I LOVED THE STEADY clap of boots on a worn wooden floor. The air inside the Boots Up Bar was thick with the scent of whiskey and beer, heated bodies, and an underlying trace of sunshine from too many cowboy hats packed in one space. The rhythm of the music blasting through the speakers settled in my bones and stirred my belly.

Tilly and Chris had disappeared onto the dance floor a while ago, but Deacon was still nursing a beer and eyeing the crowd warily. I was itching to move, but I could wait until he was ready.

Coming to Boots Up had been his idea—we'd been supposed to do this a couple months ago, after all—but now that we were here, he didn't seem too sure about actually dancing in public.

Deacon turned to me. "Did I say you look beautiful?"

I grinned. "About a hundred times." I'd never get tired of knowing how much he appreciated the effort I'd put into looking good for him.

He leaned into me, touching his lips to my cheek. "I'm gonna enjoy the hell out of sundress season."

I'd worn my favorite one for him. Red, with little white flowers all over it. It buttoned down the front, and as soon as he'd seen me in it, he'd undone a few to peek beneath.

"I guess it's a good thing I have a collection of them to wear for you."

From the throngs of dancers, Tilly appeared and grabbed my hand. "Come on, girl. If Deke won't dance with you, let me take you for a spin."

I glanced at Deacon. "Do you mind?"

He lifted his chin. "Go. Have fun. But don't wander too far. I don't want to lose you."

"Not a chance of that," I called as Tilly pulled me into the crowd.

The next song kicked in—a fast-paced two-step I could dance in my sleep. Tilly took the lead, holding one of my hands, the other on the center of my back. We weren't smooth since leading didn't exactly come naturally to her, but we found our groove quickly.

I'd danced with girlfriends plenty when we didn't feel like dealing with any of the guys at the bar, and it was always a good time. Tilly and I laughed our way through the first song, then got serious during the second. By the third, she was spinning me like a professional.

We were both sweaty and having a grand ol' time when two guys in black Stetsons got in our space.

"Looks like you ladies could use some real partners," one called over the music.

"Lucky for you, we're available," the other one said around a jaw full of chew.

"No thanks. We're good," Tilly stated, spinning us away from them.

Of course they didn't get the hint. The one who smelled like rotten tobacco put his hand on my shoulder, trying to pry me away from Tilly.

I turned my head to glare at him. "No, thank you. Neither of us wants to dance with you."

He yanked his hand away and raised his brows like he was surprised at how firm I was being. "Hey, no harm meant, darlin'. No need to get all snappy."

Before I could tell him not to call me darlin', an arm slid around my middle, and Chris appeared behind Tilly.

"There a problem here?" Deacon asked, tugging me back into his chest.

Chris glowered at the cowboys. "These women told you they're not interested. That should've been the end of it."

The first guy tipped his hat. "We're just looking for dance partners, not a fight. But a tip for you: you don't want other men trying to dance with your lady; you need to be out on the dance floor with them."

The black-hatted men wandered off, looking for other women to dance with, and Chris pulled Tilly into his arms, taking back the lead.

I turned around to face Deacon. "Thanks for the rescue. We would've been fine, though."

He took my hand in one of his, and the other claimed my waist. "I'm sure you would've, but that guy had a point. I don't want other men dancing with my lady, so I need to be out here with her."

"Are you going to dance with me, Deacon Slater?"

He lowered his forehead to mine. "I can't guarantee I'll be as good a partner as Tilly, but I'm gonna try."

His first steps were hesitant and unsure, but as he led me, and neither of us stumbled, he began to relax, beat by beat.

"You're doing it, honey," I encouraged, flashing him a smile. "This isn't so bad, is it?"

"I feel like I'm about to step on your feet."

"Don't worry. I've got my boots on. I can take it." I tapped the toe of my boot against his, and his answering grin gave me that swoopy feeling in my stomach. This man...god, did I have the biggest crush on him.

The next song picked up, and so did we, spinning and swaying across the floor. And for just a little while, everything around us faded away until it was just the two of us. No rules or worrying about hitting the rhythm just right. If he stepped on my toes, I barely noticed. Deacon set aside his insecurity to have fun with me the way I loved. My hand tucked in his, I was happier than I remembered being in a long time—and I'd been pretty damn happy lately.

When the music slowed again, he pulled me close. I turned my head and softly sang along with the love song, humming through the lyrics I didn't know. His hand flexed on my back, and he rubbed his scruff against my cheek.

"*I got you,*" I sang. "*Down to the lowest and all the times in between. I got you, hope you know it's you and me 'til the end. I got you...*"

His breath was hot on my neck. Then his lips scorched my skin as he kissed a line from my ear lobe to my collarbone. He held me so tight we were barely swaying. I kept singing words that weren't mine, but the sentiment I shared and felt deeply. I knew he was feeling it right along with me. Deacon made no bones about showing me how much he loved and adored me. Always reaching for me, caring for me, telling me when he appreciated something I did, saying the words often and unabashedly.

When the song ended and the next kicked back up, I lifted my head and smiled. "I could use a beer."

"Then you'll have a beer," he replied.

Tilly and Chris were at our high-top table, their heads tilted toward one another. From their puppy-dog expressions, I wondered how long they'd been watching us. Probably a while.

"I knew you'd enjoy yourself," Chris announced. "Nothing better than dancing with your woman."

Tilly giggled. "Well, I can think of one or two things that are better."

Chris winked at his wife. "Hell yeah, and those are pretty much guaranteed to happen after a night out dancing."

They were seriously the cutest couple. I loved how mismatched they seemed yet how actually perfect they were for one another. More than that, I loved how much they cared for Deacon.

"Agreed on all points," Deacon said, pulling me into his side and kissing my temple. "As always, once I got my head out of my ass, I started having a good time."

"It's almost like those cowboys were paid actors with the sole job of getting you out on the dance floor," I said.

His fingers dug into my hip. Not painfully, but hard enough to catch my attention. He didn't like thinking about those guys talking to us—to me. That message was loud and clear.

"They're lucky they backed off." Chris grinned. "I swear, my man vaulted over a few people to get to you, Phoebe. I've never seen him move that fast."

Deacon's chin lowered. "Funny, I seem to remember you sprinting right next to me."

Chris shrugged. "I'm a jealous beast; what can I say? Till can dance her little heart out with her girlfriends, but the day she said yes to being my girl, I became the only guy who'll lead her around the dance floor."

"It's true." Tilly put her head on Chris's big shoulder. "I willingly married a caveman."

I turned to Deacon. "I'm sorry to tell you, I can't promise never to dance with other men." His brow dropped in an instant, so I decided not to tease him for long. "I can't pass up a dance with my father and, occasionally, one of my brothers."

He exhaled, and after a beat, the corner of his mouth lifted. "I think I can handle that."

Tilly reached across the table to swat my arm. "I hear your sister's getting married. Tell me about it."

"Oh boy." Hannah wasn't a bridezilla, but she wanted what she wanted, and it was driving our mother a little batty. "She and Remi don't want to wait to get married. They've been engaged for three weeks and decided on a September wedding at the ranch."

Tilly's eyes widened. "Next September?"

"No, the one three months away," I replied.

Deacon chuckled. "Elena's making it happen, come hell or high water."

Poor Deacon had been invited with me to my family's house for brunch, which had turned into a surprise wedding planning meeting. He'd watched the whole thing, his expression shell-shocked when my mother brought out the giant wedding binder.

My father had patted him on the shoulder and said, *"Just let it happen, son. All you have to do is show up in a suit when it's your day."*

We moved on to other topics, laughing, drinking, then dancing the night away. Well…Deacon didn't do much more drinking since he was driving, but he seemed to be having just as much fun as the rest of us.

When Tilly and I needed a bathroom break, he followed us, waiting in the hallway while Chris held the table. We didn't really need an escort, but if it made him feel better, I wasn't going to tell him not to do it.

Tilly and I did our business and met by the sinks. Catching my eye in the mirror, she smiled.

"Things work out how they're supposed to, huh?"

"Yeah," I sighed. "Sometimes you have to get past all the bad stuff in the beginning to make it to the good."

We were still chatting as we stepped into the hallway. People milled around us, making it hard to see ahead. We pushed through, and it wasn't until we were almost upon Deacon I realized he wasn't alone.

The brunette looked vaguely familiar, but the shock of red hair on the man facing him made my stomach drop. Even with his back turned, Richie Slater was impossible to mistake.

Deacon saw me and, just like he had months ago, gave a subtle shake of his head. The message to stay away was clear. Unfortunately, Tilly hadn't picked up on it. She strode forward, sidling up beside Deacon with an easy grin.

"Hey, Deke." She gave his shoulder a playful punch. "Phoebe and I are itching for another swing around the dance floor before we take off."

I hovered two feet away, watching it all go down. Richie turned to Tilly first. She went stiff as a board, finally realizing who Deacon had been talking to. Then he swiveled toward Deacon, his gaze flicking past his brother, landing on me. The moment recognition set in, a slow, bone-chilling grin stretched across Richie's face.

"*Phoebe Kelly*," he called. "Don't be a stranger. Come over here, girl."

We *were* basically strangers, and though I would've rather kept it that way, I unglued my feet and trudged forward.

"Hey, Richie," I said.

The woman hanging on his arm waved. "Hi. I'm Jennifer, Richie's girlfriend."

Like she wasn't even there, his eyes dragged over me, lingering far too long on my chest before meeting my eyes. He waggled his eyebrows. "Damn. You've grown up, haven't you?"

I kept the nausea out of my expression as best I could. "We haven't seen each other in years. That's how time works."

Richie rubbed his chin, something devious going on behind his unnaturally bright eyes. "I don't know about that. Saw you in Laramie a couple months ago when I was out with Deke. I'm not much of a betting man, but I'd say the odds of you *happening* to show up where Deke is twice are pretty damn low." His gaze bounced between us, sharp as a razor's edge. "So... are you two *together*?"

Deacon immediately stepped in front of me. "That's enough. I told you I'm not gonna do it, Rich. That's all there is to it. I'm not interested in continuing this conversation with you, and you have nothing to say to Phoebe."

Jennifer frowned. "Let's calm down. There's no need for anyone getting mad."

Richie's grin became maniacal. "Whoa, you *are* together," he said, completely ignoring his girlfriend. "Congrats on landing a Kelly. I didn't know you had it in you."

"Fuck off," Deacon gritted out. Grabbing my hand and planting his other on Tilly's shoulder, he steered us away from his brother without another word.

We barely made it a few steps before Richie threw out one last parting shot.

"You might want to rethink that answer, little brother. Think *real, real* hard."

Deacon didn't flinch, and his stride hadn't faltered, though his grip on me tightened as he guided us straight to Chris, who was already standing at alert.

"Did I see Richie?"

"Yep." Deacon handed Tilly off to Chris and pulled me deeper into his side. I didn't know what exactly was going on, but tension radiated off him like summer heat on pavement. "It's time to go."

I didn't care about the night being cut short or running into Richie. I cared about the shutters that had gone down over Deacon's eyes. He'd locked himself down, and I had no idea how to find the key.

All I could do was trust he'd open back up to me.

Chapter Thirty-nine

Deacon

THE URGE TO CUT and run was strong.

But my need to be the man Phoebe deserved was even stronger. That meant staying and dealing with my problems, not shutting down or wallowing.

I sat on the end of Phoebe's bed, my head heavy in my hands. She was behind me, cheek resting on the center of my back, arms wrapped around me, holding me without a word, letting me be quiet.

I knew I needed to talk to her about this. Keeping it locked up meant shutting her out, and I couldn't do that. Not to her.

I needed my soft, pink woman close.

"I'm sorry," I forced out.

"You have nothing to be sorry for."

I lifted her hand to my mouth, brushing my lips against her knuckles. "The night got ruined."

"No, it didn't." She climbed off the bed, circling around me. Kneeling between my knees, she cupped my neck, grounding me. "We went dancing, Deke. You held me close and swung me around until I was dizzy. I got to know Chris and Tilly better and see you with your bestie bro."

I huffed a laugh. "Can't wait to call Chris my bestie bro."

She smiled. "Well, you are. There's no denying it."

She scooted forward, putting herself firmly in my space, exactly where she belonged.

"Have I told you lately how much I love Hailey? The customers adore her too. I've had more than one stop me to tell me the ways she's gone above and beyond for them. Camille agrees. We wish we could clone her."

I cocked my head, unsure why she was bringing this up now. "She's a good kid."

"Mmmhmm. Your *sister* is a good kid—the girl who shares blood with you."

I sighed, understanding where she was going. "I get what you're saying, baby."

I picked up a lock of her hair, rubbing the silk between my fingers. She was trying her hardest to comfort me, but she had no idea how deep this ran.

If I could've kept it from her, I would have, but we didn't do that. She needed my honesty, so I'd give it to her.

"When Richie called a few weeks ago, he asked a lot of questions about my job. Tonight, he told me he's creating a pipeline of road workers to transport goods and asked if he could stash something in my truck and have me drop it off on my way to Casper."

She jerked back. "*Something*—like...drugs?"

"I wouldn't doubt it. I didn't ask. It's none of my business, and I sure as hell don't plan on becoming a mule for him."

"Then you won't." Her fingers dug into my thighs. "He has no power over you, honey. He can ask you to do dirty deeds until he's blue in the face, but that's all he can do. He has no leverage. Nothing he can say or do will force you to say yes."

"He can come after you." And I would kill him with my bare hands.

"He could...but there's no closing that door now that it's open. He knows we're together. There isn't anything he could tell me about you that would make me stop loving you. And I know he's a complete asshole. It's not like that's any surprise."

I scoffed. "Understatement."

"Yeah..." She leaned forward, brushing her cheek against mine. "I think we shouldn't go looking for trouble. We'll take things as they come. And we'll do it together. You're not alone anymore, and you don't need to shoulder this on your own. I'm here. You've got Chris, Tilly, and Joy. Not to mention, my family would have your back if you needed it."

I took her face in my hands, angling it back so I could look her over. Serene as ever, she let me see her, meeting my gaze without shields. She meant what she'd said, and her sound logic was enough to knock down the flimsy walls I'd been subconsciously building.

"You stick with me; this might be something I'm dealing with for a good many years," I warned.

"I'm sticking with you." She did not hesitate. "*We're* dealing with it."

"Jesus, Phoebe." I wrapped my arms around her so tight her breath whooshed out of her, but she returned my embrace just as fiercely. "I love you so damn much, sugar. Don't know how I got this lucky, but I'm not giving you up. Not for anything."

"I'm not going anywhere. Never, ever."

Her mouth latched onto my neck, pressing hot kisses and soft suckles along my tense muscles. "Deke," she murmured into my skin. "I love you."

My hand in the back of her hair, I took her mouth in a hard, needy kiss. Our teeth clashed, tongues tangled. It wasn't enough. I needed her. God, did I need her.

She ripped her mouth from mine, panting as she shoved my shirt up. I helped her, yanking it over my head, then she went for the waist of my jeans, unbuttoning them and yanking down the fly before I could grasp what she was doing.

"Phoebe, I—"

Her hand slid into my briefs and wrapped around my cock. I was already rock hard—hell, all it took was one look from her and blood rushed below my waist. She pumped me a few times, pulling me free from my underwear, then dove down, wrapping her sweet lips around the head.

So good. My fingers slid into the sides of her hair, pulling it away from her face so I could watch her. Her eyes were closed, long lashes brushing her rosy cheeks. And those lips, pink and plump, stretched around me, working their way up and down my length. She was gorgeous, always, but damn, when she lost herself in giving me pleasure, I could barely look at her; she was so stunning.

I had no idea what I'd done to deserve to be loved this well, but I had every intention of giving it back to her tenfold.

"My beautiful angel girl," I rasped. "I love watching you sucking me, baby."

She smoothed her palms along my thighs and up my abdomen, humming as she took care of me. Her mouth was hot velvet, and it took all my willpower not to surge up into her.

I trailed my gaze over her, along the line of her arched back, to the flare of her hips and round ass.

"Pull your dress up, sugar. Let me see you."

She reached around, gathering the flowy material to her waist. Lacy boy shorts half covered her cheeks and disappeared between them. I focused on that valley. She'd let me put my tongue there—no place on her body was off-limits to me—and it'd been warm and welcoming.

"Gorgeous, Phe. So fuckin' gorgeous," I rasped.

If she kept going like she was, I'd come before I was ready, and her mouth wasn't where I wanted to finish. Not tonight.

"Baby, I need you to stop."

She sucked harder, wrapping her tongue around my length. If I hadn't been so damn determined to come inside her, I would have succumbed right then and there.

I tucked my fingers under her chin, applying gentle pressure. "It's my turn. Gotta get my mouth on you. Let go."

It took some convincing, but I got her off me and switched places—Phoebe on her hands and knees on the mattress, that pretty ass in the air, me kneeling on the floor. I peeled her panties down her legs and buried my face in her slick cunt and ass, laving her swollen flesh with my tongue and fucking her with my fingers.

She moaned for me, rocking against my touch, begging for more in the sweetest, strained voice. As I plunged my fingers inside her, I felt her get wetter and swell around me. Never imagined I'd be able to feel her like that, knowing I was making it happen, but damn if I didn't love it. And now that I'd learned what set her off, she responded to me like a flick of a switch.

I'd learned a *lot* since she'd allowed me into her life, opening her arms, heart, and body, unmasking my own desires that had been suppressed all my life. Then again, maybe they were specific to her.

No one had ever turned my head the way she did. Before Phoebe, sex had hardly crossed my mind. Now, it was rare for a day to pass without one of us reaching for the other...usually more than once.

She was the key. The only one who fits.

I coaxed a moaning, sheet-clawing orgasm out of her, then climbed to my feet, replacing my fingers with my cock. The moment I was fully seated, my hips flush with her plush backside, we groaned in unison.

"*This is* where I belong." I jerked forward, making her cry out. "Right here."

"Yes, Deke. Right here," she agreed.

I moved slowly, retreating and returning in smooth, deliberate strokes. I watched myself disappear into her, only to emerge slick with her claim coating me, marking me as hers, giving something no one else ever had and never would.

I should have let her go. But I wouldn't. Now that I knew what it was to breathe sugar-laced air and fall asleep with sweetness surrounding me, I couldn't go back. There was no *unknowing* what it meant to be loved by this woman. And I refused to live without her.

Molding my hands around her hips, I held her there, driving into her harder. She answered my call, taking what I gave her, offering herself up for more. Her arm moved between her legs, rubbing her clit the way she liked. It turned me on, watching her give herself pleasure. There was nothing she did that didn't turn me on—especially with her sundress bunched around her waist, lacy panties still wrapped around one leg, and her ass colliding with my pelvis.

"I'm so close," she moaned.

"I'll go when you go," I gritted out, doing my best to hold back. "Wanna feel you, baby. Give it to me."

"Harder. Just a little harder."

I was feeling a little unhinged after everything, so I gave her what we both needed. Her moans grew insistent, frantic, as my fingers dug into her flesh, giving me leverage to plunge deep.

She whined, her neck arched, her inner walls flooded with arousal. "Deacon!"

Yeah, she likes that.

My girl might have looked like the sweetest little cupcake, but she loved getting a little dirty and didn't mind when I left behind a mark or two. With the way I was holding her hips, she'd have more than a couple.

I felt it. The end and beginning. Phoebe clung to me, her body grasping mine as she keened. I didn't even try to resist. I came with her, spilling every ounce of myself into her. Rooted so deep, I'd found new parts of us and claimed them as ours.

We fell together, the mattress bouncing beneath us as I wrapped myself around her back. She twisted her head, our lips connecting in a slow, languid kiss.

For a while, we just lay there, sometimes kissing, sometimes with my cheek resting against hers. My knuckles traced lazy paths down her bare arm, over the curve of her breast. Eventually, we'd have to get up, clean off, and get ready for bed. But I wasn't in any hurry to end this.

"I'm liking sundress season," I murmured.

She turned just enough for me to see her smile. "Told you."

"It's going to be unfortunate when it's over."

She caught my hand, bringing it to her lips to nibble and press soft kisses on my fingers. "No sense in thinking about the ending when it only just began. Besides, if you want me in a sundress, all you have to do is ask."

"Even if it's the middle of January with two feet of snow on the ground?"

"Even then." She kissed the pad of my finger. "It'll just be sundress season in my apartment. I love you a lot, but not enough to wear one in the snow."

Laughing, I pressed my face into her hair. "I love you enough, I'd never ask you to do that."

She sighed, warm and content. "Look at us, Deacon, ending the night laughing in bed. I think that means everything's going to be okay."

"Long as I have you, you might be right."

I sure as hell hoped so.

Chapter Forty

Phoebe

We'd had a good week.

No visits from Richie. No calls. And as the days passed, I noticed changes in Deacon. His shoulders squared a little more, the weight he carried seeming a bit lighter.

I hated that he was burdened by his brother at all but held onto hope that he'd let go over time and Richie would move on.

I understood baggage. His was heavier and had wrecked his life in ways I couldn't even fathom, but I had my little carry-on bag of mistrust. I'd set it down, but it still lingered, always within reach.

Someday, we'd both be free from the chains of our pasts. We were getting there.

We'd spent the evening separately—me with my mother and Hannah, deep in wedding planning trenches, Deke working in the shed and having dinner with Chris and Tilly—but we'd reunited afterward in my apartment.

That was what we did. Deacon slept here every night. It wasn't even a question anymore.

Now we were on my couch, snuggling together. The podcast we were listening to had ended, but neither of us was in a hurry to move. His fingers were in my hair, stroking me into a coma.

He hmphed.

"What?" I asked.

"Just thinking what a waste it was for me to buy that couch."

"Should we hang out at your place so it doesn't get lonely?"

That made him laugh. "Nah, I think it's fine. I prefer your place any day."

"Well, it might not be a waste. If we move into a house and it has a den, we could use yours in there and mine in the living room."

He went so still I lifted my head to see what was going on. His brow was furrowed, and he was looking at me quizzically.

"You'd move into a house with me?"

"Yes. Isn't a house your goal?"

"Down the line, yeah."

"I'd like that too, and it would be silly for us to have two separate houses. If you think buying a couch is a waste, imagine letting your house sit empty while you're spending every night at mine."

His mouth twitched. "What if you spend all your nights at my house?"

I crinkled my nose. "There's no way your house has a better kitchen than mine. That's a nonstarter. We'll be at my house."

He chuckled. "I guess you're right. Two houses would be pretty damn silly. We'll have to stick with one."

We were joking, but I wasn't, not really. I wanted that future with Deacon. A cute little house with enough bedrooms for us, maybe a kid or two, and of course Hailey, a nice kitchen, and a workshop for Deacon.

"Glad we settled that." I kissed his chin and settled back on his chest.

He resumed stroking my hair, and little by little, I relaxed, soaking up his attention.

"You mean it, don't you?" he asked quietly.

He'd lulled me into a half-awake state, so it took a moment to register his question. "Mean what?"

"About the house. You want to find a place of our own."

"Eventually, yes. I'm happy in this apartment with you, but when it's time to take the next step, I'd only want to do that with you."

He stopped stroking my hair, but only to curl his arms around me and hold me tight. "All right. That's what we're working toward—saving money and getting sure with one another until we find a place to settle."

"Yeah," I agreed. "I think we have a plan."

"We've got a plan," he echoed.

The ache was back, but it was because I was so filled with love for this man I was nearly bursting. It probably wasn't healthy, but I couldn't imagine loving him less. It would be impossible.

The bed shifted, and suddenly, my back was cold. Deacon and I didn't always sleep connected, but him not touching me was rare.

It was the absence of his warmth that woke me. My sleep-fogged brain registered his retreating figure as he left the bedroom, heading to what I assumed was the bathroom. I drifted in and out, waiting for him to return.

Except he didn't.

The soft click of the front door sent a jolt through me.

What?

Was he leaving? Going back to his apartment? Surely, he wouldn't do that without telling me. He didn't always have good nights, but he'd never walked out.

Maybe I'd misheard. Maybe that had been the bathroom door.

I grabbed my phone to check the time. A notification from my doorbell camera caught my eye, and my stomach knotted as I tapped it. I expected to see Deacon, and I did—but he wasn't alone.

Frowning, I scrolled up to the alert from five minutes earlier. A woman stood outside my door, pacing, her phone clutched in her hand.

I switched back to the most recent clip, watching as Deacon stepped outside, grabbed her arm, and led her toward his apartment.

I...what?

Confusion swirled through me, questions stacking too fast to focus on just one.

The longer I lay there, alone, the harder it became to breathe. My lungs felt trapped in a vise, the pressure mounting, pressing in.

What was happening upstairs?

Why wasn't Deacon here with me?

Time crawled. An eternity passed before I heard my front door open again, though the clock told me it had only been half an hour.

I laid my phone on my nightstand and waited, forcing my breathing to even out. Deacon barely made a sound as he crept through my apartment, trying not to wake me.

Hold the line.

He'd explain. Any second now, he'd make this right—offer an easy answer for why he'd left our bed to take another woman into his apartment.

This was such a strange feeling—alarmed, scared, thoroughly bewildered, while stubbornly hanging on to hope everything would be okay in a minute or two.

Deacon was quiet as a mouse entering the bedroom. Through slits in my eyelids, I watched him shuck off his T-shirt and kick off his sweatpants, leaving him in his briefs. He went to his side of the bed, carefully peeled back the blankets, and slid in.

For a long moment, he didn't move.

I kept still, my breathing steady, my body frozen.

I could have said something. Could have told him I saw. But I kept my mouth shut.

This was his choice.

I wanted his honesty freely given, not because I forced it out of him.

Finally, he rolled toward me, his arm circling my middle, pulling me close. His skin was warm, his scent familiar. Relief rushed through me. He smelled the same as when we'd fallen asleep. Not fresh. Not like another woman. Just...Deacon.

He'd give me the truth.

Or he wouldn't.

If he didn't...well, that was answer enough.

Chapter Forty-one

Phoebe

SOMEHOW, I FELL ASLEEP.

And in the morning, I woke up and moved through my routine like everything was normal.

Deacon watched me the entire time.

I wasn't much of a talker first thing in the morning—he knew that—but something in my silence must have set off alarms. His eyes never left me as I dressed, got ready, made coffee—not once.

When we sat down to eat a quick breakfast, he finally spoke. "Something happened last night."

I lifted my gaze to his. "Yeah?"

"Yeah." He dragged his fingers through his hair, his expression tight, troubled.

My stomach dropped as I braced. "What happened?"

He averted his focus to his plate. "My phone woke me up. Don't know how long it'd been blowing up, but I had all these texts from an unknown number, telling me it was urgent, they were outside my apartment, and we needed to talk. I figured it was a prank, but I didn't want you waking up, so I went out to check."

Oh god, I could barely breathe. My pulse pounded. "Was it a prank?"

"Nope." He raised his eyes to meet mine. "That woman who was with Richie, Jennifer, she was out there waiting for me. Her friend knows Joy, and she passed along the information that I'm renting this place from her. She didn't know which one was mine, but she got my number from Richie's phone." He shrugged. "Doesn't matter. Fact is, she was freaking out, and I didn't want her anywhere near you, so I took her up to my place to find out why she was here."

I swallowed hard. "What did she say?"

"I don't know this woman, but she was genuinely scared. Said she'd left Richie and wasn't going back. He's gotten mixed up with someone connected to a drug cartel and owes this guy money. A lot of money. She wanted me to know he's getting desperate, and she was afraid of what he might do."

I released a shuddering breath. "To you? Does she think he'll come after you?"

"She didn't know his plans, but if I had to guess, yeah. She's worried about that, but more so that he's gonna get himself killed. Don't know why, but the woman really loves my brother, and I guess she was hoping there was some way I could help him."

A nightmare unfolded in my mind. Deacon reaching out to Richie, getting involved with him. Richie latching onto him like a lifeline and dragging them both down.

Both of them dead or in prison.

Either way, I'd lose Deacon.

"You can't help him," I rushed out urgently.

He reached across the table, gripping my hand. "No, I can't. I won't. But I need to be smart about this. If he comes after me, I have to have a plan."

I swallowed back panic and fear, focusing on actions we could take to end this. "My parents have lawyers. I think we should talk to one before even considering the police. Chris's dad should know too, but the lawyer comes first."

He nodded, jaw tight. "I don't want to bring your parents into this. It kills me even thinking about it, but it's better they know. Things like this fester when they're in the shadows. If there's light shining, it'll be harder for Richie to get to me." His eyes darkened. "Or you."

"I think you're right."

Pushing back from my chair, I moved to him. He scooted back from the table, looking up at me with worry-rimmed eyes. Dark bruises from lack of sleep surrounded them, breaking my heart.

I settled into his lap, straddling his legs, my hands resting on his shoulders as his arms wrapped around my waist.

Pressing my cheek to his, I whispered, "I love you so much, Deacon. So, so much. And I'm sorry this is happening."

Without a word, he buried his face in my throat and held me as close as he could. Guilt stirred my gut. I shouldn't have doubted him. He'd proven to me again and again he wasn't a liar, and he was all in with me.

"I know you saw me leaving last night," he murmured. "I can tell when you're not sleeping, angel."

I squeezed my eyes closed and nodded. "I wanted you to tell me."

His hand traced soothing circles on my back, comforting me when I wasn't sure I deserved it. "You thought I was sneaking out to be with another woman?"

Shame burned my throat. "I hate that it crossed my mind."

"You believe me now?"

"Of course." I pulled back to meet his eyes. There was no accusation there, just quiet understanding. The worry had lifted, replaced by something much softer.

"I *knew* that wasn't what was going on," I admitted, "but I have this stupid voice in the back of my mind that sometimes won't leave me alone. It has nothing to do with you. I trust you implicitly. It's just—"

"*He* put that voice there."

"Yes." I sighed. "But you keep it quiet."

"But I keep it quiet?"

"You do."

He cradled my face in his warm hands, his thumb brushing over my lips. "Love that I do that for you. I hope a situation like this never arises again. If it does, I won't leave you guessing for hours. We'll talk and resolve it immediately. Is that good?"

"That's great, honey." I kissed his thumb as it passed. "You've taken care of me now, so let's focus on you."

"Nope." He drew me close again, touching his lips to my throat. "I'm not done loving on you yet. You spent the last few hours thinking the worst, so let me hold you for a while." His voice was low, steady. "We've got some time this morning. There's no need to rush through this part."

"Okay." I relaxed in his arms, letting him give me all he wanted to.

His breathing stuttered as he resumed stroking my back. "To tell the truth, I needed this just as much. Maybe more."

It was impossible he needed me more, but I'd let him believe it if he kept holding me just like this.

Chapter Forty-two

Phoebe

DEACON WAS TAKING NO chances with my safety. Until we got things settled with Richie, my walks were history. As much as I enjoyed my daily ritual, I didn't have a problem with it. Me driving to work set both our minds at ease.

It had been two days since Jennifer's middle-of-the-night visit, and Deacon had been on edge since. We had an appointment to speak with a lawyer tomorrow, and I hoped it would mark the beginning of the end.

Since Hailey needed a ride home, having my car at the shop worked out well this evening. She chattered away as we went through our end-of-the-day routine, cleaning and packing up leftovers. She was taking a box of muffins home to her siblings, and I had a few of Deacon's favorites.

I couldn't make Richie go away, but I could give Deacon cookies.

"Are you seeing my brother tonight?" Hailey asked as I locked the door.

"Every night," I replied. "After I drop you off, I'm meeting him at Joy's. She's got him fixing a cabinet for her. It's really just an excuse to get him there so she can lay her eyes on him."

Hailey hummed. "I don't know why Aunt Joy couldn't have been our mom. Think of how different our lives would have turned out."

I bumped her with my shoulder. "I don't know, sweetheart. Seems like your and Deke's lives are pretty rosy these days. The Spellmans adore you."

"Yeah, they do." She grinned. "And you adore my brother."

"No doubt about that."

We walked around the back of my car together, the setting sun still warming the air. As I popped the trunk, Hailey slung her backpack off her shoulder with a grunt. The sheer size of it never failed to amaze me. I had no idea how she lugged it around, and what was inside would remain a mystery for the ages.

I reached up to close the trunk, and something hard jabbed into my lower back, freezing me in place.

Hailey yelped.

An arm snaked around my throat, locking me in a crushing grip. Hot breath blew against my ear. "Get in the truck."

My blood ran cold.

"Richie?" Hailey's voice was strangled with disbelief. "What the hell are you doing?"

He yanked me tighter against his chest. "You too, Hailey. Both of you. Get in the truck, or I shoot her. I only need one of you."

My breath caught. The pressure against my spine pressed in harder.

A gun.

It had to be.

I slid my eyes toward Hailey. Her face was flushed, gaping in shock as she stared at her brother.

"You don't have to do this," I rasped. He wasn't cutting off my air, but his hold made it hard to speak. "Let's talk to Deacon about this."

Hold the line.

"I'll talk to him once I have you somewhere safe," Richie snapped, the barrel digging into my back. "You don't move, I'll put a bullet in her head and take you anyway. You think Deacon'll keep you around after that? Nah, I don't think so."

"Fine! I'll get in the truck." Hailey scrambled backward, and before I could tell her not to, she climbed into the truck.

They always said to never go to a second location, but there was no way I would let Richie take Hailey without me. If I went with them, I could protect her.

"Okay," I whispered. "I'll come."

Richie shoved me into the back seat, closing the door behind me. I lunged for the handle, but the door wouldn't budge. He must've had the child locks engaged.

He hopped in the driver's seat and took off down Main Street like a bat out of hell, careening around a corner, nearly mowing down a pedestrian. In less than a minute, he took us away from the heart of town and onto a country road. During that time, I strapped Hailey and myself in, having zero trust in Richie's ability not to crash into a ravine.

The only weapon I had was my voice. Richie wasn't a reasonable man, but I had to try.

"This is a terrible idea," I said, keeping my tone even.

"Fuck off." He stared daggers at me through the rearview mirror, his knuckles white against the wheel.

I held his gaze, unflinching. "Deacon will never forgive you. Neither of them will."

His pupils were pinpricks—wired. He'd taken something before setting off on this disaster of a kidnapping.

Hailey's hand shot across the seat, latching onto mine. I squeezed back. We were in this together, for better or worse.

He let out a sharp, bitter laugh. "He should've just done what I'd asked him to do."

He flung both arms into the air, letting go of the wheel, sending my heart into my throat.

The truck swerved, tires spitting gravel as we hit the narrow shoulder. My body lurched sideways, my seat belt digging into my shoulder. At the last second, Richie grabbed the wheel and yanked us back onto the asphalt, overcorrecting so violently the truck fishtailed before steadying.

"All he had to do was drive a truck, drop off a package, and be done with it," he ranted, taking his eyes off the road to glare at me. "I would've given him a cut. But no. Prison made him noble or some shit."

"I never want to see you again," Hailey vowed, her chin jutting bravely. "If I have kids one day, I'm going to tell them I have one brother and that's all."

Richie slapped his chest. "Aw, Hailes, don't break my heart. You'll be all right. I don't wanna hurt you, kid. It's just bad luck you were with Deke's girl."

"Done," she hissed. "You talk about bad luck, but *you're* the idiot who decided to start selling drugs or whatever garbage you're mixed up in. Like *Mom and Dad* were great role models." She shook her head, curling her lip in disgust. "*Gawd*, how dumb are you?"

He slammed the heel of his hand down on the wheel over and over, the truck wobbling with every hit. "Shut up, shut up, *shut up*! I'm the one with the gun here. That means I'm in charge. Stop running your little mouth—it's quiet time until I say you can talk."

Richie was unraveling fast.

I gave Hailey's hand a firm squeeze, then tapped my lips with my finger. She swallowed hard, her nostrils flaring, but nodded.

There was no point in trying to talk to him. Not now.

Hold the line.

In the suffocating silence, I planned. No matter what happened, Hailey needed to get away from Richie. If I could create a diversion after we arrived at our destination, she might have a chance to run.

I just have to wait for the time to be right.

Beside me, Hailey stiffened as we turned onto a rutted dirt road. The path jostled us with every deep divot leading toward a cluster of buildings, each more dilapidated than the last. It'd been years since she'd lived with her parents, but the way her breath hitched, I knew she recognized the Slater compound.

It was worse than I'd imagined.

Dust swirled around us as Richie rolled past rusted-out junkers, their skeletal frames lining the path like some kind of ramshackle gate, trash blowing around like tumbleweeds.

The main building looked to be made of corrugated metal, and the few windows were smudged or broken, some completely boarded up. Three smaller wooden structures huddled nearby. One had half its roof missing. The others leaned precariously, like a stiff breeze might finally put them out of their misery.

I turned to Hailey. Our eyes met, and I mouthed my plan to her. After a beat, she nodded in understanding. She'd be ready when the time was right.

Richie yanked the wheel hard to the right, whipping us around the main building before gunning it toward a small, lopsided shack.

"Slow down," I mouthed. Hailey's fingers dug into mine. "Slow down, slow down—"

The last one tore from my throat in a scream, matching the truck's brakes as it jerked and skidded.

Hailey's hand clung hard to mine. I grabbed the handle above my door and slammed my eyes closed, bracing for an impact that never came.

We stopped.

I didn't have a chance to catch my breath. Richie pried my door open, waving his gun in my face.

"In there, both of you," he ordered, jerking his head in the direction of the shack.

I slid out, pulling Hailey with me. Her body trembled against mine, her grip on my hand ironclad.

Richie stayed close, the barrel pressing into my spine.

He shoved me past the door and yanked it closed behind him. "Hailey, go stand in the corner. Phoebe, sit your ass in that chair. We're gonna get you nice and comfortable, then we'll make a call to my brother."

Hailey hesitated, and Richie flashed his gun to her. "Remember, kid, I only need one of you. If you're gonna cause me trouble, you'll become the disposable one."

Her breath came out hard like he'd punched her. "Don't hurt Phoebe."

"Don't give me any reason to."

"Go," I whispered, pulling my hand from hers. "It'll be okay, sweetheart."

Hold the line.

She trudged to the corner, never once taking her eyes off her brother. He chuckled, scratching his head with his gun.

"Always were a good girl, Hailes. Keep it up, and everyone will get outta here in one piece."

His attention snapped back to me, and he shoved me toward a chair, one of three around a grimy table. A few shelves lined the walls, stacked with unmarked boxes, but there wasn't much else.

"Sit."

I dropped onto the chair, my pulse hammering.

Richie moved behind me. "Give me your hands, girl," he ordered, the muzzle of the gun digging into the base of my skull. "Hold on to the back of the chair."

I didn't want to. God, did I not want to. But this might've been my moment. If Richie was going to tie me up, he'd need both hands to do it—that meant he'd have to put the gun down.

When he did, Hailey could get away.

Slowly, I wrapped my fingers around the ladder back of the chair. Richie yanked my wrists together, something rough sliding over my hands. He pulled hard, the binding slicing into my skin.

My heart galloped.

I sucked in a sharp breath and *yelled*.

"Run, Hailey! Go, go, go!"

She bolted before I got all the words out, whizzing by us and out the door in a flash. At the same time, I slammed my head backward with as much force as I could muster, ramming into what felt a lot like Richie's chin.

Something cracked, and Richie grunted, then went crashing onto his ass.

Stars detonated, shooting across my vision. It didn't matter, though. Hailey was gone.

"Bitch," Richie roared. "What'd you go and do that for? We had an understanding."

He staggered to his feet, gripping his chin. A dark satisfaction bloomed inside me despite the throbbing in my head. I'd hit him *hard*, even with my arms tied behind my back.

"Now I gotta go chase her down." He turned, half stumbling, but steadied more and more with each step.

I couldn't let that happen.

Hold the line.

"You better not leave me here, Richie." I bounced in the chair, scooting it across the filthy floor. "If you go after her, I'm not going to be here when you get back."

He whirled around to look at me, then twisted back to the door, torn on what he should be doing.

I scooted and bounced the chair to draw his attention to me. Hailey needed more time to get off the compound, and I was determined to do anything to give it to her.

"You said yourself you only need one of us," I reminded him. "Call Deacon. Tell him you have me. Your brother loves me. He'll do whatever it takes to keep me safe."

A flicker of uncertainty passed through his eyes.

Good.

I just had to keep him here long enough.

"Fuck," he muttered, pacing a tight circuit near the door. "Fine. We'll play it your way. Besides, it'll take Hailey all day to walk back to town. By then, it'll all be over anyway."

He narrowed his eyes, pinning me with a hard glare as he placed his gun on the table. "Are you going to be a good girl, Phoebe Kelly?" He picked up the end of my braid and methodically wrapped it around his fingers.

"I'll cooperate."

He let my braid unravel. "Let's call my brother then."

Chapter Forty-three

Deacon

WHEN I FIRST NOTICED Phoebe was running late, I chalked it up to her getting caught up in conversation with Hailey or Linda. That wasn't uncommon, but she should have been at Joy's thirty minutes ago.

Nursing a Coke, I checked my phone again. No response from her yet. A sense of wrongness sat heavy in my gut.

Across the bar, Caleb Kelly leaned against the scuffed wood, his broad frame relaxed as he sipped a beer. He caught my eye, lifting his bottle in acknowledgment.

I slid off my stool and walked down to him, leaning an elbow on the bar, my phone clutched in my hand. "Have you heard from Phoebe today?"

"I haven't." He twisted his stool to face me. "Is she supposed to be meeting you here?"

My phone vibrated against the counter. A number I knew too well.

Richie.

I exhaled through my nose, rolling my shoulders back like I could shake off the weight of my brother's name. I let it ring. Hearing from Richie was the last thing I needed.

"Not gonna get that?" Caleb asked, watching me over the rim of his bottle.

"It's my brother."

He nodded in understanding. That was all the explanation I needed to offer. *No one* wanted to talk to Richie.

Caleb put his drink down. "What's going on with Phoebe?"

My phone began vibrating again. Richie's name on the screen sent ice down my spine. It wasn't unusual for him to call more than once if I didn't answer, but stacked on top of Phoebe's absence? Yeah, I was troubled.

"She's late and not answering her phone," I muttered, staring at the screen. A split-second decision had me swiping to answer. I lifted it to my ear. "Richie."

"There you are, Deke. I was beginning to get worried you were ignoring me."

"I'm trying to. You're not making it easy. Is there a point to this phone call?"

"Oh yeah. Listen to who I've got here with me."

I heard shuffling, a muffled sound, then Richie's cruel demand. "Speak, bitch. There're a lot of ways I can hurt you without you dying."

"Deacon."

My heart stopped.

No, that wasn't—

"Phoebe?" I had to be hearing things. Oh hell, that couldn't have been my girl's tremulous, terrified voice.

"Deacon, don't do anything he says. He's got me at the compound—"

Whatever else she was going to say was cut off with a roar. Richie shouted expletives at her, ranting she'd better hope I did what he wanted, or she was going to be eating bullets. He kept going, but my blood was whooshing hot and heavy in my ears, making it hard for me to catch all of it.

Caleb was on red alert, pushing off his stool and moving close enough to hear Richie's tirade. When I met his gaze, something lethal burned in his eyes.

"He's got Phoebe."

His inhale was sharp, massive fists clenching into boulders. "*No. Hell no.*"

Somehow, our voices cut through to Richie. He stopped screaming and started talking again. "You know what I need you to do, Deke. I'll keep your girl nice and safe until you do that favor we talked about. Then I'll return her to you. Not a hair on her head'll be harmed so long as you follow through."

"You think I'm going to let you keep her overnight? What'll stop me from sending the cops out there right now?"

Joy dropped what she was doing at the other end of the bar and hurried to me, leaning in so she could hear the conversation.

"Because I'm fucked if you don't do this drop for me. That means I'll put a bullet through your girl's skull and one in mine. If I'm fucked, so are you."

I should've been scared. Maybe I was. But molten, raging fury burned through every nerve, drowning out the fear.

This was my big brother. My own flesh and blood. The person who was supposed to be my friend, my protector, someone I looked up to. He should've been like Caleb—the kind of brother who looked ready to tear the world apart for his sister. Richie had never been that. He'd always been the one shoving me headfirst into trouble since we were kids. Even when I'd done everything I could to save us both.

"You'd do that to me?" I spat. "After I went down for you? You took four fucking years of my life, Rich. Four years. Does that mean nothing?"

Joy put her hand on my shoulder, and as firm as her grip was, it did nothing to reassure me. I needed Phoebe safe in my arms for that to happen.

"I thanked you," he scoffed. "You're not some kinda god just because you went to prison."

Black coated my vision. "I went to prison *for you*," I shouted. "I could've cut a deal to give you up, but I never did because you're my brother. I'd *never* sell you out. I sacrificed four years for you, Rich. Four years! And this is how you repay me? You take my girl?"

He sniffed. "I need help, man. Just one more time. Help me out, and I'll leave you alone forever."

"You leave so much as a bruise on Phoebe, I will tear you apart myself."

I slammed my fist into the bar, rattling glasses. Caleb didn't flinch, his stance coiled, ready.

"I've sacrificed enough for you. My life, Richie. You let me give up my life, and now you're trying to take more. When's it enough? You want my liver? How about my lungs? You've already got my fucking heart. Might as well take it all."

"You always were dramatic," Richie stated, like nothing I'd said had even made a dent. "Just do what I asked and everything will be fine."

"Fuck you, Rich. I don't know what I did to make you hate me, but congrats, brother, I hate you just as much."

"I don't hate you. I never have. That's not what this is about."

"If it wasn't, you'd be doing the drop yourself."

Silence stretched for a beat. Then, quieter, "I have too many eyes on me. It's gotta be you."

Phoebe's voice broke through like the sunshine on a cloudy day. "Someone's here, Richie. Are you expecting anyone?"

Floorboards creaked loud enough under his feet for me to hear them. "Shit. *Fuck.* This isn't good."

Then chaos exploded through the speaker.

Shouts, scuffling, Phoebe screaming, Richie cursing, another man yelling...

The unmistakable crack of a gunshot.

The call cut off.

I stared at the black screen in my hand, pulse hammering in my ears. Before I could move, Caleb snatched the phone and pressed it to his ear. His jaw tightened. "He's not picking up." His voice was raw, furious. "Where the hell is my sister?"

"Richie took Phoebe?" Joy asked.

A strange numbness spread through my limbs. "A gun went off." My voice sounded foreign, distant.

Joy was already reaching for her phone. "I'm calling the police."

Caleb's hand fell on my shoulder, forcing me back into the moment. "You know where she is?"

I nodded.

That had been a gunshot. Phoebe had screamed before...then nothing. *Nothing.*

Caleb's jaw rippled with barely restrained fury. "We're not gonna wait around for the police. They can follow us." His grip intensified. "You and I are going to get my sister back."

Chapter Forty-four

Phoebe

Terror ripped a scream from my throat as the door exploded inward with a single, brutal kick, wood splintering, leaving it hanging on its hinges. The man who'd entered loomed over me, over Richie, over the entire broken-down kingdom of this miserable place. A storm in human form, he was massive and angry.

Dark, furious eyes cut through the dirt and shadows, sweeping the space before locking onto me then Richie.

"Shit," Richie cried, jumping backward. "No, fuck, it's not what it looks like. Fuck, I...just let me explain."

"I'd ask where my money is, but I already know you don't have it." The man leveled his gun on Richie, steady and mean. "Time's up, motherfucker."

Richie flailed his free hand, the one not holding the phone still dangling at his side, and edged in front of me. "No, no, fuck—you gotta gimme a little more time. I got this—"

A gunshot cracked the stale air, and Richie went down, clutching his knee and cursing a maelstrom of expletives. The phone lay discarded beside him, my only connection to Deacon severed. It was better this way. I didn't want him to hear this happening.

When he found me, it would be bad enough—no, I wouldn't let myself imagine that.

I swallowed my panic and pleaded like Richie in my head.

You gotta give me a little more time with Deacon.

I'm not ready for this to end.

Injured and bleeding everywhere, Richie dragged himself to his feet, putting himself back in front of me. On purpose? I doubted it. Richie wasn't the noble sort.

The man cocked his head. "You got a girl tied to a chair?" He had an accent. Eastern European, maybe? Not from Wyoming, that was for sure. I wasn't about to waste my last moments trying to figure it out. I yanked at my bindings, my pulse hammering. One last ditch effort to save myself.

"She's my collateral. My guy's gonna get the job done." Richie doubled over in agony, breathing hard. "Christ, I'm bleeding out here, Saint. How am I gonna get that money if I bleed to death?"

"Don't care." Saint waved his gun carelessly, then took aim and shot Richie in the arm.

Richie jerked, clutching his wounded bicep as he stumbled sideways, leaving trails of blood in his wake. Saint bit his bottom lip like he was waiting to see what happened next.

Somehow, Richie managed to keep his feet under him.

Saint nodded at me. "Do you fuck that girl?"

"Nah." Richie shuffled farther in front of me. "Not my type."

Saint hummed as if considering something. I hoped like hell it wasn't whether I was *his* type. "Okay."

Then he pulled the trigger again.

A fresh spray of hot blood hit my face. I flinched, a scream lodging in my throat as Richie lurched sideways, an animalistic keen tearing from his lips. He clutched his chest, stumbled into the table, and crashed to the ground at my feet, gasping raggedly.

Saint watched the scene with detached boredom. "You're getting blood everywhere." His gaze flicked to me. "What is your name?"

"Don't talk to her," Richie choked out. "She's not part of this."

Saint chuckled, a dry, humorless sound that knifed under my skin. "She is here, so she is part of this. *You* made it so." His gaze, cold and sharklike, returned to me. "I'm sorry it has to be this way. You look like a nice person. But you understand, of course, I cannot let you leave this room."

He crouched down in front of me, dragging the barrel of his gun along my cheek. "Please don't be mad at me," he murmured, almost gently. "This is all Richie's doing."

Tears slipped down my face. I had known—*the second* he'd burst into the room, I'd known my end was coming. But knowing wasn't the same as facing it. And facing it hurts.

Fear stripped me bare, peeling away every layer of resolve and bravery. I wasn't ready for this.

There was so much left undone. So many words unsaid.

Deacon.

My sweet, sensitive Deacon.

I hadn't loved him nearly enough. He wouldn't know how he'd filled my soul to the very top. I hadn't told him I'd wanted forever with him, that I would have given him every piece of me, no hesitation. I had wasted too much time doubting him, questioning when I should have been loving him with everything I had from the very beginning.

An impossible, ragged gasp came from Richie. "You can't touch her." How was he still alive?

Saint slowly turned to watch Richie clawing his way upright, agony carved into his face. Through the blood, the pain, the fear, his trembling arm lifted his gun.

Saint's smile stretched wide, icy and amused.

This was entertaining to him.

A slow, heavy dread crept up my spine.

I closed my eyes. These men would not be the last things I saw. I reached for what really mattered. My mother's voice, warm and reassuring. My father's hugs, solid as the earth. My brothers and sister, fierce in their love, doing everything they could to protect me. And Deacon. *My Deacon.*

The smile that had once taken effort but now came easily and lit me up. The way his watchful, sometimes hard eyes always softened for me. His face. Perfect. Mine.

His love. Oh, his love.

I love you, Deacon. Always, always, always.

Gunshots cracked.

My head snapped back.

Weight collapsed against me.

And then...nothing.

Chapter Forty-five

Deacon

CALEB RACED DOWN A road so familiar I could have driven it with my eyes closed. When I was younger, I'd taken this route into town more times than I could count.

Since I'd been back, I'd gone out of my way not to take it again.

My hands were so damn numb, I wasn't sure I could have gripped the wheel if I'd tried. Caleb had no such problem. His grip was tight and steady, his focus razor sharp.

It'd been thirteen minutes since the call had cut off.

Thirteen long, agonizing minutes.

The only break in the silence had come at minute six when Caleb had said, *"She's going to be fine."* He'd been telling himself that more than me.

His words lay on my skull, not sinking in in the slightest. That scream. That gunshot. I'd seen too much. Lost too much to believe in luck. But I couldn't afford to think about what it would mean if she wasn't fine.

So, I remained numb.

Until a girl stumbled into the middle of the road. If Caleb had been less steady, he would have hit her. Cursing, he wrenched the wheel. Tires screeched as the truck veered, and he slammed the brakes just before we ended up in a ditch.

He twisted around in his seat to look at her. "Is that…is that your sister?"

The numbness disappeared in an instant, replaced by a rush of fire in my veins. I ripped off my seat belt, threw the door open, and hit the pavement hard as I rounded the truck.

Horror slapped me at the sight of my sister cowering on the shoulder, dirt streaking across her face, eyes wild and brimming with tears.

"Hailey!" I barked, rushing toward her.

She flinched at first, staggering back. When recognition hit, she launched herself at me. I caught her as we collided, her arms and legs wrapping around me like vines.

"Deke…" She sobbed into my shoulder. "Richie has her. She made me run. I didn't want to, but she made me. And my phone, I left it in her trunk. I didn't know what to do, so I just started walking."

A fresh wave of horror crashed over me. He'd done this to her. Our brother hadn't just taken my girl. He'd kidnapped and terrorized his own sister.

Suddenly, Hailey tore herself away and bolted toward the truck.

"We have to go back. We have to save Phoebe right now!"

Caleb was already moving, catching her by the arms and helping her into the back seat. I climbed in, slamming the door as Caleb threw the truck into gear and peeled back onto the road.

I turned around to scan as much of Hailey as I could see. "Are you hurt?"

She shook her head, still breathing hard. "No, no, Phoebe protected me. But Richie…he used those plastic things, zip ties, and strapped her to a chair." Her shaky hand went to her lips. "She can't run, even if she gets the chance. She's trapped, and I left her…"

I swallowed down the primal scream trying to work its way up my throat so I wouldn't scare her. Hailey had already seen one brother turn into a monster. I refused to let her see another.

"I talked to her. She knows we're coming." I gripped her trembling hand, forcing myself to be calm and keep the fear buried deep. "You did the right thing, buddy. You did all you could to get help and keep yourself safe."

Caleb cleared his throat. "Is it just Richie and Phoebe there?"

Hailey jerked at his sudden question then nodded. "I didn't see anyone else. If Mom and Dad were home, they stayed inside."

"Okay. That's good." His tone turned steely with determination. "Then we're just dealing with Richie. Between Deke and me, we can handle him."

I thought about the third voice I'd heard but shoved it aside. I'd focus on what I knew and roll with whatever waited for us when we got there. If I started worrying about the *could-bes* and *might-bes*, I'd lose it. Facts were the only thing keeping me from spiraling.

Caleb turned onto the drive leading to my parents' house, and bile burned my throat. I'd sworn never to come back here, never to have a reason to, but Richie had found a way to drag me in.

My hands clenched as Caleb sped past the house that had been just as much a prison as the cell I'd been locked in for four years.

"There!" Hailey leaned in between us, pointing to a crooked storage shed at the end of the drive. "That's where he has her."

Distant sirens howled, but sound carried for miles out here. They were too far away. I wasn't waiting for them to get here. Neither was Caleb.

He threw the truck into park outside the dilapidated structure and ran around to the back. While he grabbed his rifle, I turned to Hailey, pinning her with a stare.

"Do not move from this truck. I can't help Phoebe if I'm worried about you."

She swallowed hard and whispered, "I won't move. Just get her."

I met Caleb at the front of the truck. He shoved a baseball bat into my hands, his rifle slung over his shoulder.

"I have the gun, I go first," he said, voice like gravel.

There was no time to argue. He charged for the door hanging crooked on its hinges. I was on his heels, every muscle in my body coiled.

But I wasn't ready for what was in that room.

Blood, everywhere. Pools of it. Splatters on the walls and surfaces. At the center of it all—my brother.

Richie lay sprawled, his body unnervingly still, half of his head blown off.

"Phoebe?" Caleb's voice was cracked and broken. His rifle slipped from his grip, hitting the floor with a dull thud. "No, baby. Oh, Christ, no."

My gut churned as my gaze dropped lower. Beneath Richie, a motionless body, half-hidden—a body I knew almost better than my own. My world tilted, caved in on itself.

No.

No, no, no.

I looked at Caleb. "That isn't her."

It couldn't be Phoebe. That rope soaked in blood couldn't have been her long, beautiful hair. That wasn't her body that lay eerily still under Richie's. The silence in the room wasn't from her lungs not pulling in air. Her eyes weren't closed. Her laugh wasn't snuffed out. That wasn't her. It *couldn't* be. I was still standing, and if that were her, I'd no longer be in this goddamn world.

"Phe-Phe," Caleb rasped, dropping to his knees. He shoved Richie's body aside like it was nothing. Too bad the bastard wouldn't feel it.

And there she was. So. Utterly. Still.

Caleb kneeled beside his sister, his hands hovering over her. They shook as he reached for her, stopped, then reached again. His jaw clenched, his breath hitched, but he couldn't bring himself to touch her.

"It isn't her," I muttered again. "Not her. Can't be her."

I stumbled forward until my knees gave out. Then I crawled to her. She was on her side, still bound to her chair. There was so much blood. It had soaked into my jeans, and my hands slipped in it. In the back of my mind, I registered it was still warm.

I reached her, grabbing her fingers. Plastic dug into the soft skin of her wrists.

"She needs her hands." My gaze flew to Caleb's, wild, pleading. "She has to have her hands. We can't—we can't leave her like this."

He jolted, like waking from a nightmare. But there was no waking from this. Digging into his pocket, he fumbled for his knife and shoved it toward me.

"She needs her hands," he echoed, voice barely above a whisper.

Then he just stared at her. Like, if he blinked, she'd be gone.

She wasn't gone.

She was here—my girl, my world.

So much blood.

In her hair, on her face, her clothes, everywhere.

My hands shook as I sawed through the plastic restraints, frantic but careful. Careful not to cut her beautiful, perfect skin. The ties snapped, and her arms fell limp, lifeless.

Caleb rocked forward, catching one of her hands before it hit the ground. He cradled it between his own, rubbing her fingers, brushing her palm, his eyes locked onto her like she'd disappear if he didn't.

How could he be looking at her like she was the center of his universe when she was the center of mine?

I bent over her, brushing her hair from her face. Tears I hadn't realized I was crying fell onto her cheek, carving tracks in the dirt and blood smearing her skin.

"Angel," I keened. "Please, baby. Please let this not be real. Please, please, *please*."

The sirens grew more insistent as they approached. Help was coming, but too late.

"Where's her wound?" Caleb rasped, scanning her body. "Where was she hit?"

I shook my head, my breath ragged. "I don't know."

The sirens were nearly deafening. Almost here. They were going to take her from me. And if they did, if I had to figure out how to leave this room on my own...I couldn't do it. I knew that down to my bones.

This was it for me.

I dropped low, dragging my nose along her cheek. "I love you so much, sugar. To the ends of the earth and beyond. So far beyond, it never stops."

I kissed her cheek. Her jaw. Tilted her head just enough to brush my lips over hers.

Then she gasped.

Sharp. Rattling. *Alive.*

I jerked back, landing hard on my ass, shock radiating through me.

"Phoebe," Caleb bellowed, taking her face in his hands, sliding his fingers over her pulse. "It's there. It's beating."

Her eyes didn't open. But her chest rose. Then again. Another breath. And another.

She kept breathing.

So I did too.

Chapter Forty-six

Phoebe

I THOUGHT I WAS dead.

I was certain of it.

His face was the last thing I saw, so in a way, my life *had* flashed before my eyes in those final moments. And I had been okay with that—content with Deacon's smile and those shining amber eyes being the last thing I took with me.

When I woke up and discovered I wasn't in Heaven but in a hospital bed surrounded by all the people I loved, I was more than okay with that.

My hand ached. I looked down, finding it clutched tightly in Deacon's, and immediately decided to deal with it. After all, I was aching all over, what was one more part?

"Hi," I rasped.

Deacon shot to his feet, his eyes locked on mine. His mouth opened and closed, but nothing came out. His hand only tightened around mine, and sheer will kept me from wincing.

My mother bent over me on my other side, her lips touching my forehead. "Baby girl. You scared the shit out of us."

At my feet, my mountain of a brother folded in half, his shoulders shaking. Hannah curled around him, arms wrapped tight, while Cormac rubbed slow, soothing circles on his back.

"I'm okay, Caleb," I forced out. My throat felt like sandpaper.

As if reading my mind, my mother brought a straw to my lips. I took a sip. The cool water was the best thing I'd ever tasted. When I could finally think past my own thirst, I scanned the room. My father stood beside my mother, one arm around her, the other resting on my knee. My siblings were gathered at my feet. Deacon was still gripping my hand like he might lose me all over again.

"Where's Hailey?" I blinked up at him. "Is she okay? Did you find her?"

He nodded, but his mouth stayed pressed in a hard line.

"She's fine." My mother brushed my cheek with the back of her hand. "Cay and Deke found her on their way to you. She was checked out by an EMT. They gave her a clean bill of health and sent her home with the Spellmans. As soon as I have a minute, I'll let them know you're awake. She's been worried."

"Good," I whispered, tears burning my eyes. "I was so worried about her."

Finally, Deacon spoke. "You kept her safe. That was all you."

"Anyone would have."

He lifted my hand to his mouth, pressing his lips to my skin. "I'm so damn sorry, sugar. You wouldn't have been there if—"

"No. Don't you dare try to take the blame for this." I pushed myself up as best I could with one working hand and a throbbing head.

"What are you doing?" His eyes widened in panic. "You almost—you gotta lie down, Phoebe."

I grabbed the front of his shirt. He was wearing hospital scrubs. "Come closer to me, and I will."

His exhale fanned across my face as he bent over me, pressing gently on my shoulder until I was resting against my pillow again.

I touched his face. "I got through it so I could come back to you. If you try to take yourself away from me, none of it will have been worth it." His jaw shook as he stared at me with glassy eyes. "I know you were afraid. I was too. But it's over now. All of it."

He shook his head like he couldn't believe I was saying this. "You're comforting *me*? After everything?"

I gave him a tremulous smile. "You look like you need it."

A raw, pained sob tore from his throat as he dropped his head onto my chest. I stroked his hair, knowing I would never take any of this for granted.

My dad's warm hand squeezed my knee. "Do you remember what happened?"

"I think so." I brought my hand to the side of my head, finding a bandage. "He tried to shoot me."

Images came to me in successive, jarring bursts. The deafening crack of the gun, Deacon's face in my mind, Richie's weight crashing down on me, the burning in my scalp, then...nothing. Just darkness until I woke up here.

Caleb slammed the foot of my bed. "We thought you were gone, Phe. There was so much blood, and you weren't moving." His face was ravaged. I'd never seen my strong brother so destroyed. "I never wanna see anything like that again. My heart can't take it."

Our dad went to him, pulling him into his arms. "We need to take a walk. Catch our breath. Track down the officer who wants Phoebe's statement." Dad turned to look at me. "Are you okay if we leave for a minute?"

"I'm good. I promise."

Dad's eyes went soft. "You're always trying to make everyone else feel better, even from a hospital bed. My sweetheart."

I crinkled my nose to keep from crying. "Love you, Daddy."

"To the moon, baby girl."

Dad, Caleb, and Cormac shuffled out. A team of nurses and a doctor entered, buzzing around me, checking vitals and asking questions. They told me I had a concussion and quite a few stitches.

The pain in my head throbbed where I'd hit it, and the burn along my scalp was sharp, but otherwise, I felt...okay.

Not wonderful. But like I'd survive.

Everyone protested, especially Deacon, but I asked them all to leave when I gave my statement to the police, not wanting those details stuck in their heads.

Two officers sat by my bed, listening and taking notes as I went over what happened.

"The door was kicked in, and a man came in yelling. Richie called him"—I searched my foggy memory—"Saint. That was it."

I described Saint as best I could, though things were hazy and my mind wasn't quite firing on all cylinders. The officers exchanged glances, and I wondered if my description was more useful than I'd thought.

I swallowed hard. "Saint shot Richie in the leg first."

I wished those particular memories weren't as vivid, but I didn't think I'd ever forget the way Richie had howled. The pain had taken him down to a base level, and the sounds he'd made were inhuman.

"I think—" I chewed my lip, nausea churning in my gut. "I don't think Saint was really there for the money. He knew Richie didn't have it. He...shot him in the arm next. Then Richie went for his gun, and Saint put a bullet in his chest."

Richie had dropped at my feet. I'd thought that was it. He had to be dead.

But then he got back up. Maybe it had been the drugs in his system. Maybe he'd tapped into some hidden inner strength. I'd never know his motivations.

I blinked away my tears and fought through the tightness in my throat. "They shot at the same time. I don't know if Richie hit him. I...um, think I passed out after that."

The female officer touched the side of her head. "Did they tell you the bullet went through Richie and grazed you?"

Nodding, I closed my eyes. "I thought that was what happened."

Her partner let out a low whistle. "You got really lucky. Another inch, and it would have gone in."

It wasn't luck. Deep down in my bones, I knew luck had nothing to do with it.

Richie Slater had saved my life.

I didn't know how to deal with that, so I pushed it away and let sleep take me.

I woke deep into the night, but I wasn't alone.

Deacon's hand covered mine, his head resting on my stomach, his breaths slow and steady. I lifted my free hand, threading my fingers through his hair.

"I love you," I murmured into the dark.

His breath hitched. Slowly, he raised his head, his eyes finding mine, glinting in the low light.

"Say it again," he croaked.

A soft smile touched my lips. "I love you, honey."

He squeezed his eyes shut. "Never thought I'd hear that again." His voice cracked. "You were gone, sugar. And I—"

"I'm here, Deke. I'm not leaving you. Not ever."

He pushed up from the chair, folding over me, cupping the side of my face with his warm, calloused hand. His forehead brushed mine, and for a long moment, he just breathed me in.

"The other guy is dead."

I sucked in a sharp breath. "The guy who killed Richie?"

"Yeah." He rolled his forehead over mine. "Richie got him in the gut. Guy bled out in his truck after he crashed into a ditch."

I curled my fingers into his shirt, holding on tight. "I'm trying to figure out if it's okay to be grateful a man is dead."

Deacon exhaled, slow and heavy. "Only good thing my brother ever did was put a bullet in that man's belly. Cops knew who he was—he had connections to a lot of bad people." His thumb brushed over my cheek. "Now, he has none."

"Deacon..."

I hesitated, unsure if I should tell him the next thing. Keeping it from him didn't feel right either, though. He had the right to know. Whatever came next, I'd stand by him through it.

He raised his head, his tired eyes searching mine. "I love you so damn much, you know that?"

"I do." I touched the stubble on his chin. "There's something I need to tell you about Richie. I don't know if you'll want to hear it, but I'm going to tell you anyway."

His brow lowered over his eyes. "You think I should know, then I should. You can tell me anything."

"Okay," I whispered, rubbing my lips together. "He protected me."

Deacon jerked back slightly. "What are you saying?"

"I'm saying he stood in front of me when that other man came in. He wouldn't let him near me." I put my hand on the center of my chest. "He shot him right here, and he went down hard. But he got himself back up, Deke. He put himself in front of me when that man shot me, and the bullet went into Richie first. He's the reason it only grazed me." I swallowed the lump in my throat. "He saved me."

Deacon shook his head. "No. *No.* He's not some kind of hero. He put you in that position. Everything that happened after that was all on him."

"I know, honey. I'm not saying he's a hero. I hate what he did to me, and I *especially* hate what he did to you and Hailey. But when it came down to the wire, he did the right thing. It was his final act—he had to know it—and he chose to be brave." My voice softened. "I just think...you know, maybe there was a tiny bit of good in him, and he finally used it."

He drove the heel of his hand into his eye. "I can't take that in right now."

"You don't have to." I patted the space beside me in my bed. "Would you come lie with me? I need you closer."

His brow furrowed with worry. "I'll hurt you."

"No you won't. My head's the only thing that got banged up. The rest of me needs you holding me." I pulled on his hand. "You need it too."

I expected him to resist. But Deacon surprised me by kicking off his boots and carefully sliding into bed next to me. He lay on his side, his arm curling around my middle, his warmth comforting me, his head resting on my pillow.

Turning, our noses brushed. "I thought of you. When it was almost over, I pictured your smile."

His throat worked around a tight swallow. "It's gonna be a while before you get one of those out of me."

"I hope not." I slid my fingers between his and held on. "I didn't want to leave you, but in the last moments, I wasn't afraid because I had you in my mind."

A broken exhale escaped him before he pressed his face into the crook of my neck, his breath shaky against my skin. "I don't think I'm ready to take that in either."

"That's okay." I squeezed his hand. "We have time now."

A pause. Then, so quiet, I almost missed it, he whispered, "It'll never be enough."

Maybe not. Maybe a lifetime together would always feel too short, but that was all we had, and I wouldn't waste a second of it.

Chapter Forty-seven

Deacon

It was impossible to stop myself from thinking about my brother's final act of bravery.

Maybe the *only* act of bravery he'd committed in his entire wasted life.

I'd needed him to step up more times than I could count. He never had for me, but I'd never stop being grateful for the one time he did when it was to save Phoebe.

Two weeks of tangled anger, grief, confusion, and more anger had wrung me out. But I'd been dealing as best I could.

That I wouldn't ever know why Richie had put himself in front of Phoebe burned me up. I'd never get to ask him how he thought it would play out when I hadn't even had access to the product he'd wanted me to mule. I'd never know if taking Phoebe and Hailey had been a desperate act with no real plan or if he'd meant to hurt them.

I could have driven myself crazy trying to figure it out. But I had to accept that some questions would never have answers. And I had to move on.

Phoebe hadn't let me sit in my feelings alone. Neither had Hailey, Joy, or the Kellys.

They'd had every reason to shove me out for putting their daughter in danger, and Elena and Lock Kelly had pulled me firmly into their fold instead.

Even more surprising was my relationship with Caleb. We'd shared a trauma no one else would understand. The day Phoebe had gotten out of the hospital, he'd shown up at our door and invited me out to the ranch.

I was shit at riding, but he'd been patient.

Phoebe had spent time with her family while Caleb had taken me on long, quiet rides across the ranch. At first, there hadn't been much talking, just me concentrating on not falling off my horse and him being lost in his thoughts.

Today wasn't much different, though I'd gotten a little steadier.

We crested a hill and stopped. Below us, the river cut through the jagged landscape, stretching out for miles. Our horses grazed, tails flicking, their breath soft in the quiet.

"How do you wrap your head around this?" I asked. "Being out here, knowing all this is yours?"

"It's not something I think about," he replied honestly. "Just the way it is."

I nodded, pulling my cap low over my eyes. I'd guessed as much. I'd grown up in a different world and had felt the same way about it. It was just the way it was.

He turned his head, shadows from his cowboy hat hiding his eyes. "I've been thinking a lot since I saw your family's place. I'd heard about it—think everyone around here has—but I'd never had reason to go out that way."

"It's not pretty."

"No, not pretty." He returned his gaze to the river. "I need to remember I've been lucky all my life. I turned out all right because I have great parents and all this." He gestured toward the endless stretch of land. "But you, Deke, you made yourself into a hell of a man out of pure grit."

"Don't know about that."

"I do," he said firmly. "You could've been Richie. Would've been easier for you. But you aren't." His next breath was deep and shuddering. "I'll never forget the things you said to Phoebe when you thought she was gone. That—you're the man she deserves."

My chest twinged. I hadn't expected to ever hear anything like that, but damn did it make me feel good.

"I'm going to marry her," I said.

He turned to me again, tipping his hat. "Good. Don't make her wait too long. We've got Hannah's coming up, so my mother will already be in wedding planning mode. She'll hit the ground running for yours."

My hold on my reins tightened. "Gotta get her to say yes first."

"She will. My sister's smart, and she chose you. Phoebe's kind to everyone, but she's selective about who she lets into her heart. You're in there, Deke, and I know without a doubt she's deep in yours."

"That she is," I confirmed.

"So marry her. Give yourself the beautiful life you both deserve."

I raised a brow. "That simple?"

He looked at me for so long, I wasn't sure he'd answer. "You already did the hard part by getting out of hell. So yeah, that simple."

Maybe it would be. We were due for some easy.

After a while, I asked, "Are you doing okay?"

He shrugged his huge shoulders. "I'm getting there. I won't soon forget that sight. You understand."

"I do."

"Yeah." He rubbed his jaw, scanning the terrain. "We'll get there."

Phoebe was waiting for us at the stables. Her smile stretched wide as we drew near.

"Hey, cowboy," she called.

Caleb chuckled. "I don't think she means me."

I laughed, and it felt good. "Hey, sugar."

A ranch hand approached, taking my horse from me when I dismounted. Phoebe sauntered to me, giving me a long once-over. When she was close enough, I captured her waist and brought her against my chest.

"How'd it go?" she asked.

"He stayed on," Caleb called as he rode away.

I grinned at her. "What he said. I might be getting close to being ready to go riding with you."

She slid her hands over my shoulders. "I don't know why you wouldn't let me teach you."

"Because you're my girl, and I want you to think I'm capable of anything. Embarrassing myself on a horse wouldn't exactly instill confidence."

She poked me. "Joke's on you, bucko. I *know* you're capable of anything." Then she pressed her lips to mine in a too-brief kiss. "Next Sunday, it's you and me. You can have your boy time with Caleb another day."

"I'd never say no to you." I brushed her hair aside, my fingers ghosting over the pink scar near her temple, disappearing into her hairline. "You sure you're safe to be on horseback?"

"I've been riding since I could walk, Deke." I opened my mouth to argue, but she cut me off. "I'll wear a riding helmet, just to be safe."

"Thanks for humoring me, angel." I gave her waist a squeeze. "Ready to get out of here?"

"I am. Let's go home, honey."

Home. That was what she was. My home.

Never thought I'd have a place so sweet, but she'd given me that.

And I intended to give her everything.

With our arms wrapped around each other, we walked off, the wide-open future stretching out ahead of us.

Epilogue
Phoebe

Two Years Later

I squeezed my eyes shut against the pain. This was a mistake. A huge one. I had no idea why I'd thought this would be a good idea. Obviously, I'd been wrong.

Hannah snickered. "I never knew you were such a wimp."

"Shush, you."

"Almost done," Jett murmured. "Hang in there another couple minutes for me, okay?"

"Okay," I replied tightly.

It had taken me two years to work up the nerve to get this tattoo, even though I'd known exactly what I wanted almost the entire time. The moment I told Hannah my idea, she'd charged full steam ahead, arranging a girls' day while Deacon, Remi, and Silas—their little boy—hung out at the ranch.

A couple minutes had turned out to be an eternity. At least it felt that way. Jett finally finished, wiping my inner forearm clean.

"You can open your eyes now," Hannah said, laughing.

I cracked one eyelid open, then the other, and stared down at the colorful ink decorating my skin. I'd imagined this so many times, seeing it in the flesh—literally—stole my breath.

My lips parted in awe. "It's beautiful, Jett."

This man, who'd become my friend since Deacon and I had gotten married, was a true artist. I'd given him a description, and he'd brought it to life. A spray of watercolor flowers was the background for a wooden rolling pin—my weapon of choice.

Beneath it were the words that meant everything to me: *Hold the line.* They were a mantra, a promise, a reminder to hang on and be brave.

Hidden in the flowers was a little surprise just for Deacon

Jett swiped his forehead. "Phew. If I gave you ink you hated, Deke would disown me."

I held my sore arm out, twisting it to see from all angles. "Do you think he'll like it?"

Jett lowered his chin. "I know my boy. He'd love you in any form, but that"—he nodded toward my new tattoo—"he's going to piss his pants."

"Oh goody!" Hannah clapped her hands. "That's exactly the reaction Phoebe was looking for, piss pants."

He snorted. "You're sassy. Anyone ever tell you that?"

She feigned surprise. "Me? Never. First I'm hearing it."

He wagged a finger. "Remember, you're next to go under my needle. Too much sass and I might *accidentally* screw up."

Hannah turned to me. "He's joking, right?"

"Absolutely. When it comes to sass, you and Jett are pretty even," I replied.

Once their playful bickering died down, Jett got to work on Hannah's tattoo—a horseshoe with Remi and Silas's birth month flowers around it. He left room for more flowers when they added to their family.

We left the shop an hour later, bandaged and ready to head back home. While I drove, Hannah checked her phone.

"They're on their way to the park. Remi says Silas is in the mood to boogie. It sounds like I'm in for it," she reported.

I laughed. My nephew, not quite a year and a half, was exactly like his mother—always on the go, keeping his parents on their toes. Hannah had boundless energy, and Silas really pushed it. Deacon and I had babysat him a handful of times, and by the time he went home, we always ended up looking like we'd survived a war. We loved him to bits, but, man, was he exhausting.

Hannah put down her phone, twisting in her seat. "This was it, right?"

"What?"

"The final thing you want to do before you start trying..."

I clamped down on my bottom lip, nerves flitting in my stomach like butterflies. "This was it."

Deke and I had gotten engaged a month after Richie had taken me, and we were married six months later. We'd decided to focus on our marriage, careers, and healing before trying for a baby.

I loved being Deacon Slater's wife. Best decision I'd ever made, even better than opening Sugar Rush. He was cut from the same cloth as my father—different origins, but the same kind of man. A family man. Hardworking. A man who loved his woman with every fiber of his being.

Deacon loved me so well, so deeply, I'd never had a single cause to question how strong and unbreakable we were together.

We'd met the goals we'd set for ourselves. We had a house with four bedrooms—one that was Hailey's for when she stayed with us—and a yard big enough for a workshop. Sugar Rush was thriving, and I'd hired a third full-time employee to lighten my load. Deacon's carpentry business had picked up so much, he'd been able to quit his roadwork job. We'd gone to baseball games in Denver, taken weekend trips to California, and visited Yellowstone. Deacon had even gotten a passport, and we'd snuck away for a long weekend in Mexico.

There were miles of things we still wanted to do, but we had the rest of our lives for that. This tattoo had been the last box for me to tick before tossing out my birth control pills.

Hannah giggled softly. "Deacon's going to *really* love that tattoo."

I was excited to have a baby with him, but first came the baby-making... "Oh yeah. He's definitely going to love it."

And so would I.

We arrived at the park just as the band started playing. We didn't live close enough for me to listen to the summer concerts from my window anymore, but that was okay. Deacon and I rarely missed one. We always brought chairs, but they usually went unused in favor of dancing.

Hannah and I found Remi, Silas, and Deacon set up on a blanket. For now, Silas was transfixed by the music, his little butt parked in the grass.

As soon as Deacon spotted me, he stood, his gaze landing on the bandage on my arm. "What happened?"

Remi frowned at Hannah's matching bandage. "You both got hurt?"

Deacon looped an arm around me, dragging me close. "Did you do something?"

I nodded, biting my lip. "It's a surprise. You can look."

He peeled back the bandage, head bent close. I watched his body jolt when he noticed the honeycomb hidden in the flowers—his initials etched in the lines.

"That's..." He raised his head, eyes shimmering. "For me?"

I nodded. "You're in my heart. Now you're on my skin, honey."

It was only right. He'd inked my name into angel wings after we'd gotten engaged. Put it on his ring finger when we got married. And a year ago, he got a bag of sugar tattooed on his thigh. I was all over him. And now, he was on me too.

With a grunt, he wrapped me tight in his arms and buried his face in my throat. Over his shoulder, I saw Hannah being loved in a very similar way. My heart full, I closed my eyes and hugged him back just as hard.

Later, Remi, Hannah, and Silas danced as a trio, and Deacon pulled me close, moving his hand over my back in slow strokes.

"Have I mentioned how much I love sundress season?" he asked.

"You have, but I think it bears repeating."

His breath warmed my ear. "I love sundress season, but I love my wife even more."

I smiled. "And I love my husband most." Closing my eyes, I rubbed my face against his cheek. "This was the last thing I wanted to do before we started trying for a baby. So...if you're ready—"

"I'm ready." He pulled back, his eyes locking on mine. "You're ready?"

I nodded.

"Right now?"

I laughed. "Can we finish this dance first?"

"One dance. That's it, Phoebe." He rocked his hips into me. "Can't wait longer than that."

"We've waited long enough." I nuzzled his jaw. "I love you so much, Deke."

He sifted his fingers into the back of my hair. "Love you endlessly, sugar. Always."

I would never doubt that.

This man was my life. My home.

And as he held me close while the sun set, I knew our greatest adventure was only getting started.

Author's Note

I took a trip to Wyoming in the summer of 2024 as research for this series so it would be as accurate as possible. There's no place like Wyoming. As an East coaster, it felt like a whole different world. I hope the realistic details I added brought it to life, but I also hope you'll forgive me for any twists and tweaks I made for the sake of the story.

When I found the cover picture on Instagram, Phoebe and Deacon's story formed like a storybook in my mind. Vibrant and colorful, fully detailed, with the happiest ending. I saw this real life couple, and I knew the tale I wanted to tell. So I must say thank you to the photographer, Quincy, for capturing their love, and the couple for allowing me to feature them on my cover.

I have to shout out to Kate, my cover designer, for taking this gorgeous photo and turning it into a soft, pink cover. All I had to tell her was the vibe, and she handed me magic.

As fully formed as this story was in my mind, I couldn't have gotten the words to look so pretty without my editor, Monica, and my proofreader, Rose.

I have to shout my PA, Amber, from the rooftops. She's the very best and I never forget how lucky I am to have her.

Thank you to all the readers who took a chance on See It Through, and have been chomping at the bit for Hold The Line. If you're new to me, well hey! And if you've been around since the beginning, I love you for sticking with me through all the genres I've dabbled in.

About Julia

Julia Wolf is a bestselling contemporary romance author. She writes bad boys with big hearts and strong, independent heroines. Julia enjoys reading romance just as much as she loves writing it. Whether reading or writing, she likes the emotions to run high and the heat to be scorching.

Julia lives in Maryland with her three crazy, beautiful kids and her patient husband who she's slowly converting to a romance reader, one book at a time.

Visit my website:
http://www.juliawolfwrites.com

www.ingramcontent.com/pod-product-compliance
Lightning Source LLC
Chambersburg PA
CBHW071343300726
48976CB00006B/1754